Pas

Thank you for your
inspiration and example.
Christ's blessings!

Steve

THE LAST PROPHET:

DOOMSDAY DIARY

STEVE STRANGHOENER

"In a dream, in a vision of the night, when deep sleep falleth upon men, in slumberings upon the bed; then he openeth the ears of men, and sealeth their instruction." (Job 33:15-16)

"For then shall be great tribulation, such as was not since the beginning of the world to this time, no, nor ever shall be." (Matthew 24:21)

This book is a work of fiction. Named locations are used fictitiously and characters and incidents are the products of the author's imagination. Any resemblance to actual events or persons, living or dead, is entirely coincidental.

CONTENTS

PART 1: PHOENIX RISING

PART 2: PORTENT OF DOOM

PART 3: THROUGH A GLASS DARKLY

EPILOGUE

PART ONE

PHOENIX RISING

CHAPTER 1

TRUMPET SOUND

"Those who cannot remember the past are condemned to repeat it." (George Santayana, The Life of Reason, 1905-6) ... "If you want to see into the future, crack open your Bible." (Horace "Inky" Hermann, 2012)

Looking back, it seemed fitting that *doomsday* arrived on a Friday. It served us right since the vast majority of Americans thought Black Friday was just the day after Thanksgiving when fanatical Christmas shoppers might boost the retail sector into profitable *black ink* territory. There were still some like me who could recall Black Friday as the day the first Great Depression began on October 25th, 1929. No, I wasn't alive then, not even close. I remember my parents talking about those days even though they were just young kids back in the 1930s. It wasn't their firsthand experience as much as the mindset it imprinted upon them and their generation that stood out. They were determined, almost obsessed with not repeating that dark episode from our history. Growing up in the land of plenty made their attitudes and behaviors seem out of touch, almost comical to me. They would let nothing go to waste and could stretch a dollar like melted mozzarella. They feared debt more than the boogey man and avoided it like the plague. Even when it came to their one home mortgage and rare car loans, they'd take great care in not biting off more than they could chew. Maybe Depression anxiety prompted the Costa Grocery in our town's Hill Neighborhood to invent provel cheese to give St. Louis style pizza its distinctive topping. In any case, every time I get a clean bite of its delicious, gooey but non-stringy cheesiness, it makes me think of the thrift and sense of accountability and responsibility of my parents ... and the stark contrast to the current entitlement generation who like to devour every slice in sight with no regard for the sauce-slopped, wispy yellow strands dangling from their greasy chins.

History repeated itself but with a vengeance that rendered it unrecognizable. The Great Depression seemed almost tame compared to this go-around. It was much more widespread and went far beyond an economic and financial collapse. Third world countries were not spared this time because of their dependence on foreign aid in what amounted to international wealth re-distribution or what you might call global hush money. At least they didn't have as far to fall as industrialized nations. For them, particularly us in America, the crash was a head-on collision between the pampered life of luxury for which we had no gratitude and abject poverty that enveloped us like a hoard of locusts. It happened so fast and seemed to catch us all by complete surprise, like someone touched a glowing cigar to an overfilled balloon. But we should have seen it coming.

The Securities Act of 1933, Glass-Steagall and a million other stifling regulations enacted by Congress over the decades since then provided no security. There's no protection against human nature, especially when you've lost sight of history and government does its best to fuel our worst instincts. Even the fairly recent bubbles that exploded in the tech sector and then the housing market didn't seem to provide any lasting lessons. They called it quantitative easing. It meant that the U. S. Treasury's printing presses kept spitting out greenbacks like a demon-possessed wood chipper and we continued to spend money at a mercurial pace that outstripped our GDP by almost double. The resulting mountain of debt put Everest to shame. No problem; we just kept borrowing from foreign governments as shaky as our own with no thought that the soaring house of cards would ever collapse. Our too-big-to-fail anthem rang out as we kicked the can around the globe. The Occupy Movement hopscotched from Wall Street to the Parthenon, Paris, Trafalgar Square and beyond as the reliant rabble rebelled at each and every turn as one failing country after another tried to implement austerity measures to wean their woebegone wards from the states' barren teats. There was no courage left in the halls of government; no Churchill to decry the Iron Curtain or Reagan to demand that Mr. Gorbachev tear down that wall. By the time desperation set in to force a dose of sanity, it was too late. The maniacal game of global pass-the-trash imploded.

The world banking system from the IMF to the Federal Reserve, the Exchequer of Great Britain and People's Bank of China went belly up and burst like a bloated fish swelling in the hot sun and spewed its guts and stench everywhere. The almighty dollar, Euro, Yuan, Yen and Ruble were worth about as much as the currency of the Confederacy; maybe less since the latter was so rare, not being circulated like breeding rabbits like the others. On that first Black Friday, a lot of tycoons, barons and run of the mill affluent folks hurled themselves out of windows as the stock market crashed and their fortunes evaporated. This time around, the panic was much more pervasive. In spite of all the class warfare rhetoric that tried to paint a picture of an evil one percent of the population being filthy rich, the vast majority of people were invested in equities; if not directly then through 401ks, pensions and other retirement plans. There weren't enough tall buildings to accommodate all the suicidal lemmings who lost everything on Black Friday II.

Gazillions in wealth, at least on paper, worthless oceans of scrap, went up in a puff of smoke, just like that. The run on the banks, S&Ls and credit unions was utterly fruitless. People everywhere were numbed by the fact that everything they had was gone, worthless ... checking accounts, savings accounts, IRAs, cash on hand, mad money stashed under a mattress and even the coins in the kids' piggy banks. Sakes alive ... even plastic was rendered useless ... no credit, no ATMs! Commerce ground to a halt and businesses, those that survived, were reduced to a barter system. Commodities were king. It was as if we all went through a massive time warp back to medieval times. It was a violent shock to the global system. No one was untouched. However, underdeveloped nations had an advantage in knowing better how to deal with dire paucity and a dearth of the simplest luxuries we in the U. S. took for granted. But even the poorest countries had grown more than a little dependent on the wonders of technology and the grudging largesse of wealthy neighbors around the globe.

The financial devastation and tectonic shift in economic well-being opened a black hole that swallowed up any sense of normalcy. The change was so sweeping, swift and complete that it ravaged our world and left people as blind beggars groping for any connection to the past, like the prodigal son who was reduced to gleaning leftovers from the pig's trough. It would have been considered a godsend to reduce unemployment to twenty-five percent. Half the population was out of work and more than half didn't pay taxes anyway so government revenues tanked. If they had known their history, most people would have longed for the good, old days of the Depression. It wouldn't have helped much though since being on the dole had robbed so many people of the resourcefulness of the drifters, grifters and hobos of those bygone days. It wasn't just people on welfare. The nanny state's tentacles stretched into every aspect of society with such ubiquity that most everyone turned instinctively to Uncle Sam for a helping hand. But Mother Hubbard's cupboard was bare. The currency was worthless, crippled by runaway inflation and the flow of revenue into Washington was slowed to a trickle so much so that the government couldn't come close to meeting its massive obligations, much less take on a whole new segment of ugly step children. Medicare, Medicaid and Social Security went bust and food stamps ... hah, their only value was perhaps as a substitute for toilet paper.

This was not unique to the United States. People everywhere turned to Big Brother for protection only to be thrown out on their ears. The game was over. The Fat Lady had sung her last song ... she starved and got skinny. Nobody cared about global warming or cooling for that matter. Being *green* wasn't chic or virtuous anymore. We Are the World was replaced by Doe Ray Me and screw everyone else. The UN went out of business ... no big loss ... and the charade of one big, happy global family was put to rest. Tariffs sprang up so fast Smoot and Hawley's heads might have exploded in their graves. The world got larger instead of smaller as isolationism temporarily abounded. All this only served to speed our descent into the abyss of Stone Age economics. Here at home, shelters and soup kitchens were overwhelmed. Government assistance strained under the load. A line from an old Seventies song by Alvin Lee and Ten Years After proved prophetic ... tax the rich, feed the poor, until there are no rich no more. Violent crime skyrocketed. Naturally, panic ensued which led to anarchy.

Peaceful protest it was not. The sheer terror and viciousness of the mayhem that broke out made the Watts riots of the Sixties seem like a walk in the park. Joe Citizen unwittingly provided a partial solution befitting Scrooge's advice to reduce the excess population as death reigned supreme. We had been conditioned to disregard human life through years of worshipping at the altar of evolutionary demagoguery, the slaughter of babies inside and barely outside the womb, Kevorkianism, enviromania, terrorism, glorification of crime, non-stop warfare and open disdain for Christianity with its *outdated* morals and ethics. We're talking about a society where the knockout game … gangs of youths jumping unsuspecting, often defenseless elderly folks and beating them senseless … was considered recreational, a new way for shiftless, young slime balls to get their jollies. With government safety nets removed, Darwinism on steroids kicked in and survival of the fittest replaced the rule of law; dog-eat-dog, kill-or-be-killed. Savagery gripped the land like an assassin's garrote. Only it was worse. Even *savages* can sometimes find compassion that extends beyond the selfish confines of their own dark, cold hearts. I offer my apologies to *savages* everywhere for the lack of a better word to describe our baser elements.

It didn't take long under such horrid conditions for people to migrate to logical or perhaps illogical groupings and conclaves for safety and security. Masses of weak, unstable, bewildered wretches regrettably took what they thought was the easy way out and committed suicide. Some sought spiritual solace and sanctuary in the churches but found most were home to unfaithful shepherds who abandoned their flocks to the ravening wolves at the first sign of trouble. Legions of degenerates carved out their turf and formed alliances something akin to tribal units that preyed upon weak and unsuspecting victims. In their minds, they were fully justified in thinning the herd, so to speak, and ridding the world of weak and inferior members that had dragged down the human race. In a world that took on too much of the apocalyptic tone of a Mad Max film or zombie flick, the survivalists and doomsday preppers enjoyed their long awaited heyday.

There are survivalists then there are survivalists. The wannabes were lazy idiots who bought food insurance and gold certificates. Good luck with that! The real deal, at a minimum, squirrelled away food, water, guns and ammunition and trained like they were preparing for the Olympics. Woe to the unsuspecting barbarians, used to easy pickings, who stumbled upon one of these ready Teddies. This helped to prompt the lone wolves and small packs to congeal with other miscreants to consolidate their power. It led to more than one Custer's Last Stand for overmatched survivalists who lived up to the credo that they'd have to pry their guns from their cold, dead hands. As word spread, the survivalists responded in kind and formed alliances of their own. It was an old fashioned arms race hearkening back to more primitive times. Some of the battles resembled sieges of old with castles and moats or Wild West outposts.

At the height of this brief but bloody period, a gang of several hundred particularly ruthless, marauding nomads known as the Mercenaries, whose name struck fear into the hearts of many, cut a swath across the Deep South and happened upon what they thought was an isolated stronghold. They figured they would be easy marks for guns, ammo, fuel, provisions and a few women while they were at it. What they didn't know is that they had stumbled upon a group that had been struck by lightning once before. Consequently, they had formed a loose confederation of some fourteen heavily armed and fortified compounds in the area linked by their own private network of shortwave radios and an antiquated but effective fallback alarm system. Each compound was bristling with hidden snares, booby traps and protective ramparts that could thwart most any attack for long enough to allow reinforcements to swarm the interlopers. There were even elaborate escape hatches and tunnel systems to avoid an Alamo scenario.

The Mercenaries were more cavalier than cautious due to the overwhelming force they possessed as they approached *Ft. Sumter* as this compound was aptly nicknamed. Adrenaline-induced high spirits gripped the invaders at the prospect of bloodletting, pillaging, plunder and female conquests. This was brought to a screeching halt by the trip wire that activated shrieking sirens that shattered the silence and jolted the Mercenaries from their composure. The alarms were succeeded by a chain reaction of patchwork explosives that claimed dozens of limbs and a few eyes and testicles in their zig-zagging wake. What followed next was a hail of tear gas that would have caused pandemonium in a lessor group but the Mercenaries were battle hardened and quickly recovered and assembled for an onslaught. Their charge was met by a hail of bullets that left them scrambling for cover. By the time they were able to assess the situation and bring their heavy ordinance to the fore to mount a serious assault; units from the other neighboring compounds swooped in and surrounded them in a devastating crossfire that left no more than two dozen survivors scrambling for their lives. The carnage was a modern day rendition of Braveheart. The tables had been turned and the Mercenaries were forced to play the Seventh Calvary to Sumter's swarming Sioux. The survivalists of Ft. Sumter nevertheless showed empathy and reverence for human life that the conscienceless Mercenaries wouldn't have imparted to them and provided every one of the deceased with a proper burial.

This type of scene played out across the country on various scales, larger and smaller, with the bloodletting not sparing the *good guys* or *bad guys*. Everyone was a loser. One of the last administrations before the *doomsday* really kicked in, that had been hell bent on fundamentally transforming America, had famously declared you should never let a good crisis go to waste. This situation exceeded a crisis by light years, going well beyond the wildest dreams of the most optimistic socialists who had worked to sow the seeds of our destruction. But so be it, right ... the ends justify the means don't they? Maybe so but it backfired on the social justice crowd. History had shown that this kind of unchecked turmoil and chaos could not survive for long. The French Revolution had been consumed by its own Terror and begat Napoleon. Things were no different this time except the phenomenon occurred on a global scale. Authoritarian regimes used the worldwide threat of total anarchy to consolidate their power. Democracies across the free world were forced to declare martial law to stem the tide of violence and lawlessness. Frightened citizens everywhere were more than willing to exchange their freedom and liberty for safety and security even if it meant turning power over to opportunistic despots. There was no alternative to totalitarianism, no shining city on a hill, no Cold War between good and evil. It led to cooperation across boundaries in a way that resembled an international crime syndicate, the Five Families gone wild.

There was no place to turn to for relief; no human rights commission ... not that places like China, Russia, Cuba, Syria, Iran and North Korea had ever paid much attention to them anyway. For many of the so called social democracies it was an easy transition with the ghosts of Hitler, Stalin, Mussolini, Pol Pot, et al being welcomed back like knights in shining armor and long lost comrades. But this was uncharted territory in the U. S. In spite of the centralization of power, imperial presidency and ascendency of the nanny state, American tradition was still rooted in stubborn independence and individualism going back to colonial days when we threw off King George's yoke and sent the stiff necked red coats packing. It was one thing to voluntarily relinquish our liberties to our *benevolent* benefactors in Washington under the guise of democracy but quite another to be coerced to sacrifice any last vestiges of freedom and self-determination by circumstances outside our control.

It was okay at first; just what the doctor ordered. What people longed for most was safety and security, peace in our time Mr. Chamberlain. So what if the Constitution was suspended? Was it a big deal that the executive branch and military supplanted the congress and judiciary? When was the last time serious civics courses had been taught in our schools? What did habeas corpus mean anyway? Who cared about illegal searches and seizures when vandals were rampaging across the country? Okay, so what if we lost a few meaningless privileges under the defunct Bill of Rights? Is freedom of speech really important when your home and family are under siege? And that Fifth Amendment thing; who cares? Yeah, these things evaporated quicker than July's morning dew but gone too were the anarchy and chaos ... the real threat to life and limb from heartless marauders who roamed indiscriminately. Most were wiped out while some were quietly absorbed into the regime. You can always use a few good men with special skills, right? The new government was alien to our American way of life but it delivered the goods ... prevailing unrest and violence were stamped out with a vengeance and order was established. What would later become an oppressive yoke seemed like a light, comfy, cozy fit at first. It replaced uncertainty and ceaseless, nerve-wracking bedlam with bolted down, locked in, deliciously rigid, unswervingly consistent peace and regularity.

No one complained as Federal force was brought to bear on the lawless barbarians that rampaged across the country. No one cared if they were killed or captured as long as their threat was removed permanently. Unlike our old government with its infinitesimally slow, mollycoddling approach, the new outfit was incredibly swift and decisive. The problem was what to do with the well-oiled military/police apparatus when the task was soon completed. Not to worry; the Feds turned their sights on other perceived enemies which were not lacking in their minds. Since the Bill of Rights had been suspended, that meant there was no right to bear arms. In fact, the survivalists who had taken measures into their own hands to defend themselves were at the top of the list, considered gun-toting, Bible-clutching crazies who posed a great threat to the rest of society. People were ordered to turn in their guns at Federal reclamation centers that sprouted in every community. Many gullible air heads did just that. Those that refused were typically hunters, survivalists, constitutionalists or criminals. All but the latter were targeted by the Feds.

Janet Reno would have been proud. The siege of the Branch Davidians at Waco would have been considered just another day at the office for this crowd. Overwhelming force was brought to bear in a nationwide crackdown that opened the eyes of many. Ruby Ridges fell like dominos. Unlike roaming gangs of criminals who were wiped out earlier, many people knew these latest victims to be peaceful, law-abiding citizens. It was particularly galling and terrifying to the folks at *Ft. Sumter* when they recognized a former Mercenary gang member in the ranks of the storm troopers that descended upon them. Maybe there was something to this due process thing, even for criminals. Talk about buyer's remorse ... doh Homer, what have we done? By the time we got a peek behind the mask and got a good glimpse of the monster we had invited into the living room, it was too late. The Feds turned their sights on the *religious fanatics* too. They used the excuse that Christians in particular were guilty of hate speech against gays and others. Christians and other religious groups were labeled as law breakers who discriminated against women in violating their right to publicly funded abortion and free contraceptives. What they really didn't like was the way religious groups stubbornly maintained their first allegiance to God rather than bowing down at the Federal altar. This was unacceptable. As a case in point, many church groups and individual families came to the aid of persecuted gun owners and other citizens considered undesirable. Like Harriett Tubman, they developed a kind of modern day underground railroad to provide safe haven and refuge to innocents who had been deemed enemies of the state for the terrible offenses of things like holding on to their guns or private property, exercising the right of (un)lawful assembly, clinging to the tenets of the Bible and Constitution and proclaiming outdated, dangerous notions like eminent domain or no taxation without representation. The EPA had once employed the strategy of the ancient Romans in *crucifying* the first five villagers to make the others compliant. That was child's play. This new Federal regime could make Machiavelli blush.

Be careful what you wish for. You could avoid the harshest aspects of the police state as long as you were careful to watch your Ps and Qs but you couldn't ignore the government's heavy handed, all-pervasive intrusion into the economic fabric of the nation. The daily grind was more brutal than any short-term pain inflicted by the repressive goons in charge. The behemoth, government-run economy stalked the private sector like a gargantuan python, squeezed the entrepreneurial spirit out of the free market and devoured capitalism in one huge gulp, once and for all. I'm not sure who got the worst end of the deal, consumers or government employees. One group overlapped the other and encompassed us all so it was a moot point. The psychological depression was easily worse than the economic one, as bad as it was. Think about it. No matter where you went to work every day it was the same. You dragged your lifeless rear end out of the sack to clock in at the factory, restaurant, grocery store, retailer, gas station, school, police station, firehouse, library, bank or an endless number of government agencies and it was all the same, exactly the same.

The same mind numbing rules, regulations, policies, procedures and general bull crap. No matter where you worked, it was just like going to the post office or license bureau. It made me think of an obscure, almost entirely forgettable, old farce of a movie starring Tom Hanks and Meg Ryan called Joe vs. the Volcano. The only thing memorable that came to mind were the deplorable working conditions Hanks faced at the austere, totally drab, bleak, shades-of-gray prosthetics factory that rendered Joe as some kind of zombie-like automaton.

There was absolutely no motivation other than the money and that wasn't anything to write home about. The elaborate government leveling process made sure that, after the confusing arrays of senseless adjustments were applied for this or that convoluted reason, most everyone took home about the same amount of dough. Well, you couldn't really call it take home pay because there was no currency anymore. Everyone received Fed credits in their government held accounts and you had to use your national ID card to make any kind of transaction. Everything was linked to a single government database that tracked your every move. Before the Quickie Mart self-serve fountain would dispense your coffee in the morning, it had to read your card to make sure you had the necessary credits in your account. No tickie, no washie. The only thing more unsettling than the total lack of privacy was the fact that the government could tap into your account at any time to levy new taxes or fines or just extract more revenue for the common good as they saw it.

Everyone was the same, almost. There were really only two classes of people in this society; the insiders and outsiders, haves and have-nots, patricians and plebeians. The vast majority of us fell into the latter category. The lucky few who were the former were party elites and their relatives, friends and suck-ups who were the beneficiaries of their patronage. It made no sense to work hard to try to get ahead. Productivity vacated the lexicon of American economic measures. The trick was to do just enough to avoid draconian measures that were applied to ne'er do wells who didn't demonstrate a proper appreciation for the state's *generosity*. Such *nonconformists* would be subjected to a host of behavior modification techniques. If a good brain washing didn't bring you around, you might wind up in a labor camp or never be heard from again. So most everyone played the game and learned to go along well enough to get by. If you were the enterprising sort and really wanted to get ahead, you needed to get your nose dirty, lick the right boots and spout the proper slogans with enough manufactured enthusiasm to appear genuine. One of the best ways to join the in-crowd was to rat on a friend and help eradicate an enemy of the state. They welcomed any chance to justify reducing the excess population. Everyone was as skittish as lab rats. Who could you trust?

Government-run health care was back in full force after having been abolished by *foolish reactionaries*. There was no debate over a single payer system. We were all part of Uncle Sam's one, big, happy, healthy family now. Everyone received exactly the same slow, ineffective, heartless, costly, crappy care as the next person ... unless of course you were part of the elite. Preventative healthcare was the big thing. This cliché was used to justify all sorts of new intrusions into our lives. With the aid of our national ID cards and the real-time database maintained by Big Brother, you might be denied at Burger City even if you had plenty of Fed credits in the till. It wasn't uncommon for a clerk to give you the bad news that your cholesterol was deemed too high for the greasy, cheesy burger you desired while recommending the bland, barf-like tofu salad instead. The same could happen at your favorite bar if you wanted one more Budweiser than the FDA considered good for you. The best approach to health care was to not get sick. And heaven forbid if you were a sickly baby or senior. I sometimes chuckled inwardly, an admittedly sick and demented sentiment, in remembering how silly Sarah Palin was excoriated for warning of the death panels. Of course there was no such thing under this enlightened system. They were called life commissions. They were just looking out for us and the common good ... and dispatched unfortunate infants and the elderly with the efficiency of the Third Reich. Isn't it funny how things are labeled the opposite of reality?

You couldn't blame people for trying to escape reality. It was almost unbearable. For many it was just that; all those poor, misguided souls who feared eternity less than the current, hellish state of affairs. The regime welcomed their contribution to the betterment of mankind. In all of history, it was hard to find another situation as utterly catastrophic, terrifying and hopeless as this one. The Inquisition, Black Plague, fascism, Stalinism, Hiroshima, Nagasaki, Dresden and even two World Wars, with the widespread, intense suffering they caused, could not compare to the cloying anguish, misery, fear, gloom and despair that gripped the world in the Great Depression II's cloak of darkness. This bad movie had an unlimited engagement at theaters everywhere. It was an endless reel that kept spinning and spinning. Speaking of movies, the Feds didn't shut down Hollywood, TV or the internet although they took control with an iron grip. They allowed a certain degree of tightly monitored creativity to survive to allow enough escapism to provide a safety valve against desperation and rebellion. However, it didn't work out as well this time around. America's spirit had been gutted too severely to produce another Chaplin. The Little Dictator, Three Stooges or Groucho, Harpo and Chico mocking the tyrants didn't play well with this crowd. Yeah, life still went on but just barely. Can you call it life when you take the spirit away?

How did we go so far down the tubes so fast you ask? C'mon, think about it. Like I've been trying to say, you've got to know your history dude. This was a long time coming. Bear with me on this. You don't even have to go back very far to get my point. Humor me a bit and allow me to rewind to 2012. Not everyone was caught off guard. I for one saw it coming and wrote about it several years in advance. Ever since the Last Prophet, JD Uticus, went into hiding while presumed dead by the rest of the world, I had struggled to keep the Trumpet's head above water. At first, I was able to capitalize on the fleeting notoriety I'd gained through my association with JD but as time wore on my tiny newspaper seemed destined for failure. That is, until this old dog decided to learn some new tricks. No, I didn't relinquish my self-appointed title as the official keeper of traditional church doctrine or my practice of the lost art of focusing on Scripture as the authoritative word of God and only source of absolute truth. Let's just say I decided to get with the times and upgrade my technology to a *new release* many times removed from my antiquated ways.

I graduated from the *Dark Ages* and created my own website at InkyHermann@trumpet.org with an online edition of the Trumpet and my own blog space and even tweeted and used other social media to get the word out. Maybe I wasn't quite in league with Jobs or Gates but I was light years ahead of where the old news rag had been just a few years prior. Are you impressed with the bleeding edge approach and hip new lingo I adopted? Well, the credit really goes to Mit. No, I didn't take an extension course or two from the Massachusetts Institute of Technology. Mit's the nickname of the tech geek I hired, Malcolm Ives

Trimble. He's the oddest duck you'd ever want to meet but when it comes to technology, Mit's a nerd par excellence, a mega-dweeb extraordinaire. He provided the platform I needed to launch two new ideas. That sounds so trivial. When I say new I mean something beyond novel. Dare I say unique?

You might wonder whether venturing into the political realm was a real stretch for me but the Bible is full of all kinds of political history and drama. Now that I think of it, it's hard to distinguish theology from politics when it comes to eschatology. If I learned anything from JD Uticus and the late Dr. C. F. W. Becker, it's that tracking the Beast of Babylon and the end times prophesies of Daniel through Revelation is so intertwined in political history that it's impossible to separate them. So maybe it's more appropriate to say that delving into current events in the American political spectrum was a natural outgrowth for me. I kind of liked the sound of it ... Horace "Inky" Hermann: publisher, editor-in-chief and a political commentator to boot.

One could ask, what's so unique about another talking head pushing a political agenda? That's a fair question. Perhaps it's that I possessed a heretofore unheard of point of view? Well no, it's not uncommon in the age of 24/7 blather to cover just about every angle imaginable. While not in the majority, there were plenty of conservative commentators to go around, even those with a religious bent like mine. There were certainly an abundance of folks spouting warnings of America's demise and the political doomsday lurking just around the next corner. It was actually rather old news. Comparing the United States to the rise and fall of the Roman Empire has been a favorite pastime for prognosticators for many decades. If you turned on any conservative talk radio show, it wouldn't be long before you'd hear the dire cautions bleated over and over.

Here's where I differed from all of the others. I had no warning to heed but rather a stark pronouncement; a death certificate, if you will. We weren't in the final throes, desperately needing radical reforms, a one hundred eighty degree turn to right the listing ship of state. No, the great Republic was dead and gone, I declared. It was time to pull our heads out of the sand, I argued, and get on with the funeral. It wasn't difficult to surmise that I might be in a very small minority in taking such a position but I learned the hard way that I was completely, absolutely alone. Mine was a most unpopular notion and I received the harshest criticism and was the object of vicious name calling from all quarters; liberal, moderate, conservative, you name it. Why would conservatives recoil at my declaration? It wasn't so surprising when you ponder a bit. Conservatives were in large measure progressives too. They had just as much invested in the system as the liberals. Republicans and Democrats may have packaged their brands differently but they were both a bunch of egotistical, power-hungry, big spenders on the same trajectory when you got past the smoke and mirrors. It was okay to castigate the other side and call for massive reforms you'd be more than happy to lead in implementing but you had best not say we've gone over the edge completely and nothing offered by either side of the equation will bring us back. To Beltway denizens and political insiders everywhere, that was the worst kind of blasphemy.

Being a pariah was not all bad. Notoriety sold more papers than popularity. The trick was to survive the first wave of salvos. People of influence, especially in the media, didn't want to share their clout or see their power diluted by some new comer. Thus, the first line of attack was name-calling to marginalize interlopers and send them packing, back into the abyss of obscurity. Personal denigration is a great way to take someone's eye off the ball, to divert attention from the salient point under consideration. It's much easier and usually more effective than debating the merits of an idea on the basis of facts, if you can get away with it. Don't pay any attention to anything that kook says! The problem for the establishment was that a *David* like me had more of a fighting chance against the media Goliaths than in the past. Mit helped me to see how the internet and social media allowed small voices to be heard by going around the major outlets to reach out to the folks directly. Consequently, my army of detractors was not able to pull the plug and my aberrant manifesto was kept on life support long enough for me to state my case and gain a curious following.

Still I had a hard sell because the American people loved an underdog and were not willing to throw in the towel under any circumstances. I wasn't a quitter either. My point was not to lower the coffin into the ground, slap RIP USA on our tombstone and just discount our glorious past. I wanted people to see things in a different light and recognize that the current course was truly a dead end. In a temporal sense, the finality of death is so inescapable that many people choose to ignore it in spite of its ever present pall. But, in a spiritual sense, there is sure hope regardless of death's inevitability. Proclaiming the death of the Republic was not a message completely devoid of optimism but required a spiritual perspective to keep our hopes alive. Yes, I realized this was another radical departure from conventional wisdom. I was throwing separation of church and state under the bus and encouraging, no demanding, that God be brought back into the public square as the only recourse for our dearly departed Republic. Thus was born, AMERICAN PHOENIX: Resurrecting the Dead Republic. It was a shocking torrent of cold water thrown down the back of the establishment with a lively but completely foreign hope rooted in the type of faith that raised Lazarus.

This sounded preposterous when you consider that the majority of people, including most Americans, didn't have a clue regarding Lazarus and those that did typically considered it to be a fable which, at best, may impart some kind of symbolic meaning. However, there weren't many people in the world who were not aware of the story of JD Uticus and the miraculous resurrection of the Last Prophet. He was my connection, my modern day *corn of wheat*. There could be no better example of that biblical principle that death must precede resurrection ... that a *seed* must be buried in the ground before new life can spring forth. Thus, pronouncing the death of America was not my funeral chime pealing futile despair and cold resignation but the only way to sow the fond aspiration of a new hope with shining promise.

So many millions of people had witnessed JD's shocking death from a nine story fall through the magic of television and the world had been perched on the edge of its seat following his miraculous resurrection. Oh how things would have been different if he hadn't died a second time in the fiery suicide bombing perpetrated by Al Batin's ruthless assassins. I was the only person in the world, other than JD's parents, who knew that he was yet alive, protected from the blast by the hand of God in such a way that I would not have believed it if I hadn't seen the impossible wonder of it with my own eyes. If only the world knew of this divine intervention in preserving JD's life once again, I would not have been scratching and clawing to be heard. To the contrary, we would have been frantically scurrying to flee the spotlight's ubiquitous glare. Just think, with the snap of a finger, I could have launched the greatest PR campaign ever seen by simply revealing JD's whereabouts. So easy, yet it was absolutely unthinkable. If the powers and principalities behind that God-foiled plot knew that JD had survived, they would not have rested until they sealed his demise again, by any means necessary. That, and the safety and security of my own family, required that we maintain our clever ruse indefinitely and with the utmost care.

I had taken pains to maintain our secret. Not one peep was uttered to anyone including my precious Judith, Hugo and Adeline. It had become easy over the past few years because it was rare that mention was ever made of the Last Prophet. It was tough at first when Jude asked me for what was essentially my eye witness testimony of JD's death. I hated to lie to her and it tore me up inside but I had no choice. The most difficult time was when Gogo and Addie asked me why God had let Uncle JD die. In so many words, they wondered why God didn't protect him from the terrorists after having brought him back to life once before. What could I say? I told them that God works all things together for our good, even the bad things in life. After quoting Deuteronomy 29:29, I reminded them of how God works in mysterious ways. Worst of all, I said that God must have decided JD's work for him was finished. I had to nearly bite my tongue in two to keep from exclaiming how God had come through again and miraculously preserved JD once more. My heart yearned to give God the glory he deserved and sing his praises to Gogo and Addie to buoy their childlike faith. It gnawed at my gut too that I couldn't give any contact information to JD's parents. Even though it pained them to realize they might not live long enough to personally hear from their son ever again, they knew it was best that they not be asked to shoulder the responsibility of restricting themselves from revealing his whereabouts and putting JD in harm's way. The best they could hope for was a rare second hand greeting through me.

It always raised my spirits when I was able to connect with JD, however infrequent and brief. We had to severely limit our exchanges and take great precautions in the manner of our communications. There could be no trace left to alert our deadly foes and put the hounds of hell back on our trail. Mit unwittingly served the cause when I'd quiz him nonchalantly with no apparent purpose other than to serve my general curiosity. He got such a bang out of dispensing information that it didn't raise his antennae that I wanted to know how to communicate with someone in a way that might beat the most sophisticated system Big Brother could employ. It was all a game to him; just innocent, hypothetical what-ifs and conjecture on my part. If the truth be known, Mit liked to show off a bit, and why not? As goofy as he was, the guy was a genius. That's not an exaggeration. Mit was awkward, gangly and totally lacking in social skills. But he was a walking, talking super computer. He didn't know a little bit about a lot of stuff. Mit was able to go into great detail on just about any subject imaginable from technology, to history, to biology, to physics, to theology. You name it and he'd rattle off a dissertation if you let him. In any case, he provided some wonderful insights into clean phones, how long to connect without allowing someone to tap, safe internet connections, how to disguise and redirect web sources and even some *dinosaur* tips. Yeah, as it turned out, some of the most effective loop holes could be found in old technology like snail mail, telegrams and Morse code.

Jude and the kids were a great blessing and kept me going strong. Still, I missed that tight working relationship and close partnership that JD and I shared. There's nothing quite like the professional bond I enjoyed with JD. Mit seemed like an unlikely candidate to replace him in any capacity. He was a nice enough guy but just so weird! And he played it so close to the vest. It had been almost two years since we'd been working together and I barely knew anything about his personal life or background. I didn't know where he went to school. Was he self-taught? Mit never mentioned his relatives. For all I knew he was raised by wolves or left on the door step of some orphanage as a baby. He seemingly knew everything and could do anything but I didn't know if he held a real job anywhere. I was pretty sure he couldn't survive on what I was paying him part-time but was mostly clueless in regard to other sources of steady income.

Well, on second thought, perhaps he could get by on his meager pay from the Trumpet. He was some kind of techno-geek survivalist if you ask me. His clothes were either charitable gifts or refugees from somebody's dumpster. His threads were almost exclusively from the Seventies and Eighties but were definitely not retro-sheik; at best retro-geek. No, that's being too kind. Most homeless people dress better. At a spindly six feet, six inches tall, Mit cut a bizarre figure in his high-water corduroy pants with the contrasting square pocket patches. He had a penchant for old sweaters even when it was a bit too hot. They too were typically short in the sleeves giving him a kind of Frankenstein look with way too much wrist exposure. The fabrics were usually some outdated cable knit stuff in garish colors. He mixed plaids with stripes and seemed oblivious to any sense of fashion. Mit made the case for an adult line of Garanimal clothing on a daily basis. To save a few pennies, Mit's haircut intervals stretched out quite a ways which left his unkempt, naturally curly hair resembling the maelstrom of a youngish Einstein.

Mit's thrift knew no bounds. He could survive for a week on a loaf of bread and store brand margarine. He must have held the Guinness record for most uses from a single tea bag. There were broom closets larger than his three room apartment. I had to guess on that because, as far as I knew, secretive Mit hadn't allowed another human being to enter his fortress of solitude. I envisioned it being filled floor to ceiling with his computer junk and endless gadgets. It was the hidden lair of a mad scientist or in Mit's case a nutty professor since he was too timid, mild mannered and harmless to be the former. Once I thought I might actually get a peek inside when I brought my laptop over for Dr. Mit's diagnosis. He could fix anything and, I suppose, made a few extra bucks here and there. But he was painfully shy when it came to money matters and was reluctant to ask for remuneration for his services. He did fantastic work but refused to accept anywhere near what a tech guy or gal from one of the big box stores would charge. When he got my laptop back up and running, I had to twist his arm to accept one third of what might have been the going rate in the real world. But anyway, when I dropped off and picked up the laptop, Mit only opened the door enough to allow the laptop to slip through sideways, maybe two or three inches. When I asked a question, he stepped out onto the porch rather than inviting me in. What secrets were hidden behind those four walls? I bet the place was set up like Pee Wee Herman's playhouse. It was probably best that I didn't know.

While Mit was bashful and self-conscious in some situations, he could be almost gregarious when it comes to technical or scholarly subjects. Ask a question and he'd launch into a soliloquy with the gusto of a college professor expounding upon some pet project or favorite subject of lifelong passion. The only problem is that his speech was completely unvarnished. He said things that were not for public consumption. Oh, he wasn't trying to be controversial or grab attention by rattling someone's cage. He just had no filter and said it like it was, oblivious to underlying messages or unintended consequences. If the subject was biological in nature, he might describe some bodily function or process in precise detail without a clue as to how uncomfortable it made his audience. If the repair he just completed was the result of some bone headed mistake on your part, he would blurt it out without noticing the red flames of embarrassment he'd drawn. Mit was not vindictive in the least and never meant any harm when he committed these faux pas. He didn't understand tact, diplomacy and concepts like allowing someone to save face. I think perhaps he just saw it as part of his necessary full-disclosure policy. In any case, whether he was in his introverted or extraverted mode, there was a good chance you would feel awkward in his presence at some point. Still, he was a lot of fun because you never knew what to expect and you almost always came away scratching your head over some new revelation he'd imparted about this, that or what have you. He kept me on my toes but over the course of time I found a way to get used to Mit and actually enjoyed his company in reasonable doses.

It's pretty rare for a committed *science guy* but Mit was a devoted, outspoken Christian. As with everything else, his grasp of theology was pretty amazing. He could quote scripture like a pastor and could rattle off the chief parts of

Christian doctrine with ease. He not only knew his Bible well but somewhere along the way picked up a rudimentary understanding of Greek and Hebrew which he used frequently to divine the deeper meaning from some of the more difficult passages found in our English translations. Mit took Christ's Great Commission in Matthew 28 to heart and shared the gospel with anyone, anywhere at any time with zest and genuine enthusiasm. The only problem was that he could be overwhelming at times, providing a full-course meal to someone who may not have been ready for more than just babe's milk. Where he really excelled was bringing his vast knowledge and technical skills to bear in illuminating his theology. Mit had a special gift for harmonizing science and religion in a factual, non-threatening way. When he brought science to bear, the fantastic *fables* came to life in a way that was not only believable but wholly credible. His common sense, well-informed witnessing chased away doubt and turned skeptics into willing advocates. The creation story, Adam and Eve's fall, Noah's flood and, most importantly, Christ's resurrection took on a whole new meaning to people who previously dismissed such claims as myths or foolishness.

Mit was quite a bit younger than me and single but he never offered up any locker room guy talk. If he ever had a girlfriend, you'd never know it. Perhaps he was just being a gentleman and purposefully chaste. Maybe it was just his obsession with privacy again but it made me wonder. I'm guessing he had an interest in the fairer sex but there was no way of telling. Jude and I talked about trying to play cupid by introducing him to our niece or one of the young gals from our church but we weren't able to muster the courage. We weren't concerned about Mit's reaction so much but were worried how the girls might view such a maneuver. Mit was very talented and not bad looking if you could get past the outer trappings but it was such a shot in the dark we weren't willing to take the chance of something back firing and ending in disaster. Jude and I agreed to put our romantic scheme, Project Mit, on the back burner and hope for an opening somewhere down the road.

Anyway, I had more important things on my mind; like launching the project that I hoped would save the Trumpet and help provide a better livelihood for me and my family. It required Mit's full attention and support so I certainly didn't want to upset his apple cart with distractions of the feminine persuasion. It was time to go public with my new book, AMERICAN PHOENIX: Resurrecting the Dead Republic. I had been blogging on the topic for a while but this was different, in more ways than one. The plan was not only to publish a book digitally and provide the full detail behind my treatise that the United States of America as the Constitutional Republic crafted by our Founding Fathers was dead and gone. We wanted to do it in a way heretofore unheard of in the publishing world. You see, AMERICAN PHOENIX existed only as a concept in my mind and a rough outline in a Word file. There was no completed manuscript then. I wanted to write it bit-by-bit and release it one chapter at a time as a collaborative effort with my internet audience. Interested web denizens would be able to have input into my thought process and enjoy … or suffer through … the experience of crafting a literary tome through the eyes of an author. Of course, I'd have final say on the content but my collaborative readers would be able to see and understand how I accepted or rejected their suggestions and why. They'd get to see the finished product before anyone else, hot off the press, a chapter at a time … the ultimate in fan non-fiction.

You must admit this was a novel concept (pun intended), eh? But wasn't it like giving the kids the key to the candy store? How could I make any money if I gave away the goods for free? And was I opening myself to some kind of crazy class action suit by all my *co-authors* if American Phoenix ever achieved commercial success? The latter was easy. To enter my site as a *co-author*, you had to check the box and agree to my terms and conditions which were totally unfair and lopsided in my favor. I know, anyone can sue anyone for anything in this crazy dead country of ours but at least this would tilt the playing field in my favor and discourage some of the greedy knuckleheads out there. Achieving commercial success was another matter. This was taking a big chance. But I figured this was no different than a major retailer trying to attract customers through a loss leader. Get them in the door with a free loaf of bread and then charge them full price for their milk and butter. My hope was to attract enough attention with this approach to generate the kind of buzz necessary to attract readers later on and perhaps even entice some larger publisher to purchase the rights to the paperback and hard cover versions. If nothing else, I thought it might attract enough traffic to my web site to enable me to generate some advertising revenue from the Trumpet.com. Yes, it was risky but better, in my opinion, than maintaining the status quo and watching the Trumpet die a slow death. And, hey, if you're going to spout off about resurrecting the old, dead Republic, don't you have to practice what you preach? You know what they say about free market capitalism: no guts, no glory; you've got to bet big to win big. It was time to roll the dice.

So, I thought my latest calling from God was clear. I'd focus on the temporal doomsday I saw racing toward us while issuing a clarion call. No, I wasn't confused about the real thing. I still knew that the end of the world would not be accomplished by man's hand or necessarily be tied in any way to America's demise. Empires would rise and fall regardless. Nevertheless, I couldn't just sit back and ignore the world around us while waiting for God's judgment day. I also hadn't lost sight of the Great Commission and the need to spread the gospel. But, to me, the death of the Great Republic meant an end to God's word having free course in America. That's why I was intent upon resurrecting the dead Republic, if at all possible within God's providence. I believed that, as the old hymn writer once said, I'm but a stranger here, heaven is my home. But, what the heck, I thought … *while we're here; shouldn't we try to make ourselves at home?* No, I didn't mean to conform to the world ... you know, if you can't beat them, join them. All I wanted was to shake us from our stupor and try to restore some semblance of a better time and place where freedom of speech extended to matters of faith.

I had no lack of confidence or conviction when it came to declaring the death of the Republic. It was easy to see if you had a sense of history like me. Still, I'm only human and never could have guessed how close we were to a worldwide economic, political and societal breakdown. Consequently, I went on my merry way, as giddy as a kid with a new toy, optimistic that American Phoenix could provide a spark in turning the tide, with Mit's help, in transforming the Trumpet into a tech-induced dynamo. If I'm honest, I must admit that I was too enamored with my own *brilliance* and the savvy of my marketing plan. It didn't help matters that people really took to the idea of coming along for the ride as I penned American Phoenix real-time over the web. I guess they're right that pride comes before the fall and I took my eye off the target during those heady days when the blog took off and the Trumpet sounded with new life. What I really needed was JD Uticus

51

back by my side to provide some balance and serve as a true compass.

CHAPTER 2

Marchetti's Omen

"For a century longer, Rome still retains its outward form, but the swarming nations are now in full career." (John Lothrop Motley, American Historian 1814-1877)

In launching American Phoenix at Trumpet.com, I first had to outline the concept of collaborative, real-time fan non-fiction and post the terms required to gain entry and participation. With that accomplished, I dove right in with a bold pronouncement that was as much disclaimer as foreword … **Wake up and smell the coffee, people! The Republic is not in peril, it's not dying, it's already dead … read the tombstone and weep, RIP America. Kiss your Uncle Sam goodbye, dolts. We are already living in a Godless socialist state with communist leanings! Our electorate is largely uninformed, misinformed, ignorant and apathetic. Throwing out the bums in Washington and replacing them with a new set of bums won't change a thing. Dr. Frankenstein couldn't help this corpse. And our churches are part of the problem. And in any case, we need more than another Great Awakening … more than a complete overhaul. We need a miracle … a spiritual rebirth.**

You might even say that what followed was more than a disclaimer, perhaps a warning label. I set out to establish the ground rules and manage expectations in a no holds barred fashion. I cautioned that freedom of speech would be fully and completely exercised and political correctness would have no sway. Words, I promised, would be clearly defined and used appropriately. If, for example, someone practiced socialism (i. e, elevating the state's welfare over individual liberty and freedom and replacing private, free market capitalism with a public sector economy) or communism (i. e, elevating a ruling party over constitutional government and diminishing individual property rights by allowing the state to redistribute wealth to achieve equal outcomes rather than equal opportunities) by definition, they would be correctly labeled as socialists and communists ... in a factual, not mean-spirited way. There'd be no parsing the definition of is. A tax would be called a tax, not revenue ... terrorists would be labeled as terrorists. Also, Scripture would be treated as the authoritative word of God and quoted liberally without shame or trepidation. Moral relativism would be given no quarter. We'd call 'em as we sees 'em. The new orthodoxy of secular humanism would be challenged and popular theories would not be regarded as sacrosanct or settled science but questioned on whether they are supported by observable, repeatable evidence using common sense and objective scientific principles. Religion would not be treated as taboo or an unintelligible amalgam of coexistent goo where all steeples are presumed to point upward. We would compare and contrast the world's religions and various Christian denominations on the basis of doctrine, what they themselves teach.

Yes, I imagine that I scared off more than a few of the faint of heart. But I gambled that I'd attract many more of the curious sort or ideologues frothing at the mouth to pick up the gauntlet I'd thrown down. I welcomed the controversy and attention this would draw not fearing the open exchange of ideas from the farthest ends of the spectrum no matter how fanatical they might be. As the blog master, I was in the cat bird seat having the final say. Ah, it's great exercising absolute control and authority, isn't it? I was anxious to get into a key premise regarding American Exceptionalism. For the masses largely ignorant of the past, I thought it was critical to point out just how unique the American experience was in the spectrum of world history. My point was to show that there was nothing special about Americans as a people. We're a nation of castoffs and immigrants; our greatness was not self-derived. Rather, I needed to impress upon my readers and collaborators that our nobleness was a reflection of God's glory and our achievements, prosperity and blessings were inseparable from

God's providence. However anxious I was, I could not make this case without drawing comparisons across the world stage and annals of time. To truly appreciate the completely foreign and odd spectacle that is America, I felt it had to be seen in the light of the sordid past of our otherwise tattered world.

This post at Trumpet.com got the ball rolling as far as the collaborative dialogue is concerned and established the tone and direction for chapter one which later would be titled Bad DNA ... A Victim of History. The theme, in effect, was that apart from God's guiding hand, America would be no different than the other great powers that have littered the pages of world history, sharing essentially the same cursed bloodlines. Here's a sample from some of my initial offerings.

Most of the great empires that left their marks on the history books were not republics like the United States of America. In the ancient world, the Medes, Persians, Macedonians, Egyptians and Mongols to name a few are not remembered for their great forms of government. They were distinguished to one degree or another by their wealth, military might, longevity and magnitude. Certain aspects of their culture may have left their mark, nowadays more so as a curiosity than enduring influence. Some still remember the Phoenicians as a great naval power. Macedonia is still immortalized in Hollywood films for producing the great leader, Alexander. People flock to Egypt to marvel at the pyramids which still mystify the sages with their architectural secrets and bedazzling wealth of the pharaohs. The ferocity of Genghis Khan and the Mongol hordes can still strike terror through images on the silver screen. But these empires have long since crumbled in the dust with some remaining in name only, unrecognizable from their glorious pasts. Egypt is a tourist destination, poor, unstable and subject to the whims of the feckless military or religious zealots. The grandeur of Cleopatra is long gone and only the poisonous asp remains. A new god has replaced the idols of the past but is no less ineffectual in restoring the glory that once was. Syria is an embarrassment and an affront to humanity.

Oddly enough, memories of these ancients are kept alive in the words of the true God they've rejected and opposed. Pharaoh's stubbornness and folly leap from the pages of Scripture in his encounters with Moses, the plagues heaped upon Egypt and their crushing defeat by God's hand at the Red Sea. Babylonian hubris is still evident in the foolish self-aggrandizement they attempted to achieve with the Tower of Babel. To this day, as Saddam Hussein found out the hard way, the glory of Babylon is never again to be restored according to the curse of God. The Assyrians are best remembered as an incredibly cruel people who were spared by God and shown his grace and mercy through his servant Jonah who had to be dragged kicking and screaming to pronounce the Good News to Israel's hated enemy in Nineveh. Ever wonder why there are Christians in hostile places like Egypt and Syria? Read the history in the Bible. They aren't immigrant Johnny-come-latelies ... they're a remnant from the distant past.

God's fingerprints are all over the pages of history even though you'd never know it today. The myths of the past have been replaced with modern fantasies that are accepted as indisputable facts in the name of science regardless of how nonsensical they might appear to unfettered minds. Objective scientists admit that global warming, however it's defined, is not a man-made phenomenon. A pattern of climate change has been with us since the flood and shall remain so regardless of man's activities. Noah was told, "While the earth remaineth, seedtime and harvest, and cold and heat, and summer and winter, and day and night shall not cease" (Genesis 8:22). Yeah, that means we're going to have hot and cold trends and lots of unsettled weather patterns, regardless of anything man does, right up until the end. There is no correlation between man's production of CO_2 and climate change. Intermittent heat waves, droughts and ice ages occurred long before industrialization.

Both creation scientists and secular scholars accept that there was once a single land mass sometimes referred to as Pangea. It's not difficult to recognize the jigsaw puzzle fit between the continents. This was first publicly noted by a Christian geologist named Antonio Snider in 1859. The big difference is in explaining how this occurred. Secular scientists refer to plate tectonics and continental drift that magically happened over billions of years. This fantastic, inexplicable account is rooted in ideology rather than true science. It makes a lot more sense to say that the land mass was torn apart and mountains were formed rapidly by a catastrophic event, namely the flood of Noah.

According to God's record in the Bible, you can pinpoint the exact time when this happened, that is, by the 150th day of the earth being covered with water (that's when the waters slowly began to recede according to Genesis 8:3-4). Why ignore the overwhelming fossil and geologic evidence for the continents being divided by the flood? That's simple, accepting the obvious would require conceding God's existence and the veracity of his written record. The Big Bang Theory is laughable. How can you take something as gospel when it has such obvious, gaping holes? Where did the original matter come from and what caused the big explosion? Who created the so called god particle? Again, that's the best you can come up with if your starting point is that there is no divine Creator. History is similarly flawed when you deny the Bible and attempt to take God out of the picture. When you deny America's Godly heritage and the Christian principles upon which it was founded, all you have left is a fable.

Ancient Israel was similar to America in this respect. It was not chosen by God because of the merit or greatness of its people. Its glory stemmed from God who chose Israel to be his people to carry his promise of the Savior and be his witnesses to a lost and fallen world. This is an important distinction. Confusion ensues when you get this backward. Look at how some modern translations butcher Luke 2:14. Is God's glory bestowed on mankind because of our inherent goodness? No, God's good will is extended to undeserving mankind because of his grace, mercy and love. If you try to glean American Exceptionalism from some unique quality of our people apart from God, you'll be left befuddled and frustrated. Worse yet is to disclaim American Exceptionalism altogether in order to deny God. Why have so many immigrants clamored to become Americans and risked life and limb to join our ranks?

There are great lessons to be learned from studying ancient Israel; perhaps even more than with ancient Rome. Israel was not a republic but was certainly guided by Godly principles. It was a true theocracy guided at times by God himself. Often God provided his guidance through his prophets, just as his word in the Bible is meant for our guidance and edification today. God directed Israel in every way pertinent to daily life and faith; their law, customs, morals and more. Their sustenance, wealth and being were directly attributable to God's blessings, including their military might and victories. Their history is filled with countless examples of the fatal flaw that infects man and nations, right down to us in the United States today. When things were going good, they forgot the source of their power and blessings. They demanded judges and kings. They abandoned God's commands ... and eventually even abandoned God while turning to idols and false notions. At times they suffered greatly as a result of their own sinfulness and faithlessness. But God never abandoned them, he never forsook his promise that the Savior would come from his chosen Hebrew people.

This raises the question. Did God have a hand in America's birth and development as a nation or were we just the product of man's evolution toward an inevitably higher form of government and society? Yes, you could argue that ancient Greece provided some of the necessary building blocks. They were not a republic in the modern sense but planted the seeds of democratic principles. Rome improved upon this and created the first great republic. It crumbled in 476 AD but some of the glory was later restored by Justinian. More importantly, in

*spite of the setbacks of barbarian rule and the
Dark Ages, Rome provided a foundation for the
continuation of this grand experiment to grow
and flourish in Western Europe. The early
explorers surely brought these ideas to America,
right? Spain and Portugal must have provided
the jump start we needed. Not exactly, Spain
was an empire run amok with religious
persecution. How about France? Well, not so
fast. The French Revolution was consumed by
the Terror and begat Napoleon. What about the
Germans? Oh yeah, let's skip that one. But, ah
ha, don't forget about our progenitors, the
Brits. It took them a while to work through the
whole Aristocracy thing but they eventually got
things right. So what if they still cling to the
monarchy. It's all for show. Parliament has the
real power.*

*I won't argue that the English didn't have a
profound influence on America. We owe much
to them for our culture and unique form of
government. There's also no denying that they
provided a cradle for the Great Republic.
However, this did not spring from their minds
alone but was a product of God's providence.
The British Empire flourished as a Christian
people guided by Godly principles. That's the*

great legacy they provided us. The Anglo Saxons were no different than the other hoards that settled Europe in the vacuum that was Rome. Their greatness stemmed from God. They benefitted from being an island nation, shielded for a time from the anti-Christian secularism that swamped continental Europe. Eventually the English Channel breach was ideologically closed and Great Britain has been in decline ever since. The UK, that proud republic, is now just another run of the mill European socialist nation that has shunned God. Churches and cathedrals are vacant, converted to houses of commerce or, if still in operation, filled with worldly tripe instead of the true word of God. It used to be said that the sun never sets there. Now, if the majority has their way, the "Son" will never set foot on the British Empire.

If the fate of great nations is dependent upon their relationship with God, how do you explain the likes of China, Russia and Japan? China has been up and down throughout history but has survived for millennia and currently is thriving. One could make a good argument that they are poised to replace us as the world's greatest superpower. Japan is suffering through a malaise currently but no so long ago challenged us as an economic power. The Soviet Union was the greatest threat to the United States until it wilted under Reagan's pressure but Russia seems to be on the comeback trail too. None of these countries are Christian nations so why does God let them prosper; sometimes even at our expense? I say you're missing the point again. You need to look at things through spiritual lenses to understand God's relationship to us. God doesn't promise trouble free lives to his people. He doesn't promise peace, prominence and prosperity to any nation. The blessings he promises are not temporal but must be discerned in the light of eternity, truth and salvation. God says in Psalm 33:12, "Blessed is the nation whose God is the Lord; and the people whom he hath chosen for his own inheritance." This inheritance isn't in gold, silver or earthly might and power. It's found in reconciliation, eternal life and fellowship with God. Christ's kingdom is not of this world. Nations will rise and fall but God's kingdom will last forever after this world is ended.

It's in that sense that I can confidently say America, God's Great Republic as we knew it, is dead and gone. Look at ancient Rome. It too was vanquished well before the curtain was officially lowered in 476 AD. The parallels are many. Like ours, Rome's military might was unsurpassed in its day. Its influence was felt around the known world. Rome was the center of commerce and culture. It was built upon glorious ideas, hard work and meritocracy. The legacy of Rome lives on today in many ways. But prosperity proved to be a great curse for the Romans. It led to moral decay. Morality, not wealth served as their foundation and when it crumbled, all the wealth and power in the world could not save the empire. Honest commerce gave way to greed and corruption. The essential building block of any civilization, the family, disintegrated in the face of sexual immorality and rampant homosexuality. Rome became a crude, violent society that lost sight of the value of human life. Yes, the parallels are shockingly similar to modern American society.

There is one key difference. Rome was never a Christian empire. It was home to many Christians and, at times, was deemed Christian by edict of the emperor but was never Christian in the sense of its laws, values and institutions being founded upon God's word and principles. God uses people and nations to serve his good purposes in history. This was certainly true with Rome. The Roman Empire was not built to spread Christianity but it did nonetheless. The peace, security and stability afforded under Roman power, the Pax Romana, helped Christianity to flourish. Roman engineering and the incredible infrastructure of roads and highways they built helped the Legions to exert Roman dominion and promoted commerce that connected the world. They also unwittingly paved the way for the good news to spread on the feet and lips of Christians. Understanding Rome's true impact on us today cannot be fathomed from the history books apart from the Bible. All of history before Christ was moved along inexorably to a cross in Golgotha just outside of Jerusalem where the Lord was crucified at the behest of fellow Jews who had rejected him under the jurisdiction of the Prefect of the Province of Judea, Pontius Pilate. This was all prophesied in miraculously specific detail for many hundreds of years before the birth of Jesus. To understand where we're headed, with any surety, there is again no substitute for the revelations of Scripture. Rome again comes into play prominently in these prophesies, from the fall of the empire, the division of power, the consolidation of power and, most importantly, the spiritual battle of Armageddon that will be waged with words, truth and error, until the final day of judgment.

America as the Great Republic founded upon God's word and will is dead. In a temporal sense, the nation was always doomed and could never survive in that context. But as a home to God's people, as a Christian nation, there is yet some cause for optimism. Our best hope may lie in the fact that we're beset with great troubles and hardships. Perhaps God is just working these things together for our benefit to turn us back to him like he did so many times with Israel. As God raised Lazarus from the dead, and more importantly Jesus Christ, he can certainly resurrect our dead Republic if it is his will, if he has a purpose for us. Can we do this of our own volition? No, apart from God we're powerless. We truly are dead in that sense. But there is something we can do that will benefit our people eternally regardless of the temporal fate of America. That is, we can repent. We must admit where we've gone astray and departed from God's way. We need to turn back to God in meekness, humbleness and sorrow. Collectively, we need

to offer a most simple prayer ... Dear Lord,
Heavenly Father, thy will be done ... please
make your will our will ... show us the way.

Things got off to a rousing start and I was
pleased with the traffic that was generated at our
website. I didn't mind that a fair portion of the
audience were bitter, hateful people who spewed
the worst kind of nastiness in my general direction.
It was a little disturbing that, while these liberal
progressives were upset by my challenges to many
of their cherished paradigms, what really enraged
them was my habit of quoting the Bible to make
my case. Nevertheless, they didn't abandon the
site in anger but made repeated visits like helpless
masochists. My *heresies* seemed to energize them
and they couldn't resist coming back for more
abuse and frustration. Establishment types loathed
me more than the secular humanists. My
challenges to the status quo cut across political
parties and ideological lines. But they too made
repeated trips to Trumpet.com, not so much to
engage me as to monitor my dangerous rants that
they perceived as a threat, however small, to their
power and influence. Thankfully, I received plenty
of encouragement from earnest Christians too.
What delighted me most was not just the level of
interest shown but the type of audience we

attracted. It wasn't all fire brands from the fringes on the left and right. There were a good number of people that, judging from their comments, weren't just voicing their entrenched opinions but were sincerely seeking answers to life's important questions. I like to refer to them as the truth seekers or folks with no horse in the race.

I was thoroughly enjoying my new endeavor and making good progress. You certainly wouldn't call it an overnight success and it wasn't an instant phenomenon like some of the online videos that go virulent gaining millions of hits in a matter of hours. But there was enough traffic and interest to allow me to see that real potential existed and I seemed to be on the right track. And I was optimistic that, unlike some flash-in-the-pan video, we'd have staying power and grow larger and more influential over time. That's why I took care not to feed the beast too much. While my approach of using collaborative fan non-fiction was aimed at taking advantage of people's natural inclination toward fifteen minutes of fame, I took care to stay true to my convictions whether popular or unpopular. I appreciated gaining so many different viewpoints and adjusted some of my positions accordingly when appropriate in matters deemed adiaphorous; that is neither commanded nor forbidden by God. But I resisted the urge to cater to the whims of my readers in order to curry their favor. Bottom line, I knew that substance and character would win out in the long run. Oh, maybe it wouldn't lead to success in a temporal sense but I was certain that clinging stubbornly to the truth and refusing to compromise for personal gain was the only way to faithfully pursue this calling and serve the best interests of my readers.

It was full speed ahead at the Trumpet and I was making great progress until a bolt from the blue derailed me from my steady course. The display on my phone read "unknown caller" which was not unusual. At first, I thought it was a solicitor or perhaps one of those recorded messages that suffer a pause before completing the connection and kicking in. I almost hung up the phone but was intrigued by the silence on the other end that in twenty seconds seemed to last forever. "Hello, hello, helllloooo … is anybody there?" I repeated several times as my volume and frustration mounted.

I was unceremoniously interrupted by a voice so soft that it demanded my concentration and full attention, "Is this Horace Hermann?"

Now I was sure this was an unwanted solicitation or sales call since no one I knew referred to me by anything other than Inky, "I'm sorry but I don't accept solicitations over the phone."

The voice was filled with quiet urgency that halted my hang up reflex, "Mr. Hermann, please bear with me. I must keep this brief to avoid detection."

Perturbed by this unwanted intrusion, I interrupted and demanded, "Who is this?"

Undeterred, he would not relent, "I have information regarding the death of your friends, Carl Becker and JD Uticus." He now had my full attention. "I must end this call promptly. You will be receiving separate instructions on how to contact me safely."

I protested, "Please, who are you and what do you want?"

"I am a man who is in grave danger ... as are you. Wait for further instructions." Then there was only silence.

Dread engulfed me like a collapsed mine shaft. My hands were clasped about my head as shields and my eyes were squeezed shut like coffin lids to ward off evil thoughts. Yet frightening images flooded my mind. Try as I might, I couldn't erase the pictures popping into my head of JD falling to his death, the huge explosion that rocked his apartment, Dr. Becker's ravaged corpse and the look of horror etched on the dead assassin's face as he lay outside my home that dark, strange night years before. I was lucky that Jude, Gogo and Addie were not at home so that I had time to consider this situation more calmly after my panic subsided. As much as I wanted to share the details of such a disturbing call with someone, anyone, to settle my nerve wracked psyche, I knew it would do no good to pull my family into the fray at this point. Oh how I wished I could have a heart-to-heart with JD and seek his good counsel and steadying influence. If it were not for the bizarre and frightful brushes with death I'd shared with JD, maybe I could have dismissed the stranger's call as a sick prank. But someone familiar with Dr. Becker's murder and JD's purported demise had to be taken seriously. There was no choice but to suffer silently and wait to be contacted again. It was all I could do to mask my inner turmoil so as to not upset Jude and the kids.

Thankfully, I only had to endure one fitful, sleepless night. The next afternoon, there was a plain envelope in the mail with no postage, return address or markings of any kind other than my name. I separated it from the rest of the mail so that Jude would not see it. When the coast was clear, I walked through the house, past my home office and to the farthest corner of the compound where the Trumpet's printing press resided since it offered the most privacy. A combination of adrenaline and nerves made the simple task of tearing open the envelope seem next to impossible. I might as well have had sausages attached to my hands considering the way my fingers fumbled across the paper. Finally, I used a pocket knife to yield the contents; a single page containing the following instructions.

> *Go to the Anheuser-Busch Tour Center tomorrow. You should arrive promptly at 1:00 p. m. Browse the gift shop and museum and then depart with the 1:30 tour group. Do not tell anyone about this meeting. Do not contact the authorities. Do not talk to anyone beforehand or at the Tour Center. If you fail to adhere to these instructions, if you make contact with anyone, if you are followed, I will know it.*

*Your only chance to protect yourself and
your family is to do exactly as I say. I mean
you no harm. To the contrary, I bring you
fair warning and information that can help
preserve the lives of you and your family.
Burn this letter as soon as you have read it.*

My common sense screamed for me to take
this note to the police immediately but a small
voice inside my head bade otherwise. If I were in
this by myself it might have been different but I
couldn't put Jude, Gogo and Addie in peril so I lit a
match and set the page aflame. My heart strings
were tightened a notch or two, so taut it seemed
to tug at my skin. I thought, so this is how it feels to
be Bruce Jenner or Joan Rivers. I know, this was no
laughing matter but I desperately needed a little
levity to help me keep up my charade with Jude for
another day.

That night, my mind played terrible tricks
on me. I morphed into a conspiracy theorist
imagining the worst possible thoughts. What if
someone had discovered that JD was alive, and
thus still a threat to expose the criminals
responsible for his *death* and Doctor Becker's?
What if one of our rare contacts had been
intercepted? Perhaps JD's ruse had not been

uncovered. Maybe I was the target? Had I written something or crossed some line that caused them to perceive me as a threat? Did the perpetrators uncover a way to eliminate the *insurance policy* we'd set up to expose figures in the church hierarchy if I met with an untimely demise? Worst of all, I thought, what if this secret benefactor was really a wolf in sheep's clothing, a malefactor who was smoking me out to eliminate rather than warn and protect me? After the way the last attempt on our lives turned out, maybe they figured they needed to lure me away from the compound and my family to finish the job properly this time. I tossed and turned to the point where I woke up Jude. "What's the matter, Inky? Are you okay?"

"Sorry dear, it's nothing. I must have eaten something that didn't agree with me. A couple of Tums and I'll be good as new. Go back to sleep darling." I made a trip to the medicine cabinet for some and popped a couple of sleeping pills instead. They eventually did the job but it was not a restful sleep.

When I woke up in the morning, I was dog tired. A jolt of hot coffee was a blessing and a curse. It started my engine for the big day ahead but further irritated my raw nerves. At least the daylight calmed my wild imagination and blessed me with some common sense. I thought that if this guy wanted to eliminate me away from the compound he could just wait for the right moment and follow me when I left on business or to run some errands. Why would he go to all the trouble of calling and sending a letter to lure me out? That would only put me on high alert. It would also run the risk that I'd defy his instructions and contact the cops. Maybe my secret caller was on the level. This helped to lower my blood pressure a bit. But then my emotions and fears kicked in again. Who is this guy? How is he involved? Why would his life be in danger? It was a long wait and seemed like the longest morning of my life. Just before noon, I told Jude I was heading to Concordia Seminary to do some research for a story. I said I'd grab a sandwich in Clayton. There was no way I could eat anything and didn't want to try to get more mileage out of my supposed upset stomach. I kissed her goodbye hoping that I'd see her again in the afternoon.

As I drove east on Interstate 70 toward downtown St. Louis, my eyes kept drifting back to my rear view mirror. I imagined every car was tailing me and looked for telltale signs. My paranoia got the better of me and I exited early at

Grand Avenue in one of the roughest parts of town. Sure enough, one of the cars behind me followed me down the exit ramp. I turned right and sped up the hill toward the old water tower a few blocks away. When I made it to the tower, I made a complete circle and headed back toward 70. The car I supposed was tailing me continued past the tower on Grand. I felt a little foolish but justified at the same time. *You can't be too safe when it comes to espionage,* my juvenile mind exclaimed! I continued on to Interstate 55 and exited at Arsenal Street by the brewery. No one followed me as I turned onto Lynch and pulled into the Tour Center parking lot. I was a few minutes early and dreaded killing time before the 1:30 tour. I remembered the caller's specific instructions and only offered a smile and slight nod when I was greeted by one of the Tour Center hosts at the entrance. They probably thought I was mute or grumpy. I moved on and prayed I didn't run into any acquaintances in the lobby, museum or gift shop. I kept gravitating to nooks and corners away from the other guests and tried to busy myself with the exhibits and merchandize but my thoughts kept drifting back to that September 11th day when JD died the first time. There were no reminders of the tragedy that occurred that day, at least not inside.

There was a fitting memorial to the victims out in the courtyard. Nonetheless the images were still fresh in my mind. It was somehow oddly fitting that this meeting was about to occur on these hallowed grounds.

Even though I kept to myself, I was hyper-self-conscious over the prospect of being watched. I tried to inconspicuously scan the Tour Center to detect if I was the subject of surveillance. I must have looked awfully suspicious because my eyes darted off in every direction to avoid eye contact. The suspense was killing me. Then a horrible thought occurred. What if this was just a cruel hoax? Or worse, what if my anonymous counter-part had backed out and left me hanging? I was close to flipping my lid when the tour guide called the guests to gather for the 1:30 tour. Momentarily, I pondered an about face toward the exit but caught myself and thought better of it. My head was on a swivel as everyone shuffled together to form a loose pack near the side exit where the tours depart. Was there someone in the crowd who fit the part? Had anyone donned a long, black trench coat, dark sunglasses and matching hat with the brim pulled down low? Nothing registered. Perhaps my vision was clouded by doubts, fears and my obsession with remaining unobtrusive. I followed our tour guide out the door like one of twenty lemmings, feeling like a fool. This feeling only grew worse as we entered the fermenting cellars and still no one approached me. In spite of the mild temperature outside, it was colder than a well digger's rear end in there. It seemed like a fitting place to rendezvous without raising any eyebrows since everyone's attention was riveted on the hundreds of gigantic lager tanks stacked to the ceiling high above and across every inch of the cavernous warehouse. Each massive tank rivaled the size of an atomic submarine. Yet no one approached.

It was too late to turn back so I forged ahead. There were the Clydesdale stables with the majestic steeds standing a head taller than me at the shoulders and the wandering Dalmatians who seemed to have free run of the place. Then onto the old brew house with its gleaming, old copper kettles and wafting aromas of barley malt, hops and cauldrons of bubbling wert. Finally we made our way down Pestalozzi Street to the Bevo Packaging Plant where old world charm and the ancient craft of brewing met modern technology in a blur of whizzing, whirring, clacking and humming pasteurizers, fillers, cappers, crowners, labelers, carton erectors and palletizers that moved the precious cans and bottles of Budweiser faster than the eye could follow in a symphony of dizzying sounds befitting the mechanical magic being performed before our very eyes. My mind drifted far from the concerns of the day as I marveled at the spectacle being played out in front of me. It was at that moment that there was a slight tap on my shoulder that startled me so much I had to catch my breath.

The man next to me looked like a typical St. Louis tourist with faded jeans, a tattered Bud Light tee shirt and worn Cardinals ball cap. He drew me off to the side a bit, just far enough away to allow me to hear his voice while still masking our conversation from the other guests with the din from the production floor. He was vaguely familiar but I couldn't quite place him until he whispered his name and the memories came streaming back. Antonio Marchetti was the right hand man of the late Cardinal Riccardi who was at the center of intrigue and treachery that had claimed Dr. Becker's life and threatened JD, me and my family. What threw me off was the accelerated aging process that had claimed his youthful vigor. The lines in his face were etched much too deep and his raven black hair was beyond gray, with flecks of stark white. His erect posture was replaced with a slightly hunched look like a great cathedral in disrepair and soon to be condemned. He must have been living under tremendous stress to age at a pace akin to a U. S. president or POW. Most telling was the sadness and timidity stamped across his once proud visage. He spoke without looking at me and I followed suit staring straight ahead, "When the tour is over, bypass the hospitality room, leave through the front exit, proceed down Lynch Street, turn left on Tenth and sit at one of the tables outside the credit union. I will pass by and wait for you down at the end of the street at Tenth and Sidney." He gave me no chance to respond and melted back into the pack. I gave no thought to missing out on the free samples at the hospitality center, since I was consumed with a mixture of excitement, fear and anticipation.

I followed his directions precisely and then discreetly met him at the end of the block outside of Big Daddy's bar and grill. He motioned and I followed him on what would be a long walk through the streets of the Soulard neighborhood which was largely deserted at this time of day. We maintained a deliberate, steady pace walking side-by-side as he let the story unfold while making almost no eye contact. Although I was already spilling over with questions, I held my tongue and let him unload his burden. "I apologize for all of this cloak and dagger behavior but, trust me, it is quite necessary. Before I get to my own saga and the immediate threat we are facing, I need to set the record straight regarding everything that happened to you and your late friends, Dr. Becker and JD Uticus." I nodded as if I understood and agreed with his logic. "I was a party to the evil, dastardly deeds perpetrated against you. As you suspected and in many respects have concluded, the church was at the heart of your troubles; my church as aided by certain members of your church. The conspiracy involved individuals from several organizations but, make no mistake; Riccardi was at the heart and center ... the head of the serpent."

I wanted to scream, *I knew it*, but remained silent and somehow masked the adrenalin rush that had my senses on full alert. He continued as if he was inside a confessional, "JD's fate was sealed the first time we met. Cardinal Riccardi sensed immediately that The Last Prophet would not allow his fame and influence to be used to advance the reach of the Catholic Church. He was wary from the start and had me and others watch you closely. When the perceived threat to the papacy became clear, Riccardi was swift and ruthless in dispatching his hired assassin, a truly malevolent force of nature known only as the Sicilian Ghost. Becker was poisoned with polonium-210, a silent, undetectable weapon whose stealth was enhanced with the cover provided by Dr. Becker's cancer. We continued to monitor your every move through multiple means including the hidden bugs you later discovered with the help of your cat. If JD would have ceased his preoccupation with finishing what Becker started ... exploring the marks of the Antichrist ... perhaps things would have turned out differently. Instead, Riccardi unleashed the Ghost again. He murdered your *guardian angel*, Andrew Ogilvy, and made him disappear. His body will never be found. He was set to do the same to you, your family and JD. How you were saved we do not know. We could only surmise that it was the hand of God. Perhaps you did have a guardian angel watching over you that night."

For the first time, Marchetti glanced at me briefly with a look of true remorse. "I am ashamed to admit it but I was complicit in all of Riccardi's evil deeds, as was Dr. Kaltmann and Baker from your own church. At least I can say for them that they wanted no part of the killings, especially the threats to your children. However, once they were caught up in Riccardi's web of deceit they could not escape and followed his murderous lead. As for me, I have no such excuse. I knew what we were doing. For a time, I could say that my judgment was clouded by a sense of doing the work of the church but that can only go so far. In my heart, I knew the killing of innocent women and children had no place in the Lord's work. Still, I remained Riccardi's obedient lap dog. You would think that we, even Riccardi, would have recognized God's hand in saving you from the Ghost but we had succumbed to evil, we were blind. Riccardi's tentacles stretched far and he used the Muslims to do his dirty work. To this day, JD's death is seen as the work of Islamic terrorists but now you know the truth. Riccardi pressed the button that set their deadly plan in motion."

Marchetti sighed as a man resigned to a terrible fate, "Riccardi attempted to cover his tracks completely. It was not an accident that claimed the lives of Kaltmann and Baker on that lonely stretch of highway. Another one of Riccardi's banshees helped their car down that steep embankment and poisoned them for good measure. With JD out of the way, you were left alone since you accepted that the Islamists were to blame and offered no threat to the Catholic Church. That left only one remaining tie that could

86

link Riccardi to the crimes: me. I was dispatched on a church mission to the Middle East. I had seen enough to know I couldn't trust Riccardi even though I was his right hand man and had served him faithfully for many years. I played along with this deception knowing that he surely intended to use his fanatical Muslim friends to eliminate me. But I was prepared and took off on a globetrotting gambit as soon as I landed in Jerusalem. My hopscotching was well planned and carried out with a dizzying swiftness that left a vaporous trail. When I learned of Riccardi's demise, I knew I was no safer. In fact, I figured I was in much greater danger. Riccardi's death had to be carried out by those in the highest reaches of the church and I knew that if he was deemed an expendable threat, I was certainly destined for permanent silencing."

I hardly noticed because Marchetti's tale had held me in rapt attention but we were at the far end of the Soulard district near the Soulard Produce Market. Marchetti wisely turned our course to the west to avoid any market goers that might overhear us. It became increasingly difficult but I held my peace longer to continue the vital flow of information coming from my walking companion. "You probably won't believe this and I certainly wouldn't expect your forgiveness but I am compelled to tell you that I am truly sorry for my part in the evil plots carried out against you and your comrades." I started to object but Marchetti cut me off with the palm of his hand. "Truly, I am not seeking redemption but I need to do this to satisfy my own soul. I have paid a dear price. As you can see, I look at least twenty years older than I am. This is what happens when you live with no peace or rest, not for a moment. The litany of menial jobs I've held to make ends meet is long. Only temporary work of the lowest sort will suffice for someone on the run. I have no roots, no moss. My steps have followed every point on the compass. I've dwelled in the remotest places inhabitable on this earth from jungle vales to desert drear. I've lived off the land. At times I've hidden in plain sight, among the teeming masses, out on the streets. Even with that, the hounds have never relented. It seems I'm never more than a step ahead of my pursuers. Several times they have closed in on me and my escape has been by no more than a whisker. I can feel the noose getting ever tighter and my days are surely numbered."

Marchetti stopped unexpectedly and, for the first time, turned to look me straight in the eye. His sadness, remorse and sense of urgency were palpable, "I deserve this and in an odd way look forward to my impending doom that it may finally bring me rest. Until then, my only wish is for my soul to have some peace. I cannot change the past but there is something I can do to hopefully demonstrate the true repentance that grips my heart and soul. I want to try to spare you and your family from my fate and protect you from the danger that is lurking."

The thought of such a dire threat against my family catapulted me from my silence, "Mr. Marchetti, why would my family be in danger? If someone wanted to harm us, we would have been easy targets long ago." The thought crossed my mind that *his years in exile living under such enormous pressure ... and his unrelenting guilt ... had turned him into a paranoid basket case. Could it be that I was just the object of an obsessed, demented mind?*

He protested, "You don't know how these people think. They have not seen you as an immediate threat. But I guarantee you that they have been watching you closely. You are more valuable alive than dead right now. While they see you as a marginal threat to be eliminated for safety's sake in the longer term, for now they don't want to draw attention back to JD Uticus. The public accepted the ruse that he was the victim of Muslim extremists. If you and your family met an untimely end, it might raise new questions and open up old wounds. The last thing they want is to put themselves in the spotlight and cause anyone to link your death back to JD's. Having a closed case is a greater benefit than eliminating the potential threat posed by you. They have bigger fish to fry. With me they see a definite problem that needs to be solved immediately. Also, unfortunately, I'm unknown to the public. My death will cause nary a ripple in the public's perception of events that are dead and buried."

He had me thinking but I was still not convinced, "If I've been left alone as you say, I think it's more likely that they fear the release of the files we threatened to make public prior to JD's death."

"At one time, this was true. However, this is less relevant day-by-day. Enough time has passed that The Last Prophet is no longer at the forefront of public perception. As time marches on, they have less to fear in terms of your death being linked back to JD's assassination at the hands of terrorists. And the files you kept were short on details and prone to much speculation."

I objected, "There's still plenty of information in our files that could incriminate …"

Marchetti cut me off, "Incriminate who, my friend … Kaltmann, Baker, me, Riccardi? They are all dead and I have one foot in the grave. You have nothing that links them to the real puppet masters. Mark my word; you do not know the power and reach of your adversaries. Do you think they couldn't find and destroy your files if they saw the need? Do you realize what kind of torture they would subject your wife and children to in order to recover your files and keep your mouth shut? If your accusations ever saw the light of day, they could unleash a media storm against you that would reduce you to a laughingstock, a cheap and pitiful conspiracy theorist seeking fifteen minutes of fame or an easy score against someone with deep pockets. Please believe me when I tell you that you and your family are in grave danger."

I was frustrated and agitated and the pitch of my voice betrayed me, "So is this a damned-if-you-do, damned-if-you-don't scenario? If I rock the boat it will only speed up their timetable for eliminating me but if I keep quiet and do nothing it's only a matter of time before they get rid of the potential threat I may pose? If my goose is cooked either way, why are you bothering to tell me this?"

"I've put myself in harm's way to come out of hiding to speak to you. If we're detected, it would put you in much greater danger too. That is certainly not my purpose. I meant what I said before. I am truly repentant and I'm only risking my life to try to save you and your family." I was ready to explode and Marchetti sensed it. "Before you say anything, please bear with me a bit longer. You are correct that you're in between a rock and a hard place. That's why I'm here to help. If you remain silent it will not save you and making idle threats will only provoke them. But I'm not cautioning you against threats, just idle threats. The only thing that these people understand is danger, a legitimate threat to their power and influence."

I blew a gasket, "You're off your rocker, Marchetti! You're talking out of both sides of your mouth. That's crazy talk!"

He pleaded, "Wait before you write me off, Mr. Hermann. Please hear me out. The reason I'm here is to arm you with the facts and details. I want to put some real teeth in your threats so they will be forced to stand up and take notice and treat you with proper respect ... and fear. I can give you everything you need to make your accusations stick and blow the lid off of their conspiracy if they cross you."

I paused and pondered, "If the information you have is so compelling, why are they still trying to kill you?"

"That's a fair question. You see, in my hands this information is virtually useless when you consider the source. I deserted the church and have been living the life of a recluse, vagabond and fugitive. It would be easy for them to discredit me. And again, I'm an unknown. I'm not linked, like you, to someone with star power, someone like JD who even in death is still incredibly high in the pantheon of notable public figures. They would listen to you, by association. Remember, you lived through it. You know how rabid the media can be when it comes to The Last Prophet. As for me, I'm nobody from nowhere. I'm an easy target to be painted with the brush of mental illness. My death will be an unfortunate accident. I doubt it will make the papers. To raise a ruckus, somebody has to care. I have no family, no connections and no means. My life was the church. I was afforded a certain degree of power and influence as long as I was embedded in the hierarchy. Since I've betrayed them, I'm an outcast without an ounce of support, every prop has been taken out from under me and their vast authority and resources are aligned against me. I'm an ant under a magnifying glass."

Marchetti started to make sense to me. What he said cranked up my worst fears but also offered a slim ray of hope. My jumbled emotions released a torrent of questions. "What evidence do you have? Can it be corroborated? What about my family? Should I go to the authorities? What can I do to safeguard the information you have for me? Are you sure I wouldn't be safer just keeping my mouth shut? Should I tell anyone else about this? Who should I talk to in the church? Really, wouldn't it be better for me to just keep quiet? What are you going to do next? Should I send my family away? What should I do? What should I do?"

Marchetti touched my arm in a way that infused me with an invisible sedative to impede the avalanche of emotions that gripped me. "We do not have the time for such distractions. Our focus must be on one thing and that is how to protect you and your family. I've taken a chance in approaching you this way but it is a necessary risk. It's the only way I could see to convince you and help steer your course. However, the more time we spend together the greater the danger. I've taken great pains to elude my pursuers but I must depart soon to ensure that my trail does not lead them to you. If the church found out that I contacted you, it would force their hand to pounce immediately. We must not let this happen until safeguards are in place to deter them. Do you understand?"

I felt unbearable discomfort. It was too much for me to swallow. All I wanted was to be left alone, blissful in my ignorance of the threats. But it was too late. I was trapped like a rat and faced with a monumental decision I didn't want to make. Marchetti had been an inside man. There was no doubt that he knew the full truth and shared it with me at his own great peril. He had no reason whatsoever to lie to me; nothing to gain and everything to lose. The details he provided lined up perfectly with the facts at my disposal about JD, Dr. Becker, Andrew Ogilvy, Kaltmann, Baker, Riccardi and the mysterious stranger who died of fright outside my home. Still, a voice inside my head screamed for me to run away as fast as possible and forget everything Marchetti had said. Whether this was pure fear or wisdom speaking to me, I froze at the prospect of discounting his revelations. If what he said was true … and everything pointed clearly in that direction … could I afford to ignore him? What would this mean for Jude and the kids? Could I take the chance? Duty drove me to ask, "So, what can I do to protect my family?"

"Listen to me carefully. There is only one way. You must pose a credible threat to those that would do you harm. It must be so severe that it will utterly, convincingly dissuade them from following their reptilian instinct to eliminate you and your family." He paused to let this sink in and sober my thoughts for what he shared next was so bold it required a true leap of faith. "You must get to them before they can get to you. If you seize the initiative, you can control your own destiny. But first, I must equip you." He stopped momentarily and spoke directly, eye-to-eye in a hushed, deadly serious tone, "I have prepared a packet of information that will provide all the ammunition you need to keep the vipers at bay. It will be in your hands before I vanish again to the ends of the earth."

He instructed me carefully as if training me on how to diffuse a ticking time bomb, "I have gathered the facts and evidence that you will need to connect Riccardi to the deaths of Becker, Ogilvy, Uticus, Kaltmann and Baker. Additionally, I've included the ties linking the Cardinal to the Ghost, Kaltmann's assassin and a man named Al Batin who unleashed the Muslim fanatics who killed your friend JD. There are instructions along with the information that will help you to safeguard it and ensure the threat will remain credible, beyond detection and disposal. You cannot simply keep a copy hidden away in a safe deposit box. There must be multiple layers to your defense and you have to employ technology to your benefit. Electronic files must be encrypted and placed in safe keeping where the most advanced hacker cannot compromise them."

He clasped my arm firmly to emphasize the importance of his next bit of preparation, "You can do all of this perfectly but it will be of no effect without the next two pieces which are absolutely essential. First, you need someone you trust completely, even with your life. This person must be tech savvy. You will have to bring him or her into the loop enough so they understand the life or death importance of the task you're asking them to take on. But this person should be unobtrusive, someone who melts into the background and would never raise anyone's awareness. Whomever you choose, they will need to know that their own life could be at risk too. I cannot emphasize the gravity of your choice too much. This will either be the weak link in the chain of your defense or the glue that forms the strong bond you need to survive." As he spoke, I immediately began to think of Mit. He was perfect for the job in so many ways. But could I place my life and the lives of Jude, Gogo and Addie in the hands of such a goofy genius?

He squeezed my forearm to draw my attention further, "There is only one thing left you need to know. That is, you must issue the threat to the right person on the inside. It must be someone who is at the center, intimately involved. You must be exact. While you must get to the source, it's extremely important to keep the threat contained. A shotgun approach would be fatal ... to you and any unfortunate members of the church hierarchy outside the inner circle who might learn of the conspiracy within their midst. You should submit a copy of everything I'll provide to you to one man, in confidence ... Cardinal Cagliostro, in Rome, at the Vatican. Beware for he is incredibly powerful, extremely dangerous and deadly evil. Cagliostro resides within that small, small circle, has access to the highest reaches and is intimately involved with the plot that killed JD Uticus. I would not doubt that he had a hand in personally dispatching Cardinal Riccardi."

I literally shuddered at the thought of getting in the face of someone in a position to exercise such might unscrupulously. This seemed about as wise as taunting a grizzly bear with a sour disposition. It was all I could do to control my bladder. What had I gotten myself into? I appealed to Marchetti, "Are you sure I won't be committing suicide?"

He was resolute, "I am sure of one thing. If you do nothing, you and your family will come to know of Cagliostro in due time, through his *emissaries*. You only have one choice and that is to head him off at the pass and derail the mortal scheme he inevitably has in store for you and your family. If you do nothing, you will eventually have to face this roaring lion with nothing but a whip and chair. I'm offering you a bazooka to fend him off. In either case he will want to kill you but in the former he will only toy with you whereas in the latter he will fear and respect you. That is the only way to restrain him. I cannot make the decision for you. That is your responsibility alone. Unfortunately, we have no time. You must make up your mind right now before I depart."

I was frozen, completely paralyzed by the looming choice. It was my verdict, my ruling to issue. I was the sentencing judge. In reeling in the images of Dr. Becker, JD and the parade of mayhem and death Riccardi had strewn in his wake, it dawned on me that Marchetti was right. Who was I in the scheme of things? Why would the conspirators look any differently at me, Jude, Gogo and Addie than the others whose lives meant so little to them? Would they be any more tolerant of the threat posed by us? One final thought crossed my mind. Now that Marchetti had filled in the gaps, there was no doubt about why that strange man was outside my home and armed to the teeth when he was frightened to death by our guardian angels. They had already dispatched an assassin once to eliminate me and my family. What would stop them from doing this again? Yes, Marchetti was right. The answer was that there was nothing to stop them, unless I took matters into my own hands. Recognizing the real threat posed by Cagliostro toward my family gave me just enough steely resolve to say, "I'll do it."

Marchetti was elated with my decision but still fretted like a mother hen, "Remember, the Polonium-210. It was undetectable under the circumstances of Dr. Becker's death but it always leaves a trace. They dug up Arafat's body because they suspected foul play from Polonium-210. If you need irrefutable evidence that Becker did not die from cancer, it is always there waiting to be revealed. The same can be said of Kaltmann and Baker. Though their deaths appeared accidental, their bodies hold the truth ... the poison provided the finishing touches. Choose your techie *guardian angel* wisely. He will be the gatekeeper who protects you as your last line of defense."

He turned to go without so much as a farewell and I had to stop him, "How can I ever thank you?"

"You can thank me by staying alive."

"I mean, how can I repay you for risking your life for me?"

"My life is worthless at this point and my days are numbered. Don't forget that I was part and parcel of the failed attempt to murder you and your family."

"I forgive you for that."

"It does my heart good. It is music to my soul. I've finally learned to look to Jesus Christ for atonement. Now, please remember, as soon as you receive the information I will provide you, act swiftly. There should be no second thoughts, no delays. Time is of the essence, my friend." With that, he turned and left. I watched until he was out of sight. He never looked back.

CHAPTER 3

Smoke Rising

"We shall be as a City upon a Hill, the eyes of all people are upon us...," (Puritan John Winthrop aboard the ship Arbella in route to the new world with his fellow Massachusetts Bay colonists in his sermon, A Model of Christian Charity, 1630).

Marchetti's omen was no fantasy. I knew the pending danger he had forewarned of was very real, no figment of his imagination or mere paranoia. Yet, I did exactly what he explicitly told me not to do; I hesitated. The packet of information and computer disks materialized on my front porch the next night, just as he had promised, without a trace left behind by its secret courier. I should have jumped right into the fray, digested the information and taken immediate steps to implement our plan according to his instructions but I dragged my feet nonetheless. Did I doubt the legitimacy of the threat? Was I lacking in personal experience regarding the ruthlessness of the people behind the plot that had claimed so many lives? Were there still holes in Marchetti's story that needed to be mined? No, all of these things screamed at me to get my butt in gear. But still I dawdled as if I were impervious to the danger. I guess it was just fear and cowardice. With Marchetti there to prod and encourage me, I had stood boldly and confidently at the precipice ready to take the leap into the unknown. Then, as soon as he left, I started to backslide and take the easy way out by ignoring the peril I was surely inviting. I could only hope that my error would not prove fatal.

My weaknesses are most easily revealed when I'm alone and isolated. When Marchetti stole away over the horizon, I had no one. I couldn't share my predicament with Jude and the kids. There would be no purpose in briefing them other than to burden them with fear and anxiety. In time Jude would need to know something but not now, not while everything was so uncertain and fluid. Ah, again I thought if only I could share my burden with JD and gain his counsel, everything would be so much better. After hearing Marchetti's revelations, I recognized that contacting JD would be the worst thing possible. If the villains and plotters inside the church found out JD was alive, it would magnify the threat tenfold and certainly drive them to take drastic measures against JD, me and my family. So I was on my own; a coward paralyzed by fear and indecision. Of course, as a Christian, I should have realized I'm never alone but, due to the weakness of my own flesh, failed to turn to Jesus in my time of crisis and doubt.

No, I didn't turn to my real power source, my Savior and his quickening word of truth. Like a fool I leaned on myself, my own feeble self to weather the storm. I buried myself in my work to hide my shortcomings and insecurities and mask my jumbled emotions. I found a temporary solace by connecting with my *co-authors* and collaborators over the web. I issued a hail of posts regarding the next installment of American Phoenix and jealously gobbled up every opportunity to share a dialogue with Trumpet.com's growing band of followers. What would take shape would become the second chapter of American Phoenix: American Exceptionalism ... Manifest Destiny. Here are excerpts from the work that occupied my time and preserved my sanity.

I've said before that early America had more in common with ancient Israel than Rome and it's true for this one very simple reason. America was founded as a Christian nation guided by God's hand. No, it was not a theocracy in the sense of ancient Israel but it was conceived and born in accordance with Christian principles rooted firmly in the Holy Bible. The Founding Fathers were first and foremost God-fearing men steeped in the Christian faith. They were raised in Christian families and taught in schools that used primers filled with passages from Scripture. They recited the Ten Commandments regularly as part of their normal school routine. The Bible was their guiding light and was at the center of the debate as they hammered out the Declaration of Independence and Constitution.

If you go back to primary sources and explore the writings of the Founding Fathers that pertain to the Constitution, the Bible is quoted liberally and it's abundantly clear it was used extensively as a formative rule and guide. By way of example, the need for separation of powers was justified by Jeremiah 17:9 where God's truth is expounded that, left alone according to man's sinful, wicked nature, governing power, if unchecked, will undoubtedly lead to corruption and abuse. Now ain't that the truth! Likewise, the idea of three branches found inspiration in Isaiah 33:22 and tax exemption for churches in Ezra 7:24. The examples abound. The skeptics go to great lengths to deny the faith of the Founding Fathers and the influence of Scripture toward our founding principles. But any honest, unbiased reading of the history of those days will reveal the obvious; the Founding Fathers were by and large God-fearing Christian men who thought it good, right and natural to look to the Bible for God's wisdom in matters of life and government.

When Patrick Henry issued his famous proclamation of "Give me liberty or give me death," he was well versed in the scriptural principle of Christian liberty. In a less famous but incredibly insightful moment he later declared, "It cannot be emphasized too strongly or too often that this great nation was founded not by religionists but by Christians ... not on religion but on the gospel of Jesus Christ." John Quincy Adams, our sixth president, offered a similar sentiment, "The highest glory of the American Revolution was this: it connected in one indissoluble bond the principles of civil government with the principles of Christianity." John Jay, Founding Father and our first Chief Justice of the United States, issued this bold declaration, "Providence has given our people the choice of their rulers and it is the duty, as well as privilege and interest, of a Christian nation to select and prefer Christians for their rulers." Seems pretty clear doesn't it? These guys didn't mince words or pull any punches.

Wait, I can't stop without adding something from George Washington. He provided these wise words in his farewell address to the nation. "Of all the dispositions and habits, which lead to political prosperity, Religion and Morality are indispensable supports. In vain would that man claim the tribute of Patriotism, who should labor to subvert these great pillars of human happiness; these firmest props of the duties of Men and Citizens. The mere Politician, equally with the pious man, ought to respect and to cherish them. A volume could not trace all their connections with private and public felicity. Let it simply be asked, where is the security for property, for reputation, for life, if the sense of religious obligation desert the oaths, which are the instruments of investigation in Courts of Justice? And let us with caution indulge the supposition, that morality can be maintained without religion. Whatever may be conceded to the influence of refined education on minds of peculiar structure, reason and experience both forbid us to expect, that national morality can prevail in exclusion of religious principle." Oh, and by the way, don't believe the skeptics and revisionists when they try to tell you Washington was a deist, some kind of religionist. He knew Jesus Christ as God, Lord and Savior.

Surprisingly, the first wave of replies to this post did not attempt to take me to task on the basis of historical fact. Instead there was a sense of outrage from some quarters at my use of the term America and Americans.

Where do you get off calling us Americans? Do you mean U. S. Citizens?

Hey, what do you mean by Americans? Are you forgetting about the Native Americans? What about the Mexicans, Canadians and Brazilians?

Is God's providence restricted to U. S. Citizens? Does God prefer us over the people living elsewhere in North, Central and South America?

There was more and some of it was not so friendly. I was perturbed not so much by the political correctness being spewed at me as I was by the fact that they missed the entire point. I would have been much happier to engage the dissenters on the factual basis for claiming America was founded as a Christian nation rather than bickering over the insensitivity of my terminology. I was determined to get back on course by firing the following salvo.

My sincere apologies are offered to everyone else living in the Northern, Central and Southern parts of the continents that have adopted the Anglicized version of Italian explorer Amerigo

*Vespucci's name. However, they are not
Americans in the truest sense as used here.
There is truly something unique about our
nation, by the grace of God. Rant all you want
but people around the world know exactly what
the term American means ... and it's not a
reference to a continent. To avoid any further
confusion, please be advised that the term
America is used in this context to denote our
people, citizens and country from its inception
with the early settlers at Jamestown, VA in 1607
and Plymouth, MA in 1620 and through the
establishment of the original thirteen colonies,
War for Independence and later expansion right
up to the present day United States of America.
I also offer my apologies to Native Americans of
every tribe and culture who preceded the
European immigrants and have been
unceremoniously lumped under this single
banner. No apology is necessary to African-
Americans who adopted the term, as I've used
it here, of their own accord. The offense is not
in the name but in the manner in which they
were first brought to American shores in
shackles.*

Standing my ground and offering a reasoned
explanation without equivocating seemed to

appease most readers but a few committed ideologues persisted. I ignored them rather than spending more time getting off the topic at hand. I needed to get back to American Exceptionalism and God's role in the fulfillment of our manifest destiny. But I had touched on an issue that could not be ignored.

> How can I dare to preach God's providence when this darkest blight on our national psyche was present from the very beginning? Did God favor the fair skinned over the darker complexioned? Did the Almighty endorse the enslavement of some of his people by another? The first thing we must acknowledge is that God is perfect, not people ... including Americans. Only God's will is perfect and we do often err when we depart from his ways. Individually and corporately we have made mistakes and we've never committed a greater sin, as a nation, than the enslavement of African-Americans. But don't blame God for our transgressions. It's our bad. But, you say, couldn't God have stopped this travesty in its tracks? Of course he could ... he's the Omnipotent Creator of man and the universe. However, God doesn't operate that way. He does not force his will upon us. God doesn't

program obedience into us as if we were unthinking, unfeeling automatons. Our sins, each and every one of them ... from slavery to abortion to persecution of his church ... grieve our Heavenly Father terribly. But he permits them ... along with the consequences of sin which we heap upon ourselves.

Here again we are much like ancient Israel. God did not instill blind obedience. This was demonstrated time and again when his Hebrew people rebelled against God and forsook him for false gods and idols. They suffered tragically for their many sins ... and it grieved God tremendously to see his people suffer. Nevertheless, God was perfectly faithful. He never left their side even when they abandoned him over and over again. He allowed the Temple to be destroyed, his people to be scattered, carted off to Babylon in captivity for seventy years and enslaved by the Egyptians for four hundred years. Yes, God permitted his own people to become slaves. God never forgot his promise and worked all these things together for good so that the Savior of mankind came into the world and was incarnate as Jesus Christ, the promised Messiah from Abraham's line.

God has blessed America but that doesn't make us perfect. He has showered his grace and mercy upon us in spite of all our sins. When we've gone our own way, we've suffered the consequences. Like with ancient Israel, God has used these difficulties, tragedies and hard times to benefit us in spite of ourselves. We need to take a lesson from Joseph ... you know, the story that is still immortalized on Broadway and in summer stock everywhere in Joseph and the Amazing Technicolor Dreamcoat. God allowed his treacherous brothers to plot his murder and then instead sell him into slavery. But God used this to serve his good purposes when he raised Joseph up to a position of great influence in Egypt through the amazing power to interpret dreams. Joseph was equipped by God to provide the wise guidance necessary to avoid a devastating famine during a seven year drought. This blessing was extended to the brothers who had plotted against him. And Joseph didn't use his newfound power to punish his brothers but showed God's grace and mercy in forgiving them.

We've paid dearly for the sin of slavery. First and foremost we paid the price in blood when the Civil War claimed over six hundred thousand American lives. Slavery was ended and the union preserved but the consequences have endured, in some respects even unto today, in the form of bitterness, hatred, racism and wounds that still cause divisions among us. Yet, by God's providence we've prospered both temporally and spiritually. We've been a great force for good in this world when we've conformed to God's word and will. Time and again, at our very best, by God's grace and mercy, we've realized and lived up to the ideal that God set in motion at our nation's founding. We've come together in good times and bad as Americans to reflect the love of God toward one another and our neighbors around the world ... living up to the truth that God created us all equal, to serve one another ... basking in the warm glow of the knowledge that God loves us all regardless of our color, race, gender, age and nationality. We are a nation apart, a shining city on a hill not because of our own inherent goodness. To the contrary, we're sinners who have often departed to follow our own misguided will in opposition to God's plan. But we were still founded as a Christian nation upon the principles set down by God in his word and thus have prospered and been blessed to reflect the light of Jesus Christ, in our oft-times imperfect way, to the rest of the world.

This brings me full circle to the key point, the one lesson that I'd like for everyone to take away from this chapter. America is exceptional and we should applaud this fact of history while giving the glory to God. If you fall prey to the revisionists who claim that we were not founded as a Christian nation, you'll never understand America ... you'll be forever lost. Let's turn to the man that many people across the entire political spectrum consider the greatest American president, Abraham Lincoln. In the midst of a terrible war, Lincoln, in his Second Inaugural Address, showed without a doubt that he believed us to be a Christian nation guided by the hand of God. "It may seem strange that any men should dare to ask a just God's assistance in wringing their bread from the sweat of other men's faces; but let us judge not that we be not judged. The prayers of both could not be answered; that of neither has been answered fully. The Almighty has His own purposes. 'Woe unto the world because of offenses! For it must needs be that offenses come; but woe to that man by whom the offense cometh!' If we shall suppose that

American Slavery is one of those offenses which, in the providence of God, must needs come, but which, having continued through His appointed time, He now wills to remove, and that He gives to both North and South, this terrible war, as the woe due to those by whom the offense came, shall we discern therein any departure from those divine attributes which the believers in a Living God always ascribe to Him? Fondly do we hope -- fervently do we pray -- that this mighty scourge of war may speedily pass away. Yet, if God wills that it continue, until all the wealth piled by the bond-man's two hundred and fifty years of unrequited toil shall be sunk, and until every drop of blood drawn with the lash, shall be paid by another drawn with the sword, as was said three thousand years ago, so still it must be said 'the judgments of the Lord, are true and righteous altogether.'"

I was about to hit high gear in extolling the God-given greatness of America when a monkey wrench was thrown into the works. Philipp Melanchthon, the inquisitive kitty I had adopted when Dr. Becker died, or Phil the Pill as I called the little rascal, was following his normal routine. He rebuffed my playful pooch, Max, preferring to engage in stalking and pouncing in his own imaginary, solitary world. This was so common it barely registered until my attention was drawn to my frenetic feline by an odd pose that brought a flashback of heart-stopping proportion. Philipp froze like a pointer and locked his ultra-sensitive ears onto something indiscernible to me. My head pivoted in that direction and I locked my gaze upon him hoping for a sign that my foreboding sense of dread was unfounded. But then he cocked his head to the left and then the right like a slow motion metronome and inched forward as if entering a cobra's lair. The source of his fascination was invisible to me so I contacted the only person who might be able to help me. "Mit, can you come out to my place right away?"

"I'm in the middle of something." He proceeded to ramble on with the details which were way over my head.

"Mit, Mit, whoa, slow down for a second. I really need you."

"How soon do you need me?" He launched into his explanation again.

"Mit please, you're not listening. I need you right now. This is an emergency."

"Oh, okay, I see … I'll be right there." In true Mit fashion, he still tried to finish from where he left off. All I could do was to pretend not to hear and hang up and wait.

Philipp didn't budge from his sentry post. He barely moved except to adjust his head occasionally to home in with his radar ears. My kitty detective was as stationary as stone except for his whip-like tail which twitched and curled in rhythmic anticipation. I peered in the direction Philipp pointed me but could not see anything out of the ordinary amongst the tangle of wires hanging from my PC and printer. Then a red flag popped up in my head and I made my way outside to wait for Mit. The last thing I needed was for him to run into Jude and cause a big commotion about my *emergency*. I pondered what I would say. In the back of my mind, Mit was one of the reasons I had hesitated about following Marchetti's directions promptly. Wouldn't bringing him into the loop put Mit in harm's way? Would it be fair to expose him to such danger without him having a say in the matter? But how could I allow him to assess the danger beforehand without taking him past the point of no return? I still didn't have a good answer for that question. Well, I needed to come up with something fast because Mit was pulling up in front of me.

When I went out to meet him, he was still jabbering. I grabbed his shoulders and looked directly into his wide eyes which looked all the wilder under his tousled mound of unruly hair. "Mit, I need you to come into my office and help me with a technical issue but," I paused for effect, "don't say anything to Jude about this." I could tell it was killing him to hold his tongue but something about my demeanor convinced him to clam up. We were able to make our way to my office without coming across Jude or the kids. As soon as we entered, Mit's attention turned to Philipp. He's a cat lover … some kind of Doctor Doolittle.

He coaxed, "Hello Philipp … here kitty, kitty." Mit kneeled down and made a ticking sound with his tongue that usually brought the normally aloof cat slinking toward him purring and rubbing his sides against Mit's legs. This time, Philipp was so entranced he didn't budge.

I had to stop Mit before he went into full pied piper mode, "Mit, Philipp hears something that we can't hear. I've looked but I can't spot anything unusual. I think there may be some kind of bug, a hidden transmitter in the room." Mit gave me a look of astonishment as if I had just confessed to kidnapping the Lindbergh baby. But the prospect of the technical challenge I'd just thrown out, not to mention the intrigue it invoked, gained his full attention. He turned to leave the room and when I began to object he shushed me without a word by holding up one gangly index finger. He left to get something out of the trunk of his car. Mit returned in a flash with some gadgetry that looked like a space aged stud finder. He was silent, completely focused and I did nothing to interrupt him as he swept the room as if searching for some kind of alien life form. Mit moved rapidly and purposefully, only appearing herky-jerky because of his odd build and spidery limbs. Then he slowed as if zeroing in on his elusive prey. With the greatest of ease, Mit apprehended the puny device from behind my modem as if plucking a grape off the vine. He indulged the briefest of triumphant grins before going into analytical mode. I couldn't wait any longer, "Well, is it a bug?"

Mit raised a finger to his lips to quiet me and covered the bug between his palms, "Inky, we've got to be careful with what we say. Yes, someone is listening in." He opened his hands to study it some more and pulled a magnifying glass from his pocket that resembled a diamond cutter's loop. Again, he clamped his hands around the transmitter, "I've got to take this back to my place and give it a thorough examination. I'll call you when I've figured it out." I didn't have time to object or ask further questions. Mit was out the door and on his way. I avoided Jude and the kids as much as possible while I waited. It was only a few hours but seemed like an eternity because I was too frazzled to concentrate on work or anything productive. I alternatively vegetated and fidgeted nervously until Mit called. It took him ten minutes to get to a thirty second point. It was imperative that I know the truth so I indulged him. Bottom line, he confirmed my worst fear. It was not only a bug but in Mit's estimation a highly sophisticated transmitter, the work of a real pro. He insisted on coming back out to talk to me personally. The last thing I needed was another technical dissertation from Mit but I had to open up to someone.

This time Jude greeted Mit and invited him to join us for supper. I was scared to death that Mit would blurt something out at the dinner table but he was surprisingly disciplined until we finished dessert and went outside to digest our food. At least that's what we told Jude since we couldn't admit that we didn't want to have a conversation in the house where the walls had ears. "Inky, this is highly unusual. Someone went to a lot of expense to bug your house. Are you in some kind of trouble?" My hesitation didn't help matters. He peppered me tongue-in-cheek but halfway seriously, "Have you been paying your taxes on time?"

I tried to back myself out of a corner, "Mit, I think I know what's behind this but I don't want to speculate in front of you."

"Inky, as a Christian brother you know you can trust me. But I'll understand if you'd rather talk to your pastor about it."

"Mit it's not like that. I just don't want to drag you into something that could put you in danger, grave danger."

It didn't faze Mit in the least, "What do I have to fear? I belong to Jesus Christ. I John 4:4 tells us that, 'greater is he that is in you, than he that is in the world.'"

"That's true Mit but this is deadly serious. If I talk to you about this, there would be no turning back. I can't do that to you."

Mit displayed a lot of insight and common sense for a techie, "If you're in grave danger as you say … and I believe you based on what we found in your office … aren't I already in the same danger as you? I mean, I work for you, don't I? What do I need to do to be safe, quit my job and move to Timbuktu? No, we're in this together, brother. I can't abandon you in your hour of need. Please tell me what's wrong so I can help you."

He was right. I had already let the cat out of the bag; no pun intended Philipp; and the people that placed that bug in my office knew I was onto them and Mit was involved. "Mit, this is so, so serious. You need to realize that your life depends on what I'm about to tell you, as does mine and my family's. It may already be too late. If I'm right, the people who did this will stop at nothing. There's no place you can hide, not even Timbuktu." This jaw-dropping statement would have floored most people but Mit remained calm and resolute. I continued, "You've heard what supposedly happened to my friend, JD Uticus, the Last Prophet. Now let me tell you the real story." Mit listened intently as I filled him in completely from the terror attacks on St. Louis all the way up to my recent encounter with Antonio Marchetti. I spared no detail other than the fact that JD was still alive and in hiding. I could almost see Mit taking meticulous mental notes.

I gave Mit one last chance to back away before sharing Marchetti's file with him but he declined steadfastly and eagerly jumped on board what was essentially a runaway freight train entering a dark tunnel leading to unknown disasters. As he sifted through the evidence, Mit should have been incredulous ... and terrified ... at the prospect of being the object of the evil intent of powerful forces within the upper reaches of such a far-reaching, monolithic church hierarchy. Yet, he remained calm, anchored with the clinical stoicism of his scientific brain in full analytical mode. He stopped for just a moment to indulge in an irresistible pleasure. Mit floored me with the tidbits of information he pulled from somewhere within the vast recesses of his computer-like brain. When he came across Cardinal Cagliostro's name, he proceeded to regale me with a rather interesting slice of trivia. Mit speculated that perhaps the Cardinal descended from the famous 18th Century Sicilian alchemist and charlatan, Count Alessandro Cagliostro. Originally born Giuseppe Balsamo, the self-proclaimed count was a con artist and cheat who often posed as a nobleman and sometimes as a physician selling a magic elixir. He is most famous for the Affair of the Diamond Necklace involving King Louis XVI of France and Marie Antoinette; a crime of fraud for which he was arrested and jailed in the Bastille for nine months before being acquitted due to a lack of evidence. We needed to get back on track but I didn't discard this history lesson completely. Perhaps it was a valuable insight into the character of our current nemesis.

The grave, very real danger was not lost on Mit but he was overcome, almost ecstatic about the challenge this situation presented. When he read Marchetti's directions and realized he was being tabbed as the gate keeper, my right hand techie man, a sly smile betrayed a certain odd giddiness. In a fit of nervous energy, he burst into his strategy for ensuring our security and an avalanche of tactical details ensued. I had to bring him back to earth, "Mit, Mit, Mit … please hold on for a moment. We've crossed a very stark line and now there's no turning back. It's imperative that we move immediately to put our defenses in place. I know these people and how they operate. They know that we're onto their surveillance efforts. If they think we're a threat, they could already be dispatching a *solution*, if you know what I mean. We need to make haste … and whatever, whatever you do, please do not alarm Jude. That's for me to decide when and how to bring her into the loop. Do you understand?"

For all his quirkiness, Mit got the message, "Yes Inky, I hear you. Let's copy Marchetti's file and the discs so I can take one home with me. I won't rest until we're ready to lock things down with Cagliostro and company."

I couldn't carry on the charade with Jude any longer. It was not only the pangs of guilt I felt due to my secrecy and skullduggery but I realized my family was in mortal danger too. That night, after the kids were fast asleep, I grabbed Jude by the hand to stop her retreat toward a good night's sleep. She totally misinterpreted my gesture and gave me a coy smile, "What's on your mind at this late hour, Inky? You know I'm tired and we both need our rest." She feigned indignation as she cozied up to me like a cuddly feline, "Oh, all right ... I'll play along if you insist, mister." She turned me around and began gently pushing me backwards toward the bedroom.

I thought, oh boy, of all the times to hit the jack pot. For just a moment, I pondered to myself, what's the harm ... why not indulge in this delicious diversion first? Then I caught myself and Jude picked up on my mood-killing demeanor right away, "What's the matter, Inky."

Her antennae went up when I hesitated, "There's something I need to tell you, dear, outside." Her expression said it all. Jude sat down on the hammock as if I was about to tell her I'd been unfaithful or contracted some terminal disease. I tried to ease into it but it was more painful that way, like inching into a frigid pool on a hot summer day. "Do you remember when that man was found dead in our front yard?" Shock registered on her face and then it looked like tears would start streaming from her eyes at any moment so I took the plunge and dove right in. I figured it would be less traumatic to rip the Band-Aid off rather than tugging slowly. "I was visited by a man recently who knew the truth behind everything … Dr. Becker's death, the stranger in our yard, JD's death, everything. It was a conspiracy … it was murder." Jude was at a loss for words. I think she was physically unable to respond because the air had been sucked from her lungs. "I don't know quite how to say this other than to just spit it out. The people who committed those evil acts have returned and pose a great danger to us. They may want to do away with us to cover up their crimes."

There, I said it. Everything was out in the open. But I couldn't heave a sigh of relief as I cringed in anticipation of Jude's reaction. Then she surprised me. There were no tears, no trembling, no fright, no shock and not a hint of panic. Instead, she offered an expression that can only be described as a mixture of dismay, anger, regret and dejection. "How long have you known this?"

Caught off guard, all I could do is state the simple truth, "It's been about two weeks."

Now her face turned to pure sorrow, "How could you do this to me? Don't you trust me?"

Wow, this was vintage Jude. I just told her our lives were in danger and she was more concerned about the personal bond we shared. "I'm so sorry dear. Of course I trust you. It's just that I didn't want to worry you. I needed to sort things out."

"Don't you think that I could have helped you? Don't you have any respect for my judgment?"

"Of course I do. I don't know. I guess I panicked. I was confused."

Jude was not one to stick the knife in and twist it. She knew she had made her point so she immediately began to mend fences. "I understand honey. I just want you to know that we're in this together ... in the good times and the bad." She gave me a long, comforting, reassuring hug. "Now, tell me all about this so we can figure out what we need to do."

We had a long talk and I shared Marchetti's information with her. She held together amazingly well considering the gravity of the situation but did exhibit some fear, especially in considering the danger that Gogo and Addie were in. She agreed with the basic plan of going on the offensive with Cagliostro. Jude was very proactive in warding off problems especially when it came to the kids. She was definitely a grizzly momma. When I told her about Mit's involvement she wasn't disappointed like she had been with me. I think she marveled that motor-mouth Mit had been able to keep a lid on things. She just grinned and said, "That sneaky booger!" I was so relieved to have gotten this weight off my chest. Keeping secrets from Jude had been an incredible burden, more than I realized at the time. It felt so good to have her back in my confidence, side-by-side to face our troubles together. I could feel my emotional batteries recharging as we embraced for the longest time. She capped off this magnificent moment with a long kiss. It was so good that my libido kicked in and I wondered, hmmm, any chance of recapturing her mood, the one I had destroyed when I dropped the bomb? Nah, who was I kidding?

Once again I proved I was not very good at reading her feelings when she took me by the hand and said, "Now, where were we?" Yep, we ended the evening on a high note ... jackpot!

The next morning, Jude reluctantly agreed to take the kids away for a couple of days until our defenses were in place. Mit was true to his word. He stayed up all night working on encrypting, coding, planning and devising. I could tell by his unkempt appearance which was several notches above normal and that's saying a lot. He wanted to explain everything he'd done in minute detail as if I could comprehend it and perhaps even offer a valuable critique. He was completely wrong and I convinced him not to waste the time trying. I shooed him back to work as he promised to put the finishing touches on our preparations by the next day. Alone without Jude, the kids and Mit, you'd think I could get back to American Phoenix but it was impossible. There was no way for me to keep my thoughts straight until our informational fortress was in place. Even if I'd been able to exhibit Herculean discipline under these circumstances, I would have been blown out of the water by what happened next.

I received a UPS package from my cousin Harold in Knoxville, Tennessee. It was a gift, a rare old theological masterpiece. The thick reference book was no longer in print. Nevertheless, Volume I of Kretzmann's Commentary of the New Testament was still considered a must by many faithful seminary students, professors and pastors. There was an inscription inside the front cover, "I recall your favorite scripture passage, all the best, Harold." Now, mind you, I don't have a cousin Harold in Knoxville or elsewhere but my favorite Bible passage is contained in the Book of John, chapter 8, verses 31 and 32 so I flipped through the commentary to page 458. There I witnessed the intricate work done with painstaking care by none other than JD Uticus. Somehow he had managed to acquire several pages of blank paper identical to the stock used in the commentary; same size, thickness, weight and even texture, except, of course, it was lacking in yellowing from age. These pages which contained a type written letter were meticulously inserted in place of the original sheets so as to draw no attention to the unsuspecting eye. If this seems rather extreme, it was actually still quite risky considering the type of scrutiny I was under. Thankfully, no one yet suspected that the Last Prophet was alive and well.

I'll explain later but, at this point, there's no harm in revealing JD's hiding place. He had gradually made his way to the East Cherokee Nation in their adopted homeland of western North Carolina along the Tennessee border. This sheltered area of the Great Smokey Mountains had afforded an exemption to a relatively small number of Cherokee who became U. S. citizens rather than being forced to follow most tribe members along the Trail of Tears to parts of present day Oklahoma in 1830. The land was poor in terms of agriculture or other forms of 19th century commerce but they were able to scratch out a meager living. Today it offers better opportunities, abounding in the tourist trade; souvenir shops with kitschy collectibles, white water rafting, fishing, gas and grub mobile marts and a variety of other tourist traps. Revenues pale in comparison to the nearby highly commercialized hillbilly havens of Gatlinburg and Pigeon Forge but it was perfect for JD, well off the beaten path. It attracted just enough folks passing through who were interested in *real Indian culture* to sustain JD and his Cherokee hosts but there wasn't enough outside contact to draw any special attention that could snare JD in its web.

Unlike some politicians and freeloaders who claim minority status for personal gain, JD was the real deal. He was one eighth Cherokee on his mother's side and could prove it through the genealogies and oral traditions she'd passed along to him. As far as the Cherokee were concerned, he was their brother and they were duty bound and felt honored to bring him under their protection. Forfeiting one's identity and living in seclusion far from home is difficult but, all things considered, it was an ideal situation for JD. He earned just enough to get by on doing odd jobs for his benefactors; everything from tour guide to manning a register at the local trading post which dealt in *authentic Indian treasures*. It was far from a nine to five grind and allowed JD plenty of time to work on his compilation of Dr. Becker's many theological works. JD adored the people; simple, straightforward and honest. He also loved the beautiful scenery. Some called it economically depressed but he looked past that to enjoy the natural allure of the rock formations, majestic trees, rushing mountain streams, elegant waterfalls and scenic vistas. JD felt blessed every time he guided a group of hikers in the early morning hours when the mist hung around the peaks like billowing smoke shrouding enchanted mountaintop cathedrals.

Some of the local inhabitants were so isolated from the outside world that they had not heard of the Last Prophet. But some had followed the story and word eventually spread about JD's powerful medicine. Some feared him but others sought his counsel. Everyone did their part to hide his true identity and protect him. Living in the Nation allowed JD to skirt government authority and intrusion. He didn't have a driver's license or social security card … didn't pay taxes or vote. His pay was in cash and he owned no real property. JD lived here and there on someone else's land in a barn, garage or shack for a time. He finally settled into a small loft room above the souvenir shop where he worked. It gave him the bare necessities and a place to write and study. In time, many learned that JD was a man of God and he took advantage of the many opportunities to spread the gospel of Jesus Christ … or Tsi-sa as he is called by the Cherokee or Tsalagi. He was able to connect on a spiritual level using Cherokee culture as the starting point. They believed in a monotheistic God before white men stepped foot on the continent. Many of their oral traditions dove tailed with the Bible. For example, they had passed down a story of a great, worldwide deluge that closely resembled Noah's Flood. They marveled at the way

JD constantly referred to his Bible and gave it such great reverence. It helped them to give him his new Cherokee identity, John Bookman. It was from this safe cocoon that JD penned the following letter that was sent to me within the folds of Kretzmann's masterpiece.

Dear Inky,

I pray this letter finds you, Judith, Hugo and Adeline joyful and safe in God's grace and mercy. I hope God will forever bless your efforts to continue the Lord's work through the Trumpet. Here in the seclusion and tranquility of the Smokey Mountains under the protection of the Nation, so far from the hustle and bustle of our crazy world, it seems almost paranoid to go to such lengths to disguise my letter to you. But I know you will forgive me since, no matter how much time has passed, it can't erase the danger we faced and the evil that still lurks far off in the distance.

Life here remains good and fulfilling even though, at times, I long desperately for my family and dear friends like you. Thankfully, it's impossible to remain sad for any length of time here since I'm surrounded by the wonders of God's creation at which I marvel anew each day. Just yesterday, as the 'smoke' was rising from the mountain tops, I and a group of hikers came across a black bear foraging through a rotted stump for larvae. The magnificent creature took one glance at us and then went on about his business as carefree as, well, a bear. He almost seemed to smile as he lapped the wriggling white worms from his snout with his happy, pink tongue. My work also keeps me occupied and joyful. I'm making great progress, by the grace of God, in compiling a summary of Dr. Becker's work. I'm amazed every day at the wisdom and insight imparted to him by God. He was a beacon of light that illumined the cavernous treasure trove of God's Holy Bible. I can't tell you how many times I've come across a passage that I've read a hundred times before only to find new and deeper meaning with the help of Dr. Becker's guiding hand. It's such a privilege to carry out this joyful task. I can only imagine the blessings that God may impart to many hungry souls who might be freshly exposed to Becker's writings.

God has also blessed me with many opportunities to witness to my Cherokee brothers and sisters. So many doors have been opened. I've been astounded by the depth of

Christ's legacy that I find here. I guess it should be no surprise since we all originated from the same parents as part of God's creation and benefited equally from his atoning sacrifice for all mankind but still I've been pleasantly surprised. Even with the oral traditions passed along by my mom, I must admit I've been influenced by the media and pop culture to believe that Native Americans are somehow separate, believing only in false gods and idols, ignorant of the truth and lacking in real faith. To the contrary, the Tsalagi people are monotheistic and well aware of God's role in creation. They understand sin and have knowledge of the Savior in spite of having lost touch with the Scriptures for a time. They see and understand the amazing parallels when I open the Bible to them and are eager for the gospel. Sharing with the Cherokee in this way has been quite a blessing to me ... it has strengthened my faith immensely.

While my life and work are in a good place, there is something new I need to share with you. This calling that God has given to me among the Tsalagi is meaningful and fulfilling but I'm starting to feel that God is pointing me in a new direction. Lately I've had dreams ...

strange and powerful dreams. Yet, it's not just my subconscious imagination. The dreams seem much too real. I'm guessing that you, like just about everyone, have experienced dreams that seem real. You know the feeling, where you seem to be awake and fully conscious during the dream, perhaps encountering physical affects corresponding to the dream like limbs being paralyzed or breathing being restricted. But this is more than that. I know I've been awake and conscious while receiving dream-like visions. It's like watching a very weird movie. I hesitate to say this but it makes me think of the visions and revelations the Apostle John saw while exiled on the island of Patmos.

I can hear you now, Inky. Maybe I'm just going batty while secluded here in the mountains amongst these strange people? Let me remind you of some of the unbelievable, remarkable, miraculous things that have happened to me ... things that you've witnessed personally. I've already been resurrected from the dead once and then protected from a bomb blast that should have most certainly killed me. I'd say that, in that context, receiving a few strange visions from one of God's 'movie reels' is not much of a stretch.

In any case, I'm left with the clear impression that God wants me to move in a new direction. You and I both know that he resurrected me and preserved me for a reason. The years I've served here have been a blessing but I've nearly finished my work on the Becker compilation and planted many seeds among the Cherokee. I truly feel that God is ready for me to come out of hiding and get back on that big stage he provided to the 'Last Prophet' to spread his message of warning and hope. However, I can't be sure. I need to talk to someone. I need your counsel. Is this the right time? Can I come back without putting you and your family in harm's way again? I just don't know. But I do know this ... God is sending these visions for a reason.

I realize we must continue to take every precaution for the sake of your family's safety and security. But we really need to talk, brother. Please call this number on this safe line, a disposable phone, at your earliest convenience. I am thankful to God for you.

In the grace and mercy of our Lord and Savior, Jesus Christ,

JD

As if I didn't already have enough balls in the air, this really muddied up the waters. Everything was on hold waiting for Mit to give me the green light but I felt compelled to do something rather than waiting another day or two. To me, it seemed urgent that I warn JD not to come out of hiding. If he knew what I knew, he'd probably have a change of heart. There was no reason to wait until we dropped the bomb on Cagliostro. It sounded like JD had taken proper precautions with a clean, disposable phone so I purchased one on my end too and called right away. "Hello, Inky ... it better be you Inky because no one else has this number," he chuckled.

"It's good to hear your voice, JD. It's been a long time. How (I paused for a long time until JD got the point of my sophomoric, rather tasteless Indian-speak joke) are things on the reservation?"

"Very funny ... as you well know, the Nation does not live on a reservation here in North Carolina. But, yeah, things are going very well ... except for that bit of trouble sleeping I'm having, that I mentioned in my letter."

"Hey, I kind of picked up on that, bro. By the way, thanks for the Kretzmann Commentary. Can you send me the pages you cut out?"

"Nothing doing Inky ... I expect it back when I return. The letter is yours to keep but the *envelope* belongs to me."

"Okay, wise guy ... I'll hang onto it until I see you in person." The jaw-jacking was fun but I paused to gather my thoughts on the serious matters at hand.

JD struck a concerned tone, "Hey, what's the matter guy? Is something wrong?"

I tried to ease my way in without beating around the bush too much, "Man, there's nothing I would like more than to see you come back here. I miss working and collaborating with you. But I'm not sure it would be a good idea right now."

"I don't know, Inky ... I really feel like God is pushing me to move forward. You know me ... when in doubt go with God's plan no matter what else the world may say."

I didn't have time to be tactful or diplomatic, "Hear me out, JD. Some things have happened recently that may change your mind. Do you remember Riccardi's right hand man, Marchetti?"

I could hear the uncertainty and trepidation in his voice, "How could I forget? What does that have to do with anything?"

"He contacted me out of the blue recently. He confirmed all of our suspicions and then some … conspiracy, murder, the church; it's all true. Marchetti provided me with hard and fast evidence to prove it all."

JD was thoroughly confused, "Why would he do that? He was right in the middle of the whole, sordid thing."

"He came to warn me. Marchetti told me that the church was trying to do away with him as part of a cover-up, just like they did with Kaltmann, Baker and Riccardi. I guess he was making amends or seeking redemption but he came to warn me and protect me and my family. Marchetti urged me to use the evidence he provided to confront the church, a new nemesis named Cardinal Cagliostro who is apparently cut from the same filthy cloth as Riccardi only more powerful and dangerous. I've decided to take Marchetti up on his advice. It's the only way."

"But Inky, won't you just stir up trouble by confronting them and invite more danger, the deadly peril we faced before?"

"That's what I thought too but there really is no choice. You remember Philipp don't you … old eagle ears? Well, he uncovered another wiretap the other day. They are at it again. This convinced me that Marchetti is right. It's only a matter of time before they decide I'm an unacceptable threat. Plus, I opened my big mouth at the wrong time and they realize I've discovered the bug. I hate to say this but, if you come out of hiding now, it may tip the scales completely. It would put you in danger too and perhaps make me, Jude and the kids more of an unacceptable risk."

There was a long pause as this stark reality sunk in, "I'm really torn, Inky. I felt compelled to come out of hiding but this revelation changes everything. I know I should follow what God has in store for me and I was pretty sure about what he has in mind but I can't do something that might put the safety of you and your family in jeopardy. I guess I'll just stay put for now and try to be patient."

"Thank you so much JD. This means a lot to me. We're forever grateful and indebted to you. I know our minutes on these phones are almost up but let me leave you with this. In just a matter of days, we will have put our plan in motion and then the fog will lift one way or another. If we've miscalculated, God help us. If Marchetti was right, this could ensure our safety for the foreseeable future. I will call you at the other clean number you provided once the dust settles. If you don't hear from me within two weeks, you'll know the worst has happened."

"I'm so sorry it has come to this again, Inky ... but take heart and remember that he who is in us is greater than he who is in the world. He will never leave us or forsake us."

I tried to leave things on a lighter note, "Amen to that, JD! I just wish God would make this all go away. But I'm sure he has our best interests at heart and will turn this into a blessing somehow. When things get back to normal ... whatever that means ... I can't wait to tell you about my new book. You won't believe it but I've become somewhat of a techie over the last few years. I have my own web site and even a blog with a few devoted followers. The Trumpet has blasted off into the 21st century!"

The last thing I heard before our minutes expired was a hearty guffaw and, "Wonders never cease!" I immediately took steps to destroy the phone as I was sure JD was doing too. In the midst of all the incredible peril and uncertainty, my spirits had been greatly uplifted by talking to JD. I turned back toward the house feeling secure in knowing that we'd preserved our great secret regarding JD's fate and hiding place. I had no way of knowing then that the eavesdroppers had already adapted their strategy to overcome the discovery of the wiretap in my office. At the edge of the woods, just outside my line of sight was a ghost of another sort, a techie ghost if you will, armed with a parabolic microphone that picked up and recorded my entire conversation with JD. Ignorance can be blissful. In this case, it was also very dangerous.

I felt so good after my conversation with JD that I decided to get back to blogging and American Phoenix rather than wasting the next few days twiddling my thumbs or chewing my finger nails down to the nubs. I was in the middle of the chapter on American Exceptionalism and our manifest destiny but I felt I needed to rattle some cages to grab people by the ear and get them thinking again. So I went off topic a bit and lobbed a bomb to stir up the natives about the wretched state of our republic. I figured once I had their attention in regard to the current mess, it would be easier to lead them back to what once was by comparison. Rather than laying it all out there at once, I threw this teaser at them to raise awareness.

Imagine the Worst Lyrics Ever

*John Lennon's Imagine tops the list of the
songs with the most misguided, despicable,
offensive and un-American lyrics of all time.
Stay tuned for more to come.*

This had the desired effect. Vocal devotees
emerged with pitchforks and torches in hand to
slay the monster. I let them rant and vent. Then I
hit them with the full post.

Imagine the Worst Lyrics Ever

*Let me preface this by saying that my
favorite band of all time, the band that I
think is by far the greatest of the 20th
century, ahead of the Stones, Beach Boys
and all the others, is the Beatles. As a third
grade kid, the first 45 rpm single I bought
with my own allowance money down at the
neighborhood grocery store in 1963 was
Please, Please Me with Ask Me Why on the
flip side. Everyone had their favorite Beatle
with Paul being the most popular but mine
was always John Lennon. Even at that
young age I could discern that special
something in his voice and lyrics. Thus, it's
with some regret that I must deem one of*

his most popular, beloved songs as having the worst, most despicable and sickening lyrics of any song ever written. Well, can you imagine that?

The United States has become the land of the freeloader and home of the depraved so isn't it about time that we dispense with the Star Spangled Banner? I think Lennon's Imagine would be the perfect anthem for what we've become. I know, my sarcasm and criticism sounds crazy. Hey, I used to listen to it all the time and loved it. No, I didn't pay that much attention to the words. On the surface they seemed to speak for a generation with the haunting, prophetic voice of a modern day Gandhi, struck down in his prime by Mark Chapman. Wasn't it all about peace, love and brotherhood? And that melody ... it was so simple, pure, innocent and child-like ... like Peanuts' Schroeder pecking away at the piano keys. What kind of bum doesn't like Imagine, much less tries to label it as something evil rather than saintly?

Bear with me for a minute, please. Let me break it down for you and let's scrutinize the message. Then tell me if this doesn't reflect exactly what we've become … it's the perfect anthem for our fallen Republic.

- ☐ *Imagine there's no heaven. Can you imagine anything worse? Is the nihilist's view really what you want? There's no soul, no spiritual realm, just this sorry world and sad life and then, poof, it's over. Just a bunch of happy atheists headed toward oblivion!*

- ☐ *Imagine there's no hell. There's no justice … no God to make things right once and for all? O. J. and Casey Anthony get off scot-free?*

- ☐ *Imagine all the people living for today. Do whatever you want; whatever makes you feel good. Live for today and to hell with tomorrow. Never mind your neighbor who is married to a giraffe. Anything goes, mate!*

- ☐ *Imagine there are no countries. Kiss the USA goodbye. Say farewell to our Constitution and God-given rights memorialized therein too. Think about it … it will be almost like living under the UN's mandate … nothing but peace, love, brotherhood and justice. Yeah, right!*

☐ *Nothing to kill or die for. Sounds nice but I wonder how the French, British, et al would have felt about this if we would have taken this approach instead of helping to fight the Axis Powers in WWII? Is there no killing or dying under communist rule like Stalin's Russia, Mao's China or Pol Pot's Cambodia??*

☐ *And no religion too. There you have it folks … no religion. All we have to do is rid ourselves of God and Jesus Christ and all of our problems will be solved. I guess that's why we have to ditch our country and Constitution. That 1st Amendment is a real problem with the free speech, freedom of religion and all. What were those crazy Founding Fathers thinking?*

- *And the world will be as one. Yep, one world government is the ticket. Oh wait, there's no government right? I guess it will just be some kind of utopia. Somebody will figure it out for the rest of us dolts. Maybe one of those Washington elitists will lead us all to the Promised Land.*

- *Imagine no possessions. Yeah, this is really coming into focus. If our taxes go up much higher I won't have any possessions anyway. Reminds me of another British rocker, Alvin Lee of Ten Years After ... tax the rich, feed the poor until there are no rich no more.*

- *No need for greed or hunger. Whoa, there you have it in a nutshell ... the Big C ... communism. Get rid of religion, sovereign nations and property rights and everyone will have everything they need. But if you get rid of greed (i. e, free market capitalism), who's going to work to produce all the goodies we need, the*

Morlocks? I hope this doesn't mean we'll all be equally destitute.

☐ *Imagine all the people sharing everything in the world. This one worries me a bit. Can we really trust human nature, for people to be naturally kind, gentle, caring and sharing? The Bible says we're evil, sinful, greedy and desperately wicked by nature apart from God. It sure seems to jibe with my experience. Oh yeah, never mind, that Bible thing will be done away with so no worries.*

☐ *You may say I'm a dreamer, but I'm not the only one. You're darn tooting you're not ... at least not anymore. Remember John when you were battling it out with Richard Nixon? Today you'd find a lot of allies in the White House and Halls of Congress. The old US she ain't what she used to be. It's not too far-fetched to imagine your Imagine being our new national anthem.*

- *The brotherhood of man. There's just one small problem. Do we really want to hold hands with the folks running Syria, North Korea, China, Russia, Iran, Somalia, etc. and sing Kumbaya? The Islamic nations have outlawed Christianity and the commies have done away with religion altogether. So how come there's so much bloodshed and poverty out there??*

No, I'm not boarding this Love Train. If you want a revolution, I'd suggest one of Lennon's other lyrics that he penned before Yoko got into his head. If you talk about destruction, don't you know that you can count me out? If you go around carrying pictures of Chairman Mao, you ain't gonna make it with anyone anyhow. You say you have a real solution, well, you know, we'd all love to see the plan. When someone submits the plan, especially any of those scoundrels in DC, you might want to read the fine print. Yeah, you should demand some details, a little meat on the bones ... not just some warm and fuzzy hope and change baloney. Until then, we best stick

with our Bible and Constitution. Let the
rockets-red glare ... is our flag still there?

What can I say? I rest my case, with apologies to my favorite Beatle, the late John Lennon. This helped me to get a few things off my chest but more importantly, took my mind off of the real problems I was facing, the demons lurking just outside the door. It killed time while Mit worked feverishly to dig a moat around our defenseless castle.

PART TWO

PORTENT OF
DOOM

CHAPTER 4

Hunter's Prey

"And Cush begat Nimrod: he began to be a mighty one in the earth. He was a mighty hunter before the Lord: wherefore it is said, Even as Nimrod the mighty hunter before the Lord. And the beginning of his kingdom was Babel, and Erech, and Accad, and Calneh, in the land of Shinar." (Moses, Holy Bible, Pentateuch, Book of Genesis 10:8-10, about 1445-1405 B. C.)

Mit was driving me crazy. He had this maddening habit of calling me several times a day to update me on his progress ... in painful, mind-numbing detail. It only served to slow him down in spite of his earnest efforts and considerable toil. I tried to get it across to him that I was okay, that I was feeding my patience and sanity by concentrating on American Phoenix and the blog. My politeness was counter-productive. And Mit's conscientious, well-intentioned updates only served to remind me of the fear that should have gripped me while we were yet exposed to whatever the plotters might be hatching. Finally, I had to hit him right between the eyes. I know it sounds ungrateful to unload on someone who was busting his tail on my behalf but it was the only way to get through to him. It was like Mit was suffering under the influence of Spock's Vulcan mind meld. When I finally came right out and told him to knock it off, Mit got the message and didn't seem the least bit offended. My insistence that he devote the time to the task at hand instead and not stir up my fears seemed to appeal to his pragmatic nature. Never mind the rudeness, Vulcan Mit would have only been perturbed if I'd said something purely emotional, illogical.

I really was better off waiting in blissful ignorance rather than fretting. The only periodic calls I wanted were from Jude. Knowing that she and the kids were safe and sound, far off with her parents, provided all the peace I needed. After my dissing of John Lennon kicked up such a hornet's nest of protest, I was excited to get back to blogging and press forward with American Phoenix. I had made my point, rather bluntly, about the sorry state of affairs in our country and it was time to circle back to what had been and why.

> Now, where did I leave off, history buffs? Oh yeah, ideologically motivated revisionist nonsense aside, as we've shown in the Founders' own words, America was settled, founded, nourished and flourished as a Christian nation. This was not by fiat but through the pervading faith in Jesus Christ. This faith was not coerced or followed blindly from birth through rote indoctrination. It came as a precious gift of God by the power of the Holy Spirit working through God's word, the Holy Bible, which was central to American life in most every aspect including governance and education. This may seem odd from our 21st century perch where the Bible is blacklisted in government circles but to understand America,

we need to see it from their 18th century viewpoint.

The Christian faith that pervaded early America was not a program or policy. It was a way of life. Were all of the early settlers and founders Christians? No but they formed the overwhelming majority. More importantly, Christianity was at the core of our very culture. Its principles guided family life and education in our homes and schools. It wasn't something that was practiced in church on Sunday only by a portion of the population. It provided a code of conduct for every aspect of society including commerce. It set our moral compass and laid the foundation for our system of justice. It defined right and wrong.

Our culture was undeniably Christian in every way. We were a melting pot more than a salad bowl where 'diversity' is lionized. Cultural differences were embraced where tomatoes, mushrooms, onions, peppers and radishes maintained their own identities and contributed to making the whole better but we were one at our core and shared the same lettuce; a common set of values uniquely American. Christianity is not a religion of forced conversion

... not a kingdom of this world but rather a spiritual one. Yes, it presented societal pressures from a cultural standpoint but was open to everyone and tolerant of others. People of other faiths were respected and many doctrinal differences existed within the various Christian denominations. (That was the whole point of the Danbury Baptists and the concern that was later hijacked to propagate the false notion of the separation of church and state. There will be more on that later.) American Christians were tolerant, loving and understanding but not shrinking violets. While others were treated with respect, people understood the differences between the various religions and weren't afraid to take a stand for the truth.

Yes, one odd, very special thing set America apart and opened it to the rich blessings that have been imparted by God. That is, we were a Christian nation where the word of God as contained in the Holy Bible was not only given free course throughout the land but was revered and respected as God's authoritative, inerrant, inspired word of truth. You may not like the sound of this. You can say that was then but this is now. But you cannot truthfully deny the historical fact of the matter. You can say this was just coincidental and America's success was driven by other factors such as our vast natural resources, the character of our people, etc. That's baloney and you know it. Just look at history and you will see that there are many countries with great resources and smart, hard-working people. Something else set America apart. The real cynics and scoffers amongst you might say that we succeeded due to a lack of character and morals. You can cite the revisionist fables which paint us as evil imperialists who benefitted solely off the blood and sweat of others; through genocide, enslavement, dirty dealing, tyranny and wanton militarism. You're wrong again, swamp breath!

I'm not saying we were perfect. No one is. We didn't always follow Christian principles. As I pointed out previously, slavery was a horrible, sinful stain for which we endured terrible consequences. But in our essence, in spite of all our imperfections and misdeeds, America was great because of Christianity and we prospered by the hand of God. How did we defeat the vastly superior British forces, survive the War of 1812, conquer the West, tame the land, develop cities that flourished like mustard seeds, not only survive but provide forces that tipped the scales in two great world wars, amass such incredible wealth and become the centerpiece for such mind-boggling technological advances? Did we do this on our own or just get lucky? No way my friend! Abandon your ego and give credit where it's due ... give the glory and honor to our good and gracious God. All of these things were accorded us due to God-given faith ... the faith that allowed us to offer national Thanksgiving, national prayers that echoed in the halls of government, the words 'In God We Trust' emblazoned on our currency, the freedom to worship God enshrined in our Constitution, the word of God taught in our public schools and the reverence afforded to the authority of God's inspired, inerrant word, the Holy Bible, in homes and hearts across the land. This is the treasure we've lost.

We've lost sight of our manifest destiny. It was a feeling that bonded us, a foundational belief held by most Americans across generations. We didn't focus on the insurmountable odds we faced from such humble beginnings with outcasts logging months across treacherous seas to land on hostile shores. We didn't cave in to legitimate fears the colonists faced under the *yoke of a tyrant whose power was unsurpassed in the 18th century. We dared to dream the impossible as we peered westward toward the vast expanse of wilderness containing innumerable, hidden dangers. Nor did we shy away from the worldly menaces like the Nazis and others who threatened the entire planet. We weren't afraid or ashamed to admit that God was on our side. As Yanks we exhibited a brash confidence that was borne of something more than foolish ego. We believed in the providence of God. We could clearly see his guiding hand. We were never bashful about this special relationship with our God and heartily, cheerfully gave thanks, praise and glory to God. Our God-given faith was strong. It helped us to endure, by his hand, through droughts, depressions, grave dangers and all manner of hardships. It was by God's providence that our manifest destiny was to grow and prosper as a people beyond our wildest expectations. Our omnipotent God was the power source for our irrepressible American optimism. Call it Supreme confidence in the highest sense. If God be for us, who can be against us?*

Some of the responses were heartening. They gave me some assurance that I was getting through to a good number of folks. Most seemed to be older people closer to my generation where they were able to tap into memories I'd stirred from their youth. They had a foundation, perhaps buried deep but still there nonetheless, which allowed them to recall past optimism and American pride. But was I getting through to the youth whose only base was the shifting sand laid by the media and our woeful public school system? I could only hope. There was no doubt about the cynics and scoffers. They were riled up and let me know it in no uncertain terms. That was okay. I wasn't about to try to deny them their voice. I let them vent but always came back to the same place. Could they support their claims with historical evidence? Most were stopped in their tracks by this challenge. Others though picked up the gauntlet and let fly with revisionist garbage that was easy to pick apart. Most of the stuff was internet junk without proper references and usually devoid of any primary sources. I'd fight the anecdotal gibberish with solid primary reference material but had to spend more time ferreting out the truth from those with purported primary historical evidence. It took some work but most were easily refuted. Many were taken woefully, intentionally out of context and some were blatant fabrications.

I was having a lot of fun with the whole exercise and, more importantly, felt I was doing some good in trying to turn back the clock and set the record straight. Then, I was stopped in my tracks, not by any comments posted on the blog but a call from Mit. This time he reported proudly that he'd finished his work and was ready to pull the trigger. This meant, unfortunately, that I had to sit through another meeting and get pummeled with more techie minutia but it was worth it. All the mumbo jumbo aside, the meeting served an essential purpose. While I didn't understand much of the nitty gritty, Mit was able to convince me that he'd done everything possible to safeguard the data we were about to release and protect the evidence that was so vital to our survival. Most importantly, this gave us a final chance to put our heads together and consider the plan one last time before crossing the point of no return. There were pros and cons but one thing tipped us both whole heartedly in favor of the former. We were already in danger. If our plan was too aggressive it might accelerate things but not create a dynamic that didn't already exist. If we shied away from the plan and were wrong, it could result in certain death. We both knew we had to give this our best shot.

Everything was set. Marchetti had provided rock solid, damning evidence. Mit had incorporated every possible defense against detection, compromise or destruction of the data. And Marchetti had identified the head of the snake, Cagliostro, the object of our offensive. But there was one thing missing. How would we know if it worked? We would surely know if the plan failed … at least in that split second before death. How would we gauge success? Would Cagliostro contact us or send an emissary? Marchetti had been so sure of the plan that he had not commented on this in his instructions. We were left with, I guess, another leap of faith. No news is good news? As we pondered this it seemed unlikely that Cagliostro or one of his henchmen would dare to make contact and leave any possible trail leading back to the church. We'd be forced to live with the sword of Damocles hanging over our heads. If we heard nothing, we'd have to assume that the deterrent was effective. This, we agreed, would surely drive us both mad. Plus, I lamented, how could I bring Jude and the kids back without getting some indication that we'd arrived at a truce? We eventually decided that the best way to communicate would be through the wire taps, assuming that others were in place besides the one we'd found behind my modem. Mit could confirm this. We'd wait a few days to make sure the package arrived safely at the Vatican office of Cardinal Cagliostro and then speak our piece throughout the house and assume the eavesdroppers would hear us. We'd ask for a sign, an olive branch, painted black, to be delivered to a safe, remote location to seal the agreement.

In the meantime, it was back to my safe harbor in the storm, American Phoenix. Having pulled no punches in extolling the cause and effect relationship between the good fortune and past glory of the Republic and our gracious God, it was now time to call a spade a spade and unearth the ugly truth about what we'd become. It was time to make the case that the Republic, as we knew it, was dead and gone. With the help of my able readers, I decided to label chapter 3, The Descent … Smoke, Fire and Fiddles with the latter referring to a succession of feckless American leaders who presided over our demise like Nero fiddling while Rome burned. Often, historians point to the late 1960s as the beginning of the end for America. Chapter 3 was to be devoted to the notion that our demise started much earlier and, as such, I spit out a spate of blog posts going back to the 19th century and ending with the Great Society in the mid-

1960s. This struck my opponents as ironic since the Great Society, for them, marked a real break-through from our oppressive past. What to them was a clarion call to social justice … a term not really in vogue then … was, according to me, a death knell.

It wasn't hard to convince people that the roots of Progressivism extended way back. History was on my side. The tougher part was demonstrating the downside of the movement. To many, all I accomplished was to open their eyes to the fact that … from their perspective … the U. S. had been on the right track much earlier than they realized. Not many people remember publicist and politician Horace Greeley whose heyday was back in the mid-1800s. Some recalled his most famous quote urging us to "Go West young man," but didn't realize he wasn't some kind of rugged individualist or John Wayne conservative. To the contrary, he loved to adopt liberal social views that were considered quite radical at the time. Greeley looked not to the West but often abroad for his inspiration like the early French feminist, Fourier. The concept of setting up a utopia fascinated him and, accordingly, he corresponded with Karl Marx and Friedrich Engels. He wasn't a classic Marxist but must have been influenced by them in some fashion although his views were geared more toward agrarian populism. It's funny what we remember and forget from history, isn't it?

I didn't want to get bogged down too much but couldn't resist a few sharp jabs. I reminded them how it was more so the GOP than the Democrats who championed Civil Rights legislation. I hearkened back to a time when the Southern wing of the Democratic Party put up the fiercest opposition. I really got under their skin by recalling how Alabama segregationist Governor George Corley Wallace, Jr. was a longtime Democrat until the very end when he ran a fourth time for President as an Independent. Boy did they howl when I pointed out that on most counts he was a typical tax and spend liberal who was the bane of well-known conservatives at the time like William F. Buckley, Jr. and Barry Goldwater who deemed him a "New Deal Populist". If you looked at the man's record, he was a modern day Democrat through and through with that one little glaring blemish by today's standards; he was a rabid segregationist best known for blocking the doorway to Alabama University on June 11, 1963 in a vain attempt to halt the tide of desegregation. Sorry 'Bama fans but I couldn't resist the Tide pun.

I drew similar derision from the Left ... and some enthusiastic it's-about-time boo yahs from the Right ... for a host of pointed attempts to destroy some of the most popular myths about our nation's *advancement*. Take the League of Nations for example. Today, young people ... if they've ever heard of it ... think the League was just a precursor that spawned the UN. They don't realize it was an utter failure and the brain child of Woodrow Wilson, one of the first true progressives to occupy the White House. The term progressive is applied, I guess, as a polite way of avoiding his socialist leanings. If socialist policy and Marxist ideals are so laudable, why do their proponents in America, to this day, squeal at the very mention of these labels being applied to them? That's because you can spin policy talk to sound deliciously inviting but once you apply clear terminology there are still a lot of Americans who associate these isms with bad, bad characters like Hitler, Stalin, Mao, Castro, Ho Chi Min and others. It's kind of tough to get people to warm up to movements we fought against, enemies who claimed so many lives of valiant American heroes. Again, I say let's call a spade a spade. If it waddles like a duck and quacks, it's a duck ... not an eagle. Some of the loudest jeers came when I drew a simple comparison between Woodrow Wilson and a more recent President. This brought out the race card but hey, I was only pointing out the fact that they both were academics with little practical experience whose actions seemed to place a greater value on the brotherhood of nations than American sovereignty and exceptionalism.

I drew similar comparisons between the aforementioned Harvard Law professor and the grand poobah patriarch of the Dems, Franklin Delano Roosevelt. Normally there would have been cheers instead of reproach for casting any beloved contemporary Democrat in such an angelic glow but, horror of horrors; I didn't cast FDR in a favorable light either. The New Deal, according to me, drove one of the biggest nails in the Republic's coffin. It created the welfare state and laid the foundation for our entitlement society. Like our 21st century, not so shovel ready stimulus package, the New Deal prolonged our misery. FDR's strategy must have been cloned because he too seemed to believe you should never let a crisis go to waste; the bigger the better. The Great Depression and World War II were much like our wars in Iraq and Afghanistan and the financial crisis and resulting Great Recession. Both paved the way for progressives to make monumental strides in fundamentally transforming America.

One of the most vilified villains in American history is Joe McCarthy. The former WWII Marine and Wisconsin Senator who rose to prominence in the 1950s was forever painted as an extreme right-wing fanatic who spear-headed a witch hunt against innocent, freedom-loving liberals. The hearings he led to expose communist subversives earned the term McCarthyism an infamous place in the American lexicon of the Cold War. I posted one simple question that earned me an avalanche of derision and hateful invectives: could it be possible that Ol' Joe was right? From hindsight, Joe doesn't look so crazy, does he? The Soviets once boasted that they wouldn't have to conquer us militarily; that instead they would defeat us in a war of attrition by winning minds and hearts, by destroying our institutions and values through internal decay. Yes, Ronnie made them tear down that wall but we just won a battle. They've won the war in the long run just as they promised. And how did they do it? Look at Hollywood, the mainstream media, our universities and public education system, the unions and our own government. McCarthy is long dead and gone, just an asterisk in the history books, but you don't need hearings to ferret out subversion today. It's all out in the open. Frank Marshall Davis, a card carrying communist, was a mentor to the future president during his youth in Hawaii. A prominent, self-proclaimed communist, Van Jones, was pegged for a key White House post. A 1960s radical anarchist, William Ayers, is a close pal of the President. Saul Alinsky, the original *community organizer* who literally wrote the book on Rules for Radicals, has become the patron saint and guiding light for Democratic strategists. The Soviet strategy has been carried out by Americans not Russians well after the fall of the USSR.

In one post titled, We Miss You John, I staked a claim that John F. Kennedy was the last true Democrat. Americans of every stripe including conservatives and patriots could vote for him with a clear conscience. The vast, impassable gulf between Republicans and Democrats, conservatives and liberals was a shallower gulley then and Kennedy was able to bridge the gap. He was a Democrat who clung to his Bible and guns ... unthinkable today. It wasn't just rhetoric or some bloviating speech writer that caused him to utter those famous words, "Ask not what your country can do for you." Yes, he was a *bleeding heart liberal* when it came to lending a helping hand to those truly in need but he didn't believe in an entitlement state. Religion was not a dirty word to Kennedy. He even understood the concept of lowering taxes to boost the economy. Imagine that … Democrats used to believe we paid a portion of our money to the government, not that the government allowed us to keep a portion of their money. JFK fought in WWII and knew the good guys from the bad guys. He understood the threat of communism and backed his words with actions. He stood eyeball-to-eyeball with Nikita Khrushchev and made him blink. Don't get me wrong. I'm not trying to trivialize the differences between the Parties back in the early 1960s. They existed but were fly dung in the pepper compared to today. Kennedy was a uniter because, when push came to shove, he championed our national banner, the red, white and blue. He was looking to change things for the better when it came to causes like civil rights but he would have fought to the last breath against the fundamental, transformational changes being pushed by the Dems today. I'm not much of an Oliver Stone fan but, when it comes to JFK's assassination, it's hard not to smell the stench of conspiracy.

My last post before moving on to the late 1960s was, Then Came Johnson. I let LBJ have it with both barrels and deservedly so. In my estimation, he was as influential as FDR in fostering progressivism as our new religion. His Great Society created the entitlement society … not a helping hand to a needy few but a mindset that our country owed us something and not vice versa. He exchanged upward mobility for class warfare. Lyndon Johnson, in my opinion, was not looking out for the little guy. He was a crass, self-centered, power hungry politician who used a crusade cloaked in altruistic banners to carry out a Machiavellian agenda. LBJ pitted Americans against Americans along class, race and gender lines to benefit the Party. His Great Society ushered in a new era of slavery with the government being the plantation owner. He planted the seeds for big government, the nanny state and perpetual minority dependence. I believe LBJ, more than anyone, adulterated our good intentions in halting the tide of communism in Southeast Asia and set us on the course for a misguided, avoidable, devastatingly harmful and completely regrettable outcome in the Vietnamese War. As they used to say, LBJ all the way … right down the tubes for the USA. Look at the Democrat presidents since him … all anti-American in the traditional sense and largely anti-capitalist although President Bubba, bless his roguish, fun-loving heart, was an economic pragmatist who pulled a lot of the right levers with major prodding from Newt and the then GOP majority on the Hill. The Republican presidents since LBJ, with the exception of Ronald Reagan's breath of fresh air, were a bunch of misguided, feckless wanderers all too eager to compromise with the progressives.

I didn't make a lot of friends on either side of the equation with this succession of posts but drew quite a bit of rabid attention so I forged ahead with another string of blog bombshells to take us from 1969 to the bitter end. Chapter 4 of American Phoenix would be the coup de grace and nail down my central premise that the Great Republic we once knew and loved is already dead and gone. The title fittingly became, Death Throes … Stick a Fork in Mom's Apple Pie. For this era, I didn't need to refer solely to the history books. This was my coming of age memoir since I lived through this most wild and chaotic period in our American saga. I was a little young to be on the cutting edge back then but old enough to get caught up in the wake of a revolution unlike any other. There were so many facets to it that just about everyone was caught in the net eventually … gender rights, civil rights, anti-war protests. Of all the causes involved and sources of divisiveness that could have splinted the movement, the one thing that provided the glue that held everyone together, in my opinion, was the generation gap.

The whole thing ultimately rested upon the youth of America, an entire generation rebelling against the old order and demanding the premature passing of the proverbial torch to the next in line. The generation gap provided the cover and rallying cry for each and every disparate special interest crusade. It united the whole incredible mess under one umbrella. There was a sense of comradeship that exceeded family ties in many instances. Everything the older generation stood for became anathema. The establishment was bad just because. It included religion, social mores, economics, politics, education … everything. The hard core hippy types who were a few years ahead of me were wrapped up in their causes. The younger ones like me were swept up in the general idealism of the time but largely clueless. We were attracted to the fun and excitement of it all. It seemed like a great way to dodge the harsh realities of the real world. While I didn't outright reject my religion or turn on my parents, no one was immune to the trappings of the Psychedelic Sixties. Everything was designed to draw clear distinctions between the generations, none more so than our hair and music. Looking back, I was lucky that my parents grounded me in God's word and a good appreciation for American history. You might say I swerved across the yellow line now and then but didn't go completely off the deep end. But I was young and sympathized with a lot of stuff that later, from hindsight, made me question my sanity. I don't know; it just seemed fun, frivolous and thrilling at the time ... togetherness, a shared sense of purpose ... kind of a hope and change thing. Most of us didn't realize we were being led down the primrose path. Some still haven't caught on to this day. Looking back now it reminds me of a Tale of Two Cities ... it was the best of times; it was the worst of times.

The greatest sham of the era was the notion we all bought into that we, the younger generation, were forging the transformation by ourselves from the bottom up. Talk about naïve ... we didn't realize we were being used; led by the nose by our invisible handlers, the next generation of establishment types. One Party in particular pandered to the youth for those age old temptations of greed and power. This myth of the Dems being the party of the people and the GOP being the guardians of the establishment helped foster the great divide and deliver us to today's gridlock of irreconcilable differences. The ugly truth is that both Parties have had a hand in our demise. The Founders were right ... as later captured so succinctly by Lord Acton, "Power tends to corrupt; absolute power corrupts absolutely." This death struggle for power between the Parties reared its ugly head in taking down Tricky Dick. Think about it; the Watergate Scandal is child's play compared to the stuff the pols pull off today. People have completely forgotten his most egregious transgression. If Richard Nixon was such a staunch conservative, then explain to me how he could completely abandon the free enterprise system and put government dictated wage and price controls in place. Where did he get that idea, on his trip to China?

By today's warped standards, Nixon should be remembered fondly as the hero who presided over the end of the Vietnam War. Who cares that we lost and wasted American blood and treasure? It doesn't seem to bother anybody with the way we skedaddled from Iraq with our tail between our legs. Vietnam was the first war that we unquestionably lost. But we lost much more than a war. If the generation gap provided the glue, Vietnam more than anything else provided the impetus and focus for the revolution. In the beginning, we were willing to acknowledge and overtly confront the threat of communism that General Patton so famously exposed in the aftermath of WWII. It had the tone and tenor of a holy war with our values and cherished, deeply held beliefs pitted against Godless aggressors bent on world domination. My, oh my; how things unraveled!

It was a perfect storm. Everything came together under the banner of peace, love and brotherhood. Who wasn't anti-war? It was an easy case to make. Was communism really a threat to our way of life? What were we doing halfway across the world blowing up villages and maiming innocent women and children? Weren't the Vietnamese just like our American Revolutionary forefathers, standing up against colonial imperialists? Then the media weighed in with daily coverage of the carnage. At home, we were hit with oppressive inflation while the military-industrial-complex spent wildly on an *unjust* war. The pied pipers had a field day firing up the flower power legions at home ... Edwin Starr asked, "War; what is it good for?" ... John Lennon demanded that we "Give peace a chance," ... Country Joe McDonald and the Fish chortled sarcastically, "What are we fighting for? ... Whoopee, we're all gonna die!" It started out as care for our men in arms ... why were eighteen year old boys being sent off to some God-forsaken hell-hole to get killed for nothing? Then it morphed into an indictment of our soldiers as baby killers who were shunned and spat upon when they returned from their tours of duty. This fallacy was fed by the visions of storm troopers back home and forever cemented in the American psyche by the tragedy at Kent State when four university student protesters were gunned down.

The anti-war movement became the eye of the storm. It was altruism at its best. The real heroes weren't the goons running around the steamy jungles of Southeast Asia. No, the glory went to the long-haired, bearded protesters putting their necks on the line for the cause celeb, the greater good of mankind. Sounds good but admit it ... it was a lot of fun. Sex, drugs and rock 'n roll were the ubiquitous perks of the movement. Tearing up the streets surrounding the 1968 Democratic National Convention was a great way to release tension ... until that damned Mayor Daley let the Chicago dogs loose. Woodstock was a much better gig than humping patrols looking for Charlie in the bush. Love-ins and protests on college campuses were much more entertaining than going to class or pulling an all-nighter during finals. Vietnam was costly in more ways than one … going far beyond the lives lost and money squandered. It completely altered the favorable view of the American military. It caused us to let down our defenses. It opened the flood gates for the psychological and sociological war of attrition the communists preferred over guns and bullets. We lost our sanity, our common sense, our moral underpinnings … we lost our souls.

Not everything about the upheaval in America was bad. There was some good, especially in the beginning but it was taken to extremes or perverted in a way that sowed tares that eventually choked out the wheat. Take the Civil Rights movement for example. We started with Martin Luther King leading peaceful protests to claim equal rights for blacks that were long overdue and horribly denied in spite of the Constitution. He didn't demand special treatment … only the equal opportunity afforded to all of God's children under the law of the land. He spoke for all Americans in calling for an environment where people could be judged by the content of their character rather than the color of their skin. His voice of reason, truth and justice was silenced; gunned down in his prime. We could sure use his encouraging, uplifting words today. But the movement was hijacked, in some quarters, by violent people, opportunistic people who gave into vengeance, divisiveness and racial bigotry. Then, worst of all, Civil Rights and race relations became a pawn in the struggle for political power. Good and pure intentions were corrupted by political pandering and payoffs. There's a new plantation with slave quarters called the entitlement society and race relations are ashamedly poorer as a result of our misguided efforts. Thank God that Dr. King is not here today to see this sorry state of affairs and perversion of his legacy.

Many other movements that we thought were based on good intentions have ultimately led to our demise. Equal rights for women turned into another unholy cause leading to a war between the sexes. Helen Reddy sang the anthem and we heard the women roar ... but are women and men better off than before? What's become of the traditional family, the linchpin of any civil society? Look at the divorce rate, teen pregnancies, millions of dead, aborted babies, single-parent households, frazzled moms trying to raise kids and bring home the bacon, domestic violence, drug addiction, the skyrocketing rise in STDs, suicide rate and endless succession of young mass murderers who've gone off the deep end. I'm not laying this at the feet of women seeking equal rights. But the movement went way beyond this, for the express purpose of nuking the family unit as we knew it and as God defines it. Are we better off today? You be the judge.

At one time we could say, never fear, Jimmy Carter is here. Underneath that toothy grin and aw shucks, John Denver-ish, Southern, country boy charm, beat the heart of a liberal progressive every bit as committed as FDR or LBJ. He wasn't as blatant but was just as committed to fundamentally changing America. Jimmy carried the torch that kept the flame of utopia burning. Instead of walk softly and carry a big stick he espoused talk a lot and carry no stick at all. He was a classic tax and spend, big government guy who saw the UN as having moral authority that trumped American sovereignty. I must admit, I was caught up in the hype and actually voted for him the first time around. It was the idealism of youth. What do they say? If you're young and conservative you have no heart but if you're old and liberal you have no brain. I came of age under Carter thanks to outrageous gasoline prices, long lines at the pumps, runaway inflation and seeing the American flag dragged through the dirt all around the world.

The promises and expectations of the progressives never seem to wash with reality. I especially didn't like mea culpa replacing American Exceptionalism.

Yeah, I jumped on Revivalist Ronnie's bandwagon when he promised to restore our shining city on a hill. It paid off immediately when the Iranians thought better of putting President Reagan's resolve to the test and released our hostages. Look back and it's amazing. The turnaround was nothing short of miraculous. Dumb old Ronald Reagan is now lionized by members of both Parties. How did he do it? It was simple really. Ronnie got back to the basics. First, he restored pride in America. He extolled American Exceptionalism and gave us renewed confidence. He hearkened back to a simpler, purer time when it was okay to acknowledge our Creator and give glory to him. He held people accountable and applauded responsibility. Who can forget how he handled disloyal, unfaithful public employees when he handed the striking air traffic controllers their pink slips? The guy had big, brass balls. As Commander in Chief, he restored the honor of our military men and women and backed words with actions as he rebuilt our sagging defenses. President Reagan eschewed moral relativism and called a spade a spade … with us as the good guys and the Soviets as the head of an evil empire. He fired up the engine of free market capitalism and showed that you could increase government revenue by cutting taxes and putting money back in the hands of entrepreneurs, job creators and regular citizens. Reagan restored the American dream. Rocky really could defeat Apollo Creed against all odds.

Ronald Reagan was an oasis in an otherwise parched, lifeless desert. He stemmed the tide and actually helped us reverse course for a while but, without him at the helm, it was only a matter of time before the immutable forces already in place would continue the onslaught toward our inevitable destruction. The links to our sure foundation were cut by public schools and universities bent on ushering in the new age. Free speech was undermined by political correctness. American Exceptionalism was again colored as something evil and corrupt, a myth used to justify colonialism, imperialism, greed, war mongering and genocide. Religion was removed from the public square and God was replaced by a fable called evolution. Earth worship was formalized via an environ-maniacal EPA tasked with putting Mother Earth's well-being ahead of mankind. The churches threw in the towel without much of a fight. They incorporated the absurdity of God-authored evolution into their doctrine and departed from the truth of the Bible on most fronts. My own church, the Lutheran Church-Missouri Synod was no exception. We didn't cave to the pressure and held fast to the truth but faced a devastating split when the Bible doubters under the banner of Seminex pulled many members away to form heterodox bodies like the ELCA. The LC-MS wilted under the pressure and eventually allowed false teachings to creep in. The quest for popularity trumped the truth and the progress of error marched on.

The Trumpet was on a roll. Readership and traffic increased with each succeeding post. Unfortunately, civility was often sacrificed at the altar of popularity but at least the flow of ideas was unrestricted. Everyone got their two cents worth in. Not too surprisingly, there wasn't a lot of squabbling over history. There was some revisionist babble that was easily disputed but most people recognized the battleground was not in the data. In a sadly amusing way, the same basic facts were spun to support any number of viewpoints. Analysis is in the eye of the beholder. At the end of the day, I achieved my primary goal in reaching a consensus across the political spectrum that the old American Way was dead and gone. That aside, it appeared there would continue to be endless squabbling on the merit or lack thereof of the Republic's demise. Some applauded it and others decried it while everyone acknowledged the corpse. My job was not to sway public opinion, so I was content to claim victory and move on. Some might favor the old and others the new but so be it. My sights turned to a new mission ... to outline what needed to be done to resurrect the Republic. Then I was derailed once again, this time by an email from Cagliostro's elusive prey.

It shocked me that Marchetti would take the chance of sending an email and possibly revealing his whereabouts ... not to mention putting me and my family at further risk. I guess he figured I'd acted promptly and had my precautions in place for quite a while. As I read his surprisingly frank and detailed note, it became clear that he felt time was of the essence. Also, it was obvious that maintaining secrecy was no longer at a premium. Oddly, the email was dated several weeks prior to the email transmission date. That's because Marchetti did not have access and had used a jungle courier of sorts to transport his handwritten note on foot to a place many days travel away where an ally with access to the web transcribed the message and sent it to me over the web. I had to keep telling myself this was not fiction as I read Marchetti's fantastic account.

Dear Mr. Hermann,

Please excuse me for emailing you this way but I'm sure you will see that it's in your best interest for me to contact you directly at the first opportunity. My travels as a fugitive from Cagliostro's henchmen have taken me around the globe to some of the darkest corners of the world but never anywhere near as remote as this. I'm deep in the Amazonian rainforests of Brazil in a tiny reserve set aside for the handful of remaining members of the Akuntsu Tribe. This place and these people are so far removed from anything you and I would call reality that it's hard for me to put it into words.

We live off the land, mostly fishing and hunting for game while practicing the most rudimentary form of agrarianism. It's a long way off from the rat races we're familiar with in America and Europe. Here the rats are very real and danger lurks everywhere ... not from layoffs, car accidents, crime, taxes or the occasional power outages. Here peril waits up close and personal in the form of bugs, snakes, bats, wild animals, carnivorous fish and a host of unknown diseases. There is no time to dwell on anything but immediate troubles, not even encroachment from farmers or the threat of neighboring tribes. The main focus of life is to stave off hunger one day at a time.

I'm still amazed that I was able to survive the journey and make contact with the Akuntsu without losing my head, literally. It would have been impossible without knowledge of their language. Yes, I've had a lot of time on my hands in recent years and took up the study of Tupari. I'm guessing that there are no more than two dozen outsiders in the world who can speak the language fluently. There are no roads leading to the reserve and it requires weeks of travel over rough, treacherous terrain to get here. That is, if the animals or neighboring tribes don't claim you first. The Brazilian government agency, Funai, in charge of maintaining the welfare of indigenous people, jealously guards their rights and privacy. No one from the government has had contact with the Akuntsu in many years, much less outsiders. I'm here without government permission but, oddly enough, I'm not the first of my kind to live among them. Many years ago, another missionary made it this far and, thus; I'm pleased to say that the gospel is not totally foreign to them. Thankfully, my faithful predecessor left them with a good impression or otherwise my head might be on a pike.

Given all of this, you can imagine how astounded I was to find that an assassin dispatched by the church made it this far and tracked me down. I'm sure this man was very good at his profession and handsomely paid but, unfortunately for him, was out of his element here. He was discovered and met with a terrible death at the hands of the Akuntsu. They really do not take kindly to intruders. His superior weapons and vaunted street smarts were useless in these primitive surroundings. He never knew what hit him when the poisoned missiles were launched by blow guns hidden deep in the brush. The assassin was treated humanely in that multiple darts made sure the natural toxins took effect swiftly. I knew the moment I saw his dead body with his guns, knives and paraphernalia that he had been sent to kill me.

I hope my sharing this gives you comfort in knowing that you did the right thing. If

Cagliostro is willing to go to these lengths to rid of me ... and has the wherewithal to even track me down in such a hidden sanctuary in this lost corner of the world ... he would certainly have no qualms about eliminating the threat you pose. Be on your guard my friend but know this; you are much more secure with the safeguards we've put in place than any hiding place could afford. Look at me. There is no more cloistered confine I could possibly find. Thus, I plan to stay put. They may know my location but they've proven they could find me no matter where I might go. My best chance is to remain here with the Akuntsu as my benefactors and protectors. Only a small contingent can steal past the watching eyes of the Brazilian government and, with the home field advantage, I'll cast my lot with the Akuntsu any day.

Christ's Blessings,

Antonio Marchetti

If I hadn't had experience with such deception, treachery and ruthlessness under Riccardi's watch, Marchetti's revelation might have totally freaked me out. Instead, it gave me an odd sense of security. Sure, it was frightening to see the extreme measures they were willing to take but, as Marchetti said; it confirmed what we were up against and showed me that we were on the right track in taking aggressive counter-measures. Coincidentally, a short time later, Mit knocked on the door and handed me a package that had been left outside anonymously. There was no message, only the lone content ... a small twig of an olive branch sprayed with black paint. This undeniable sign could have been taken as a portent of doom but I chose instead to see it as another assurance. I thanked the Lord for Marchetti's foresight, repentance and earnest desire to make amends by offering his wise counsel and the ammunition necessary to keep Cagliostro at bay. Jude and the kids returned and Mit and I went about our business with the Trumpet and American Phoenix in spite of our bizarre circumstances. As each day passed, a sense of normalcy returned, at least as much as one could expect with that blasted Sword of Damocles still hanging over our heads.

I might have missed a bit of obscure international news if Mit had not brought it to my attention. I almost wish he would have missed it too. Blissful ignorance would have been preferable in a sense. The small headline from a back page article read, Missing Vatican Official Found Dead.

According to the press release, Antonio Marchetti had been on a humanitarian mission for the Catholic Church when he was abducted in Jerusalem several years back. He had been held hostage by fanatical Islamists who made impossible demands that the Vatican renounce Jesus Christ, proclaim Allah as the one, true god and issue official apologies for everything from the Crusades to various Papal decrees over the centuries. The church had kept this all from the news to protect any slim chances Marchetti had of being released, as they explained it. Now the details could be shared. Marchetti had been brutally beheaded and was declared a church martyr. In typical, Christ-like fashion, the church denounced the senseless act of violence against brother Marchetti while offering forgiveness to the sorry souls who carried out his murder. It couldn't have been more ironic. Marchetti had joked about literally losing his head to the Amazonian *savages* and wound up instead meeting the same fate at the hands of *civilized* religious zealots.

I knew for a fact that the Vatican's account was a bunch of hooey. Marchetti's worries and warnings proved prophetic. It gave added weight to his advice and the level of sacrifice he made by coming to my aid. Mit and I ... and Jude ... were left to ponder how Marchetti wound up dead in the Middle East at the hands of Muslim terrorists. Yes, I included Jude in everything. She had proven that she was up to the challenge and certainly deserved to be in the loop. We shared a trust … I had her back and she had mine. I needed all the allies I could get. And we all needed to remain vigilant, on high alert as much as possible without crumbling under the constant pressure. We surmised that Cagliostro learned and adapted quickly. The odds of pulling off an assassination under the watchful eyes of the Brazilian government and the protective shield of the Akuntsu were long. But the Catholic Church is very influential in Brazil and the Vatican has many important, close ties in high places. It's not inconceivable that the Church was able to work through someone in the government to secretly extradite Marchetti. It would be much easier for a government spook to get his hands on Marchetti by reaching out under the auspices of the Funai. The Akuntsu were beholden to the agency for their land and ultimate protection. Once in the hands of the church's Brazilian agent, it would be a snap for Cagliostro to make arrangements with Al Batin to play out the final act of the drama and eliminate the threat posed by Marchetti without a hint of suspicion for anything other than another pointless act of terror. I wouldn't want to be Cagliostro's Brazilian patsy. Like Riccardi, Cagliostro liked to cover his tracks and was not prone to leaving loose ends alive.

In the end, Marchetti was regrettably proven right. He hadn't been suffering from paranoia when he likened himself to the prey and Cagliostro the hunter. For some reason, this made me think of Nimrod who was the son of Cush, grandson of Ham and great-grandson of Noah. Nimrod was a very significant man in ancient times. He set up one of the first kingdoms in the post-flood world beginning in Babylon. Our English translation of the Bible refers to Nimrod as a mighty hunter before the Lord. The proper term would be rebel rather than hunter. Many, including the ancient historian Josephus, believed the Gilgamesh Epic told the story of Nimrod. Although he descended from Noah and Ham who were spared by God on the ark, Nimrod built his kingdom in opposition to the God of his fathers and, like godly Adam's son, Cain, departed from the faith. Like Gilgamesh in the epic tale; Nimrod became a tyrannical ruler bent on using his wealth, power and influence to draw his people away from trust in the Lord. So, in a way, he was a mighty hunter before the Lord … an evil hunter of men's souls. Likewise, Cagliostro was a hunter; not just in tracking down Marchetti. In spite of all the trappings of godliness and his lofty title as a man of god, Cagliostro too was an evil hunter of souls; doing the devil's work while posing as a gentle lamb.

I tried to make sense of Marchetti. Here was a man who had served Riccardi and was complicit in his evil deeds including the murder of my dear friend, Dr. Becker. He had been steeped in the false doctrine of works righteousness, possibly leading innumerable souls to destruction. Yet, he wrote about sharing the gospel of Jesus Christ with the Akuntsu and died a martyr at the hands of his former cohorts. When we met he seemed truly repentant and bore the good fruit of his faith by doing everything he could to make amends and protect me and my family at his own risk. John 15:13 reads, "Greater love hath no man than this; that a man lay down his life for his friends." Yes, he had made that ultimate sacrifice knowingly and willingly. He was a true friend and brother in the end. The power of God to transform is miraculous. A smile broached my lips as I thought of the prospect of Marchetti and Becker together in heaven. That must be some reunion! Then I wondered what Marchetti thought about JD. He was not there to greet him in heaven so did he think JD was suffering the torments of hell? Or did he now somehow know that JD was yet alive? God only knows. I'd have to wait until I made it to heaven to find out.

CHAPTER 5

Cascading Death

"And there sat in a window a certain young man named Eutychus, being fallen into a deep sleep: and as Paul was long preaching, he sunk down with sleep, and fell down from the third loft, and was taken up dead." *(Luke the physician and companion of Paul, Holy Bible, Book of Acts 20:9, Approximately 60 A. D.)*

Little did I know at the time that Cagliostro already knew that JD was alive and well … and his whereabouts. The surreptitious taping of our last conversation had provided him with everything he needed to set the rusty, grimy, sludge-soaked gears spinning in his head. The pulsating swarm of creepy, crawly spiders that infested his mind began casting off webs of deceit and treachery while the venom from their sharp fangs dripped down the folds and crevices of his cerebral cortex and thoroughly marinated his putrid brain through to the basal ganglia core where the poison collected into a cesspool of evil intentions. Thinking our secret was secure and still needed to be safeguarded, I used a disposable phone to contact JD at the clean number he had given me the last time we spoke. We each had thirty minutes but I didn't want to beat around the bush. I got right to the point and filled him in quickly on the way Cagliostro had been able to stretch out his tentacles to apprehend Marchetti and stage his death at the hands of Muslim fanatics. My sole purpose was to keep JD abreast of the continuing threat emanating from the late Riccardi's overseers in Rome. He was his cool, calm and collected self and took it in stride. JD told me he was still gripped by the uncanny, surreal dreamscapes that illuminated his nights and a compulsion to go public but reiterated his understanding of the need to remain in seclusion. He really didn't want to dwell on Cagliostro and we had almost twenty-five minutes left on our disposable phones so we took the opportunity to catch up.

Apparently, JD didn't notice Damocles' sword because he launched into a lighthearted, airy conversation as if we were at a high school reunion, "Hey Inky, have you ever hiked in the Great Smokey Mountain National Park near Gatlinburg?"

"Yeah, I went with my family a couple of times when I was a kid. It's been a long time though."

"Do you remember any of the trails you took?"

"Nah, not really ... but I remember it being really cool ... very quiet and peaceful with lots of big trees going up the mountains forming a canopy ... like an enchanted forest out of some kind of kid's storybook."

This seemed to please JD and get his juices flowing, "Well, you know, I get to do this all the time now as part of my job ... or at least one of my jobs. I actually get paid to lead small groups of hikers up some of the best trails in the area."

"You're a lucky dog, JD ... at least as lucky as someone can be who's in hiding from a murderous killer."

He shed this unpleasant reminder like it was water rolling off a duck's hind end. He carried on as happy as a lark, "A lot of the time, I'm stuck with beginner or intermediate hikes geared toward your average tourist. Even though they're not too challenging, some are still pretty awesome. Take the Grotto Falls for example. The other day, I led a party of eight people. We had to take it pretty slow because of a couple of couch potatoes in the group but it gave me a chance to catch a few things we might have missed if I was really humping it. A huge snake zipped across the path right in front of us giving everyone the willies. Then we had to step around some bear poop and I made a joke about keeping an eye out for Smokey. Funny thing, on the way back down the trail, we sighted a big, lumbering black bear no more than fifty yards off the path. It was so cool! Anyway, back to our trip up to the falls. There's so much tree cover I don't know how we saw it but one of the younger kids in the troupe blurts out, 'Hey, look at the monkey in that tree!' We all turned and, sure enough, there was a mutated tree branch that had taken on the shape of a Dr. Seuss character perched casually on the limb with one leg crossed over the other. I've got to show you the picture I took some day."

I was enjoying his colorful travelogue and didn't take advantage of his brief pause to interrupt. "Anyway, in spite of the trail being pretty much a walk in the park … only a mile and a half to the top … when you get to the falls; it's well worth it. It's aptly named because, even though it's not very tall … about fifteen or twenty feet high … the falls are wide and cascade over what looks like a grotto. You can actually walk behind the falls. The kids love to climb on the giant boulders standing guard in the pools that form in between a succession of descents leading down from the grotto. Now here's the cool thing. Grotto Falls is near the take-off point for Mt. Le Conte. If the group is willing, able and up to the challenge, it doesn't get much better. Le Conte is the third highest peak in the Great Smokey Mountain National Park at 6,593 feet behind Clingman's Dome and Mt. Guyot, although it's the tallest mountain in Tennessee."

I had to interrupt him in spite of JD being on a roll, "Wait a minute, JD. How can it be the highest mountain in Tennessee if it's behind Clingman's Dome and Mt. Guyot? Aren't they in Tennessee too?"

JD adopted his best Ed McMahon impersonation, "You are correct sir … almost! The answer is yes and no. Clingman's Dome and Mt. Guyot are both in Tennessee but they overlap into North Carolina. That's where their tallest peaks reside."

I sneered in a Carson's Karnack falsetto, "Ah, I see, monkey breath."

JD rambled on, "The view from Le Conte's High Top peak is incredible … it's a slice of heaven … like being on top of the world. It's so high up that you can look down on the mist that blankets the Smokies in the morning. It's like sitting on top of the clouds."

I wasn't being sarcastic when I said, "You're bringing my memories back to life. It's like reliving a bit of my childhood. I can see the rocks, streams, trees and grand vistas."

I was soaking up JD's animated, kaleidoscopic description. He was my mind's tour guide and we had more than five minutes left so I let him continue on with me in rapt silence. It was great therapy for him … and me too. "There's a group of gung ho climbers that want to do a *real* hike in a few weeks so I've started my preparation to tackle a new trail called Ramsey Cascades. I've only hiked it once so far but I hope to make two or three treks before leading anyone else. It's not as high up as Le Conte at 4,200 feet but is, in my opinion, more challenging since it gains over 2,000 feet in elevation in just four miles along the trail. And most of that is in the last mile. It is less than intimidating, almost tame at the start. The trailhead is deceiving. There's a fairly broad, gravel-covered path that seems quite inviting due to the shallow ascent. At first I thought it might be just another couch potato's haven. Boy was I wrong! I find it hard to believe that some brochures deem it an intermediate trail. It is short compared to Le Conte and others so I guess it's a sprint rather than a marathon … but still tough if you go at it hard."

JD caught his breath and I could almost sense his eyes growing wider, "After about a half mile of ho hum hiking, there's a dramatic change … not so much in the elevation as the scenery. The path goes natural with the gravel gone and meanders like a sidewinder crisscrossing the Little Pigeon River here and there. The natural soundtrack is unbelievable with the rushing water breaking the peaceful calm that is otherwise only interrupted by an occasional bird calling out to mark its territory. The trees take on monstrous proportions like something out of the Lost World and the cliffs grow steeper and steeper offering amazing outposts to luxuriate in the lush, rugged surroundings. Then I came to a long, wooden bridge that was hewn out of a natural, fallen oak that must be traversed to make it across the steep gorge below. It was thrilling to feel the sense of real danger that would have been completely lost on a more secure structure of concrete and steel. It was other worldly on this stretch up the mountain. Everything was cloaked under the vast, majestic, green canopy formed by the endless treetops but, within this secret world, there was nothing claustrophobic. It was like a gargantuan circus tent that offered incredible, far-reaching, scenic landscapes within the magical, hidden confines. Around every corner, I expected to encounter a lumbering brachiosaurus, ravenous T-Rex or skulking raptor."

JD paused, I assumed, to gauge the time left and this caused him to forge ahead with a bit more urgency. "You have to see it to believe it. There's so much to soak in. But the final stretch is enough to snap anyone back to reality. The last mile and especially the final half mile is a bear. The path narrows to just a few inches in spots and winds like a steep staircase. Think back to your days in high school running stadium stairs during two-a-day football drills and multiply it by tenfold. It seems to go on forever and made me even question the whole point of the exercise. That is, until I finally reached the top and spied the cascades. It's a one hundred foot drop where the rushing water skips and bounces from one rock ledge to another like a nervous Slinky, shooting a fine mist that gives a hint of the cool refreshment. If you dare, on hot days you can stick your head under the falls but be prepared for a shock from the bone-chilling, frigid water that spills off of Mt. Guyot another 2,000 feet above. Yes, it's all worth it. I can't imagine a more idyllic scene for a picnic lunch, lounging on top of the boulders at the edge of the pool that forms below the falls. When you gaze up at the cascades, you can't miss the numerous signs warning against climbing up on the rocks for a bird's eye view. Since there was no one in sight, I couldn't resist bucking authority and making my way to the top. It was foolish, I admit, but when I reached the stream above, I walked out on a tree that had fallen over the rushing water just on the very edge where the stream plummeted over the precipice. I couldn't help myself. I let out a Tarzan yell that made the birds go silent. I wondered what any hikers below thought when my bellowing call of the wild reached them."

JD noticed our time was about up and briefly apologized for running off at the mouth. He gave me the number of the next disposable phone he had cued up and said goodbye. I rushed to say no problem; that I had thoroughly enjoyed listening to him before we were cut off. After we hung up, an imaginary reel kept entertaining me with the Smokey Mountain images JD had loaded into my mind. Then the ghost of Johnny Weissmuller swung into my psyche on a jungle vine and unleashed his patented, ear splitting, jungle thumping, ululating Tarzan yell. How did JD come up with a Tarzan reference anyway? He was way too young even for re-runs and the once popular ape-man flicks had fallen completely out of favor. Perhaps he had been watching AMC or TMC on one of those rare occasions where they ran the jungle classics, in spite of objectionable content, for educational, historical purposes.

The Smokies went up in smoke as a switch flipped in my head and I wondered why Tarzan had become persona non grata. A little voice tempted me to think that is was just another example of political correctness or unfair reverse discrimination. I couldn't honestly make the connection though. As much as I enjoyed those movies as a kid, I had to admit that I had to cringe at some of the scenes now. The African characters were painted with a pretty broad, ugly brush. This made me think of a lot of other movies and shows from that 1940s-1950s period. Black folks got a raw deal. They were typically portrayed as lazy, cowardly, stupid and superstitious. The crazy thing was that it didn't seem malicious. It just reflected the poor attitude of the general population back then who accepted such black characterizations as normal. Were the Three Stooges politically motivated racists with an ax to grind? Of course not … they were good hearted funnymen who were a product of the times. It still didn't make it right. Black people had every right to be ticked off. For that matter, so did Native Americans for the way Indians were often portrayed in Westerns and popular culture.

I really could sympathize with them. That's because I was now on the receiving end. Don't get me wrong, I'm very happy that the entertainment industry finally got it right and started depicting minorities in true-to-life roles as doctors, lawyers, sleuths, educators, leaders and heroes. It's great that scripts evolved to allow other points of view to be aired. But like a lot of other admirable causes, this well-intentioned, long overdue correction of the many injustices perpetuated in the past was hijacked and turned into something ugly. Why is it that to elevate one group, we think we need to drag another group down? To give the black man his due respect and honor do we need to make every white man a devil? Does restitution for Indians require all cowboys to be made bloodthirsty, genocidal bigots? Must we denigrate all men to uplift our women? Maybe I'm being too sensitive but I don't think so. As a white, Christian male, I feel like I'm part of the most downtrodden segment of our society ... and not just in Hollywood's eyes. The scales are tipped against us in the media, workplace, government and classroom. I guess it's just a symptom of our fractured society's obsession with us-vs.-them mentality where every splinter, every special interest group feels the only way to get ahead is by pitting themselves against someone else instead of pulling together for the good of all. Yeah, we're the Divided States of America today and you can thank the opportunistic politicians who don't give a damn about unity. It's all part of the grand scheme ... the big power grab.

I started to sink into the quicksand of self-pity. Who were our male role models today? Was there anyone more loathsome than Homer Simpson? Yeah, he was a lovable loser compared to the detestable Family Guy, Peter Griffin. As poor as these guys are for the male image in general, no one's character is defamed quite like Homer's neighbor, Ned Flanders. What is his greatest flaw? He's not just a white, male father but ... oh by Jiminy ... he's a devout Christian on top of it! Peter Griffin's misogynist, pervert pal, Glenn Quagmire, receives better treatment than Ned. Family Guy creator Seth MacFarlane and Simpson guru Matt Groening take special delight in portraying Jesus Christ in the worst light possible. How did we arrive here? I guess it really got rolling with Archie Bunker and then Al Bundy helped along the way. It's all good clean fun. There's no agenda here folks. Yeah right ... tell me another one, Mother Goose!

It may take a village to raise a child but you don't need fathers anymore. That's the message boys. Single moms, gay couples, anyone is more qualified to rear the next generation than dear old, outmoded pop. What ever happened to dads that weren't deadbeats, slobs, buffoons and sociopathic, self-centered, lazy, worthless losers? Where are Ozzie Nelson, Jim Anderson of Father Knows Best or Dr. Alex Stone of the Donna Reed Show, Bill Cosby as Dr. Cliff Huxtable and Ward Cleaver as Beaver's dad? None of these guys were perfect. They got into plenty of jams and provided lots of laughs. But they were all grounded in traditional American principles and set a great example for all of us. There was always a moral to the story ... always an outcome that helped show us how families should be and could be. Even when mom wasn't around, dad got the job done. Look at Andy and Opie. Somewhere out there in cyberspace, Ben Cartwright is riding herd over Adam, Hoss and Little Joe; setting the gold standard for dads everywhere from the Ponderosa to Poughkeepsie.

I thought about blogging something about dads but was too depressed. What's the point? Anyway, I had already made my case about the Great Republic. It was dead and gone; a victim of the culture war. Yeah, there were still a few skirmishes here and there but it was nothing more than a progressive clean-up detail mopping up the last vestiges of days gone by. I shook my head to cast off the gloom. What was wrong with me? I sounded like Elijah on the run from Queen Jezebel. Hey, God and one Christian still form the majority! Elijah had been outnumbered 950-to-1 by the Prophets of Baal and the Prophets of the Grove ... not to mention King Ahab and all of Israel except for a remnant of 7,000. Yet he prevailed mightily by the power of God. I told myself to get my chin off the ground. Yes, doomsday is coming … but Christians win in the end … God has already sealed the victory. I was uplifted as I recalled Revelation 19:6 … the comforting, assuring message in the midst of the tribulation of the final days … "And I heard as it were the voice of a great multitude, and as the voice of many waters, and as the voice of mighty thunderings, saying, Alleluia: for the Lord God omnipotent reigneth."

With my head back on straight, I was able to replay the pleasant images that were left by JD. I was also able to concentrate and get back to work. I had made the case for my premise but had to complete the history. Chapter 5 was dedicated to our last hoorah and was aptly labeled Ronnie's Respite … Gipper Offers One Final Glimpse of a Shining City on a Hill. This was the most satisfying chapter to write even if it seemed like just a fairy tale. Chapter 6 was back to being grim: United We Fall … GOP and Dems are Birds of a Feather. It started with Bush I's saga which can be summarized as, Read My Lips … I'm a Big Spender. Then I chronicled the epoch of Prez Bubba. He was like the Wizard of Oz. Never mind that man behind the curtain. He worked his magic under the mantra of It's the Economy, Stupid while hastening the death of American morality. I can still hear the indignation in his voice as he declared he did not have sex with that woman, Monica Lewinski. Finally, there was Bush II. He was a God-fearing president who had a chance to turn the lights back on in Ronnie's shining city especially after the wake-up call our nation received on 9/11. But then he got 'Gored' by the media and derailed by a Democratic Congress ... and his own sad tendencies. His legacy will unfortunately be, Hey, I'm a Compassionate Conservative which is Code for I'm a Big Spender Too. He caved to the pressure, panicked and got the ball rolling for *stimulating* Hope and Change while America went back to being asleep at the wheel.

Chapter 7 wrapped up all the loose ends. I called it America RIP ... the Final Nail in the Coffin. It was a long, long chapter that evolved from a cornucopia of contentions posts that kept my blog buddies busy for days on end. For the sake of time and your weary eyes, please allow me to give you the condensed version in outline form.

- ☐ Redistributor in Chief
  - o If it walks and quacks like a Marxist, it probably is.
- ☐ Flip-Flopper in Chief

- o Traditional marriage, gay marriage, traditional marriage, gay marriage.
- ☐ Hypocrite in Chief
  - o Abortion should be rare but let's not ban partial-birth abortion.
  - o I'm pro-energy but for us to succeed the price of electricity and gasoline must necessarily skyrocket.
  - o Mine will be the most transparent administration in history unless I invoke executive privilege to cover the Attorney General's butt.
- ☐ Non-stimulating, non-shovel-ready "stimulus"
  - o If at first you don't succeed, try, try again.
  - o It's all free! (By the time the kids and grandkids get the bill, I'll be long gone.)
- ☐ Nero's Fiscal Policies Revived
  - o Nero was a big spender who devalued Rome's currency to fund extravagant public works projects and dole out charity to the lower classes to increase his popularity.
  - o There's nothing new under the sun.
- ☐ State-run everything

- o Hey, I'm running GM. Let's push the Volt whether people want it or not.
- o Obamacare ... if you like the way the Post Office runs, you'll love this.
- o Why not spend half a billion on Solyndra?
- Nanny State
  - o Goodbye to Big Macs, Big Gulps, salt, sugar.
  - o Don't like tofu? Too bad!
- Tipping the scales ... haves and have-nots
  - o Now cell phones are a basic human right?
  - o More than 50% don't pay federal income tax.
  - o More than half are on the dole, just wards of the state.
- Occupy movement
  - o These are the good guys? Why are they taking a dump on the American flag?
- Diversity, tolerance, inclusiveness ... death of the first amendment
  - o Forced contraceptives (another basic human right?)
  - o Marriage redefined
  - o Anything goes ... except Christianity

- Social justice
  - Just what did Obama learn from Rev. Jeremiah Wright?
  - Is this really why Christ took on human flesh ... to preach social justice?
- Collective salvation
  - Whoa, what Bible have you been reading President Obama?
- Coarse society
  - Knock out game ... TV ... Movies ... video games ... filth and more filth.
- All steeples point up?
  - Then why did Jesus say he's the way, the truth and the life and no one can come to God the Father except through him? Was he dissing Buddha, Mohammed and the rest?
- Evolution
  - This is the new state-sponsored religion.
- Earth worship ... this is the altar for the new state-sponsored religion.
  - All the paraments are "green".
- Media and universities are breeding anti-Christian, anti-American anarchists.
- Wussification

- o Everybody wins the gold!
- o Don't proclaim American Exceptionalism … you might offend someone in Timbuktu.
- ☐ Crushing debt
  - o We've kicked the can off the cliff.
  - o For the first time in history, the next generation of Americans will digress to a lower standard of living than their parents.
  - o It didn't happen by accident.
- ☐ No personal responsibility … no one is held accountable.
  - o Blame someone else, blame society.
  - o Don't hesitate to litigate.
- ☐ Rule of law undermined.
  - o Saul Alinski's pragmatism … end justifies means.
  - o Activist judges.
  - o Executive fiat.
- ☐ War on Free Speech.
  - o Government targets hostile news outlets.
  - o If you disagree, it's deemed hate speech.
  - o Media Matters is an arm of the White House.
- ☐ War on Christianity
  - o Separation of church and state … code for elimination of the church.

o   You can "worship" all you want within the four walls of your church but don't try to practice religion in the public square.

I know that's a lot to swallow and you're probably glad that I gave you the *Reader's Digest* version. If you want more, you'll just have to read American Phoenix. That is, except for two strange concepts that I think deserve just a little more ink here. What in blazes is social justice? According to the Wikipedia definition: "social justice is based on the concepts of human rights and equality and involves a greater degree of economic egalitarianism through progressive taxation, income redistribution, or even property redistribution. These policies aim to achieve what developmental economists refer to as more equality of opportunity than may currently exist in some societies, and to manufacture equality of outcome in cases where incidental inequalities appear in a procedurally just system." Did you catch that? I just heard that duck quacking again. Income/property redistribution and managing the economy to ensure equality of outcomes is, by textbook definition, the Big C. Okay, I hear you ... what's the big deal? Well, this is what is being passed off as Christianity in churches filled with community organizers. Is that what Christ taught? Don't you remember where ancient Israel went wrong? They lost sight of the gospel and began looking for Messiah to kick some Roman butt and re-establish David's earthly kingdom. Christ certainly teaches Christians to help the less fortunate but he wants charity to come from individual hearts, cheerful givers. Jesus didn't teach that we should give everything to Caesar and let him divvy up the goodies as he saw fit. Keep your eye on the ball people! Christ's message is a spiritual one. His kingdom is not of this world. It's much, much better.

Another one that mystifies me is collective salvation, a term that was used by President Obama on occasion. This one is summed up succinctly by gotanswers.org: "Basically, 'collective salvation' means 'unless we are all saved, none of us will be saved' or 'we as individuals must cooperate and sacrifice for the good of the whole.' Another way to state what collective salvation means is: 'I can't be saved on my own. I have to do my part by cooperating with the group, even sacrificing, to ensure everyone else's salvation. It is then that we're all saved together.' Scripture, however, is clear that salvation is a process by which God saves individuals through the sacrifice of Christ on the cross. Each person must come (be brought) to Christ individually, not collectively." Amen to that last sentence.

Apparently, based on at least one interview I saw, President Obama believed in collective salvation. Listen up; I'm not making this stuff up! Again I must ask, what Bible was he reading? It's not a package deal. There are sheep and goats ... believers and unbelievers ... heaven and hell ... the saved and the damned. Those that are saved owe it to God's grace, not by going along with the crowd. Those that are damned have no one to blame but themselves for their stubborn lack of repentance and unbelief. Mark 16: 16 says, "He who believeth and is baptized shall be saved, he who believeth not shall be damned" not y'all who believes. John 3:16 says, "For God so loved the world, that he gave his only begotten Son, so that **whosoever** believeth in him should not perish, but have everlasting life." He didn't say anything about the whole kit and caboodle putting their collective heads together before being saved.

I didn't realize it but in the midst of my feverish blog-a-mania, I must have seemed pretty worked up ... face red and steam hissing from my ears and nostrils. I didn't notice that Hugo had crept into my office and was watching the whole spectacle intently. "Daddy, why are you so mad?"

I calmed down immediately but my face remained red, with embarrassment, "Hey Gogo, what's up buddy?"

"What's the matter daddy?"

I regained my composure and slipped easily into daddy-mode, "Nothing's the matter bud. Sometimes I just get a little excited when I'm working. You know, it's kind of like when we play football in the back yard. We get fired up when we're having fun sometimes don't we?"

This explanation seemed to satisfy his curiosity and, as kids can so easily do, he jumped to the next thought in line. "Wanna play catch with the football daddy?"

"You bet Sport … let's do it!'

Before we could make our way through the back door, Jude intercepted us, "Don't go too far. Dinner will be ready in about thirty minutes. Honey, Mit called earlier and he has a surprise for us. I hope you don't mind. I invited him over for dinner."

I didn't notice that she had set six plates out on the dining room table as we bounded into the back yard. I guess Mit had already tipped her off. The last thing I expected was for Mit to show up with a young lady in tow ... and a fine one at that ... if you ignored her rather Mit-like apparel. I wanted to ask if they'd met at the nerd-of-the-month club but resisted. Mit was beaming with pride, "I'd like you to meet Kit." She didn't seem to notice or care about his awkwardness as he blurted the obvious with a button-busting grin on his face, "She's my girlfriend!"

I resisted busting Mit's chops in front of her, "Well, hello Kit, it's a real pleasure to meet you." Jude chimed in too.

"Thank you Mr. and Mrs. Hermann. It's a pleasure meeting you too."

"Come on now, Kit. We'll have none of that Mr. and Mrs. Hermann stuff. Please call us Inky and Jude."

She looked down, blushed and actually shuffled her feet in a refreshingly shy way and offered a barely audible, "Okay, if you insist."

"Kit, that's an unusual name."

Before she could respond her knight in shining armor came to the rescue, "Actually, her name is Katarina but her dad used to call her Kitten and it kind of stuck and was shortened to Kit."

I was amused at the thought that perhaps Kitten's dad was a fan of Father Knows Best too but resisted the temptation of mentioning Jim Anderson's youngest daughter, Kitten. Something told me that Mit would jump on the trivia train and I'd never hear the end of it. So instead I opted for, "Mit and Kit … how quaint." Kit noticed my sly smile and blushed again.

Thankfully, Jude saved us all from another awkward moment, "I'm sure you two are hungry and the boys have worked up a good appetite playing football in the yard so why don't we grab a seat and dig in." I was used to home style cooking but still appreciated the simple but delicious fare Jude had prepared for us … pot roast; mashed potatoes; fluffy, hot, cornbread slathered with melting butter; green beans; corn and crisp, fresh, green salad with home-made dressing prepared from scratch. Mit's thankfulness made mine seem almost ungrateful by comparison. I was surprised that he had enough self-control to wait until after our table prayer to make his happy assault on the banquet. It did my heart good to see the look of sheer delight on Mit's face as he prepared to gorge himself like a hungry lion that had just happened upon a zebra. He was so used to monumental scrimping to make ends meet that this truly was a special treat for him. I felt like turning the lights out to catch the glow coming off his beaming face. For someone so lanky, I was amazed at the amount of food he packed away. I could have sworn there were sparks flying off his knife and fork as he shoveled the feast into his gaping yaw. We probably didn't need to wash his plate because of the efficient way he used a roll to lap up any last trace of velvety brown gravy that had graced the roast and potatoes. He washed it all down with a third glass of Jude's fresh squeezed lemonade. I was still marveling at his accomplishment when Jude brought out the piece de resistance, cherry pie hot from the oven and a carton of vanilla ice cream. Mit left enough room somewhere in his hollow leg to gobble two large, steaming slices with heaping scoops of the fabulous, frozen confection on each.

Jude and I couldn't get up from the table just yet. We were both basking in the incredible feeling of satisfaction that came from seeing how our hospitality had been received. Gogo and Addie just sat there in awe of the display Mit had put on for us. Jude had really knocked herself out. In spite of the huge dent we made in the *zebra*, there was plenty remaining for left overs and care packages for Mit and Kit. When Mit finally came back down to earth he was uncharacteristically quiet. His ravenous hunger was satisfied so he turned his gaze upon Kit with big, puppy dog eyes that caused her to smile shyly and look down at her folded hands. In my mind's eye, there were bright red, heart-shaped bubbles floating up from Mit's head and popping with zest as they rose toward the ceiling. We were all silent captives of the good feelings emanating around the table. It was as if no one wanted to break the spell. Just then, a knock on the door startled us out of our hypnotic, food-induced stupor. We shook off the pleasant lethargy and I rose to get the door and Jude rushed to start the clean-up while Mit continued to make goo-goo eyes at Kit.

As I strode from the dining room to the living room, I thought it was odd to get a visitor out in our far-flung neck of the woods at suppertime. Perhaps it was a UPS delivery. As I opened the door, I received the shock of my life. There before me, in the flesh, was none other than the Last Prophet, JD Uticus. I stood there with a dumb look on my face, stunned. JD broke the silence, "Hey, I'm hungry. Is it too late for dinner?"

I stuttered hopelessly, "What ... are you ... how did ... I mean?" I rubbed my eyes as if it would make the apparition go away. I was still completely flummoxed, "Are you out of your mind?"

Mr. Cool just laughed, "I guess you're not happy to see me?"

I gathered myself and noticed that I was blocking the door leaving JD standing on the front porch. Even though I was still in shock, I managed to smile broadly and give JD a big bear hug before moving aside to let him in. "Of course I'm happy to see you ... c'mon in JD!" The wheels started spinning and worries flooded my brain. I paused before leading JD toward the dining room, "JD, we have guests in the other room. Do we need to talk first?"

JD acted as if it was perfectly normal for him to pop in after years of living in seclusion, presumed dead in order to avoid detection from murderous plotters. "No, no ... we can talk later. I want to see Jude and the kids. And hey, I really am hungry."

Then JD paused for a moment and asked, "Who are your guests."

"One is Mit whom you've heard about and the other is his new girlfriend whom we just met for the first time."

JD tugged at his chin, "Well, maybe we should talk to Mit separately about his girlfriend before you spring me on them."

I asked Mit to step into the living room and ignored Jude's inquiry about who was at the door. I spoke in a hushed tone so as to not tip off Jude or Kit, "Mit, this is JD Uticus." His jaw dropped and it took several seconds for him to extend his hand to JD. "Mit, you know the danger we're in. But Kit knows nothing about any of this so perhaps you should find an excuse to leave and take her home before JD comes in."

Mit understood immediately and simply nodded before turning to explain to Kit that something had come up. He stopped just short of the hallway and said in shades of Schwarzenegger, "I'll be back." JD and I stepped outside and around to the side of the house while Mit grabbed Kit, offered his excuses and apologies and headed out. Jude was disappointed but not suspicious since Mit was so prone to odd behavior. She was curious about what was taking me so long but was wrapped up in getting things back in order. When I walked in with JD, you could have knocked her over with a feather.

JD tried to downplay his dramatic entrance with more of his droll humor, "Hmmm, something smells good. Can a guy get something to eat around here?"

She was still frozen, unable to comprehend. I tried to bring her back to reality, "Don't you at least have a hug for JD?"

"Oh, I'm so sorry JD. You just caught me so off guard." Jude rushed over to welcome JD and feverishly ushered him into the dining room. In no time, there was a plate stacked high in front of him. The kids tip toed into the room, rather wary but soon I was able to coax them into hugging JD. I'd explain *Uncle* JD's latest *resurrection* later. We could tell that JD was famished by the way he heartily satisfied his appetite although it paled in comparison to Mit's gluttony. We had a million questions but, with the kids present, restricted ourselves to chit chat and catching up. It was easy to see how thrilled JD was to be home and in the company of close friends again. It was his first stop. JD had not contacted his parents.

By the time JD was finished eating, the mess was cleaned up and the kids were put to bed, Mit was back from dropping off Kit. I asked JD if we should go outside to avoid eavesdroppers and he said not to bother. This was another unsettling shock to my system but I took his suggestion as sound advice and the four of us gathered around the kitchen table. JD started on an ominous note, "I'll tell you why I'm here and, when I'm done, you'll understand why there's no point in us trying to hide or avoid detection from the *ears* on the walls. Normally, I'd only share what I have to say with Inky but it's clear that the four of us are in this together and there's no turning back. Mit and Jude, I'm sorry that you have to be involved but you'll be safer being fully informed against the danger we're facing."

JD really set us back on our heels, "Someone has been watching you and listening in to everything. Inky, they already knew I was alive and where I was hiding. Somehow they got past our precautions and knew about everything we discussed over the clean phones. Marchetti was right in his assessment and you can thank him for your safekeeping to this point. I don't mean to sound melodramatic but I'm convinced you're only alive today because of the evidence Marchetti provided to you ... the threat of them being exposed saved you." Jude gasped ever so slightly in thinking about the kids. "The people behind the threats we're facing are ruthless. Your aggressive stance caused them to back off of you but it didn't stop them from seeking me out when they learned of my condition and whereabouts. They will stop at nothing to protect themselves and preserve their power, nothing."

I felt a horrible, sinking feeling in the pit of my stomach. I didn't want to relive the horrors and helplessness we'd experienced at the hands of Riccardi and his ilk but had no choice. Jude seemed composed, at least on the surface, and intent upon getting our defenses ready. Mit was in analytical mode, ready to take mental notes on another fact-finding mission. You couldn't tell from his demeanor how much was at stake; our very lives. JD began to take us through his ordeal. "The fact that I was still alive was not the greatest threat to Cagliostro and his gang of cut-throats. They might have hesitated since, until recently, I was intent upon remaining out of the limelight, for all intents and purposes dead to the world. No it wasn't just them overhearing our conversation and realizing I was alive that set things in motion. What really put them on edge was hearing that I felt compelled to come out of hiding to share the message of the visions I'd received. Having me back in the public eye is simply unacceptable, the risk too great. It was an easy decision ... but the method was very complicated. Killing me was not the difficult part but what would they do if my death became public? How would they explain it away so as to not dig up all those old skeletons they'd buried in their closets?"

"My cover was somewhat similar to Marchetti's in South America. In such a remote area, embedded into the fabric of the culture, it was next to impossible for them to kill me and dispose of my remains without someone knowing and leaking the news to the public. Finding me was much easier than eliminating me without a trace. They could murder me but not without repercussions; lots of loose ends. What could they do, eliminate the entire Nation? There was no way. They had to find a chink in my armor. Blood is definitely thicker than water in the Nation so they had their work cut out. I'm still amazed at their reach ... and swiftness. Even within the reclusive confines where I was sequestered among the hidden peaks and valleys of the Smokies; they were able to secretly uncover that one small crack in the dam they needed to plot my demise. His name was Painted Pony, a crazy horse of sorts. He was the lone Tsalagi that might betray me and they sniffed him out like hounds on a fox."

We girded ourselves with coffee as JD let the intriguing saga unfold. "Painted Pony was not given to greed which would have been unseemly for a member of the Nation. He also could not have been coerced by threats. Such an intrusion by outsiders would have been met with stiff resistance by any Tsalagi. No, Painted Pony's only weakness was jealousy and they found it. He accepted me as part of the Nation but was beset with envy due to my relationship with his grandfather, Morning Sky. He, more so than anyone, took me under his wing. Morning Sky was my mentor and protector. He treated me like a son and I respected him like a father. Painted Pony was not an outcast but was looked down upon in some quarters because of his mental deficiencies. He was slow and simple minded; not incapacitated but rather challenged in ways that made it difficult for him to fit in. Perhaps the worst thing for a Tsalagi male was to be considered dependent and child-like. His support system collapsed when his parents were killed in an accident at a young age and the responsibility for raising Painted Pony fell upon his grandfather. Morning Sky met his obligation faithfully but Painted Pony never felt they shared a true father/son bond. He became a loner with only a precipitous grip on reality. Painted Pony often soothed his demons with alcohol and drugs, further alienating himself from the Nation."

JD mused, "It must have been easy for them to gain his confidence through booze and weed and then turn him against me. I can imagine them painting me as the villain and source of all his problems; the wedge that had been driven between him and Morning Sky. Of course, that chasm had been formed long before I joined the Tsalagi but in Painted Pony's unbalanced mind it made perfect sense. All of his frustration and anger was aimed toward me. He couldn't be influenced by greed or intimidated by fear but the thought of regaining the love and companionship of his grandfather must have been very intoxicating. The only thing standing in the way of this idyllic picture coming into focus was my intrusive image. Painted Pony was easy prey for my devious foes. There's no telling what kind of justification they provided to him. I suspect they told him I was a fugitive from the law, using the Tsalagi as my unwitting pawns in eluding the authorities. Perhaps they convinced Painted Pony that they needed his help in luring me to a secluded spot where they could capture me and whisk me away before I could get lost in the crowd or put others in danger. Yeah, that would have appealed to Painted Pony's twisted sense of duty. By helping them to apprehend me in such a fashion, it would protect his Tsalagi brothers from certain danger, maybe even a hostage situation. In any case, they somehow persuaded him to lure me off to a rendezvous point where they could snatch me and take me away for good. Getting rid of me must have seemed like music to Painted Pony's ears."

Obviously, JD had escaped his captors somehow so I was itching to hear how he eluded them or whether God had once again intervened in a miraculous way. Both Jude and Mit exhibited great discipline and concentration and didn't interrupt. In spite of her relatively calm exterior, Jude's muted expressions were enough to betray that she was on pins and needles as the story unwound but Mit's poker face revealed nothing. He could have been studying a bug under a microscope. JD offered an explanation, "Bear with me and eventually you'll see how I'm able to relay the details and motives behind the plot. It was odd when Painted Pony approached me because he normally avoided me or stared at me with a contemptible look in his eye when we crossed paths in the presence of Morning Sky. He never said why he wanted me to take him on a hike in the mountains. I thought perhaps he overheard me recounting one of my adventures to Morning Sky and was enticed to see for himself or more likely Morning Sky had encouraged him to spend some time with me in the hope it might break down the emotional barrier Painted Pony had constructed between us. Rather than second guessing, I simply took it as an opportunity to win him over and agreed to take him on an early morning trek to Ramsey Cascades to soak up the scenery and enjoy some peaceful time alone together."

"I was totally unaware that Painted Pony passed along the time and location to my pursuer almost immediately giving him ample time to map out a deadly strategy. When the day came the next week, we set out bright and early just as the dawn was breaking. We'd be at the falls by nine o'clock and back to the trailhead by lunchtime. At such an hour, I knew we'd have the trail to ourselves … just us and nature, unfettered by noise, crowds or other unwanted incursions from civilization. I figured there'd be no better setting for me and

Painted Pony to seek common ground and perhaps have a chance to weave the first threads of a new friendship. Nothing could have been further from the truth. One reluctant tourist was already well ahead of us on the trail, near the top. He'd made his ascent while braving the darkness knowing that there was no one or anything more lethal than he lurking nearby. He was out of sorts but had made his way to the cascades twice in the prior week to get acclimated. Cagliostro had chosen him carefully for this crucial mission. A Sicilian of the same pedigree as the Ghost, the Viper, as he was known, was young as assassins go and incredibly fit and strong. But he already had a well established reputation as a trusted professional who lived by the ancient code of silence, Omerta."

JD shuddered at the thought of the heartless killer. "The Viper was not a disposable killer. There would be no need to eliminate him to cover their tracks. Like the Ghost before him, the Viper was considered a valuable asset ... the ultimate problem solver to be kept under retainer so to speak ... Cagliostro's Luca Brazzi, *most trusted friend*. The name Viper suited him well. He was silent, deadly and a cold blooded killer. He was armed to the teeth for this mission, I guess, to ward off bears, snakes or any unfortunate park authorities or nosey tourists who might accidentally stumble onto the scene at the wrong time. However, he had no intention of using them. This was to be a most unfortunate accident. I was the perfect target. I'd already disregarded the prominent warnings once to scale the cliff and peer from above the falls. It wouldn't take much urging to command a repeat performance."

JD laughed derisively, "In spite of his limited mental acuity, Painted Pony was expertly coached and played the part well. During the first part of the hike he was morosely quiet and gave me an uneasy feeling. Then he opened up, I thought, at my prodding. It was all planned including the way he shared tales of his boyhood with Morning Sky. As he took me into his confidence, I let my guard down and didn't dare caution him against ascending to forbidden cliffs for fear of losing the ground I'd gained with my new companion. Instead, I jumped right in and showed him the safest way to get to the top by climbing sideways off to the right of the falls and then up, over and around to get back to the water. Only for a moment did I get to experience the euphoria of gazing out over the precipice where the crystal clear water began cascading downward. Painted Pony seemed oddly distracted at such a pivotal moment at the zenith of our hike. Then as quick as a steel bear trap snapping shut, the Viper leapt from the bushes and struck. His startled victim was not me but Painted Pony. With cold, carefully calculated malice and one precise, powerful shove, Painted Pony was launched over the falls. I'll never forget the ghastly look of terror that overtook his face. He did not have time to scream. The last sound I heard before the sickening splat on the wet rocks below was Painted Pony gasping for his final labored breath."

The shock registered on all of our faces including normally stoic Mit. Even JD's countenance dropped as he re-lived that terrible moment, "The killer turned toward me and there was no doubt that he had the same fate in mind for me. I don't know if it was my military training coming back to me but, by the grace of God, I backed away from him immediately. He inched forward carefully with the grace of a gymnast, ensuring his footing as he moved in for the kill. As I ran out of real estate, I had no choice but to step gingerly onto the wet, slippery log that lay over the stream at the edge of the falls. It sounds crazy but I couldn't help but picture Cary Grant desperately holding onto Eva Marie Saint's outstretched hand in Hitchcock's thriller, North by Northwest, dangling off of Mt. Rushmore under the indomitable gazes of the four presidents as the Viper crept closer and closer. I pictured Martin Landau's cold, blank stare as he ground his shoe into Thornhill's clinging fingers. Maybe I needed the distraction to maintain my sanity ... and precarious balance. It had been a long time since I'd seen hand-to-hand combat and my training never prepared me for a do or die battle on a slick perch high above a roaring waterfall. My confidence ebbed as the assassin moved forward with the stealth of a jungle jaguar. Yet, I never lost faith because I'd cheated death twice before at the hand of God."

JD stopped to catch his breath. We could see that it was emotionally draining for him to share such a painful memory with us. "I thought about trying to jump to the other side or even out into the stream to avoid his clutches. Just the way he moved reminded me of one of those Special Forces guys who can wrap you up into a pretzel. Could I survive the water and make my way out to escape before being swept over the falls? I looked down and saw Painted Pony's grotesquely contorted body below and lost any hint of courage. Hysteria held me in its cold grip for a moment as I thought about my fall from AB's tall headquarters building years before. There must be something in the name Uticus because, like that other Eutychus, there I was again facing death from a fall. Finally, I said a silent prayer and steeled myself for the struggle … thy will be done. At that, the log gave way unexpectedly. Was it a tremor, just too much weight to bear with two grown men atop it or just the hand of God again? I don't know for sure this time but I suspect it was the latter. Otherwise, we should have both plunged to our deaths. Instead, it dropped hard at one end and twisted sharply when it hit the water and catapulted me to the far bank. The Viper was not so lucky. He was swept over Ramsey Cascades in the furious, rushing torrent. His rag doll descent was interrupted multiple times on the uneven rock ledges until he came to rest violently near Painted Pony."

Jude couldn't help but let "Praise the Lord God Almighty" slip across her lips.

Mit offered an "Amen!"

JD raised a finger as if to say, wait there's more. "As you can imagine, my heart was racing a mile a minute. I laid there on my back, breathless, staring up at the early morning sky thanking God for saving me yet again. Then I heard moaning. I cautiously peered over the edge and saw the slightest movement from the Viper's prone shape below. I collected my senses and gathered my strength to make my way back down to the rock slab surrounding the pool below. There was still life in the Viper's broken body. I approached him slowly and knelt down and put my ear close to his mouth to catch his tortured utterances. I asked if he could hang on while I made my way down to seek help but it was clear he knew he was in his death throes and had one thing on his mind. For all his evil deeds, the Viper somehow clung to a knowledge of God and was deathly afraid to meet his Maker. Unlike his predecessor, the Sicilian Ghost, he had a sliver of a conscience remaining. It was buried deep but he knew his *work for the church* was in no way redeeming but rather sacrilegious and evil. He was desperate to make last minute amends and spilled his guts to me. He said he had been hired to kill me. My death was supposed to be seen as a senseless act of violence by a crazed Indian seeking vengeance against a white traitor. It was meant to be staged as a struggle gone wrong where both the victim and perpetrator slipped during the altercation and fell to their deaths."

I couldn't bite my tongue any longer, "Did he say how he located you?"

"Yes, he said our last phone call had been intercepted and relayed."

"Did he reveal anything else, JD?"

"I asked him his name and if he wanted me to contact anyone. He was true to the code and said he was only known as the Viper. He said he had no family and pleaded that I say a prayer for him. He was losing it at that point, drifting in and out of consciousness. I felt very sorry for him. The Viper was only concerned with one thing … facing God. I held his hand and said a prayer out loud. I exhorted him to ask God for forgiveness in the name of Jesus Christ. He said 'Lord God, Heavenly Father, please forgive me in Jesus' name'. He only spoke once more before dying. It was as if he wanted to make his final amends. Facing eternity, he broke the code of silence and said these last words to me, 'Beware Cagliostro'."

CHAPTER 6

Unholy Truce

"Doveryai, no proveryai"(Russian proverb meaning trust but verify often cited by Soviet Revolutionary, Vladimir Lenin) … "Trust but verify"(Ronald Reagan) … "You repeat that at every meeting" (Mikhail Gorbachev) … "I like it" (Ronald Reagan, Intermediate-Range Nuclear Forces Treaty signing between President Ronald Reagan and Soviet General Secretary Mikhail Gorbachev, December 8, 1987)

We were physically spent from the emotional fatigue. I felt it personally and could see it written on the drooping faces and slumped shoulders of JD, Jude and Mit. There was an odd sense of relief in hearing JD's harrowing tale; getting it behind us. We all stared into space sharing catatonic empathy toward one another in our mutual plight. JD was the first to break the spell before we drifted off too far, "Unfortunately, this doesn't mean we're out of the woods by any means." As this sunk in, there were double takes, raised eyebrows and a few giggles that turned into uproarious laughter. Sometimes being dog tired can have that effect … you know … it can turn you into silly putty where the slightest little thing seems hilarious.

I was the first to weigh in between the snickers, "No pun intended, right?" Everyone busted up again. "You're absolutely wrong, JD! Actually, you are out of the woods, literally!" In our weakened condition, this rather benign comment had us doubled over holding our stomachs while an avalanche of guffaws brought tears to our eyes. Maybe it was a cathartic thing where we needed to cleanse our systems of all the bad vibes. Perhaps it was just contagion … we were feeding off of each other's delirium. Whatever the case, Rodney Dangerfield couldn't have done a better job of keeping us in stitches. JD was laughing so hard that he not only was crying but started leaking at the nostrils too. Jude did the humane thing and handed him a tissue not realizing that this would bring another round of uncontrollable belly laughs. JD tried to halt his chortling so abruptly that it produced a huge snot bubble that caused everyone to stop and stare in disbelief. Then everyone completely lost it and the boisterous ballyhoo erupted all over again. It finally stopped due to sheer exhaustion and cramping pain in our rib cages and diaphragms. It took several minutes for us to catch our breath and regain enough composure to carry on.

JD exhaled and issued a long sigh of relief which signaled an end to the merry mayhem. He waited another good minute before speaking to make sure our giggle boxes were disarmed. JD was able to muster enough fortitude to set a serious tone again, "Marchetti, God rest his soul, provided wise counsel. The steps you've taken at his urging were crucial to our safety and security. But it's not enough."

This was quite a downer and effectively killed the mood. I reacted with something bordering on anger, "What do you mean? What else can we do?"

JD responded in typical fashion with his wonderful knack for avoiding unnecessary conflict, "Don't get me wrong. You've done just the right thing. It has very likely saved your lives. However, when they discovered I survived the attack by Al Batin's fanatics, it changed the dynamics completely. As the Viper's failed attempt shows, they will stop at nothing to eliminate anything that threatens their position of power and influence." JD paused in deep regret, "I'm so very sorry to have come back here and, in the process, put you all in danger again."

My anger subsided immediately and reason prevailed, "JD, you shouldn't talk like that. It's not your fault. You had no choice but to come back here and warn us. When they overheard our phone conversation, it turned their sights on us too. If they had succeeded in killing you, it was only a matter of time. They knew I'd learn of your death and trace it back to them. In spite of our precautions, they'd have pulled out all the stops in seeking a way to silence us all permanently."

"Thanks Inky ... that means a lot to me. We truly are in this together whether we like it or not. I came back here for two reasons. First, I believe that it is God's will that I come out of hiding and get back to the business of spreading the good news. These visions he's shared with me have a purpose. Second, I needed to warn you so that we could close ranks and take whatever measures are necessary to get them to stand down."

"You're right on target JD ... united we stand, divided we fall ... we either hang together or we'll hang separately. But what can we do? Do you have any ideas on how we might turn up the pressure a notch or two on Cagliostro and company?"

"Right now I'm thinking that perhaps it would be better to dial back a bit rather than ratcheting things higher."

"I don't know JD. Do you really think appeasement will work with these devils?"

"No, not at all but I'm not talking about appeasement. I have something else in mind but need to flesh things out a bit. I think we should sleep on it and start fresh in the morning. Anyway, we need to find someplace where we can strategize in private, outside of earshot of any eavesdroppers."

"I agree, JD. Mit, can you stay here tonight so we can get a jump on things in the morning?"

"Sure Inky, I'd be happy to spend the night here … assuming chef Judith will be on duty in the morning." He wasn't saying this in jest. Mit was the practical sort and was thinking solely of his stomach. There was no intent to be charming or funny.

Jude chimed in, "No problem Mit … would you boys like some scrambled eggs, bacon and hot cakes for breakfast?" There were eager nods all the way around. "I'll have to drop the kids off at a sitter before we head out though." I didn't object. Jude was up to her eyeballs in this like the rest of us and needed to be a part of our crucial strategy session. Plus, she's great at brain storming and would be a valuable asset to the team.

JD had one piece of unfinished business which he preferred that our malefactors hear, "Mit, I take it that your new girlfriend is clueless about our situation with the church?"

"That's right JD … she doesn't know anything about the past other than what she might have read in the papers or heard on the news. She's never brought it up though. Also, she has no idea about you … she still thinks you're dead and gone."

"That's great … let's keep it that way … for her own good."

Goofy Mit replied, "Aye, Aye captain" and offered a sorry excuse for a salute.

Jude showed everyone their arrangements for the night and offered a tired, "Good night" to all.

There's nothing quite like waking up to the smell of a hearty country breakfast in the making. The wafting aromas, soothing sizzling sounds of frying bacon and splattering of batter hitting the griddle as Jude flipped the hot cakes had us all salivating like Pavlov's dog. The scrambled eggs were a thing of perfection. Jude liked to add a splash of pancake batter to make the eggs fluffier and had a special knack for cooking them without leaving any dry, burnt spots. She gave the flap jacks a special touch by heating the Log Cabin syrup. It helped to melt the butter into gleaming pools atop the steaming, feathery, golden stacks heaped high on our plates. Luckily, we were still groggy enough from our slumbers that we didn't bust into a fresh fit of laughter when Mit approached the table. He was a sight to behold. His hair which was normally tousled was somehow even more frazzled in the morning making him look like a cross between Sideshow Bob and Seinfeld's Kramer. All in all, it was a great start to an important day and the hot, black coffee gave us just the jolt we needed for the challenges ahead.

JD and I handled kitchen duty while Jude dropped off the kids and Mit did his best to avoid a bad hair day. Everything was ship shape before Jude returned and we passed notes to determine our destination. We didn't want to tip off any eavesdroppers and give them advance notice even though we realized they could tail us if they wanted. That danger gave us inspiration for our plan. Jude had a friend who taught at a local high school and was sure she would help us get access to a table in a commons used for study hall and general gatherings. It was perfect in that it was very public and noisy. The teens, normally suspicious of older types, kept their distance and eventually paid us no attention as they snacked, chatted and studied. They probably figured we were some kind of committee of teachers or administrators working on another new program to make their lives more difficult. Mit certainly looked the part of a physics or chemistry teacher. In any case, it gave us just the right cover to strategize. It would have been easy to detect any interlopers in that environment ... except in the unlikely event our adversaries had some teenage lackeys on the payroll.

To me, it seemed like we were in a real quandary. "I don't know how we can get them to back off. They've already played their hand. They might have been willing to tolerate the rest of us for a while but your return has boxed them into a corner. After the latest attempt on your life, we just can't trust them."

JD was ever thoughtful and pragmatic, "You hit the nail on the head. I'm the wild card in this mess ... the thing they fear the most. Do you know why that is?"

"You're the Last Prophet."

"Bingo Inky ... that's the bottom line! If I was a regular Joe they wouldn't be so hell bent on killing me. It's my celebrity that scares them. For any other face in the crowd, they'd have easier, less extreme ways to eliminate the threat. They can marginalize any anonymous *kook* without spending big bucks on professional goons or doing things that can raise the wrong eyebrows. My Achilles heel is my strength. I can control the media ... I can garner limitless attention. That's way too dangerous of a proposition for them. They can't have me running around all over the air waves digging up their skeletons." JD paused and asked the sixty-four thousand dollar question, "So, how can we minimize this unacceptable threat?"

I couldn't see a way out of this trap but to Mit, the analytical pragmatist, it seemed easy, just a matter of common sense. "I'd do what mortal enemies do all the time. Just sign a treaty with them."

I was still stuck in the box and couldn't see the wisdom in Mit's remark. "Are you kidding ... a treaty?"

Mit was unaffected by my harsh retort. "The Russians were hell bent on destroying us, weren't they? That didn't stop Reagan and Gorbachev from signing a treaty and putting the Cold War somewhat on the back burner. It bought us enough time to eventually get the upper hand."

I was about to strike again when Jude chimed in, "Wait, I think Mit is onto something. Think about it. Ronnie was able to pull off the deal by negotiating from a position of strength. Right now, we're in as strong a position as possible thanks to

Mr. Marchetti. Maybe it's time for Let's Make a Deal."

It still wasn't clicking for me but I was smart enough to show Jude more respect than I'd extended to Mit. "Don't you think it's dangerous to try to cut a deal with people like Cagliostro?"

"Do we have a choice? What's more dangerous; cutting a deal or sticking with the status quo? Is there a risk in playing Deal, No Deal? The worst thing they can say is no and that only leaves us where we started, not worse off. They're holding most of the cards right now and we need to tilt things more in our favor. You know what they say … if you can't beat 'em, join 'em."

While I pondered Jude's logic, JD offered, "Yes, we need to stick to our strong suit which is the threat of exposure through the evidence provided by Marchetti. We need to make it clear that I'm under that umbrella too and any attempt to harm any one of us will result in us going public with that information. But at the same time, we can offer assurances that, when I come out of hiding, I won't do anything to put them in the spotlight."

I finally saw the light and began to warm up to the idea. "Okay, I think I get the picture. We're not going to cozy up to this brood of snakes. We'll just agree to play nice. Like we did with the Russians, we'll practice détente publicly while ensuring our mutual assured destruction behind the scenes. If they don't back off, we'll drop our Fat Man, Marchetti's bomb, on them. If we break our vow … well, you know what that means." I scratched my head over one thing. "This could work except that we won't be able to contain the media firestorm that will erupt when you come out of your *tomb* for the second time."

"You're right Inky … we've seen this movie before. There will be no escaping the glare once word gets out. But we can still manage the message. It won't be easy but it's our best shot."

Mit just smiled smugly seeing how things had unfolded. He seemed to wonder what took the rest of us so long to grasp the simple solution he'd figured out minutes before. "So it's settled then. We'll call a truce." He proceeded to ramble on explaining why it was the logical thing to do. We had to tune him out.

Thankfully, Jude dammed the babbling brook, "So how do we go about calling a truce with a Roman Catholic cardinal a continent away?"

Mit applied his impeccable logic in typical goofy Mit fashion, "If the mountain won't come to Mohammed, then Mohammed must go to the mountain."

JD saw I was building up to another outburst and gently held up a finger to stem my reaction. "You've got a point there Mit. Cagliostro is not apt to make the same mistake as Riccardi did by coming here to meet me. He can best keep all of his options open by leaving no trails that lead to my door. Plus, it's difficult for a high ranking cardinal from the Vatican to come to the US without causing a fuss. Riccardi had good reason since church leaders from around the globe were beating a path to see the Last Prophet back then. Now, with me still in hiding, supposedly dead, it would be next to impossible for him to come here without exposing my latest *resurrection* prematurely. No, our best chance would be to allow Cagliostro to maintain home field advantage. On his turf, he could ensure secrecy."

I didn't disagree but raised a caution, "This makes sense but wouldn't it be awfully dangerous to venture into the lion's den?"

JD never got ruffled, "No doubt there'd be a risk. But are you forgetting one of my name sakes,

Daniel? I won't be alone in the lion's den ... God will be with me."

I had to object, "Whoa there John Daniel! Nobody said anything about you going alone. You have to have a witness. I've got to accompany you to discourage them from pulling a fast one."

"Like I said, I won't be going alone. God will be my constant companion."

"Maybe so but God won't mind me tagging along. I'll make sure you don't wind up permanently in the catacombs somewhere."

JD could see I wouldn't relent so he appealed to my sense of family duty, "Who's going to watch out for Jude and the kids?"

"I'm sure Mit wouldn't mind enjoying more of Jude's home cooking while we're away, would you Mit?" He just offered a euphoric grin. JD acquiesced silently. "There, it's settled then." I didn't look at Jude, wanting to avoid the scowl she must have shot at me at the prospect of listening to Mit's incessant chatter for a week.

We had a lot of wrinkles to iron out but left the school with our mission accomplished; a plan of action. As soon as we got back to my house, we dug out Marchetti's papers and poured through them looking for the right contact. It seemed Rafael Benedetto was the best candidate. From the way Marchetti referred to him, it appeared he was Cagliostro's Marchetti. Getting through to him presented a challenge. It took several phone calls and then numerous holds and transfers before we could get someone to acknowledge that Benedetto existed. And even at that, we could not convince anyone to put us through to his office at the Vatican. We had to leave a message from me, Horace Hermann, and hope for a return call. We guessed that, after verifying the legitimacy of our call, curiosity would get the better of them. It took two days of pins and needles before my phone rang. I presumed they had taken precautions to set up a clean, untraceable line. The conversation was brief and sketchy. No names were given, no point of reference. We didn't want to say or do anything that might scare them away. "I am returning your call."

"Thank you, this is ..."

"I know who this is. There is no need to name names. Please get to the point quickly."

I'd be lying if I didn't say I was a bit rattled but did my best to maintain my composure. "We would like to set up a private meeting with you and your superior."

"I'm sorry but I don't think that would be possible."

"It would be completely private ... no media ... no publicity of any sort. We would be happy to come to you. It would be just the two of us ... me and your friend from the Smokey Mountains."

"I understand but cannot promise you anything."

"We want to offer you certain protections and assurances ... a peaceful co-existence. There is no need for us to be at odds."

There was a long pause but I could tell that the call had not been interrupted. Benedetto was considering. Finally, he broke the silence, "I will contact you if there is any desire to meet." Then he hung up without further ado.

What followed was dead silence, a long Maalox moment for us. Had we screwed the pooch and sped up the timetable for our own execution? Let me tell you, there were some sleepless nights at the Hermann household. After a couple of days I couldn't take it anymore and asked Jude to take the kids away just in case. The walls closed in on me, JD and Mit. Every strange sound, any odd movement of a windblown branch or limb or squirrel skittering across the yard brought a portent of doom. Was there a successor to the Ghost and Viper lurking outside plotting his plan of attack? The interminable waiting grated on our raw, irritated nerves and we became short tempered with one another. None of us could keep our minds on anything productive and there's just so much television you can watch before going bonkers. It was like being stuck inside a prison knowing someone had put a contract on your life. We were trapped like rats waiting for some goon to spring out of the shadows and plunge a shank into our necks. After a week of this hell, JD decided enough was enough and declared that we had to get out and away for a while. He suggested, of all things, a trip to the links for eighteen holes.

Mit was terrified at the idea. He had never touched a club in his life other than one miniature golf outing that didn't fare well. We disregarded his caterwauling about being athletically challenged and assured him he'd have a blast. We guaranteed we'd just play for fun and it didn't matter how well or poor he played. The point was to get out in the fresh air and enjoy the beauty of the fairways and greens. Boy did we lie! Well, not intentionally but we didn't realize just how bad it would be. Mit wasn't athletically challenged. Let's be honest. He was clumsy and awkward. It didn't help that he wore flat tennis shoes instead of spikes and had to use rental clubs that were at least three inches too short for his elongated body. His shoes slipped so much when he swung that a couple of times he came close to falling down. I'm ashamed to admit it but he got so contorted trying to smack that little white ball that we couldn't help but laugh. Mit was mad enough to spit nails and threatened to walk off the course. We pleaded with him to stay and promised to help him. It's not that we were good at the game … far from it. But we knew enough to give him some basic pointers.

We were lucky that the course was empty that day and no one got upset because of our slow play. Patience paid off and Mit made some progress. By the fifteenth hole, he was starting to have a little fun. Once he understood the importance of swing mechanics, trajectories, angles of approach and such, he settled in and applied his command of advanced physics to help overcome his shortcomings in execution. On sixteen he strung together four decent shots, one putted and scored a bogey which we considered a major accomplishment after a succession of snowmen or worse. I dropped the pin in the hole and we celebrated the victory with high fives all around. It took JD two tries to get some skin because Mit missed connections on the first elated hand slap. We shared a hearty laugh heading back to the carts as if Mit had just won the Masters championship. One thing was sure; golf had been the right tonic to take our minds off of Cagliostro. Just as it seemed every care in the world had melted like an April snow shower in Missouri, my cell phone rang. I scrambled to the cart to get it before it went to voice mail.

There was no introduction. There was no need. I was already familiar with Benedetto's raspy, sinister voice. It sounded like thick phlegm was perpetually lodged in his throat. My bile rose and I felt like hurling. "His eminence has graciously agreed to grant you an audience. There will be a private jet to pick you two up at Parks Airport in East St. Louis tomorrow evening at 6:30 p.m. You should pack for two nights. All of the arrangements have been made. You will be told the time and place of the meeting once you have boarded the plane. If you are not there promptly at 6:30, we will assume you have changed your mind. Repeat back to me what I have just shared with you."

I repeated the particulars to ensure Benedetto I had heard correctly and asked, "Where will we be staying?"

He repeated, "All of the arrangements have been made." Then the line went dead.

We all felt uneasy about the private jet. What was to stop them from dumping us somewhere over the Atlantic Ocean? It didn't seem wise to put ourselves so completely in their control. However, it was apparent we were in no position to negotiate. It was understandable that they would want to maintain strict control of the situation. Perhaps it was best that way. It would help to ensure that our visit remained completely confidential. JD never seemed to get rattled ... his faith never appeared to waver. He tried to make light of the situation, "If they wanted to make us disappear, they wouldn't need such an elaborate scheme with a private jet and trans-Atlantic flight. We'll be lucky to survive East St. Louis." Mit thought that was funny but all I could muster was a nervous laugh. We'd come too far to turn back so we finished the last two holes, headed back to pack and called Jude to come back home and babysit Mit.

We exchanged hugs, kisses and handshakes all around and left early for Parks. It was a good thing. As we headed across the bridge on I-64 East into Illinois there was a delay due to construction traffic. We made it through the maze of twists, turns and signs and exited toward the East bank of the Mississippi River. Luckily, we didn't have to go through the heart of town to get to Parks. I laughed and JD demanded to know what was so funny. I said I'd just received a vision … a vision of Clark Griswold's wrong turn into East St. Louis in the movie Vacation on their way from Chicago to Wally World. That got a smile out of him. We'd never been to Parks before but it was small and easy to navigate. I guess the private jet crowd is a pretty exclusive club. There was an intercom by the gate leading to the tarmac and we gave them my name and it opened automatically. As we drove around to the back of the terminal there were two guys waiting for us that looked like Secret Service agents. They took my car keys, grabbed our luggage and escorted us quickly to the jet. I should have been nervous but couldn't resist commenting on the special treatment, "Wow, valet parking, no waiting, no security check points … we've got to do this more often."

JD was a little skeptical even though he at least had some experience with private jets of the military transport type. "Yeah, it's the only way to fly," he said glumly.

I had no idea how long the jet had been waiting. My guess is that it had just touched down long enough for a quick maintenance check and refueling. There were no distinguishing features on the outside of the plane to offer a clue as to whether it was a charter or Vatican-owned. We assumed it was the latter because it seemed to be top of the line. JD figured they preferred to keep it incognito. It was a Gulfstream G650 and looked brand spanking new. The interior was immaculate with plush white leather seats. There was plenty of room for eight passengers and we only had four including our two baby sitters. The pilot and co-pilot said hello but didn't introduce themselves and closed the cockpit door. Mutt and Jeff took the front seats and pointed us to the back and told us to buckle up. Just that quickly it was wheels up and we were winging our way to Italy. The back seating area was retrofitted with a comfy couch that folded out to a sleeper. There'd be no snoozing on this ride. We didn't want to wake up in mid-air, sky diving without parachutes. And anyway, we were too jacked up having fun posing as high rollers. As decked out as our ride was, it wasn't like taking off in a commercial airliner. It was more like riding a Corvette instead of a Caddie. It was windy outside and we bounced around quite a bit until we reached altitude and leveled off.

I guess we could have slept since our two large, scary companions both nodded off rather quickly. Still we didn't want to take any chances. We had more than eight hours to kill so JD and I took advantage of the goodies at our disposal. There was plenty of free food and drinks on board and no waiting in line for the restroom. There was TV, music, newspapers from major cities around the world, magazines and cards, all of which we didn't let go to waste. With plenty of time to burn and running out of trivialities, we used the time to map out our strategy with Benedetto and Cagliostro. I whispered as if we were trading state secrets then, quite to my irritation, JD responded in full-throated glory as if we were in a loud bar. "JD, you've got to keep it down. Those guys may not really be sleeping."

"Do you think I give a rat's rear end?"

"C'mon JD, we really need to keep it close to the vest."

"Look, those two guys are out like lights ... they're sawing logs up there. But if someone wanted to eavesdrop, I'm sure they could. Do you think this plane isn't bugged?" I shrugged and twisted one side of my mouth upward to grudgingly agree. "We don't have anything to hide at this point. If they can't hear us, I'd be happy to write it down for them." I was exasperated and air rushed from my pursed lips as if someone had just released a pressure valve. "Inky, you know what we're going to say. We're going to lay our cards on the table so there's no use in holding back now."

"Yeah, I guess you're right. I'm just tense because I don't trust these people; not a one of them."

"I don't trust them either. They've tried to assassinate me twice, duh." I nodded in agreement. "Inky, we've gotta have faith. There's no reason for us to make things worse than they are. Ever heard of jet lag my friend? Why do you think those two lugs are sleeping? We need to catch a few hours of shut-eye or we won't be worth a plugged nickel when we get to Rome." With that, JD fell asleep almost instantly. I fought it for a while but soon succumbed to the inevitable. It was pitch black when we hit the hay and bright and sunny when we awoke giving us the false impression of a full night's sleep. I wasn't that hungry since it had only been a few hours since our last snack but JD said it would help acclimate our bodies to the new time zone by cramming *breakfast* down the hatch so I dove in to some awesome Danish and fresh fruit and cleared the pipes with some OJ and coffee.

Our landing wasn't much different than the takeoff in the small jet. It seemed precarious and jumpy compared to a commercial flight aboard a Boeing jetliner. I'm a white knuckle flyer anyway so I was pretty tense. That is, until there was some comic relief in the form of the lavatory door popping open and a roll of toilet paper barreling down the aisle past us. JD couldn't resist a wise crack, "Here you go Inky. They think of everything on these private jets ... even an auto TP dispenser in case you drop a load in your pants during the landing." I managed to laugh in spite of being tied up in knots. My attention was drawn to the windows by something odd. Then my antennae went up completely when I noticed JD was concerned too. Leonardo Di Vinci airport looked like a parking lot for Alitalia. Luckily, the runways were clear as was our path to our remote hanger but still I'd never seen anything like it before. One of our escorts who spoke fluent English with a noticeable Italian accent took note of our concern and assured us there was no need to worry. He said it was a wildcat strike by the pilots' union and a common maneuver where they pull off the runway, park on the tarmac and walk off the job in a show of defiance and solidarity. He said it happens more often than you'd think. I thought *if this is European socialism, you can keep it.*

Thankfully, we didn't have to go through the main terminal. It was jam packed with thousands of miserable travelers caught in the crossfire between airline management and the union rank and file. With just about every Alitalia flight canceled the only fortunate ones were the few people that were able to switch to another carrier like British Airways. The rest of the poor schmucks were relegated to finding a spot to recline on the floor for hours on end. As for us, we might as well have been foreign dignitaries. The VIP treatment continued as we deplaned, waltzed through the small private hanger and hopped in our limo with Mutt and Jeff along to get us to our destination. The limo bar was fully stocked and JD said playfully, "This round is on me fellas." Our tour guides weren't amused but stoically started to comply when JD commanded tongue-in-cheek, "Two glasses of your best single malt, straight up." It was much too early in the day for such shenanigans so when JD saw they were taking him seriously he quickly back tracked, "Just kidding fellas. Hey, what's next on the agenda?"

Mutt answered robotically, "The local time is currently 10:32 a. m. You are scheduled to meet with Cardinal Cagliostro at 3:00 p. m. We are taking you to your hotel so you can check in, rest and freshen up. It is not far so we will pick you up outside the lobby at 2:20 p. m. to drive you to your meeting." That was all they were willing or able to share. They weren't too big on idle conversation. When the limo pulled up to a grand hotel with ornate features just dripping with history we thanked our escorts and tried to grab our own luggage. They insisted upon handing our bags over to a bellman and left without as much as an arrivederci. The lobby was just as impressive as the exterior and I wondered how much one night in this place would set us back. To our surprise, we were told that everything had been taken care of including any bills we might incur during our stay. Visions of unlimited room service calls and indiscriminately raiding the minibar danced in my head. Though well-appointed and luxurious, the room was small by American standards. It didn't take us long to unpack and clean up so we talked about strolling around the area nearby for a while. JD noticed a red light flashing on the phone. We already had a voice mail. Who could it be? It was probably just some recorded welcome from the front desk, right? No, it was a bland one liner from Benedetto encouraging us to not leave the room prior to our meeting ... bummer. It made sense that they would not want us out and about drawing attention to ourselves.

We whiled away the time nervously until 2:10. Well, I was nervous but JD seemed unaffected by the magnitude of it all. Like clockwork, Mutt and Jeff strode into the lobby just as we exited the elevator and showed us to the limo which was parked neatly out front. JD and I had speculated about where the meeting might take place, thinking that, most likely, it would be some dark, secluded, off-the-beaten-path cubbyhole that could offer the utmost privacy. Boy were we surprised when the limo turned into the Vatican and dropped us within a healthy stroll of St. Peter's Basilica. We put our differences with Roman Catholic theology aside for a moment and marveled at the splendor of the surroundings. Sometimes places you've seen on TV look smaller and less impressive in person but that didn't apply here. If anything, it was more stunning than expected and everything oozed pomp and circumstance. St. Peter's Square was huge and the surroundings were laden with history and tradition in every direction ... the colonnade and statues of the saints, Apostolic Palace, Sistine Chapel, the Roman obelisk secured from Egypt by Caligula and so much more right down to the Swiss Guard in their traditional garb. They could have been on a casting call for a remake of Camelot adorned in their bright, multi-colored vests, plumed knee-pants and ornate berets and equipped with long spears and swords.

We were turning every which way trying to soak in the incredible images, so engaged in sightseeing that we didn't notice when our hosts approached. For all we knew, they could have materialized out of thin air. They were unmistakable in their black cassocks highlighted with scarlet piping, buttons and sashes. However, in this setting they did not seem out of place or draw special attention since many people in clerical dress were coming and going throughout the Square. Surprisingly, they were unescorted except for Mutt and Jeff who maintained a discreet distance from us. Everything was purposefully understated so that we would not stand out from the crowd. I immediately assumed the large, portly man was Cagliostro but he introduced himself pleasantly as Benedetto. The gravelly voice didn't match his cuddly, non-threatening façade. He offered a formal introduction of his senior fellow, his eminence, Cardinal Cagliostro. He was a slight man with rat-like features that reminded me of a low-level wise guy in a mobster movie. Yet, his voice was soothing as silk and put us immediately at ease. That is, we were momentarily caught off guard until remembering this was the man who just recently was responsible for hiring the notorious Viper to carry out his death wish against JD. The dissonance between his evil reputation and gentle, fatherly image had us off balance.

Cagliostro did not treat us as mortal enemies or terrible skeletons to be buried deep in a closet somewhere. To the contrary, everything was quite open and highly transparent and he feted us with the dignity and graciousness that might be expected for visiting heads of state. We were not whisked away to some hidden catacomb where we could get right down to the nasty business at hand. Cagliostro extended open arms and smiled demurely, "Gentlemen, welcome to our church home. Will you allow me the pleasure of taking you on a personal tour?"

What could we say? We both nodded and JD returned the pleasantries, "Of course, thank you very much." What followed was truly amazing. Cagliostro was the perfect tour guide. There in the midst of St. Peter's Square he was able to point out for us the Papal Apartments, Papal Palace and other less descript edifices where business was conducted by the Curia, College of Cardinals and various Papal offices and commissions. JD had done his homework and asked if one building housed the Governorate of Vatican City. He impressed the Cardinal when he inquired, "Didn't the Pope appoint you to a term in the Governorate?" JD knew that Cagliostro occupied one of these important posts in what might be deemed as the administrative executive branch of the Vatican. Cagliostro nodded in a humble fashion incongruent with the power and influence he exercised. We knew well enough to greatly fear him although, in the scheme of things, he was a small, inconsequential man. The College of Cardinals occasionally exercises authority in selecting a new Pope and the Governorate holds sway over certain aspects of day-to-day administration and governance but when you get right down to it, the Vatican is run as an absolute monarchy under the Papacy. We maintained a healthy respect for his power as ants in the presence of an elephant but kept in mind also that, like Riccardi before him, Cagliostro had his masters too.

We made our way toward the buildings and Cagliostro shared his wealth of knowledge in pointing out many secret treasures that would have otherwise eluded our attention. One of the highlights was the Sistine Chapel. Gazing at Michelangelo's masterpieces, the elaborate frescoes adorning the walls and vaulted ceilings were something to behold. The vivid colors and bold images were breathtaking. It was very tough for me to contain my skepticism and disgust for the way the Roman Catholic Church had strayed from the word of God over the centuries and relegated it to second or third class status behind the authority of the Pope and their man-made traditions. I couldn't escape the irony of the Bible being brought to life in all its glory overhead in the brushed images of Michelangelo ... Jeremiah in meditation, Zachariah with papyrus in hand, Isaiah in meditation, Jonah exulting over being expelled from the great fish's belly, David and Goliath and the apostles. I wondered how the Roman Catholic Church could accept the heretical theory of evolution. There for everyone to see was the true story of God's creation ... the earth, the heavens, the creation of Adam, Eve's creation from Adam, the fall into sin, their expulsion from the Garden of Eden and Noah's Flood. Instead of letting this eat away at me, I took solace in the hope that, in spite of the damnable lie of works righteousness, these images might draw many to the truth of the Bible and God's revelation of his plan of salvation accomplished through our Lord and Savior, Jesus Christ.

Speaking of irony, how about the magnificent scene splashed across the back wall of the Sistine Chapel. The Last Judgment provided a sobering reminder to all that there will come a day when God's word will be fully vindicated and Jesus Christ will be universally recognized as true God, the Second Person of the Holy Trinity. There will be no doubters, scoffers or naysayers. Every knee will bow and every tongue will confess that Jesus is Lord over all. As depicted through the mind of Michelangelo, it will be a terrifying and glorifying day of judgment and triumph ... a separation of the wheat from the chaff, sheep from goats. Yes, the irony was palpable. There we were with our gracious host who was in reality a ravening wolf seeking to destroy JD ... the Last Prophet, resurrected from the dead to renew God's biblical message of warning and hope regarding the coming judgment. Cagliostro somberly intoned as we stared at the grand tapestry, "Prepare for the day of judgment comes."

JD couldn't resist a respectful retort as we departed the Chapel, "Come quickly Lord Jesus, come."

Cagliostro saved the best for last: St. Peter's Basilica. The sheer enormity of the cavernous interior was breathtaking and awe-inspiring. While incredible impressed, I couldn't help but think, *no wonder so many people buy into the heterodoxy of the Papal system ... signs and wonders.* It seemed every inch of the massive structure was replete with incredible artwork and intricate, hand-wrought designs and details festooned in gold. The sculptures were so lifelike and expressive; none more so than Michelangelo's Pieta. It was all brought together in a crescendo of opulent reverence in Michelangelo's imposing dome. It had the effect of making the individual Christian seem small and irrelevant in the presence of God. I thought to myself thankfully, *God's love is hard to comprehend. This structure, so mind-boggling by human standards, is just a pitiful pile of dust in God's eyes. Yet, in spite of our sinfulness ... in spite of deserving to be washed down God's cosmic drain ... God came up with a plan to rescue us. And that plan cost him dearly. He fulfilled the law where we could not and then sacrificed his own life to pay the terrible price we owed and imputed his righteousness to us poor, miserable sinners while we were yet in total enmity toward him ... all out of pure, unconditional, Godly love.*

Cagliostro knew all about the Last Prophet and his *blasphemous* attack against the Papacy. He knew exactly what he was doing by steering us to the last stop on the tour. Off to the side in a much more secluded corner of the Basilica was an arched doorway leading into what could almost be termed a very luxurious grotto. Above the archway was a banner sculpted from stone that read "SEPULCRUM SANCTI PETRI APOSTOLI". It was the tomb of St. Peter who, according to their contorted view of history, was the first Pope. There was no doubt in my mind that this was not the final resting place of the great apostle. I knew that Matthew 16:18 had been taken shamefully out of context to perpetuate the lie of Papal authority. In the context of the whole counsel of God, it's clear that the rock upon which Jesus established his church was the God-given faith Peter had demonstrated prior to Christ's pronouncement. The rest of chapter 16 alone shows that Christ didn't build his church on any such shaky, fallible, human foundation. As promised by Jesus, the Holy Ghost came on the day of Pentecost to inspire Peter's great sermon and miraculously transform some 3,000 Jewish converts. Looking at the tomb, surrounded by the buried bones of so many Popes nearby made me think of Judgment Day again. What a shocking surprise they would have in store if they had put their trust in Peter or anyone else other than Jesus Christ, the one Mediator between God and Man, the way, the truth and the life.

The cordiality seemed to evaporate as we left the Basilica and Cagliostro announced it was time to meet. Mutt and Jeff closed ranks and four other security types coalesced with us as we left the square toward two black SUVs nearby. I thought we might retire to Cagliostro's office in the Governorate but I was wrong. My spider-sense tingled as we left Vatican City. Was the charade going to end with us being dumped in a dark alley somewhere in the bowels of Rome? Benedetto hissed, "For the business we need to discuss, we will go to the Cardinal's residence for privacy." JD seemed at ease and whispered to me that most of the Cardinals had private residences outside of Vatican City. We pulled into a garage beneath a stately building that reminded me of pictures of the Dakota in New York where John Lennon lived out his last days. Half of the security contingent preceded us to make sure we'd encounter no one in the parking lot or elevator. They radioed that the coast was clear and we headed upstairs with Mutt, Jeff, Cagliostro and Benedetto. The apartment was spacious and suitably appointed for someone of Cagliostro's station in life. After ensuring that the apartment was safe and secure, Mutt, Jeff and the other brutes stationed themselves outside. There would be no witnesses to our conversation.

Cagliostro waved us to a couch that was built more for looks than comfort before taking a throne-like chair off to the side. Benedetto served a cup of tea to the Cardinal and offered the same to us but we declined. It was Benedetto who sat in the less ostentatious chair directly facing us. He, not Cagliostro engaged us, "Gentlemen, you've called this meeting so please kindly state your business." Benedetto was impeccably professional and polite but still his voice created a sinister impression that was unsettling to me.

JD was not intimidated in the least, "Thank you sir; as you suggested I will get right to the point." He then turned his gaze momentarily to Cagliostro. "I know that I represent a danger to you, such a grave threat that you sent one of your henchmen to kill me." Benedetto feigned great insult at the offense but Cagliostro was completely placid. JD eased ahead, "I mean no disrespect. I'm only stating a fact. And I understand why you would perceive me as a threat. But I'm here to hopefully persuade you that you have nothing to fear from me."

Benedetto eased back into his chair, "Go on then."

"As you know, Marchetti has provided us with powerful evidence that could lead to devastating consequences for you if it were made public. Nevertheless, you were willing to take the chance of setting this most undesirable chain of events into motion by seeking to take my life." Benedetto tensed again and JD almost set him off, "Why is that?" It was a rhetorical question but Benedetto seemed to squirm as if searching for an answer. JD let him off the hook, "It's because your worst fear is the Last Prophet getting back into the public eye and bringing worldwide attention to bear." I could have sworn that I heard Benedetto's sphincter pucker while Cagliostro sat stationary as a gargoyle and showing no more emotion that a crocodile waiting to strike. I looked at the old serpent out of the corner of my eye hoping to catch a glimpse of his forked tongue flitting in and out. "Well, I'm here to tell you that I am going public." Benedetto strangled a gasp. JD paused for a long time to gauge their reaction. Benedetto's squinted eyes shot daggers at him but Cagliostro remained stoic. "But here is the key. You have my word that I will not say a word about the Roman Catholic Church ... not a word ... if you agree to leave us alone. You must guarantee our safety."

They never confirmed or denied our accusations. They simply would not broach a subject that might leave them in any way culpable. But contrary to his dour, skeptical expression, you could tell that Benedetto was warm to the idea because he went into negotiation mode. "Of course we would like to avoid any attacks on the Church or Holy Father. In the past, you have laid claim to charges against the Church, under the guise of theology, that are false and scurrilous. We are fully prepared to refute such blasphemy but nevertheless it's difficult to protect many uninformed, vulnerable souls from clever, enticing lies. If you've had a change of heart, we are pleased. You say these fine words and make them sound so sincere but how can we trust you? As you

Americans say, once the horse is out of the barn, it is too late … the damage is done."

I was surprised at JD's confidence and boldness. If I were in his shoes, I may have floundered. "Let's be realistic here. Do you think I'd say these things to buy time just to gain a chance to speak out against the Roman Church and Papacy in public? Do you really think I'm that foolish? Believe me; I know from experience what the consequences would be. I'm not about to do anything that would put me, Inky, his family or anyone else in jeopardy."

Benedetto again sidestepped the implication toward their violent intentions and reasoned with JD. "Our only concern is the Church. You do strike me as sincere and I'm beginning to believe that you would do your best to honor your commitment to avoid causing the Church any harm. But once you are in public, you have no control over the media and the questions they will surely raise. What would prevent you from falling into one of their traps?"

"You are right. They will ask what they will ask. But I have learned to be selective. I don't need them. They need me. If I don't like the venue, personnel or content, I can shut things down. I don't need or want to be in the public eye."

"Then why must you go public. You could adopt a new identity and live a wonderful life without the rigors of celebrity. We could help you to shape such a new life."

"I appreciate that very much but I need to go public as the Last Prophet."

"I do not understand."

"You may find this hard to believe but God has given me visions. He has a new purpose in mind for me to again share his message of warning and hope regarding the end." This was the last thing Benedetto wanted to hear. He screwed his face into the most unpleasant, pained contortion and crossed his arms tightly across his chest. "Please, hear me out. I've said my peace on the tribulation leading up to the end. The visions are not focused on Armageddon or the Anti-Christ this time. The message is centered in a picture of the last day, the final judgment. It's a message that transcends denominations. I'm not here with a doctrinal treatise. It's a vision of the culmination of the plan of salvation, the gospel end game."

Benedetto relaxed and seemed to strike a reflective pose. "It appears you have repented of your misguided ways and wish no harm to the Church or Holy Father." JD bit his tongue and I held mine. Benedetto warned with a stern look, "We would be most displeased if you repeated that horrible debacle you perpetuated with Nick Phace."

"I will not limit my exposure to carry the message as stated here. It could very well be that I make a return appearance on Mr. Phace's program. But you have my word that we will not retrace old ground. My mission is a new one and it doesn't involve taking your church to task in any way. All we want is peace, a peaceful co-existence. As long as there is peace, you have nothing to worry about from us." I noticed the slightest nod from Cagliostro.

Benedetto formed a steeple with his fingers, rested his chin there and smiled broadly as if a piece of the finest chocolate was melting in his mouth. "We have an understanding Mr. Uticus."

The warm façade returned to Cagliostro like a theater curtain descending. He stood and clasped JDs hands, then mine. "Gentlemen, my driver will pick you up in the morning and take you to the jet for your flight home. In the meantime, you have the evening to see Rome. If you don't mind, I've made arrangements for you to dine at one of my favorite restaurants. Just mention my name to the maître de and everything will be taken care of for you. I hope you enjoy a safe and peaceful flight home." With that, as if by magic, the door opened and Mutt and Jeff entered to show us to the car and back to our hotel.

Before we could exit, Benedetto offered one last chilling bit of advice, "Gentlemen, enjoy the evening and the sights of Rome but I suggest you keep a low profile … and, of course, there is no need to mention this meeting to anyone." He shut the door unceremoniously.

When they dropped us off at the hotel, Mutt said, "You are on your own tonight." He handed me a slip of paper, "These are the directions to the Forum Restaurant." We tried to say thank you but they were gone before we could form the words.

JD grabbed me before I could enter the lobby, "Let's take a stroll."

I guessed that he didn't want to talk in the room since it was likely bugged. "What's on your mind?"

"Do you feel as filthy as I do?"

"Yeah, I know what you mean. It's kind of like we just made a deal with the devil. But look JD, we had no choice. They tried to kill you man … and they were following me and my family!"

"You're right Inky but that's not what bothers me the most. I feel like we've compromised the truth."

"How do you figure, JD? It's not like we've endorsed the Papacy or bought into their false teachings."

"No, then how come I feel like a slimy worm?"

"You shouldn't feel that way. JD, I was proud of the way you stood up to them under the circumstances. I would have wilted under the pressure. You didn't back down an inch in telling them that you're going to go public with the visions you've received."

"It's not that we caved into them but, you know, when you remain silent it's just like you've compromised truth and error."

"JD, you never repented as they said. You never renounced the truth of everything you said before including the message you delivered on Nick Phace's show. You were right to say you were moving on. God's given you a new mission … a new message. That's your calling now, not putting our lives in jeopardy by retracing the steps you've already taken. You spoke the truth about Armageddon and the Anti-Christ before and that record still stands. Remember, God has bound Satan with a chain but that doesn't mean he's harmless. God has warned us and given us the good sense not to get too close, within the length of his leash."

"Thanks Inky, that really helps. We've gotta stay focused on the mission at hand. Let's head back."

"Do you think we're safe now, JD?"

"Do you trust those devils? I wouldn't put anything past them. I feel we're safer now … for a time. We've eliminated the immediate threat that had them on high alert. Let's say we've been given a stay of execution. But make no mistake … the best solution for them is to remove the threat completely."

"Do you think we should can the Forum Restaurant?"

"Are you kidding? Do you think we'd be safer at McDonald's? If they were going to kill us they could do it without treating us to a gourmet meal. Let's go back, clean up, change and soak up the grandeur of Rome ... at least as much as possible in one evening."

Just as we were beginning to feel at ease, almost lighthearted, someone tapped JD on the shoulder causing both of us to nearly jump out of our skins. A short, cheerful fellow with a broad smile and German accent said, "Forgive me, I'm so sorry if I startled you. Aren't you JD Uticus?" We just stared at him, at a loss for words. What if we were being followed? What if someone from the Vatican saw us talking to a stranger? Would they think we'd betrayed their trust so that all bets were off? The German did his best to ease the panic on our faces, "Do you remember me? I'm Stefan Shultz from Deesen, Germany. I was in the audience when you appeared on Nick Phace's show and we chatted briefly after the program. Remember I told you that I'd treat you to a real beer if you ever visited the Rheinland-Pfalz?"

The happy beam of fond recognition slowly glowed from JD's face and the chain reaction drove the looks of concern from me and Stefan. "Ah yes, now I remember. I'm sorry that we must have looked like we saw a ghost. We weren't expecting to see anyone we knew."

Stefan bellowed, "I think I'm the one who saw a ghost!" He laughed in a way that made it seem natural to cross paths with a dead man. Perhaps he was not surprised after seeing the way JD was resurrected following his harrowing fall from Anheuser-Busch's headquarters building years before.

JD grew very serious, "Stefan, no one knows that I'm alive. I've been in hiding since my purported death … for my own safety. It's crucially important that you don't tell anyone that you've seen me. Can you do that for me until the time is right for me to go public?"

"Of course, my friend … your secret is safe with me. But, may I ask, can you tell me how you survived death a second time?"

"Are you alone? Can you meet us later for dinner?"

"Yes, I am here alone on business. I've wrapped things up and am just enjoying some sightseeing before heading back tomorrow. Where would you like to meet?"

"We're going to the Forum Restaurant at 7:00. Do you know where it's at?"

"Oh yes, it's a very famous place. You know how to live well!" Stefan laughed in amusement.

"We've never been there before. It was recommended by a … an acquaintance. We look forward to seeing you there."

After Stefan departed, we returned to the room and debated what to do. We had no choice since the cat was out of the bag. We had to trust Stefan and hope that he could keep a secret. We'd have a chance to convince him further over dinner but would need to be very careful not to reveal anything about the situation with Cagliostro that might jeopardize our safety or put Stefan in harm's way. There was a lengthy back-and-forth between us until we agreed the best thing to do would be to be completely upfront about it and let Benedetto know we'd been the victims of an odd coincidence by being spotted by a casual German acquaintance in Rome. We had to run the tedious phone gauntlet to get through to Benedetto. We explained what had happened and told him how we asked Stefan to keep a lid on things for the time being. They say in for a penny, in for a pound so we went the full disclosure route and advised Benedetto that we had invited Stefan to dinner so we could reinforce the need for secrecy. We assured him that there'd be no mention of our meeting with the Cardinal or anything of the sort. Benedetto didn't say much other than an I-told-you-so admonishment for not staying in the room until dinner. He was a cold fish. Benedetto left us with some regret for opening up to him but it was a case of damned if you do, damned if you don't. It might have been worse if we said nothing and he received a report back from one of his lackeys at the Forum that we were joined by a third party.

We hopped a taxi to the Forum and Stefan was there promptly at 7:00 like you'd expect from any good, punctual German. "Wie gehts Herr Shultz!" Our feeble attempt to greet Stefan in his native language caused him to throw a stream of German back our way. We were quickly overwhelmed and raised the white flag of surrender.

A gregarious guffaw emanated from deep in his belly, "I'm not so proud of my English … but it beats your Deutsch, eh?"

JD sheepishly conceded the point while I gave my name to the maître de. He was a bit surprised that we had three in our party but did not make a fuss. There was a healthy crowd waiting to be seated but he immediately escorted us inside and took us to an elevator that carried us to the preferred seating outside on the rooftop where only privileged guests were allowed to dine. Stefan mugged at us to show he was properly impressed by the pull we had at such a fine, landmark restaurant. If only he had known! Our table was perfectly situated to offer stunning views of the ancient city. Directly beneath us were the ruins of the Roman Forum. As we gazed upon the remains of a few stark columns left standing as lonely sentries alongside their smaller companion statues, the remains of what was once a vibrant marketplace and the largely intact Via Sacra, Basilica Aemilia and Temple of Antoninus and Faustina, we discovered that Stefan was quite the historian. He explained how the prestige and glory of the Forum area had been restored under Maxentius and Constantine with the construction of the Temple of Romulus and the great Basilica of Constantine. Then he went on to describe how the decadence of Rome and Barbarian Invasions, especially the Goths in A. D. 410 and Vandals in A.

D. 455 brought about the damage still so evident today. Stefan was a wealth of information in addition to being a good hearted ton of fun.

Off to the left were the ruins of the great Colosseum which were so close it seemed we could reach out and touch them. We could see inside the remaining walls to view the cavea and subterranean passages. Visions of Barabbas, Spartacus and Russell Crowe's General Maximus Decimus Meridius floated through my brain. Then my thoughts turned to those early Christians who were martyred on these very grounds; some torn limb from limb by wild beasts in front of the bloodthirsty hoards. Just past the Colosseum stood the massive War Memorial topped by twin chariots, each drawn by four majestic steeds manned by an elegant warrior. Illumined by spotlights against the backdrop of the evening sky, the Wedding Cake as it was sometimes called echoed with glorious ghosts of the past. In addition to the unbelievable scenery, the food was spectacular. Authentic Italian fare was quite different from the Americanized version. We shared one glass of wine but then switched to beer to celebrate our shared German heritage with Stefan. It was an evening to be remembered. At the end of our meal, we were pleasantly surprised to find that our money was no good there. Benedetto, under instructions from the Cardinal, had settled our bill in advance.

As if that wasn't enough, we were then escorted to an even more exclusive spot on the corner of the roof. It was an elevated patio area only large enough for four tables. This is where the crème de la crème retired for their after dinner drinks and good conversation. It was surrounded by a wrought iron gate that afforded an air of exclusivity. Thanks to Stefan who was fluent in several languages, we were able to engage some of the other preferred guests. Stefan was savvy enough to introduce us as American business associates by our first names only. The conversation was light and spiced with plenty of humor, some rather salty. Several countries were represented in this little *League of Nations* and the international flair made the whole experience that much more special. We consumed just the right amount of alcohol to enter an uninhibited state of silliness and fun without crossing over the line into the danger zone. So what if we had to fly out in the morning? The night was still young. So with Stefan as our expert guide we took off to see the sights.

There was the Circus Maximus and then on to the catacombs. We burned up quite a bundle in cab fare but didn't care since we hadn't spent hardly anything with our room and dinner being charged to the Vatican's deep pockets. Next, Stefan suggested the Piazza Navona, the most famous square of Baroque Rome standing on the site of Domitian's stadium. We gazed in wonder at the Neptune Fountain and Bernini's magnificent Fountain of the Four Rivers dating all the way back to 1651. Yes, Mr. Encyclopedia Stefan knew that the four rivers referred to the Danube, Ganges, Nile and Rio de la Plata ... go figure. We stopped at one of the outdoor cafes and grabbed a table so we could enjoy a couple more beers and watch the people go by. Let the good times roll! Stefan lit up a cigarette like is the custom of so many other Europeans and JD and I, who abhor smoking, asked Stefan to include us in his unholy ritual. We couldn't stand to inhale but laughed until we choked when he showed us how to smoke like Germans with palm up and thumb and forefinger circled. Just about then, a street troubadour walked up with his guitar playing something unrecognizable and we demanded something American. He proceeded to warble the only song he knew in English, Bad; Bad Leroy Brown. It sounded so ridiculous with his thick Italian accept and rolling R's that we laughed until we broke down in tears.

The magic evening continued until we scaled the Spanish Steps and ended the tour at the Trevi Fountain just past midnight. It was hard to say if it was the most beautiful fountain in all of Rome but there's no disputing it is the most famous. Even at that late hour there was a large crowd of people mingling and gazing. The bright lights enhanced the gleaming beauty of the white marble statues. Our friend, Bernini, had a hand in this celebrated masterpiece too. The palace of Neptune with its four Corinthian columns and sober Arch of Triumph dominated the scene from on high but the grand structure with its imposing centerpiece of Neptune atop a seahorse drawn chariot didn't detract from the intricacies below. The aquatic tritons seemed to guide the mythical god toward the reflective pool which shimmered in a stunning, iridescent blue that could draw envy from the most crystalline waters of the Mediterranean or Caribbean Seas.

It was late; we had more than enough beer in our systems and were facing a long flight home in the morning. Thus, we had to say our goodbyes.

We had grown so close to Stefan in such a short time that handshakes seemed inappropriate. We exchanged hugs all around. JD reminded Stefan of the importance of maintaining our secret and thanked him for being so understanding and faithful. We exchanged contact information and vowed to stay in touch. JD promised Stefan he would be the first to know when it was okay to go public. After we dropped Stefan off at his hotel, JD and I heartily agreed that our unfortunate coincidence had turned out to be a blessing. We had gained a good friend. The next morning, it took several cups of coffee to boost us out of our lethargy. The plane was once again stocked with plenty of food which helped us make a comeback from the prior night's revelry. We read all of the papers on the plane to kill some time but saw nothing about Stefan. Reports of his dead body being discovered by the housekeeping staff at his hotel the next morning were lost on the back page of local newspapers. We had no idea that our unfortunate coincidence hadn't turned out so well for our new friend. It wasn't until later when JD tried to contact Stefan to let him know we were going public that we learned of his demise. Apparently, Benedetto wasn't willing to trust our promise that we wouldn't share anything with Stefan that could come back to haunt the church.

PART THREE

THROUGH A GLASS DARKLY

CHAPTER 7

Strange Bedfellows

"And Jesus knew their thoughts, and said unto them, Every kingdom divided against itself is brought to desolation; and every city or house divided against itself shall not stand:" (Jesus Christ, approximately A. D 33 as recorded in the Holy Bible, the Book of Matthew 12:25).

My reunion with Jude and the kids was fantastic. Private jets, limousines, the grandeur of Rome and fancy restaurants were no match for home, sweet home. It warmed my heart to be so well received with long, warm, cuddly, bear-like hugs. The only person who didn't seem too thrilled was Mit. For him this meant an end to Jude's home cooking and a return to his Spartan lifestyle in his tiny, cramped apartment. Jude loved Mit ... in small doses ... but I could tell she was anxious to send him packing. I could imagine how sore her ears were from his incessant yacking. We exchanged Mit for JD, a much more low-maintenance house guest. I was looking forward to working closely with him again. I was anxious to involve him in American Phoenix and hear about the visions he'd received. Before moving forward, we had some unfinished business.

We gathered around the table and tried to assess our current position. Everyone agreed that we had done the right thing and improved matters by offering a truce to our enemies in Rome. That was pretty easy considering that only a couple of weeks before they had us under close surveillance and dispatched a hit man to stage JD's death. The much tougher part was in discerning whether we were truly safe for now or just being set up for the kill. We went round and round bouncing from one end of the spectrum to the other without reaching anything close to a consensus. I don't think any of us were able to make up our own minds much less convince anyone else. Leave it to Mit though. He never got stuck in an emotional quagmire, not when logic and science could be applied. "It's a simple matter really. If you want to know how our actions, the stimuli you introduced in Rome, have impacted our environment, then you need to conduct an experiment." His smile was matter-of-fact but not arrogant.

I snidely challenged, "What might that be, *professor*?"

"We want to know if the other side will honor the truce; right? What were the terms of the deal?"

I obliged, "In a nutshell, we said that although JD would be going public with a new message regarding the final judgment, there'd be no talk of the Papacy or Roman Catholic Church as long as they left us alone."

Mit continued on without a trace of indecision, "Then all you have to do is go public and hold up your end of the bargain. You'll be able to judge by their reaction."

He was right. It made sense. But Jude was quickly able to point out the downside, "There's only one problem. If this is just a tactic and they don't intend to hold up their end of the bargain, this experiment could have disastrous results for us."

Mit couldn't argue with the logic, "That's true."

JD weighed in, "There's really no choice. We have to know one way or the other if they'll keep the truce. At least this way we can find out on our own terms and be prepared to face the consequences rather than getting caught off guard."

Thanks to *Mr. Spock*, I mean Mit, we achieved the elusive consensus. But we had a lot of work to do before hatching our experiment. From past experience, we knew we had to be totally prepared before unleashing the media firestorm that would erupt with the second *resurrection* of the Last Prophet. We had to refine the message, choose our audiences and outline a sequence of events that would help us to control rather than be controlled by the media. For now, it was important for us to keep the Last Prophet dead, buried and out of the public eye to allow us a free hand and plenty of time to develop a clear strategy and effective plan of action.

JD offered some wise counsel and good leadership. "There's a lot to be done but we don't have an endless amount of time. We know we can't trust Cagliostro and Benedetto. But they may live up to the truce as long as they see it as being in their best interest. We have to test them and do it as soon as possible. This should be weeks rather than months. If they plan to betray us, it won't be long before they develop their plan of attack so we must beat them to the punch and smoke them out. Let's develop a short-term and longer-term plan for hitting the airwaves with the former being something small and easily manageable. If it works, then we'll know we have more time and can adjust accordingly. If they betray us, then all bets are off."

Scientist Mit wanted details, "What is the control in our experiment? How will we know if it worked, short of them making another attempt on your life, JD?"

"That's a good question. I think we can start right away by sweeping our surroundings. Mit, I'm guessing you know how to figure out if they're still bugging the place." He nodded as if to say no problemo. "If we're not wired for sound, that's a good sign but doesn't mean we're not under other forms of surveillance. For that, we need help from some of my old Army pals. Obviously, I can't contact them but Inky you could approach one of the guys from Ops Ogilvy's old unit and ask for help in seeing if anyone has eyes on us. Just tell them you've seen evidence of someone prowling the grounds around the compound. Play it down and tell them it's probably just kids or someone trespassing but, given the past, you'd appreciate someone checking things out to give you peace of mind. Blame it on Jude. In any case, that would tell us if they've backed off and are only watching us through the media or long-distance, less threatening intelligence gathering methods."

I thought it was a reasonable plan but wanted to tie up one loose end. "JD, what about Kit? Is it safe for Mit to continue seeing her or should he cut all ties?"

"I think it's best for us to resume our normal lives. It might raise more of a red flag than not if Mit were to break things off for no apparent reason. It could tweak their suspicions. They already know about her so I think Mit should continue to see her. That is, Mit as long as you never say anything to her about me or what we're doing here." Mit nodded his consent and a look of concern crossed his normally studious, meditative countenance. If we had known what Benedetto did to Stefan for befriending us so briefly we would have told Mit to send his *Kitten* far, far away and pronto.

It didn't take Mit long, only a couple of days, before he was able to assemble his gizmos and gadgets and sweep the compound. The results were completely negative and this gave us a glimmer of hope. We'd have to wait until we were ready to go public to see if other forms of surveillance were in use. After that announcement, we'd also bring Mit back to see if anything changed. In the meantime, this small shot of assurance provided a springboard for me and JD to get down to business. He was impressed at how far the Trumpet had come and got a kick out of the website and blog. It was late in the summer of 2012 and I wanted to show JD the power of the new technology we'd adopted by firing up the blogosphere with a piece called Random Thoughts I posted about a variety of current events.

RANDOM THOUGHTS

I can't think of a better way to make my point about the sad state of affairs in our dead

Republic than to offer some random thoughts on recent events that have bubbled up from the political cauldron during this election year.

Immigration: *Are we really fighting over the rights of illegals? Let me see if I understand this. The Federal Government and individual states like Arizona are battling in the courts to determine whether illegals are entitled to free tuition, medical care and food stamps? But what about the children, you say? Let me ask you a question. What do you think would happen to American citizens, young or old, who illegally entered Mexico ... or just about any other country in the world ... and demanded free anything at their taxpayers' expense? Here, let me help you if you can't figure it out on your own. They wouldn't be allowed to sue anyone in court and they sure wouldn't be given the right to vote in their elections. They'd most likely be stuck in a Mexican jail getting Coca Cola squirted up their nostrils until their eyes popped out.*

Mediscare: *Ah, the third rail of American politics. You've gotta love it! Anyone who raises the specter of Medicare or Social Security going broke ... a well-known, undisputed fact ... is* demonized as someone who wants to throw granny off a cliff in her wheel chair. In a new low, now we're seeing ads with Congressman Allen West punching old ladies. By the way, he's African American and she's lily white. It's okay though to play the race card because he's a conservative. Romney's VP pick, Paul Ryan, is the latest and biggest target of the Left for wanting to reform Medicare for people under fifty-five. He's pushing this wild and crazy notion that maybe they should have a choice, you know some small say in how their money is invested for them to cover their health care needs in their golden years. He's assured everyone that he doesn't want to hurt current seniors because his mom, who is retired and living in Florida, depends on Medicare. I'm sure it won't be long until there's a commercial showing Ryan throwing his mother off his yacht into shark infested waters. So help me figure this out. What would be wrong with letting me take my own money and invest it in my own savings account that I control to sock away a few dollars for my own health care needs? Oh, I see, I can't be trusted to look out for myself. Instead, I should turn it over to Uncle Sam to put in a lock box for me? Yeah, that's the ticket.

Let's trust a bunch of big spending DC politicians to guard my piggy bank for me.

Transparency: *President Obama entered office in 2009 declaring that his would be the most transparent administration in history. Hmmm, it's been over two months since he's granted a press conference to the White House Press Corps. Instead he's granted interviews to those hard hitting news outlets like the Tonight Show and Entertainment Tonight. Isn't that what you really want to know about our President ... his favorite type of chili and the type of superhero he'd like to be? Oh wait, he finally graced them with his presence and they rewarded him with fawning and softballs. I guess we're good through the election.*

Gasoline Prices: *Has anyone noticed that a gallon of gasoline costs nearly $4.00? It's odd that this is not getting much critical air time in the mainstream media. The President thinks the private sector is doing just fine. All we need to do to get our economy going is to spend more taxpayer money on hiring teachers, police and firefighters. At least the President's plan to produce more hybrid cars and ethanol is forging ahead. If you have any money left after filling* the tank, wait until you see your electric bill after charging your car battery. I'm sure you don't mind paying more for ethanol since it supposedly helps the environment. So what if it uses more water and drives up the price of our food ... go green baby! I know you're not concerned about the billions of your tax dollars that have been spent on foreign car manufacturers or green energy companies that have gone belly up. It's all part of the plan. Hey, the President saved GM didn't he? What do you mean they still owe us $25 billion? Thank Obama for the Volt!

Hate: I caught a brief blurb on cable news about a shooting at the Family Research Council's office in Washington, D. C. I flipped over to the networks to get more details but oddly couldn't find anything about it. It was like it didn't happen. I was perplexed so I turned back to cable and finally the fog lifted. You see, the Family Research Council is a hate group. Yeah, they're a bunch of Christians who actually believe what the Bible teaches about traditional marriage and that homosexuality is a sin. They deserve to be shot. It's too bad that security guard stopped the shooter before he could cause more damage, right? The funny thing is *that, unlike the recent shooting in a Colorado movie theater, no one came out to decry guns and attack our 2nd Amendment rights. I guess it is okay for people to use guns to take the law into their own hands and shoot Christian haters. No, I'm not kidding. Some militant gay/lesbian/transgender groups came out in support of the shooter ... really. I'm confused ... who are the haters?*

Chain of Fools: *With apologies to Aretha Franklin, VP Joe Biden has stolen her thunder with his own rendition. It's not unusual for the race card to be played during an election season but this was different. White boy Joe was addressing a largely African American audience and made the claim that when the Republicans said they wanted to reduce regulations harmful to business and the economy it actually meant they wanted to unchain Wall Street to prey on all of us innocent victims. To drive it home, Connecticut Joe adopted a Southern drawl and said the GOP wants to put "yawl" back in chains. A lot of people, including African Americans in the audience and elsewhere were appalled by the crude method of race baiting. Nevertheless, the President and White House defended Crazy Old*

Uncle Joe. Can you say double standard? No, then just ask Missouri Senate wannabe Todd Akin. He said something pretty offensive too but at least apologized.

Romney the Felon and Murderer: *Our President has often lectured us on the necessity to restore civility to public discourse. It reminds me of when my parents would preach do as I say and not as I do. First, hatchet man Harry Reid said he had a good, unnamed source who assured him Mitt Romney was a scofflaw who hadn't paid any taxes in ten years. Then a White House Aide, Stephanie Cutter labeled Mitt's disclosure regarding when he stepped down as CEO of Bain to run the Salt Lake City Olympics a felony. That wasn't enough so one of the PACs supporting President Obama came up with an ad featuring a guy named Joe Soptic who claimed his wife died of cancer thanks to Mitt Romney and Bain Capital. Never mind that Romney was gone from Bain nine years prior or that his wife had her own health care coverage after Joe was canned when Bain had to shut down his employer's steel mill. Romney was labeled a murderer. Stefanie Cutter claimed the Obama Campaign had nothing to do with the PAC ad and had no knowledge of Joe Soptic. She* *must have forgotten that only a few months prior she talked to him personally after the Campaign had produced a separate ad with basically the same content. Hey, has anyone noticed that unfortunately lots of people die from cancer and other things every day whether or not they have health care coverage? I guess if Obama is re-elected we won't have to worry about cancer or death anymore, right?*

Class Warfare: *Have you ever wondered how the German people went along with Hitler's mad plan? It's hard to imagine sane people falling for such a lie. Perhaps we'll never know but one thing is for sure ... it could never happen again; at least not today in a place like the USA. Have you ever heard of the Occupy Movement? Yeah, you know ... I'm talking about those wonderful folks that the President has endorsed on numerous occasions. You know the ones. They've disrupted commerce and behaved very badly in a number of ways including drug abuse, rape, public defecation and general anarchy. They've resorted to violence and shattered store front windows in making their case against those horrible One Percenters. But it's all for a good cause. Those One Percenters are a bunch of greedy fat cats*

*who've gained their success by lying and
cheating the rest of us. They didn't get there by
their own hard work, initiative and risk taking.
They took unfair advantage of what the
government provided in the way of schools,
roads and bridges. Occupy is just giving them
what they deserve. Does this sound familiar?
Isn't this what Adolph said about those nasty
Jews just before Kristallnacht in November,
1938?*

*Okay, okay that's enough for this rant. I can't
wait to hear your responses.*

JD was truly surprised, "I don't know what's
more impressive ... that an old dinosaur like you
has embraced such new-fangled technology or
your hard boiled approach to politics. The way
you're stirring things up, our biggest threat may
not be in Rome." JD was right. It didn't take long
for angry reactions to begin to pour in. I let him
sort through them as they popped up on the
screen. He noticed how, as the site administrator, I
had the power to approve or disapprove comments
before they were posted. We read together as one
vitriolic reply popped up.

*You're a complete idiot if you think any
business can succeed today without the*

government's help! Speaking of fat cats, how about you Inky; you disgusting, bloated pig? You sit there all high and mighty, spouting your capitalist propaganda on your fancy blog. Where do you think it came from? Did you build the internet? No, without the government, there'd be no internet and we wouldn't have to put up with your crap! Ozzie Occupier

JD couldn't believe I approved it. "You're going to let that guy attack you like that? Are you crazy?"

"Maybe I'm crazy like a fox. Can you think of a more effective way to hammer my point home? The door swings both ways on freedom of speech. I'm just giving him some rope. What better way than to hoist him with his own petard?"

"I hear you but are you going to leave it at that or fight back?"

"I'd almost feel guilty since it's like shooting fish in a barrel but okay. Do you want to help?" We had some fun in collaborating on the following reply.

Dear Oz,

What's your real name, Al Gore? Do you really think the government created the internet?

Sure there were research grants here and there and some of the work may have been done at public universities. Who do you think financed those efforts? Where do you think the government gets its money? No it doesn't grow on trees or even printing presses. It comes from hard working tax payers. And do you know who pays over fifty percent of those taxes? Believe it or not, it's those nasty One Percenters.

Before you give the government too much credit, remember that they jumped on the band wagon. They didn't build the wagon or even supply the planks, nuts, bolts, axels or wheels. Those things came from private entrepreneurs ... innovators and risk takers like Bill Gates and Steve Jobs. It's just like those roads, bridges and schools out there. They were financed by our tax dollars and, you know what? The government didn't build them. The real work was done by contractors ... many of them private companies run by One Percenters who employ all those tax payers who support government largesse with sweat equity.

Hey, here's another question for you. How come you only want to give the government credit for the efforts of successful businesses?

Shouldn't we tie the government to everyone who uses the roads, crosses bridges, browses the web or attends a school? Using your logic, then the government is also responsible for drug dealers who ply their trade using our streets and highways. The same must be true for perverts who use the internet to prey on little kids. Bernie Madoff couldn't have run his Ponzi scheme without infrastructure and the web. So, Uncle Sam must have his hands in all kinds of slime, eh?

No, the government is no more responsible for these crimes than they are for the successes that private businesses eek-out every day through their own ingenuity and elbow grease. It's called individual responsibility and accountability. Oz, if you'd like to gain some firsthand experience, I'd be happy to let you serve an internship down here at the Trumpet to see just how much help we're getting from Uncle Sam and what it's like to be a "fat cat".

We laughed like naughty, rebellious teens who had just published an edgy editorial in the high school newspaper decrying bad cafeteria food. "Inky, it's not fair. You're having too much fun. I could get used to this. So how is the new Trumpet doing?"

I sobered up pretty quickly. "Readership is definitely up. But that alone doesn't pay the bills. The hard work is in selling ad space."

"And how's that going?"

"It's fair to middling. We're getting by but still have a cross to bear."

"How's that, Inky?"

"The bottom line is the Trumpet is still a Christian news outlet and Christianity is a hard sell. A good chunk of my readership is non-Christian and a growing portion is made up of hard left ideologues like Oz who like to rant and stir the pot but don't attract marketers."

"Oh, I'm sorry to hear that."

"Don't get me wrong, JD. We've reversed the trend and stemmed the tide for now. We're not getting rich but at least bankruptcy doesn't seem inevitable. And I have my ace in the hole. If our country continues on the current trajectory, I think there'll be a decent market for American Phoenix as long as my attempt at collaborative, real-time fan non-fiction doesn't blow up in my face."

"Maybe I can help, Inky."

"I'm all ears, JD."

"You may have solved the biggest problem facing us. We have to go public, right? And we have to do so in a manageable way that we can accomplish quickly without a big, time-consuming production. Why not the Trumpet? We did it the last time around and it gave you a boost, didn't it?"

"It sure did JD but this is different. This is going to be huge. The Last Prophet is back from the grave!"

"Oh, like it wasn't a big deal the last time around? No, I think the Trumpet is the perfect vehicle for our coming out party. And if it helps you get firmly into the black ink, it's all the better."

"JD, I don't know. This is bigger than the Trumpet. I really appreciate the thought but shouldn't we work with someone who can handle what should easily be the biggest news story of the year?"

"Don't forget our plan … short-term and longer-term goals. The big splash will come in time. For now, we need to run our experiment. If we go whole hog out of the blocks it might backfire. We need to exercise maximum control. The Trumpet can afford us that luxury."

"Well, you've got a point there."

"You bet I do. We don't want to jump right into shark infested waters. No, if we handle this properly we can have the media sharks eating out of our hands. Think of what this could mean for American Phoenix. This reminds me … we need to craft our message before we can go live with the Last Prophet's coming out party."

"Do you mean we need to capture the essence of your visions?"

"Yes, that's part of it. But I also need to understand your book if we're going to shine the spotlight on American Phoenix too."

"That's easy enough. How fast can you read?" I showed JD how to access my online files for the completed chapters and the outline for those yet to be written."

"I guess I should ask you the same question, Inky."

"What do you mean, JD?"

"I have something for you to read too. I've kept a record of all the visions I've received. I guess you could call it my doomsday diary. It's rough around the edges and might need some explaining but you should go through it while I tackle American Phoenix."

"It's a deal."

I think JD's job was a little easier than mine. American Phoenix was pretty straightforward. The visions in JD's diary were not always so clear, even to him. But he inserted footnotes here and there to help. It was kind of like a commentary explaining what he thought the visions meant. It was fascinating reading, other worldly. I jotted down questions and saved them up rather than interrupting JD constantly. He did the same. The time passed quickly and we made fantastic progress in just one week. When he got to chapter six, JD couldn't resist picking my brain a bit.

"I'm sorry to bug you Inky but something hit me in reading through chapter six."

"No problem man."

"By the way, I like the catchy title: United We Fall ... GOP and Dems are Birds of a Feather. United We Fall ... it's an appropriately ironic and sarcastic play on words."

"It sounds like you get the idea then."

"Yeah, you make a good case that we're only united in the worst, most destructive ways ... an otherwise hopelessly divided, pluralistic nation drowning in our own greed and special interests whether the Republicans or Democrats are in charge. But I'm wondering if you shouldn't go into more depth about what is dividing us rather than showing how the Left and Right have converged on the wrong path."

"Well, I get into that more in chapter seven."

He flipped ahead and zeroed in on the section regarding the fallacy of diversity. JD waded through it like a machine, like a human scanner. As he flipped through further, I waited patiently for his pronouncement. "Inky, I don't mean to be critical. But I still think it would be helpful to devote more time to the divisions among us."

"Okay, you may be right."

"Here's the thing though. I'm thinking about how everything's going to fit together."

"Do you mean in American Phoenix?"

"No, I'm thinking ahead to when I go public and we turn the spotlight on my visions alongside your *vision*; American Phoenix." He could tell by the look on my face that I was perplexed but I didn't raise a specific question so he proceeded. "The premise of your book is right on target in my opinion. Our downfall has already occurred even though we may still seem okay, relatively speaking, in temporal terms. We still have a powerful military and enjoy prosperity that is the envy of most of the rest of the world. However, it's a hollow shell. The USA has collapsed in a spiritual sense. You've also hit the bull's eye in declaring that we can't reform our way out of this mess through political machinations of the liberals or conservatives who are birds of a feather when you get right down to it. No, it will take a spiritual transformation, a resurrection to get our Republic back on the right track. That's all well and good." He paused to gather himself and figure a diplomatic way to offer a constructive criticism.

"Okay, I'm waiting for the big but."

He laughed nervously. "Okay, think about it Inky. Aren't we both writing about doomsday?" JD gave me a moment to consider.

"Yeah, I guess you're right in a way."

"What's the difference then?" JD didn't wait for me to answer. "Yes, one is temporal and the other is spiritual."

I let this sink in. "Now that you mention it, you're right. But what are you saying? Do you think I need to switch gears and write about Judgment Day rather than the downfall of our Republic?"

"No, that's not what I'm saying. That would basically gut American Phoenix."

"What then ... what are you suggesting?"

"All I'm saying is that maybe you can tweak chapter six a bit to make it easier for our audiences to bridge the gap."

I pursed my lips and nodded slowly, up and down, over and over. "Yeah, that would make sense."

JD saw I was stuck and helped prime the pump. "Do you remember when the Pharisees accused Jesus of being in league with the devil in casting out demons? They were jealous and fearful of his power and growing influence and wanted to discredit the miracles he'd performed. He showed the folly of their remarks with simple logic ... a kingdom divided, fighting against itself, is brought to desolation. Even though the Pharisees and perhaps many in the crowd were not spiritually discerning this truth, they could understand it nonetheless. How could Jesus serve Beelzebub by casting out his demons? Abraham Lincoln applied this same truth and logic in his house divided speech to maintain the Union. People today can grasp this logic and see your point that our divisions are killing us and ripping the nation apart. But can they see the spiritual ramifications? Just like with ancient Israel, that's a much tougher proposition. Almost everybody was on board with Jesus when he was feeding the five thousand, healing the sick and raising the dead. They wanted an earthly Messiah who would use his miraculous power to drive out the hated Romans and re-establish the glory of David's kingdom. When he talked about the Bread of Life instead of real loaves and fishes, proclaimed his kingdom was not of this world and foretold of his suffering and death, his followers left in droves except for the faithful few."

"I hear you loud and clear, JD. So what should I do?"

"You've done a great job of showing how the Dems and GOP are walking hand-in-hand down that broad path to destruction. Now, all you need to do is lift the veil a bit more and show what's happening behind the scenes … shed a little celestial light on the invisible world, the powers and principalities behind it all. It's not a battle between Democrats and Republicans or the Left and Right. We all need to fix our spiritual eyes on the battle between good and evil … the Savior of the world versus Satan, the prince of this world."

The light bulb came on. "Yeah, I get it. I've got all the pieces in place. I just need to feature the spiritual dilemma more prominently. And I agree that it needs to come earlier, in chapter six like you've suggested. That way, it will tie together better with the later chapters where I offer the solutions. Otherwise, it might not jibe if I'm offering a spiritual fix to what they perceive as temporal issues." JD was pleased that the message hit home and I wasn't offended by his critique. "But JD do you think that's enough for our messages to dovetail?"

"I think so, Inky, or at least I hope so. We're still dealing with two separate but related topics. You're writing about an earthly collapse rather than the final judgment. But your doomsday is rooted in spiritual causes and can only be rectified by spiritual means. If people can grasp that concept, with their spiritual lenses firmly in place, they should be able to make the leap to the earth's inevitable end, the final judgment and Christ's everlasting kingdom."

This put me in a contemplative mood. "Politics makes for strange bedfellows, doesn't it?"

"Is that so, bro?"

"I mean, look at the mess we're in. This country is in real trouble whether you're viewing it from a practical or spiritual standpoint. Everyone can see it. We should all be pulling together to save our collective bacon. But that's impossible, I guess, especially in an election year. Look at the way the GOP hopefuls eviscerated each other during the primaries. Now they're all behind Romney like nothing ever happened. I'm betting it won't be so easy to span the divide between the Republicans and Democrats once the general election is behind us but you know they will. At the same time they're on the Hill and in the White House figuratively plotting and planning to stab each other in the back, they'll hold their noses and choke down legislative compromises necessary to keep the ball rolling. It's a big game of survival while the pendulum of power sweeps back and forth in Washington."

JD always seemed to have a unique take on things. "Are we any different, Inky?"

"What do you mean? I abhor politics … and I think you do too."

"We're playing politics of a sort, aren't we? Look at our truce, our compromise with Cagliostro and Benedetto. It's a game of survival … a power play where the stakes don't get any higher."

"C'mon, JD; this is different. We're battling for the truth. We're fighting for our lives."

"Is it really so different?"

I thought long and hard before answering. "Maybe you're right. It's like American Phoenix and your doomsday diary. There's more in common than meets the eye, especially when you're coming from a spiritual perspective."

Things were getting deep. Thankfully, we were interrupted by a knock at the door. JD quickly retreated into the printing press room. It was Mit and Kit, cavorting like two lovebirds ... or should I say love-nerds. They had their arms around one another with their hands tucked into each other's back pocket. Had they just come from the halls of Bayside High School? Were they literally joined at the hip or was this a public display of spooning reserved for my benefit or intended to make me jealous? It would have been nauseating if they weren't so genuine. I could hear Donnie Osmond singing Puppy Love in my head and imagined more little pink hearts and Cupids floating all around them. It was enough to make me squirm uncomfortably. I had to break the spell. "Kit, it's so good to see you again. Hey, I bet Jude would like to chat with you. She's over in the house." Kit smiled and started bounding happily in that direction with Mit in tow. "Kit, if you don't mind, can I tear Mit away from you for a few minutes? I would like to talk to him." She reluctantly released her grip while momentarily flashing sad puppy dog eyes at Mit before skipping out the door to find Jude. I called JD back into my office. I almost had to slap Mit across the chops to shake him out of his love sick stupor. "Mit, mum's the word with Kit, right?"

He immediately went serious on me, almost as if snapping to attention. "Oh yes, I haven't said anything to her, not a word." He paused and seemed to recalibrate something in his head. "I wanted to tell you that I did a sweep of my apartment too ... just to be safe." He then started to ramble into a detailed, techie discussion which was totally unnecessary and unwanted.

"Mit, please spare the details. We need to finish up before Kit comes back. Get to the bottom line. What did you find?"

"There was nothing. My place is as clean as a whistle."

I knew what he meant but almost choked on that one. I guessed that his apartment always looked like a typhoon swept through it. And that was on the good days. However, I resisted the urge to take a shot at him. "That's good to know. Now here's the latest. In about a week, we'll be ready to go live. We're going to announce JD's miraculous comeback through trumpet.com. At that time, I'm going to contact Ops' old comrades and ask them for a deeper dive on surveillance. Don't say anything to Kit until then. You're going to have to pretend to be just as surprised as everyone else about the news on JD, okay?" Mit nodded eagerly. I think he liked the whole secret agent thing. "Once this is out in the open, we'll introduce you to Ops' guys so you can offer any technical assistance that might be helpful." Kit hadn't returned so JD stayed put and Mit and I went back to the house and found Jude and Kit at the kitchen table commiserating over coffee and orange pop. You guessed it. Jude had the big girl coffee.

The next day, JD and I put our noses back to the grindstone. Within a couple of days we were ready for another pow-wow, this time on his doomsday diary. I started where we left off the last time we'd talked when JD was still tucked away in the Smokies. "So tell me again how these visions came to you."

"It's hard to describe, Inky. They were what I'd call dream-like. It was like having dreams while being awake."

The seriousness wasn't lost on me but I couldn't help cutting up with my old pal, "Now think hard. Are you sure you weren't dropping acid or snorting coke?"

"Oh you're killing me ... very funny, squirrel breath."

"I'm sorry man. I couldn't resist. But seriously, what were you doing when this happened? Could you see it coming on?"

"No, there was no way of predicting it. It seemed totally random but was always late at night or early in the morning when I was sleeping or should have been sleeping. When it happened though, I was always made wide awake. But it was like I was in an altered state … even though I was as sober as a Baptist judge. It was as if I was magically transported into a cavernous, dark IMAX theater and then the images swept around me like lightning fanning out across the heavens. My body was paralyzed but my mind was free to roam."

"Did you know whether it was God's doing?"

"He didn't speak to me from a burning bush or anything but somehow I knew it was God. There was no doubt."

"Did you wonder why he was coming to you in such a way rather than simply opening his word to you?"

"Definitely … it was the first question that popped into my mind. I worried at first that maybe it was the work of an evil angel. Knowing that God has chosen to work through his means of grace, the word and sacraments connected to the word, it didn't make sense that he'd try to give me a new message apart from the revelations of the Bible. I prayed over and over for God to protect and guide me. Yet, the visions continued so I prayed that God would make his will clear to me. I began to document what I'd seen and went over my notes repeatedly. As this process continued over time, it dawned on me that I wasn't being lured away from the truth but drawn to it. There was nothing new in the visions; nothing that contradicted the Bible in any way. It was just a fresh, personal perspective on the end times ... the same prophesies that God revealed to his people from the beginning until the close of the holy canon; in the Old Testament and New in Daniel, Thessalonians, Matthew, Revelation and other books of the Bible."

"From what I read, the visions seem to be limited, very narrow in scope."

"You're right, Inky. That's why I felt secure in promising not to get into a full-blown eschatological discussion this time around. We've already covered Armageddon, the Beast of Babylon, the tribulation, Satan's little season, the interpretation of the books from Daniel through

Revelation, the history paralleling the prophesies and the signs of the end times. For some reason, God focused my attention on that final day alone, doomsday, the final judgment."

"In looking at your diary, it seems like the visions were repeated many times."

"Yeah, it reminded me a lot of the Revelations to John on Patmos. As you know, the Book of Revelation is often horribly misinterpreted by so many people who see it as a series or succession of stand-alone visions when, in fact, the same vision is repeated multiple times from different perspectives. It completely changes the meaning. Perhaps God was doing something similar here. It was a single vision of the end repeated for emphasis, for my understanding."

"Your footnotes, all the commentary your diary contains about the visions draw many parallels to the way Scripture describes the final judgment. It seems completely consistent. Again it makes me wonder why God would share this new vision with you."

"I wrestled with this quite a bit until I realized just what you saw too. God didn't provide me with a 'new' vision of the end. It's the same vision that's been available to mankind throughout the Scripture since the fall into sin. Adam and Eve were told that the Savior, Christ, would do battle with Satan, the serpent, and win the victory in spite of being mortally wounded. The plan of salvation and faith alone in the coming Messiah, the Savior, Jesus Christ, was there from the beginning … before the beginning from God's perspective. It was revealed in more and more specificity over time including the triumphant Second Coming and final judgment before the end of the world and new heavens and earth. You see, God wasn't providing a new revelation or steering me away from Scripture. These visions drew me deeper and deeper into the truth of the Bible."

"I'm sure you've thought about why God would do this in this way."

"Absolutely, this was the other burning question. I think I know why. I had to go back to that September 11th and the terrorists' attacks on St. Louis and my death in the fall from Anheuser-Busch's headquarters. He brought me back to life for a reason … to share his message of warning and hope about the end times. God gave me worldwide notoriety and an incredible forum to spread his word. We accomplished that mission, by

God's grace and might, in spite of the church's determined attempts to silence me. You were there and witnessed the bomb blast at my apartment that should have ended my life a second time. We both knew the Lord miraculously saved me again ... and for a purpose. We just couldn't figure out what God might have in mind back then. Now we know. God wants me to make another clarion call and share the gospel. This time he's focusing me in a new, narrower way. The message is judgment. The message is the divining line between heaven and hell, salvation and damnation."

"Why is he focusing your attention on Judgment Day?"

"Maybe the end is near? We'll never know for sure the day or the hour. No matter what I might say or do, we know that many people will be caught unawares as if by a thief under the cover of the darkness of night. There are so many unanswered questions. Yet some things are certain. God has miraculously preserved my life again for a purpose; the purpose of spreading his word. He's given me these visions to focus my attention on the truth of Scripture in a very specific area … the last day. That's what we're going to do."

"Do you think the visions will help in getting the message across?"

"I really think they will help, by the grace of God. Look at John's revelations. They must have been so much clearer to him and people of that time. My visions from God, although narrower in scope, are no different except they're more contemporary. In a way, perhaps it's like reading the KJV versus the original Autographs, Septuagint or some other version. Maybe God's just translating his word regarding the final judgment in a language I can better understand and share with others. When this notion came to me, it made me think again that perhaps God was trying to tell me the end was near. But we know there's to be no special warning other than the signs of the end that have been present in every age. Also, when you consider the visions, God has put the images in a modern context that make his truths easier for me, you and others to discern but he's taken care to cloak the visions too. There is nothing geographical, chronological or demographical in the visions to offer a clue about when the Judgment will occur or, for the most part, who will be goats or sheep. God never lies. No one will know the day or the hour besides our Heavenly Father. That's immaterial. What's important is that we get the message out. And we can't worry about threats from some evil people within the church. Jesus had the Pharisees to contend with and we have Cagliostro and Benedetto. God has brought us this far. We need to continue to trust in him for our guidance and protection."

There was only one thing I could add, "Amen!"

JD switched gears, "We know our purpose and the message is clear. The time has come for us act. Are you ready ... is the Trumpet ready?"

I wasn't as resolute as JD, "I'm ready but there are a lot of loose ends. Am I just supposed to post something on the blog and see what happens? Our readership has grown by leaps and bounds but our audience is still miniscule in relative terms. As far as the experiment is concerned, how can we test Cagliostro and Benedetto if we're not sure they'll even see or hear about the announcement since the Trumpet's reach is so limited?"

"The Trumpet will be our platform but I'm not saying we shouldn't have links to other outlets. We'll need to stream some video and post it on

YouTube. Once the word spreads, we can funnel the release to various media outlets. I'm not suggesting we try to keep a lid on things ... just that we steer everyone to the Trumpet as the wellspring. It will not only drive your numbers through the roof but will ensure the control we need."

I felt a little silly. Here I was the supposed media guru and JD, the Last Prophet, was providing the savvy we needed. It was time for me to get with the program and step up my game. "I'm with you, JD. Now, we've got to make sure these initial ripples don't detract from the big splash that will follow. There will be nothing live, only the recorded video we'll carefully craft for the website, YouTube, news outlets and other media. It will be not much more than a teaser intended to draw interest and generate buzz."

JD was pleased to see me hit my stride, "Now you're talking!"

"Before we can do anything else, we need to know the end game. Where are we going to make the big splash?"

JD smiled slyly, "It will be more than a big splash … it will be a tsunami. Are you thinking what I'm thinking?"

I was thankful that he didn't steal my thunder. "Has there ever been any other choice? You have a standing invitation from Nick Phace."

"Yep, we'd never be able to top my first go-around on Nick's show without Nick."

"Okay JD, here's the deal. In terms of a live interview with the Last Prophet back from the dead, we'll offer Nick an exclusive. Once he's on board, we're in like Flint. But we've got to clue him in now so he can be prepared. Do you think we can trust him not to let the cat out of the bag before the Trumpet piece?"

"There's only one way to find out. Let's get him on the phone, Inky."

Getting in touch with Nick Phace was tougher than getting through to Benedetto at the Vatican … really! We couldn't use JD's name for confidentiality's sake. It probably wouldn't have helped anyway since they would have surely hung up on a *crank caller* posing as a dead man. Thankfully, Nick remembered my name and made the connection to the Last Prophet "Hello Mr. Hermann. How can I help you?"

"Please, call me Inky." Nick agreed in a non-committal, curious tone. "I've got some very important news for you but first I need to know if you'll promise to keep it strictly confidential."

Nick sounded slightly perturbed and hedged, "I'm in the news business. It's against my nature to promise something like that."

I tried to sound more polite than insistent, "Trust me on this, Nick. What I have to tell you could be the biggest news of the year but I can only share it if you'll give me your word to keep it between us for now."

His snarky laugh was very familiar, "You have the biggest news of the year and you want me to keep it under my hat? Are you kidding? You're not helping your own case by tantalizing me, Inky."

Beads of sweat gathered as my desperation set in. "Listen Nick, if you'll just trust me on this, I'll guarantee you exclusivity on the biggest story of the year ... of many years."

He still resisted, "Can you tell me why you need me to keep quiet?"

"If I told you that, the secret would be out."

"I'm sorry Inky but you'll have to do better than that."

JD could see my frustration and that I was close to losing it and he grabbed the phone and blurted, "Nick, do you know who this is?" I was so shocked I couldn't hold back an audible gasp even though I should have been used to it. JD was like the Apostle Peter … always the brash one who operated on such zeal and faith that he often leaped before he looked. By the silence on the other end of the line, it seemed that Nick Phace was putting two and two together but didn't dare to make a fool out of himself by venturing a wild guess. "Nick, this is me, JD Uticus … the Last Prophet."

A nervous laugh turned to derision. "Look, if this is your idea of a practical joke, I don't find it the least bit amusing." JD was afraid he'd hang up on us so he told him what he'd said to Nick during one of the commercial breaks on his show. Then he quoted word-for-word what he had said to Nick in the closing paragraph of his final letter to him.

Nick was silent for the longest time. It wasn't unbelief. He was stunned because JD had shared things that no one else knew. "I don't know what to say. Apparently, you truly are the miracle man of God … not once but two times over."

JD chuckled in an infectious way, "How about that … Nick Phace is speechless for the first time in his life!"

We all busted out in laughter. "You weren't kidding Inky. This is bigger than big. So gentlemen, what have you got in mind?"

We explained the game plan to Nick and how we were planning on going public in a few short days with the teaser that there would be more to come. But the only live interview would be available exclusively through Nick Phace. It was music to his ears. "Of course, I'd like to be the one to break the news but, you know, I think this will be even better. Yeah, let's whet their appetites on … what is it called … the Trumpet? Then, when they're ready for a feeding frenzy, Nick's all-you-can-eat-diner will be open for business as the only game in town. This will give me just enough time to prepare. But we've got to hurry. This is going to be bigger than the first visit from the Last Prophet and that drew the single biggest rating ever … anywhere."

JD momentarily interrupted his euphoria, "There's just one more little catch, Nick."

You could hear a pin drop, "Yeah, what might that be, JD?"

"I want Inky to be on the show too. Will you help him hawk his new book?"

Nick breathed a sigh of relief, "Sure, no problem, JD. What's the name of the book?"

"It's called American Phoenix: Resurrecting the Dead Republic. It's about doomsday in a temporal, political sense. It should fit in quite well with my message … about the real doomsday, the Final Judgment."

He was elated, "Perfect, I can make that work." Then he returned to character and sternly re-established his authority, "But there'll be no more than ten minutes on the book. Do you hear me?"

JD grinned like a Cheshire cat and gave me a reassuring wink, "10-4 good buddy!"

After we hung up the phone, I remembered something JD said about the visions. "Hey, what did you mean when you said 'for the most part'? You know, about the goats and the sheep?"

JD smiled uneasily, "I guess you noticed where I redacted a few things from the copy of the doomsday diary I gave you. Those were the names of real people. I'm not sure if they were revealed to me for my personal edification or are meant to be shared with others. So, for now, I'm keeping that to myself."

CHAPTER 8

Thirty Pieces

"When the morning was come, all the chief priests and elders of the people took counsel against Jesus to put him to death: And when they had bound him, they led him away, and delivered him to Pontius Pilate the governor. Then Judas, which had betrayed him, when he saw that he was condemned, repented himself, and brought again the thirty pieces of silver to the chief priests and elders, Saying, I have sinned in that I have betrayed the innocent blood. And they said, what is that to us? See thou to that. And he cast down the pieces of silver in the temple, and departed, and went and hanged himself. And the chief priests took the silver pieces, and said, it is not lawful for to put them into the treasury, because it is the price of blood. And they took counsel, and bought with them the potter's field, to bury strangers in. Wherefore that field was called, the field of blood, unto this day. Then was fulfilled that which was spoken by Jeremy the prophet, saying, And they took the thirty pieces of silver, the price of him that was valued, whom they of the children of Israel did value; And gave them for the potter's field, as the Lord appointed me." (Matthew the Tax Collector and Apostle, Holy Bible, Book of Matthew 27:1-10, First Century A. D.)

I contacted the fellow who took the reins at Ops Ogilvy's old private security firm after his passing at the hands of the Sicilian Ghost. Like Ops, he and the members of his crew were ex-Special Forces and still dealt almost exclusively with one key client, Uncle Sam. I can't tell you their names for confidentiality's sake so I'll just refer to him as Cary Grant and his right hand men as James Mason and Martin Landau. I think you'll understand the North by Northwest reference and the appropriateness of these monikers later. I couldn't reveal that JD was alive quite yet but wanted to give them some prep time so I asked the favor with the promise that they'd understand why in about a week. It was easier than I thought. I didn't have to beg, lie or come up with excuses about needing to assuage Jude's concerns. Cary and company were willing to take my word and conduct the sweep once I gave them the green light for one simple reason. Cary felt they owed it to Ops and believed any friend of his was a friend of theirs.

Everything changed in a heartbeat the day we went public. Our lives went from zero to one hundred miles per hour as if we'd jumped aboard a rocket sled. At first, the Trumpet was derided for pulling what was thought to be a gratuitous, self-serving hoax. A bit later, as people viewed the video of JD we posted and the frenzy spread through the various media outlets, skepticism turned to curiosity and then to wild speculation and finally a ravenous appetite for more details. The YouTube video went viral. So much traffic was driven to trumpet.com that the website was actually shut down for a time. A nationwide and presumably worldwide phenomenon kicked in when we cut Nick Phace loose to begin promoting the upcoming exclusive, live interview. The national media descended upon St. Louis and, along with their local brethren, began scouring the countryside looking for the Last Prophet. We had notified JD's parents just in time to brace for the firestorm that swept away the immense joy they'd felt during their reunion with their long lost son. It didn't take long for the media hounds to find their way to my home and the Trumpet production compound out in the sticks of New Haven. We knew the only way to throw them off JD's scent was for me to open up to them. I addressed the gaggle and confirmed that JD was in fact alive and well; again the beneficiary of God's miraculous, protective hand. I'm sorry to say that I lied and said JD was not with me; that he was in seclusion under the protective care of Nick Phace pending the announcement of the time and place for the upcoming live broadcast.

Unfortunately for JD, this meant he had to stay inside, well secluded for more than a week since the media was keeping an eye on me, the only known link to the Last Prophet other than Nick Phace. He took it in stride and used the time to prepare. I wasn't under *house arrest* like JD but took similar advantage of the situation to work on American Phoenix and prepare for Nick's show. It didn't take long for Cary Grant and crew to assess the situation and report back to me. It was a good-news, bad-news story. There were no electronic devices or other forms of covert surveillance found anywhere near my home and compound or Mit's apartment. We weren't being followed or spied upon in any fashion. However, much to our surprise, they found several bugs at Kit's place. Immediately, the alarms went off in our heads. Why would they leave the rest of us alone and focus in solely on harmless little Kit? Mit was especially troubled and lost his typically stoic composure. We finally soothed his ragged nerves by postulating that perhaps it made sense. She was the new kid on the block. They probably just wanted to confirm that she was unaware and uninvolved. Yeah, that made sense.

This notion gave us somewhat of a sense of security but it also reinforced the truth that Cagliostro and Benedetto were dangerous and couldn't be trusted. Whatever peace we found in our rationale was completely shattered the next day when we called our German friend, Stefan, to see if word about JD had reached him across the pond. His wife answered the phone in a suspicious tone. Once she established who we were, she became very distraught and informed us that Stefan's body had been discovered in his hotel room in Rome; the victim of an apparent armed robbery gone awry. We tried our best to console her but were not very effective since we had suspicions of our own. The only thing we could do was to assure her that, in the brief time we had known Stefan, he had expressed his faith in Christ in a most bold and joyous fashion. After leaving her to her grief, JD and I agreed that the robbery was surely a bogus cover-up for the evil deeds of Cagliostro and Benedetto. It sent chills down our spines to realize just how ruthless they could be. Apparently, to them, Stefan was just a meddlesome loose end. Although they surely must have realized he posed only the slightest potential threat, they deemed it better to dispose of him rather than taking any chances.

We were completely unsettled by Stefan's death which we rightly supposed was a murder. We tried not to feel guilty for putting him in harm's way but felt anger more than anything else that he was executed simply for being befriended by us. At the end of the day we had to accept the harsh reality that our experiment had proved successful. Surely Cagliostro and Benedetto were well aware of the way we had gone public and how we were planning on making a gigantic splash on Nick Phace's show. Yet, they had taken no action against us other than to keep a watchful eye on Kit. It appeared they were holding up their end of the bargain and honoring the truce, for now. Nevertheless, a stark warning issued forth from poor Stefan's grave ... remain ever so vigilant ... do not let your guard down for one minute. We took this brutal lesson to heart but, thankfully, did not have time to dwell on our fears. There was so much work to be done. Then we received a call from Nick Phace himself. He was planning something bold, completely unprecedented. His hour-long exclusive with the Last Prophet would be broadcast live from one of the most iconic monuments in the world: Mt. Rushmore.

He asked us to pack up everything we needed and head to Rapid City, South Dakota the next day.

Our transportation and security were already arranged. For privacy's sake, the show had rented out an entire lodge nestled in the foothills alongside Rapid Creek. We'd be safe and secure there, tucked away from the glare of the media for the next few days until the location was announced only two days before the broadcast. This would provide just enough time for the crew to build a temporary set under the gaze of Washington, Jefferson, Teddy Roosevelt and Abe and screen and distribute passes to lucky local audience participants they'd chosen and select members of the media. Phace was sparing no expense. By broadcasting from the national monument at Mt. Rushmore, Nick's staff must have been forced to wade through oceans of government red tape and surely it was driving the cost through the roof. It probably didn't bother him though since he knew from experience that this would not only boost his ratings into the stratosphere but cause the show's revenues to skyrocket. Obviously, he thought it was worth it. Instead of using his New York studio with its sedate portraits of the Founding Fathers adorning the walls, we'd be in the shadow of the four presidents with the sun gleaming off their sixty foot high, awe-inspiring countenances, etched from the perfect, pale granite protruding from the

Black Hills under azure skies. What a gas! JD was the main attraction, no doubt. But still, I couldn't think of a better, more meaningful place to unveil American Phoenix.

It was hard to contain our excitement but, for me, the thrill of it all was tempered by my concern for Jude and the kids. That night, I met with Cary and explained the situation. He assured me that they would keep a close eye on my family in my absence. I was still nervous but had to admit Jude, Gogo and Addie couldn't be in better hands short of perhaps the Secret Service. We got clearance from Nick to bring Mit along as our aide de camp and general jack-of-all-trades for anything techie. Of course Mit was excited but dreaded leaving his Kitten behind. We assured him that she was in good hands too since Cary and the boys were on top of the situation involving the bugs planted in her apartment. We didn't have time to fret. To avoid the media, Nick arranged for a driver to pick us up in a black SUV at 3:00 a. m. We were whisked away to Spirit, a small, private airfield in West County to board his personal jet. Wheels were up before anyone knew better. There we were again, in the lap of luxury, this time with Mit along for the ride. Yeah, as you might have guessed, he took full advantage of the free food. The two security guards sent along for our protection marveled at the bottomless pit as he gobbled everything in sight.

Before we left, we had tried to assure Jude and Kit of their safety in our absence. There was no longer any need for pretense with Kit because she knew about JD by then and she deserved to be clued in as much as possible since she had wound up on Cagliostro's radar screen in spite of our previous efforts to shield her from any involvement. We briefly introduced them to Cary but not James or Martin at Cary's request. It was bad for business for anyone to become too well acquainted with his guys. Cary said they might never see them but promised that they would be close by in case of any trouble. He left with Jude still feeling uneasy. I did my best to convince her that Cary and his crew were the tops in the business. Jude was savvy enough to recall how Ops had fallen to the Ghost in spite of his skills and training which had been equal to if not better than Cary or anyone else he might have on his staff. I was thankful that Jude declined the opportunity to put me on the spot. What was the use? I did better in comforting her with the fact that I'd be gone for only a week.

I knew we couldn't trust Cagliostro and Benedetto but figured they'd be held at bay by the threat we presented to them if the information we'd gained from Marchetti leaked out. From hindsight, boy was I wrong! They had no intention of honoring our unholy truce. What appeared as principled restraint was just another well-calculated tactic on their part. They were quietly testing our defenses, exploring, prodding and probing for soft spots. Unbeknownst to us, Benedetto was dispatched to our nation's capital to seek out another more practical alliance within one of the many labyrinths of our government where the sun doesn't shine. He met with a NSA boss to convince him of the threat posed by JD Uticus. Let's call him Brutus. You know, like the back stabber of Rome who revered party politics over the rule of law and honored allegiance to the cause over his friendship to Julius Caesar. JD was deemed dangerous not because of his theology but more so his intention to promote American Phoenix and the notion that both Parties are in cahoots to maintain power at the expense of the American people, our culture and the basic liberties and freedoms framed in our Constitution. Granted, this was just a splinter group within our vast government bureaucracy but it had ties to important higher ups ... and, more importantly, a couple of former spooks, James and Martin, who had worked for Brutus during his days in the CIA.

It didn't take long. The first day we were away, Jude had just put the kids down for the night and was taking a shower before hitting the hay. Cary was perched outside, hidden in the woods and keeping watch like a guardian angel. He was settling in for a long night of surveillance when he received a call from James. He had noticed something suspicious going down at Kit's apartment and requested back up, just in case. Cary called Martin to cover for him and Martin said he could be there in twenty minutes. Martin was actually close enough to be there in two. When Cary arrived outside Kit's apartment, James told him he'd seen a couple of suspicious characters casing the joint. Wasting no time, they knocked on Kit's door and she answered wearing a tattered terrycloth robe, no make-up and a turban-like towel wrapped around her freshly washed hair. She recognized Cary and let them in. He offered no introduction other than to say, "This is an associate of mine. We really hate to bother you but just wanted to check in and make sure everything is okay."

"I was just getting ready to go to bed. Is there anything wrong?" She didn't notice as James put one hand behind his back to retrieve a gun from his waistband while the other slipped a silencer from his pocket. Just then, the tea kettle on Kit's stove began to whistle indicating her warmed milk was ready. It was just loud enough to cover the clicking sound as the silencer was set into place.

"No, everything is fine. We just thought we should check in on you since this is the first night and all. Again, we're sorry to have bothered you." He smiled as if to bid her adieu. Cary never saw it coming. Neither did Kit, that is, until she was startled by two muffled pops that zipped through the back of Cary's head and sent blood spattering across Kit's robe and freshly scrubbed face. In a flash, James pumped one more slug into Cary's back, into his heart for good measure before he crumpled to the ground releasing a pool of blood seeping into the well-worn carpet. Kit gasped deeply but, like a jungle cat, James thrust his hand over her mouth to stifle the blood-curdling scream she was about to release. He held his hand there tightly over her mouth as her eyes bulged in horror and caught her with his other arm to prevent her from collapsing.

He eased her onto the couch and whispered sinisterly, "Don't say a word, not a word. Do you understand?" She nodded with tears forming in the corners of her eyes. As he slowly removed his big paw from her mouth, her bottom lip trembled terribly. "Listen carefully because I'm only going to ask you this once. Where are your boyfriend and the other two guys?" Staring at Cary's lifeless body lying prone on the floor and the expanding blood stain, there was no doubt what would happen if she failed to cooperate. But what if she did? She was a witness to murder. The odds weren't good in either case. So she summoned every ounce of courage in her being.

Her sobs were tainted with defiance, "Why should I help you? You're going to kill me either way."

James' lips curled into a reptilian smile. "I've got to admit; you've got a fair point there sister. But here's the deal. I can kill you now and then it's your friend Jude's turn in the barrel. Or you can tell me and at least live long enough to see your wimpy boyfriend once more before you go."

Kit had no choice. She certainly didn't want to put Jude, Gogo and Addie in any danger. She had to buy some time. And, in any case, it would only be three days before their location was revealed by Nick Phace. "Okay, I'll tell you but please don't do anything to harm Jude Hermann and her kids." He was not at all reassuring ... he didn't even nod. James raised his gun ever so slightly and seemed to caress it like a baby bunny. "They're in South Dakota." He pressured her without speaking, solely with his eyes. "They went to Rapid City, near Mt. Rushmore."

He was expressionless except for a slightly satisfied smile. James called to Martin, "Okay, you can move in."

Jude was completely relaxed. The kids were sleeping peacefully and her head was tucked under the shower head rinsing the last remnants of velvety suds from her hair and the warm, pulsating water caressed her skin as it cascaded the length of her body. She turned the faucet off and squeezed the water from her thick head of hair as the clouds of steam were dissipated by the bathroom fan. As she pulled the shower curtain back she was jolted by what seemed like a thousand volts as she encountered the hulking figure of a strange man leering at her naked body. Panic and terror swept over her in an instant. Her first instinct was to shout at the top of her lungs but she held back. The last thing she wanted to do was wake Gogo and Addie and put them in harm's way with this demented pervert. She pulled the shower curtain toward her to conceal herself. The intruder reached out and pulled the curtain in one swift motion snapping the shower rings in rapid succession. It sounded like shell casings from an automatic weapon hitting the floor, clattering and pinging. The only thing more unsettling than having your home invaded by a stranger is the total vulnerability of being confronted without a stitch of clothing, bare to the world.

Jude's hands and arms moved reflexively into position to cover her private parts. Even though it was anything but cold, she began to shiver uncontrollably. She had to wonder, *how could this man be so calm? Was he so practiced at his nefarious art that he could stare at her without a hint of emotion?* He was taking his time and obviously enjoying himself. Could anything be more degrading, disgusting and dreadful to a woman? There was only one thing worse; the thought of what he could do to Gogo and Addie if they were roused from their slumbers. She steeled herself for the inevitable, to grin and bear it.

Then her natural instinct to fight kicked in. Jude reached out and grabbed a pair of scissors off the vanity and clutched a heavy ceramic soap dish in her other hand. As awkward and embarrassing as it would have been under other circumstances she forgot her self-consciousness and held her makeshift weapons out in the strongest defensive posture possible. Her expression was a manic cross between a frightened rabbit and a belligerent badger ready to tangle to the death. Still, the beast calmly eyed her up and down as the drops of water fell from her glistening bare skin. He calmly reached inside his windbreaker and pulled out a gun. Jude gritted her teeth, ready to face rape and death. Then he did something so unexpected she almost fainted. He turned the butt end of the pistol toward her, reached out and offered her the gun. "Go ahead and take it."

This had to be some kind of sick trick. She was frozen except that her body, juiced up with fear, anxiety and adrenaline, started to tremble violently. He drew the gun back, pulled back on the top sliding a shell into the chamber and cocked the hammer. Jude was still frozen with fright and confusion. Then he moved toward the door and began to close it. Instead of shutting and locking it, he retrieved her robe from off the hook behind the door, turned and tossed it to her. Perhaps this was a clever maneuver to get her to discard the scissors and makeshift bludgeon? She did it anyway. Jude set them aside and threw the robe on and tied the belt so tightly it pinched into her slim waistline. Again he offered the gun. "Go ahead, take it. I have no intention of harming you in any way. I just want to talk." Jude took the gun nervously. It was completely foreign to her. She knew he probably had another one so it didn't give her any sense of confidence, safety or well-being.

Her voice was shaky, "You want to talk? You want to talk? What kind of maniac are you?" Jude remained tense and tight as a drum as she motioned him toward the kitchen with the gun. "Have you ever heard of knocking?" Her Irish was up, "You sneak into a woman's bathroom while she's showering and say you want to talk? I ought to shoot you right now!"

Her newfound anger-fueled confidence was short lived. Martin lowered his chin and stared straight into Jude's eyes and spoke in a deadly serious voice. "If I wanted to kill you, you would already be dead. Thankfully for you, there's something I need from you. If you cooperate, I'll do no harm to you, your husband ... or your children."

When he paused for effect and lowered his voice in mentioning the children, it sent shivers down Jude's spine.

"What is it that you want?" Jude was thankful that she was seething with anger at the implied threat to her children. It helped to counter her debilitating fear.

"You have some information from Mr. Marchetti that you've tucked away for safe keeping. There are people who do not appreciate such threats. They will not be tolerated. You will help me to remove these threats if you want your family to live."

"How dare you threaten my family?" There was no reaction. She might as well have been talking to a rattle snake. Her mind was racing and she took another, desperate approach. "I'm of a good mind to call the police. I'm of a good mind to release the Marchetti file to the authorities and media."

Martin remained calm and resolute. "That would be a big mistake." To emphasize the point he reached under the table and began to slide his hand under her robe and up her thigh causing her to clench. He removed it just as quickly with a devilish smile. "My client wants the same thing that you do … simple peace of mind. Take away the threat and yours will be likewise removed." Jude was between a rock and a hard place and had to stop to consider. He sensed an advantage, "Think of your family. I'm giving you the chance to ensure their safety." Martin paused to let this sink in. "No one will have to know … not your husband, not anyone. It will be our secret. They can go on with their lives none the wiser but completely free from danger. If it makes them feel better they can keep on thinking that the Marchetti file is their ace in the hole. You and I will know the truth … that the Marchetti file served the opposite purpose of putting all of your lives on the line. With it gone, there will be no reason for anyone to fear you and, thus, no purpose in wanting to harm you. You'll have the peace and satisfaction of knowing you did what was needed to keep your family out of harm's way. You'll be the brave one; the true hero in this matter."

He knew he had her when Jude bowed her head and offered a silent prayer. "Okay, what do you want me to do?"

"Atta girl, Mrs. Hermann … now you're being sensible. Believe me, you won't be sorry. You've just done a wonderful thing for your family. I'll meet you tomorrow morning at 10:00 and you can help me retrieve the files."

Jude was relieved and drained. Her intentions were good and worthy. It helped to mask the gnawing doubt. She had no choice. Jude tried to rationalize. She tip toed into Gogo's room then Addie's. Seeing them nestled in their beds convinced her that she had made the right move. Still, as tired as she was, it took a long time for sleep to overtake her. The next morning she met with Martin and turned everything over to him. She retrieved the hard copies and thumb drives and granted him access to electronic files. "I'm sure the e-files are heavily encrypted. I can't help you with that."

"That's okay Mrs. Hermann. You can leave that to me." He sounded creepy but Jude just nodded and let it go. She wanted to get away from him as soon as possible. With their business concluded, Jude turned to go. Martin seized her wrist and added, "Oh, there's just one more thing. Don't try to get in touch with your friend Kit."

Panic swooped back in, "What do you mean by that? What have you done to her?"

"Now, now, there's no need to worry. Your friend is just fine. We've just taken her on a little vacation."

"You promised you'd leave us alone if I cooperated."

"That's correct Mrs. Hermann. Just think of this as an insurance policy. No harm will come to your friend. As soon as your husband and friends return from their trip, she will be released. That is, as long as you don't change your mind and go blabbing to the wrong people. And as long as your husband and his friends watch their Ps & Qs about what they say to the media."

Jude was frustrated, scared and angry but bit her tongue. "Whatever you say, Mr. um. By the way, what is your name? What should I call you?"

"Never mind, that won't be necessary. You'll hear from me if we need to talk again. One more thing; don't say anything to your husband or his pals about little Miss Kitten. There's no need to upset them." With that, he turned and left.

We were oblivious to Jude's dilemma, Kit's abduction and the peril confronting us. From hindsight I've wondered what I would have done in

Jude's position or Kit's. Did they foolishly betray our trust or bravely take extreme, self-sacrificing measures to protect us out of love and devotion? I couldn't come to any other conclusion than the latter. After turning it over in my head a million times I always wound up at the same place ... I would have done exactly the same thing. They really had no choice. Compared to Jude and Kit, we three *bachelors* didn't have a care in the world. We were living in a protective cocoon. With the secluded lodge all to ourselves and plenty of security surrounding us, we were pretty much free to do as we pleased. Most of the time was spent working and preparing but we had some fun too.

One afternoon we ventured out back and decided to take a dip in Rapid Creek. The water was only about waist high but it was still difficult to navigate on foot. The name Rapid Creek is completely appropriate. The rocky bottom was smooth and slippery and the current was surprisingly forceful so it took deliberate concentration and extreme care to stay upright. It was also shockingly cold ... so frigid that I felt like we were in a commercial, ready to head to the mountains and pluck a few Busch beers from the sparkling depths. Mit was the first one to lose his footing and take a chilly plunge. He was dragged twenty yards downstream before he was able to emerge with teeth chattering and wet hair going every which way. The look on his face was priceless and we roared with laughter. Going under helped acclimate Mitt to the water which was so crystal clear that you could literally see your toes on the bottom. Mitt began to spy the water for fish. All of a sudden, he voluntarily thrust himself under again and stayed down long enough that we began to worry. Finally, like some distant cousin to a hillbilly hogger, he rose slowly as if Neptune was ascending from Atlantis with a wiggling trout in his hands. To our delight, he raised the trophy triumphantly above his head and let out a Tarzan yell before slipping and falling again. We busted a gut until the violent laughter caused me to fall and I was swept downstream taking JD's feet out from under him. It was Mit's turn to laugh at our expense.

We cackled all the way to the hot tub. What a welcome relief! We raised our body temperatures to where we were able to enjoy a couple of cold Buds. The mood was loose and light. That is, until Mit looked at his phone with consternation and proclaimed, "Something's wrong."

I didn't want to kill the mood, "What do you mean?"

"Kit hasn't called me today." The absurdity tickled our funny bones and JD and I snickered like Beavis and Butthead.

"I'm serious … Kit calls me at least once a day. It never fails."

The look on his face choked off our laughter and I said soberly, "Mit, maybe her battery is low or the service is bad."

"No, I've got two bars and Kit would never let her battery run down that much." Apparently, over the relatively short period of time they'd known each other they'd developed an odd but very special relationship because Mit was truly worried.

"I'm sure there's a good explanation. Listen, I'll call Jude and ask her to check on Kit." I did so and she said she'd talked to Kit earlier in the day and everything was fine. Jude even offered a suggestion that Kit didn't want to interrupt our important work as we prepared for Nick's show. She was so convincing that I didn't pick up a hint of the pangs tearing at her gut. When I passed this along to Mit it helped somewhat but he was still troubled by Kit's uncharacteristic lapse.

I tried a little levity to clear the air, "Hey Romeo, did you ever think that maybe Kit has found a new nerd to hug and squeeze? You know what they say … when the Mit's away the Kit will play."

JD could tell that my weak attempt at comedy didn't help. In fact, it had the opposite effect. "Don't listen to him, Mit. Jude's probably right that she doesn't want to bug you while we're gearing up for the big showdown with Nick Phace. You know what they say … absence makes the heart grow fonder. The reunion will be that much sweeter when you get back to St. Louis."

Mit seemed to perk up a bit. Thankfully, he had plenty to keep himself busy now that he was in contact with Nick Phace's staff and had several homework assignments to accomplish before they arrived in two days. We grabbed some dinner then peeled off to get a few things done before bedtime rolled around. JD abruptly stopped me before I could get to my room. "Hey Inky, could you do me a big favor?"

"Sure man, what do you need?"

"Now that there's so much traffic flowing through your website, you could really help set the table for something important that I know will not get enough airtime on Nick's show."

"Okay, what's that?"

"Can you post something to get people thinking about the Ten Commandments? It needs to be eye catching and relevant ... not too stodgy, you know?"

"Yeah, I can do something a little more contemporary than Cecil B. DeMille and Charlton Hesston. What's the deal?"

"I figure at some point I'm going to have to get into the silver lining of Judgment Day with Nick Phace but it will mean tackling the concepts of contrition and repentance. How can you cover repentance without an understanding of sin and how can anyone understand sin without the Commandments? You know as well as I do that there won't be enough time during a one-hour show to get into the Commandments in any length. So maybe you can help prep the audience and our viewers with an advanced primer."

"Ah, now I've gotcha."

I really wanted to put the finishing touches on my outline of the fix, the details of what a spiritual reawakening, the resurrection of the dead Republic would entail but it wouldn't take long for me to post something to help set the stage for JD. I was just thankful to get second billing on this gig. JD was the headliner and his message was infinitely more important than what I had to say about America's lot in the world. So I dove into the assignment and came up with something I thought would fit the bill.

An Idiot's Guide to the Ten Commandments

Hey, can you recite the Ten Commandments in proper order? No, well how about a reasonable facsimile thereof? No, then can you get five out of ten? What, you don't care? C'mon I don't believe that! You don't need to be embarrassed. Look, I'll help you out ... it's really pretty easy. Okay, okay, don't worry ... I'm not going to make you memorize Exodus or Deuteronomy. I'll put it in simple language that anyone can understand.

Oh, but you think it's a waste of time, outdated and irrelevant? You may want to reconsider. God thought it was important enough that he gave us the Commandments twice. Yeah, after Moses got ticked off at the slackers who were the intended beneficiaries and broke the original tablets, God came back with a second set. It seems to me, that alone warrants our attention. But I hear you. That was a long time ago and, today, in this country, we're not even allowed to post the Ten Commandments in a government building even though they're still the basis for our system of jurisprudence. I'm sorry but this is no excuse to ignore the Commandments. As we're told in Romans 2:15, God doesn't care about government restrictions or even our ignorance or apathy toward his Bible for he has written his law on our hearts and in our consciences. Even when we sear over our consciences we can still know right from wrong. In I Chronicles 16:14 we're told that we can see God's judgments just by looking at the evidence in the world around us.

No, don't fret. I'm not going to quote a bunch of Bible passages to you (maybe just a few). Here are the Commandments in plain English dude.

1) *Hey, don't forget who is number one. I'm not just talking about wooden and stone idols here. Keep your priorities straight and don't let your career, money, fame, creature*

comforts, pet causes or anything else shove me to the side.

2) Watch what you say. I really don't like this GD stuff. But it goes further than that. Don't use your mouth for dropping F-bombs or any such stuff. You wouldn't let someone shove gunk or poison into your mouth, would you? Then why put it in there yourself? It makes both of us look bad.

3) Get into church every week. No, it's not the same if you watch some TV preacher or read the Bible by yourself. Those things are fine too but you need to worship with other Christians. No, this isn't an ego thing. It's not for my benefit. It's all about what I can give to you when you go to church to hear my true word preached and taught. Try it, you'll like it. Trust me on this.

4) You should respect proper authority. This includes your parents but it goes beyond that. Give some props to government servants, your boss, teachers, the police, your pastor and anyone else I've put in a position of authority for your well-being. That goes whether you like them or not. And remember, nobody's perfect so cut them some slack along the way.

5) *I won't tolerate murder. Don't do it and don't even think about it. Life is precious to me, every life; no matter how old or young, healthy or feeble, including life in the womb from conception. I'm the Lord of life, not you. Don't play God. Yes, you have the right to defend yourself and exercise justice and national defense through legitimate authority. In your messed up, sinful world these things can't be avoided. But please, try to see everyone as I do ... precious children created in my image with a living, eternal soul.*

6) *Stay faithful to your spouse if you have one. If you don't, please stay faithful to me. I didn't create you to live immoral lives. Don't shack up or sleep around. Don't give into perverted desires. C'mon, control yourselves people. Do things my way. You'll be a lot happier.*

7) *Keep your mitts off other peoples' stuff. Ultimately, everything belongs to me. I made it all. I'll divvy things up the way I see fit. Trust me; I know what's best for you. Have faith in me that I'll make sure you have everything you need. I'll also make sure to withhold things that would harm*

you in the long run. Some people can handle wealth and put it to good use for my purposes. Others can't and just get into trouble.

8) *If you don't have something good to say, keep your mouth shut. Don't go around cutting down your friends, relatives and neighbors. I don't like lying in general. It reminds me of the biggest liar of all. You know who I'm talking about, that Devil. Even if you know something bad about someone that is true, you don't need to blab. Unless it's a matter of law enforcement that you need to share with the authorities, put a lid on it. Try to accentuate the positive and say something good about that person.*

9) *Green is not a good color for you when it means you're clothed with envy. Don't waste your time thinking about your neighbor's big house, nice yard, hot tub or pool. It will just eat away at you. Just be thankful for your own place; whatever you've got.* Remember that my Son never even had a place to call home. *You may not have a lot but I guarantee you that you'll have something priceless if you learn to*

appreciate what you have: true peace and eternal life.

10) *This may sound redundant but it's a real problem so I've got to hit this one again in more detail. Don't be so jealous or greedy for what other people have. Don't think about how great it would be to have someone else's spouse, their peeps and helpers, their car, boat, fancy clothes or snow blower. The grass may look greener on the other side of the fence but it's not. They have lots of weeds in their lawn too. Remember, be thankful for what you've got and don't get too wrapped up in the things of this world. You can't take it with you. What I have in store for you in the next life will put everything in this world to shame.*

Now, do you see what I mean? Yeah, you kind of knew this already. And don't forget that you don't always need to remember this word for word. God has made it easy for us. Do you remember Christ's Reader's Digest version, his Commandments for Dummies edition? Here's how he boiled it down for us in Matthew 22:37-39 ... "Jesus said unto him, Thou shalt love the Lord thy God with all thy heart, and with all thy soul, and with all thy mind. This is the first and great commandment. And the second is like unto it, Thou shalt love thy neighbor as thyself."

Okay, there's one last thing. Do you know why God gave us these Commandments? Well yeah, in part as a guide for how we should try to live. But he knows we can't always stick to the rules. So don't make the mistake of thinking God gave us the Commandments as a way to salvation. No, these rules are primarily given to show us how far short we fall from keeping the law perfectly. They show us that it would be impossible to save ourselves. The law was given out of love to show us how much we need a savior ...Therefore by the deeds of the law there shall no flesh be justified in his sight: for by the law is the knowledge of sin (Romans 3:20). The law points us to the one, true Savior of mankind, Jesus Christ. He is the only one who can satisfy God's admission requirements for us ... For Christ is the end of the law for righteousness to everyone that believeth (Romans 10:4). This is why we can honestly say like the Psalmist that we delight in God's law.

I let JD have a peek at the finished product before posting it. He read it once and then a second time which worried me. Then he smiled,

"You've come a long way baby. A few years ago, you would have penned something that old men in ivy covered halls might have read on a slow day."

This was music to my ears, "You've gotta get with the times, right? It may look and feel a little different but the message is the same. This way I may get through to a few more people, eh?"

"Good job Inky. It's just what the doctor ordered."

"Do you think Dr. Becker would have approved?"

"Well, it's not really his style ... but it's true to the word and that was the most important thing to him. I think he'd be in favor of spreading the gospel in a way that reaches out to another generation." We both reflected fondly on the memory of Dr. Becker.

The next day our work was cut short when Nick Phace showed up a day early to spend time with us. This was very unusual for the top rated talk show host in the country. He was as popular as ever and his media empire had expanded in every direction; beyond TV and radio to publishing, the web, his own production company and even a fledgling network. To say he was busy would be the understatement of the year. That was normal and didn't even account for the height of the political season as the election year neared its climax. An exclusive with the Last Prophet, back from the dead again, was a big, big deal but even so it didn't warrant him taking a full day out of his schedule. It would have sufficed for him to wait and touch base when the rest of the production crew showed up the next day. Something else was driving him. It didn't take long for it to become apparent that he considered JD to be more than a high profile guest. It wouldn't be too far-fetched to call it friendship. There was something different in his demeanor too. The uber-confident, sometimes bombastic, occasionally self-absorbed, whiz kid turned mogul seemed oddly humble and reverent. Had there been a spiritual transformation? One thing hadn't changed; Phace's offbeat sense of humor. We were huddled inside, oblivious to the buzz outside where security was ramped up at least double. Nick entered alone, stopped, opened his arms wide, tilted his head and offered a patented, goofy, self-deprecating, smart aleck grin. He gave JD a warm hug, extended his hand to me and shrugged as if to say, what the heck, I'll hug you too, and wrapped his arms around me.

Phace was in a gregarious mood, "Look at you, the Last Prophet! No wait, don't tell me. I know what you're going to say … 'I'm baaaaaaack!' Yep, back from the dead again; the cat with nine lives. That's two down and seven to go. How in the heck are you JD?"

JD downplayed it with his best deadpan, "I'm just happy to be here Nick. How are you?"

"Whoa, now wait a minute Mr. Prophet. You know I'm not going to let you off that easy. So tell me, how did you survive the bomb blast that blew the top off of your apartment building and burned your suicide killers to a crisp?"

JD teased, "Details, details … I don't want to bore you. The important thing is that I survived." Nick didn't even have to speak. All it took was one of his looks of mock indignation and JD recounted how God miraculously shielded him as if with a force field akin to Daniel's account of how God saved his pals Shadrach, Meshach and Abednego from King Nebuchadnezzar's fiery furnace. "So, once again God delivered me, Nick."

Phace just shook his head in silent wonderment for almost a good minute. It was hard to tell if he was amazed by God's miraculous power or overwhelmed by the potential this offered for the upcoming show. Then a puzzled look gripped him, "But what happened then? Where have you been for all this time?"

"I've been in hiding. The only way to protect myself and ensure the safety of Inky and his family was to let the world think I was dead and gone."

"Couldn't you have gone to the police?"

"Trust me Nick, there's no way they could have protected us."

"Protected you from what, from whom? Are the Islamists still out to get you?"

JD squirmed, "Nick, this is something better left alone. I can't talk about the people behind this, the forces that still want me dead."

"I don't get it. Aren't you leaving yourself exposed? Why in the world did you come out of hiding then? I just don't understand."

"Nick, you'll have to trust me on this. We've done everything possible to protect ourselves. I simply can't talk about it, period, or it would put us in grave danger. As for your other question, that's easy. God saved me to deliver a message. This time the message is very specific."

Nick grudgingly conceded from digging further, in part, to keep us out of harm's way but also his appetite was whetted by JD's last comment. "Tell me about the message JD."

"Much like the last time, God wants me to share the Bible's message of warning and hope regarding the end times but this time he wants me to focus on the last day, the final judgment."

Nick salivated at the prospect. We could almost see the wheels turning in his head as he surely envisioned how this could play to an enraptured, worldwide audience. "JD, how do you know this? You seem so certain, so determined."

"All right Nick, hold onto your hat because you're going to have a hard time believing this." JD paused to give Nick a chance to mentally prepare himself. "God sent visions to me."

Phace's jaw dropped, "What ... what do you mean by visions?"

"It's hard to explain but it was like dreams on a big IMAX screen but I was awake."

Skeptical Nick challenged JD, "Now wait a minute. Aren't you the guy that preached over and over how God doesn't change his message and wants us to stick to the Scripture alone?"

"Yes, I'm that guy. Hear me out though. God didn't give me a new message. He simply opened my eyes to his revelations in the Bible about the end times in a new way. It's kind of like the images God showed to John on the island of Patmos but updated in a contemporary way that shed's new light on the original meaning. And again, he has homed in on one particular piece; Judgment Day."

Nick understood but was having a hard time wrapping his head around how this might play out. "Oh boy … how are we going to sell this? Will people believe you or think it's some kind of hocus-pocus? Who'll sponsor us, Joe the Snake Oil Salesman and Colonel Rupert's Traveling Medicine Show?"

JD remained calm and resolute, "Nick, you're forgetting the most important thing. Why did people believe me the first time around? Yeah, dead men tell no lies. It's hard to doubt someone who survived such a deadly blast at ground zero."

Phace's confidence was immediately boosted, "You're exactly right JD. We'll have to open the show with enough detail to unveil your second miraculous resurrection."

"Well it's not really a resurrection this time. I wasn't brought back from the dead like before but I was definitely shielded from the blast by the hand of Almighty God." JD pondered our dilemma and offered, "I think we can tell the story of how I survived and went into hiding without trespassing onto forbidden ground but please remember we can't get into who tried to kill me or anything about us remaining in danger."

"Okay JD, I've got you covered. Now tell me about the visions. How can you remember what God showed you after such a long time? Are you claiming to be divinely inspired like the writers of the Bible?"

"No, it's nothing like that. What God showed me was certainly inspired or provided by him but from there it's pretty simple. I kept notes to help me remember the images. It's like a diary." JD chuckled, "I call it my doomsday diary."

The light bulb came on in an instant and Nick was absolutely thrilled. "The Last Prophet is back

from the dead with his doomsday diary in hand."
Phace wiggled his fingers and mouthed some
spooky music sounds, "Hollywood couldn't have
scripted this any better. The doomsday diary ... I
love it!" I felt like a third wheel at this love fest
until Nick suddenly turned toward me. "Now,
American Phoenix is a horse of a different color,
Inky." I wasn't sure how to take his comment since
he maintained a poker face so I held my tongue.
"You know, I used to think JD was the crazy one ...
but you make him look like vanilla pudding, you
radical you." Finally he smiled giving me a chance
to exhale. "Inky, in all seriousness, I agree with you
for the most part."

This gave me the confidence to join the
conversation, "So Nick, did you get a chance to
skim some of the manuscript ... at least the
chapters I've finished so far?"

From the look on his face I think I accidentally
offended him. Phace was known as a voracious
reader who gobbled up pages like a monkey on a
bag of potato chips. "I don't skim. I either read
something or not depending on whether I like it."
There was another pregnant pause and I tried not
to lean toward him. "I read the whole thing. It's

really good, even if I disagree with the basic premise."

I took a chance, "How so, Nick?"

"We're simpatico my friend when it comes to the Republic being in deep trouble. I also think you've hit the nail on the head in saying we need a spiritual reawakening to get back on track." This shouldn't have surprised me. Over the years since JD last appeared on his show, Phace had taken on a more serious tone regarding the depth of our national predicament. He too was preaching doom and gloom. Phace had also shifted from the pragmatism of a policy wonk to a spiritual guru of sorts trying to lead the country back to the *Promised Land*. He argued that the solutions had to come from the people rather than Washington, D. C. My impression was that he was focused on our national character and morality more so than what I'd call spirituality. In any case, I could see why he felt there were some close parallels. "But here's where we differ, Inky. You think it's too late, that the Republic is history; dead and gone. We're close to the edge but we haven't fallen off the cliff yet." He affected the tone and cadence of a Southern Baptist preacher to mock me affectionately, "It's not too late for a revival, Brother Hermann!"

I wasn't afraid to argue this point and defend American Phoenix, "It all comes down to what has made this country great in the first place. The way I see it; those days are over barring a complete resurrection from the dead."

"Are you kidding me? Have you been paying attention lately? I know it's still close but the tide is really starting to turn. Did you see the conventions? Have you seen the latest polls? Do you remember what things were like under Carter just before Ronnie took over? I think we're in for a Romney/Ryan revival. I know it will take more than just getting back on the right track. A lot of bad, bad stuff has to be eradicated or reversed but you can't give up yet. Don't lose hope, man!"

"Nick, you know history as well as anyone. Switching parties in D. C. isn't going to cut it. You've said yourself that the change has to come from us as a people, not Washington."

"I don't disagree with you Inky but don't you think we need a catalyst to get the ball rolling on this revival ... or resurrection as you call it?"

"Nick, that's a good way to put it. We do need a catalyst ... but it won't come from political leaders or even from a grass roots movement. As a people we need to repent … to turn back … to have a true change of heart. The only catalyst that can make such a thing happen is Almighty God by the power of his Holy Spirit. Scripture says that, as individual human beings, we're dead in our trespasses and sins. A dead man can't do anything to help himself. That's what I mean when I say the Republic is dead. We're too far gone to bring it back on our own. Lazarus needed Christ. We need God to quicken us too … to make us alive again."

"I hear you Inky but let me ask, are you pulling for a change in Washington?"

"Sure, I'd love to see any change that might give us some respite and hope. But that alone won't change anything."

"Wow, I thought I was a pessimist! I'm Pollyanna compared to you."

"Nick, I just have a different perspective. I'm not looking for Romney or anyone else to be our bread king. It will take more than lower unemployment, cutting into the deficit and balancing the budget to pull us out of our tail spin. We need to somehow get people to look through spiritual lenses. If people would seek the Bread of

Life instead of just loaves and fishes for their bellies, then we'd have new life."

"It sounds to me like you've been eating too much pie in the sky pal."

"No Nick, I'm the real realist here. What do you think made our country so exceptional? We didn't do it on our own. It was the providence of God that made us great. Our God-given faith in Jesus Christ is what brought us power, prosperity and all the blessings we've enjoyed. The resurrection I'm talking about is simply that … we need to put our faith and trust back in God and listen to his word in the Holy Bible."

Nick was not one to back down easily or shy away from a good debate but I think I wore him into submission, at least temporarily. Perhaps he just realized we needed to move forward on preparing for the show. "I understand your point, you stubborn, crazy son of a gun. That doesn't mean I completely agree but I get you." He smiled to let me know there were no hard feelings. "Here's something we can agree on for sure. Between JD's doomsday diary and your doomsday novel, this is going to be one heck of a show. Now, where's the outline for the rest of American Phoenix? Maybe I'll warm up to your thesis more after I've had a chance to see what kind of solutions you have in mind."

I snapped to attention and offered an exaggerated salute, "Yes sir, general … coming right up!"

JD jumped in, "I'm dying to know, Nick. Why'd you choose to broadcast live on location from, of all places, Mt. Rushmore?"

"Hey, call me sentimental. You know how I feel about the Founding Fathers. For something this big, the New York studio didn't seem right. I thought about the Mall in D. C. on the steps of the Lincoln Memorial, in front of the Jefferson Memorial or maybe in the shadow of the Washington Monument. But I just couldn't bring myself to feature *sin city*, ground zero for everything that ails this country right now. Plus, with the current Administration in power, do you think they'd let me put on my biggest program ever right under their noses? This is incredibly expensive and no piece of cake when it comes to red tape but you'll see. When we get set up, with Washington, Jefferson, Roosevelt and Lincoln as our backdrop, spanning the horizon like patriotic thunderclouds … well, nothing could be more fitting to spark the kind of revival we need. Oh, sorry Inky, I mean resurrection."

We were in a good place … literally and figuratively. There was a ton of work to do over the next couple of days but it would be a labor of love. My blood was pumping at the thought of what lay ahead. Nick told us that tomorrow morning they would begin the media blitz to publicize the return of the Last Prophet. It was about to get insane but it was a good crazy. The excitement was tangible. I could almost taste it. We didn't need coffee. Adrenaline alone would carry us through the monumental tasks that lay ahead (sorry, yes, pun intended). With the glad tidings and electrically charged atmosphere we were oblivious to anything close to danger. We had no idea of the deal that Jude had been forced to make with the devil. Even Mit's concern over Kit going incommunicado subsided amidst the hubbub. It would have been another matter altogether if we'd known that Kit was hostage to James, one of the NSA's plants in Ops' old organization, and much, much closer than we could have guessed.

CHAPTER 9

Life and Death

"Then certain of the scribes and of the Pharisees answered, saying, Master, we would see a sign from thee. But he answered and said unto them, An evil and adulterous generation seeketh after a sign; and there shall no sign be given to it, but the sign of the prophet Jonas:"(Jesus Christ speaking to the Jewish religious leaders, approximately A. D 33 as recorded in the Holy Bible, the Book of Matthew 12:38-39).

The next morning, I turned in my *homework assignment* to Nick. It was an outline of **Part II of American Phoenix: Raising Lazarus ... Ten Steps to Resurrection**. The headings for chapters eight through seventeen along with some crib notes were enough to bring Nick up to speed and generate some fast and furious dialogue aimed at preparing him for the interview. He was in full-speed-ahead mode and necessarily much more serious than the day before when we were able to exchange some lighthearted banter along the way. Here's the synopsis I provided.

> *Chapter 8: De-Wussification ... With the exception of our military, America has become the land of wimps thanks to political correctness, historical revisionism and progressivism. We need to regain our pride, identity and belief in the exceptionalism of America. Americans need to recapture our bold spirit and sense of adventure. Instead of apologizing for all of our supposed ills, we need to recognize the essential value of American leadership and the hope we offer to others in the world according to the providence of God.*

America needs to wave its banner ... we're not the villains ... we're the good guys. Say it loud, we're America and we're proud! Glory to God on high!

Chapter 9: Cleaning Up Education *... Education has become an ideological tool of the Left. Teachers need to be professional educators and not bleating union sheep. We need to wrest power from the Feds and reel education in, back to where it belongs as a local matter where parents have the greatest influence, not partisans in DC. The three R's should come back front-and-center in place of gobbledygook about diversity and such. American history should be featured as a cornerstone before exploring other cultures. Ours should be the standard by which others are judged. Civics is a must ... learning about and gaining an appreciation for our system of government and the Constitution is essential. Finally, and most importantly, God must be brought back into the schools. The faith of the Founding Fathers should be discussed openly and the basis for our justice system cannot be glossed over or ignored.*

Chapter 10: Restoring State's Rights *... This one is simple. It's all about shrinking the size of our bloated government and getting power back into the hands of the people. The best way to reduce the cost of government and make our representatives more accountable to us is to bring government back closer to the people; where we live. If you want to cut back on wasteful spending, let the states control the purse strings more. People are much more apt to spend their own money wisely versus someone else's tax dollars. In America, one size does not fit all. We need to give more discretion to the governed. This goes for education, abortion, school prayer and a host of other important issues. We need to get back to government of, by and for the people.*

Chapter 11: Restoring Free Speech *... Political correctness has got to go, especially the most pernicious aspect; that is, limiting thought, speech and the free exchange of ideas. People are too easily offended. We need to man up and stop being so sensitive. If you don't like what someone is saying you can offer a different viewpoint or ignore then, not silence them. We need to be able to say whatever we want, wherever we want, whenever we want and to* *whomever we want ... period, no exceptions. Of course, we should try to do so in a civil, respectful manner and avoid doing anything that would put people in danger such as yelling fire in a crowded theater. But such behavior should be self-disciplined only and not subject to government restriction. The notion of hate crimes and hate speech needs to be eradicated. These are just excuses for curbing free speech. Most importantly, there should be no restriction whatsoever against God's word, the Holy Bible, having free course throughout the land in public or private. And we should have no qualms in speaking the truth to foreign fanatics who want to put limits on our freedoms of religion and speech, or worse.*

Chapter 12: Restoring the Family *... This is the fundamental institution upon which civilization and our country is built. It is the essential building block, instituted by God, upon which everything else stands. If you take it away, all else will crumble. No empire, republic or society has ever been able to survive without it. God created the family and he alone can define it. The family is meant to consist of one man and one woman, husband and wife, and their children. It extends from there to grandparents,* aunts, uncles, nieces, nephews, cousins, etc. We need to stop tearing down the traditional family and doing things aimed at redefining and perverting the family. The most important family of all is the family of God; all of us living under our Creator's grace and mercy. All of our blessings and rights are God-given.

Chapter 13: Restoring Our Culture ... Ours is a Judeo-Christian culture rooted in the inspired word of God in the Old and New Testaments. We are a nation of immigrants but still one nation under God. We are tolerant of different beliefs and accepting of all races, creeds and religions. But this does not mean we should sacrifice our culture for the sake of the false notion of diversity. We applaud and honor our different backgrounds and enjoy the blessings of many roots but should not divide ourselves. English is our national language. We need to reunite as Americans and embrace and trumpet the things we share in common. We cannot live by the Constitution and Sharia Law or international law. It is impossible to say in God we trust while denying the existence of God. America exists by the providence of God and we are all guided by his purpose and blessed to live under our Constitution. We believe in free *market capitalism. We are the land of opportunity and believe in the American Dream. We should celebrate who we are and thank God for the blessings he has bestowed upon us and the rest of the world through America.*

Chapter 14: Restoring the Rule of Law ... *Republics cannot exist where rights are deemed to be privileges granted at the whims of men, whether despots or democratic governments. Executive fiats and judicial activism are symptoms of a much deeper, more dangerous problem. Left to the will of man, the law will always be elusive and a threat to freedom. The elites in power always think they know what is best for the rest of us and inevitably force their view of utopia upon us no matter how hellish it turns out to be. The most important precept is the knowledge that we have a Creator who has endowed us with certain inalienable rights not the least of which are life, liberty and the pursuit of happiness. We need to embrace this principle again and look to the Constitution rather than the fleeting fancy of men.*

Chapter 15: Separating Business and State Rather than Church and State ... *Read the Constitution you jack-wagons! It's freedom of*

*religion not freedom from religion! How is it
that the wishes of an entire community can be
trumped by the evil, misguided desires of one
atheist? Is that what you call democracy? The
so called separation of church and state is the
biggest, most dangerous lie ever perpetuated in
the history of these United States (okay, maybe
global warming and enviromania is a close
second). Thomas Jefferson advised the Danbury
Baptists that they need not be concerned
because the government wouldn't pick and
choose between Christian denominations and
effectively set up an official religion of the
United States akin to Henry VIII establishing the
Anglican Church for his own libertine purposes.
There was never any intention on Jefferson's
part or any of the other Founding Fathers or
their successors for almost two hundred years
thereafter to dredge our Godly heritage from
the national landscape. This was a relatively
recent revelation driven by Secular Progressives
intent upon fundamentally transforming
America. We need to put an end to this foolish,
dangerous notion and focus on separation of
another sort. That is, we should echo the
Founding Fathers in re-establishing a cherished,
long-held principle. That is, the separation of*

business and state. The state exists to serve the common good in a very limited capacity so that life and commerce can thrive freely. That's what makes America the land of opportunity. Government controlling the means of commerce is a formula for sure disaster that will concentrate power in the hands of a few. We need to honor the free enterprise system once again and let the market, made up of all the people, determine our wants and needs without the stifling, misguided influence of the government or any group of elites.

Chapter 16: Restoring Morality *... Our culture has become very course. This ties in closely to education and the family. It takes parents to raise a child, not a village or the government. The diminished influence of parents has left our children to fend for themselves in a moral wasteland. They've been educated in school and by the media to believe there is no God; that we've evolved by chance and are no different than the animals. It's no wonder that the murder rate is so high and abortion is considered a choice. Without God to provide our moral compass, we and any other society are doomed to remain adrift in a river of depravity until we plummet helplessly over the* falls. We need to recognize our Creator and hear his voice. We're made in the image of our Creator and endowed with immortal souls. We need the golden rule instead of mob rule. The Ten Commandments should be revered, not reviled. We should delight in God's commands.

Chapter 17: Humbling Ourselves before God ... We need to recognize where we would be without God. We owe everything to him. Our nation would have been snuffed out or withered and died long ago without his protection and loving care. Every day should be a day of national thanksgiving and prayer. Instead we have turned our backs on God. We've despised his word and driven it from the public square. We've passed laws in direct disobedience to God's commands. We should drop to our knees and thank God for his mercy and divine patience with us. America needs to beg God's forgiveness and rededicate ourselves to his word and will in our government and every aspect of our life. No, I'm not talking about a theocracy or any such thing. It's our attitude. We should be humble, thankful and ever mindful of God's providence.

To sum up: Blessed is the nation whose God is the LORD; and the people whom he hath chosen for his own inheritance (Psalm 33:12).

The whirlwind spun ever faster and, before we knew it, it was show time. Nick wanted to start by grabbing everyone's attention. He planned to take us back to the miracle of the Last Prophet's resurrection with footage of JD's death in the fall from that tall building during the terrorist attacks on St. Louis. Then, without compromising our security, he wanted to fast forward to the present with a brief stop along the way to reveal how JD had been shielded from the terrorists' suicide bomb before going into hiding for the past several years. Nick knew how to work the audience, create frenzied interest and tantalize them with the revelations of the Last Prophet's doomsday diary. Then he'd need to deftly segue into America's doomsday by introducing me and dissecting American Phoenix in fifteen minutes or less before shifting gears back to JD's message from God regarding the coming judgment. I was keyed up and trying to fight the butterflies but JD was, as usual, cool as a cucumber. He tried to calm and encourage me by expressing his trust in Nick Phace's unique, Svengali-like ability to manage an audience. I had to agree that if anyone could pull it off, it would be Nick. If I was lacking any confidence, Nick took care of that when he asked if I'd like to have his company publish and distribute the hard copies of American Phoenix. Of course I was thrilled by such an unexpected windfall and vote of confidence and managed to sputter my thankful consent.

The production crew had done a fantastic job with the setting. The stage was elevated enough to provide a clear view to the audience from any of the more than two thousand stadium-style seats that had been erected in a semi-circle stretching from one side to the other. Everything from our simple stools to the microphones and camera wells were bare bones; muted to accentuate the magnificent backdrop of Mt. Rushmore looming behind the stage almost six thousand feet in glorious elevation. The gleaming presidents were framed in perfect, blue skies interrupted only by a few wisps of clouds that lent a heavenly ambiance to the proceedings. Great expense had gone into mechanizing the jumbotrons on either side of the stage so they could be lowered out of sight when not in use.

Every seat was filled; some by lucky locals and others by people who had traveled long distances to be part of the spectacle. There were run of the mill folks commingled with celebrities and dignitaries. Careful screening had been conducted to keep out undesirables who might have posed a security threat. To maintain the proper mood and atmosphere, security was unobtrusive as possible but there were metal detectors at the entrances and plain clothes personnel sprinkled about the premises, visible to only the most discerning eyes. Al Batin's men were in the crowd too with carefully forged identities and Americanized facades. There were no cues hinting at fanaticism or martyrdom … they melted into the audience even better than the security staff. They were also unarmed. Their automatic weapons had been planted days before in broad daylight amongst the ductwork in the rafters above the welcome center restrooms. This was accomplished with the help of Brutus' boys, James and Martin, posing as part of the team tasked with securing the site. There's nothing like a little cooperation between government agencies, is there? So what if it was a rogue branch of the NSA supposedly helping out the National Park Service with security?

There was a constant buzz of anticipation as the crowd readied for the top of the hour to approach. A loud roar erupted when Nick Phace finally took the stage. Then a reverent hush fell over the place as if we were in a large, open-air cathedral at the beginning of a church service as the jumbotrons were raised into place. Nick took everyone back in time to the second 9/11 in St. Louis and the silence was shattered by a collective gasp as the video made the crowd relive the horrible sight of his terrorist captor and JD plummeting from the rooftop all the way down to the unyielding ground below in a stunningly abrupt and devastating scene of death. The audience members were frozen stiff as the video shifted to a picture of JD's apartment building, demolished by the massive blast with plumes of smoke rising to the heavens. It ended by panning JD's tombstone in the cemetery where his shattered remains were purportedly laid to rest. With everyone's eyes riveted on the gripping scenes splashed across the screens, no one noticed that JD had taken the stage until the jumbotrons were lowered. Nick brought the crowd to its feet by announcing that JD Uticus, the Last Prophet, was back from the dead once again.

"Welcome back, my friend. It's so good to see you again. Please, tell the audience how you survived the bomb blast at your apartment ... that horrific scene we just saw up on the screen moments ago."

"Thanks so much Nick. It's great to be back." There was a brief pause and apologetic grin. "I'm sorry Nick but I have to correct you on one thing. I'm not back from the dead for a second time. Yes, I was in the apartment and should have been killed when that bomb went off but I survived unharmed. I was shielded from the blast by something like an invisible force field. It was God's work."

Nick sensed the audience's underlying skepticism and jumped in, "Forgive me for saying but, if you were in our shoes, would you believe such a story? I mean, there were no witnesses this time. Perhaps you were knocked silly and imagined God helping you out of this fix. Is it possible that you were shielded by something else like a bathtub or piece of heavy furniture?" There was a smattering of applause to indicate the audience was happy to see Nick challenge JD.

"I can understand how people would have difficulty believing me. However, I can only tell you the plain truth. I was fully conscious throughout the ordeal and within arm's length of my attackers when the bomb detonated. It was God who shielded me."

Nick's warped sense of humor and showmanship kicked in. "JD, we saw it happen once with our own eyes. There was little doubt then that God had something special in mind for you. But unfortunately, no one saw the second miracle other than you. You're from the Show-Me State of Missouri so surely you can understand that to see is to believe, right? Maybe you can ask God to do something right now to convince the doubters. What do you think, JD?"

JD didn't think this was the time for levity. "How many miracles did Christ perform in front of all those witnesses including the scribes and Pharisees? He healed the sick, blind, deaf, dumb, drove out demons and even raised people from the dead. Yet they demanded more signs. Do you remember the story of the rich man who died and went to hell and saw his servant, a beggar named Lazarus, in heaven afar off in Abraham's bosom? He asked that Lazarus be sent to his five brothers so they might be persuaded to have faith in God and avoid eternal damnation like him. Do you remember Abraham's reply as recorded in Luke 16? 'And he said unto him, if they hear not Moses and the prophets, neither will they be persuaded, though one rose from the dead.' I'm not here to convince people through parlor tricks or miracles. I have one purpose and that's to share the word of God in truth and love."

Nick took his cue from JD's gentle admonishment and struck a serious tone of his own. "We hear you JD ... we'll just have to take you at your word."

"With that in mind, I'm sorry but I have to correct you again. You said there were no witnesses. That's not completely accurate. My friend Inky Hermann saw the whole thing."

Nick seized upon this tidbit to make the perfect transition, "You know, that's right. I forgot about Inky." Showman Nick went back into chucklehead mode, "Folks, we're going to break but then when we come back I'm going to bring out none other than JD's friend, Inky, Horace Hermann, and we can ask him about the miracle man, the cat with seven lives left." JD raised his arms with palms upward and another sheepish grin on his face. "C'mon JD, what now ... what did I say?"

"Sorry Nick but it's actually the cat with six lives left. I haven't told you this but God saved me a third time while I was in hiding." JD could see that Nick was nonplussed. "It's not important. Sorry for the interruption."

Nick didn't like being caught off guard but you'd never know it. He went to the break with more comedy and affected his best Ronald Reagan impersonation, "Well JD, there you go again."

After the break, Nick did his best to be a gracious host by greeting me warmly with both his hands on my one in an effort to calm my nerves. As he turned to the audience and the cameras, he kept one hand gently on my shoulder, "Folks, it's my pleasure to introduce JD's close friend and confidante, Horace "Inky" Hermann." There was a polite round of applause. "Mr. Hermann is here to provide an insider's view of the Last Prophet and tell us about a new book." We took our places on our stools and Nick waded in. "So Inky, tell us about that day back at JD's apartment when the suicide bombers attacked."

My voice was a little shaky at first, "Thanks so much for making me a part of this show."

Nick did his best to help me steady the shakes with some Rickles-like sarcasm. "That's quite alright Inky. Now don't let me down ... speak boy speak!" The audience laughed and Nick kept firing away, "And what kind of name is Inky anyway? Is your mother some kind of weirdo?" More laughter erupted and I readied myself to explain where I got the nickname. Nick didn't want to get off the subject, "Never mind INKY ... nobody cares ... now speak boy speak."

Nick's stunt worked like a charm. I forgot about my butterflies and tried a little comedy of my own. I played dumb while mugging for the camera, "Sure thing Nick ... uh, what did you want to know?" This got a few laughs which really put me at ease.

"Hey funny boy, leave the jokes to me. The apartment ... the apartment ... tell us about the bomb, INKY!"

I laughed to give Nick his due before turning serious. "Yes, I was there that day. I was in the parking lot in my car waiting for JD to get some things out of his apartment when the blast occurred. It was like a volcano erupted. The concussion shook my car and the roof was pelted with debris like I was in a huge hailstorm. When I looked up and saw the devastation it caused, I just knew JD must have been dead. When I got up there to the third floor in the midst of the smoking ruins and saw JD without a scratch, I thought I was seeing a ghost."

"What did he say?"

"He was in shock like me. I asked him how he survived and he told me the same thing; that God had placed some kind of invisible force field around him."

"Did you believe him or did you think he was out of his mind?"

"Trust me on this, Nick. After hearing the blast and seeing the destruction and the charred, mangled bodies of the bombers, there was no doubt in my mind that I'd witnessed another miracle."

Nick knew better than to poke into the wrong subject but had to make some kind of transition for the audience's sake. "We don't have time to get into the details but suffice it to say that you helped JD go into hiding to get out of the media's harsh glare. I think everyone can understand why you helped perpetuate the myth of JD's death to remove him from the eye of the storm and allow him to return to a more normal life."

"Yeah, at that point the last thing he wanted was more fame, publicity and celebrity. The Last Prophet had fulfilled his calling from God on your show and just wanted to fade back into anonymity."

"So Inky, JD goes from being perhaps the most recognized figure in the world to living, I guess, almost like a hermit. And you were the only one to have regular contact with him? You guys must be tight, eh?"

"Yeah, going through what we did together will do that to you. Other than my family, there's no one to whom I'm closer. It was tough. We stayed in contact but it was not what I'd call regular. It was the only way to protect his privacy and not compromise his identity or location."

"That's fascinating Inky and I'd like to ask a thousand questions but unfortunately we've got to move on. Everyone's dying to hear about what brought the Last Prophet back into the limelight. But before we do that, I want to touch on what you did to keep busy during JD's long hiatus. When we come back from the break, I want to talk about your new book, American Phoenix." Nick gave me a knuckle bump to show his approval and provide some encouragement for the next segment. The jumbotrons were raised featuring the cover of American Phoenix. It showed a large, star-spangled tombstone surrounded by smoke, fire and rubble and etched with the words: America R. I. P. I should have felt like a rock star but remained self-conscious. My strength didn't wane though. I girded my confidence by reminding myself that it wasn't about me ... it's the message that's important.

Nick resumed, "Welcome back folks. We're just minutes away from talking to the cat with ... uh six ... more lives left, the Last Prophet, JD Uticus. Yes, the miracle man of God is going to share a message about Judgment Day from what he calls his doomsday diary. But before we get to that, I want to talk about another sort of doomsday, call it America's doomsday with the Last Prophet's best friend and author of the soon to be published book, American Phoenix: Resurrecting the Dead Republic. Please welcome once again, Horace "Inky" Hermann." This time the applause was enthusiastic. Nick dropped any pretense at comedy and turned studiously serious. "Inky, in one sentence, please summarize the premise of your book."

"Nick, in a word, our great Republic is not in deep trouble; it's not in need of reform ... it is already dead."

Nick let the grumble work its way through the shocked and confused audience before attacking. "Let me get this straight. You think America is dead? There's no use in trying to dig ourselves out of the hole? Are you saying, let's stick a fork in it?"

"What I'm saying is that our great Republic, as it was founded and on the basis under which it thrived and prospered for so long, is already a thing of the past."

There was another murmur throughout the crowd and Nick rightly sensed they didn't like someone pulling the plug on America this way. It's one thing to critique our faults and problems and offer solutions but not okay to say it's all over and there's nothing we can do to change it. "Inky, everyone knows we have problems, very serious problems. But this isn't the first time. Don't you think it's pretty extreme to say we're beyond help?" Nick scanned the audience as if to say I feel your pain and chided me on their behalf, "Frankly, I think the audience is offended by your premise. Right now, we're looking ahead to the presidential debates and a pivotal election in November where everything's on the line. We think our future is at stake and you're saying we have no future."

My backbone stiffened at the challenge and I was on message and any hint of stage fright evaporated. "I'm here to tell you that if you think we can secure our future by putting our faith in political parties or one candidate over another, you need to wean yourself from the Kool-Aid." My momentum temporarily stalled as a chorus of boos descended but I persevered. "Let's just assume for a moment that we play musical chairs in November and put the GOP back in control of the White House and Senate while hanging onto the House. Do you think things will really change; that we'll avoid the doomsday we're facing?" I answered before Nick could interrupt, "Watch and see what happens. Yeah, there will be some policy changes that will make some folks feel good and tick others off. But within the first one hundred days, it will be time to kiss and make up. Compromise will be the watchword in the halls of government. Out of control spending will slow down for a time but it won't stop. There will be a few Band-Aids applied to our sacrosanct entitlement programs but the bleeding will continue. As both sides of the aisle hold their noses and choke down the fetid compromise banquet for public viewing, the partisan positioning and backstabbing will continue. Under the thinly crusted, smooth surface, the fissures of division will grow and widen. Even the mounting unrest in the Middle East will not draw us together."

Nick finally had to stop the freight train I was on. He looked to the audience for support. "Whoa, whoa, whoa ... and you guys thought I was pessimistic! Inky, this is one heck of a bleak picture you're painting." Nick's indignant tone channeled the audience's sentiment and they cheered him on. "Okay, so, according to you, we're headed down the crapper and this election is meaningless. Then what's next?"

I tried to keep the audience at bay by adopting a reasoned, measured tone. "Granted, this election could provide us with a temporary respite. And to the naked eye, things don't look so bad right now. I mean, yeah, unemployment is through the roof and our national debt is scary any way you slice it but, all-in-all, Americans don't have it so bad. For all intents and purposes we still look pretty strong and prosperous." I let this soak in for a moment. "But you've got to dig deeper and look inside. Our biggest problem is not political, social or economic. We have a spiritual problem. Look at our churches. Look at the way we've turned our backs on God and banned his word in the halls of government and the public square. That's our real problem. American has lost its soul."

This didn't bring boos. It was a thought-provokingly sober message that left the audience somber. This was just what Nick wanted. He didn't want to push my premise on them. He wanted the crowd to come to their own conclusion. It was almost Last Prophet time and we had to wrap up. "Judging from the silence, it seems you've struck a chord. Maybe we do have a spiritual problem in this country. I guess I've been harping on this for more than a year now. But I'm not ready to write us off." There was a long, thoughtful pause and Nick stared up toward Washington, Jefferson, Roosevelt and Lincoln as if seeking affirmation. "And do you know what folks? I don't think Inky is ready to write us off either. I've got the advantage of having seen an advanced draft of American Phoenix. Inky I call it a revival and you call it a resurrection … but you still see hope for America, don't you?"

I could almost feel the tension in the audience ease. "Absolutely, there's hope for America. We just have to look in the right place for the solution."

Nick was back in selling mode. "Your book is full of solutions … a spiritual makeover … but that's for another day." He offered a goofy smile to let everyone in TV land know he was making an unapologetic sales pitch. "If you want to learn how we can get out of our spiritual fix, you'll just have to buy the book. You can go to trumpet.com for an e-copy or, better yet, in a few weeks you can order the hard copy through my website. Of course, I'd prefer the latter so poor, little, old me can get my cut." Then he turned serious once more, "Don't get me wrong. This book isn't all peaches and cream. There are lots of solutions but there's also a grave warning. If we don't wake up, there's an American apocalypse on the way. According to Mr. Hermann we will be facing an economic meltdown, complete anarchy and totalitarianism in America in less than twenty years. Again, you'll have to read the book to get the full story. Speaking of the apocalypse, coming up next the Last Prophet will be here to tell us about the real doomsday, the final judgment. Stay tuned folks."

With JD making his way to join me and Nick on stage, we were unaware that Mit was about to be drawn away from his backstage perch by an unexpected visit from Martin about Kit's whereabouts. Unbeknownst to any of us, she was just a couple of miles away in a rented cabin with her captors. Kit was at the end of her rope. Being transported almost halfway across the country in the back of a van and held against your will for days will do that to you. The loss of her freedom and constant threat of death had taken its toll and she was close to a nervous breakdown. "Who are you people and what do you want with me?"

Her shrill outburst was met with cool indifference and cruel humor. "Hey now little lady, that's kind of impersonal don't you think? With all the time we've spent together we should be on a first name basis. You can call me James as in James Mason."

Martin smirked and was equally smug, "And you can call me Martin Landau. Oh, sorry, you're probably too young to get the connection."

Kit was no longer timid and seethed, "Yeah, I get the joke … Alfred Hitchcock and North by Northwest. I know; you're the bad guys."

"Very good Kit; you catch on real quick." James' heavy lidded eyes squinted in a menacing way. "That's enough fun and games. I'm glad you asked the question because there's something we need. The information we received from your pal Jude isn't going to be much help to us without the encryption key."

Kit was sincere in her panic, "I don't know anything about an encryption key!"

"I know that. Don't worry Hon; we know where to get the key. We just need a little help from you. We need your boyfriend. He's the only one who can break the code for us. All you have to do is get him here."

"I won't do it! Just leave Mit out of this!"

James smiled confidently, "Oh, you'll help us. It's your only chance ... and Mit's." Kit tried to look away defiantly but James grabbed her wrist and squeezed it so hard she thought her bones might be reduced to dust. Grudgingly she returned his gaze which was a frightening no-nonsense look. "Here's exactly what you're going to do, down to a T. In a minute, Martin is going to go to Mt. Rushmore and tell Mit you're being held hostage. He's going to enlist Mit to help him come to your rescue. When they arrive here to save you, I'm going to hold a gun to your head to fend them off and demand that Mit give me the encryption key code in exchange for your release. You better play along like a good girl. If you try to pull any funny business, I'll put a bullet in Mit's head." Kit lowered her head and began to sob. James put her wrist in his vice grip again until she raised her head and collected herself. "Do you understand me?"

Kit meekly sniffed, "Yes."

Martin played the role superbly. Mit didn't know Martin from Adam but was aware that I had made the arrangements for members of Ops' old crew to provide security so he wasn't surprised that part of the surveillance team had followed us out West. "Mit, my name is Martin Landau and I've been assigned to your security detail. I've been tailing you for the past week. Please pay attention carefully because we don't have much time." Mit was dumbfounded but followed his instructions. As a trivia buff, Mit was well aware of the irony in having a guardian angel named Martin Landau here in the shadow of Mt. Rushmore but didn't pay it any heed under the dire circumstances. He listened as Martin delivered the shocking news in hushed tones, "It's about your girlfriend Kit." Mit gasped reflexively and concentrated on Martin all the more. "She's been taken hostage and is being held in a nearby cabin." Mit nearly fainted and Martin grabbed him by the shoulders to steady him. "Pull it together man! I need your help." Mit was still wide eyed like a startled child but nodded compliantly. "I don't have any back-up in the area and don't have time to call anyone in. Can you come with me and help in setting up a diversion?" Mit nodded numbly again. "Okay Mit, that's good … everything is going to be okay."

On the short drive over to the wooded cabin, Martin outlined the simple plan that would allow him to gain access through the back of the cabin while Mit drew their attention to the front door. Of course it worked perfectly and Kit played her part in the ruse obediently. Mit was overjoyed to see Kit until James raised the gun to her head and gained a stalemate with Martin. None of it made sense to Mit until James demanded the code. Then logic kicked in. Ah yes, James was apparently in league with Cagliostro and somehow gained access to the Marchetti files but was foiled by his encrypted defense. It all made sense now. In a weird way, Mit was most relieved to know there was a good reason for Kit failing to make her daily phone calls to him. But he was drawn back to the task at hand. He knew he'd be inviting grave danger by giving up the code but had no choice given Kit's situation. The logical thing to do was avoid the immediate threat and buy time. He could always figure out another counter-measure to secure their longer-term future. As soon as Mit gave up the code, James and Martin completed the charade with the latter being forced to drop his weapon while James made his escape. In reality, Mr. Mason was hurrying to a point above Mt. Rushmore where he would deploy his skills as a sniper. Martin retrieved his gun and urgently asked Mit if he'd given the actual code to James. Mit replied in the affirmative in a manner as if to say he was incapable of lying, even under such trying circumstances.

Martin was happy that Mit confirmed the authenticity of the code. The only thing left to do was to terminate Mit and Kit before heading to join his comrades at the site of the show to finish the job they'd started. Kit sensed the danger but played along helplessly. Martin didn't like to leave any loose ends or leave anything to chance. He wanted further confirmation that they had full access to the data. "Mit, you did a great job. That creep got away but that's okay. The important thing is that you and Kit are safe now. We'll deal with him later. I just wish there was a way we could keep the data from being compromised." Martin hesitated as if deep in thought as he stared at the laptop James had left behind. "Wait a minute! Mit, can you log in and get access to the data?"

"Sure, as long as the file hasn't been wiped clean."

"I'm sure our traitorous *pal* James won't have access to a computer for a while so we should be good, right?"

"Yeah, that's true, unless he's called ahead to someone else and passed the encryption key along."

"I doubt he'd be that savvy. I imagine he's totally focused on his getaway. In any case, let's give it a try. If you can get in, we can download everything onto a disc before it's gone forever."

Mit went through the motions and Martin paid close attention as he keyed in the code to make sure it was the same one he'd given to James. "Viola, we're in!" Mit popped in a disc and hit copy to file. With that done, he turned his attention to Kit. Martin was positioned between them and was about to reach for his gun to finish the job as soon as they were conveniently side-by-side.

As Mit approached, Kit suddenly and unexpectedly stopped him in his tracks with an urgent request, "Mit, can you please get me a cup of coffee. I need a pick-me-up." Kit never drank coffee and had a bad aversion to anything with caffeine. Mit knew this but didn't let on.

He stared at her briefly while replying, "Sure sweetie, I'd be happy to pour you a cup." In just a few seconds during what appeared to Martin as a longing gaze between the two love-nerds, Kit blinked out a warning. Yeah, call it the revenge of the nerds but, believe it or not, in the few months they'd known each other the two brainiacs had worked out a secret code. I guess it wasn't really secret in that it was simple Morse code but leave it to Kit and Mit ... they were both fluent and communicated the code in Russian, just in case Martin suspected something. With Mit duly on alert, they had a fighting chance but were facing insurmountable odds with Martin having a gun. Kit needed a diversion. She did the only thing she could do, no matter how out of character it was.

After Mit handed her the coffee, he knew to put some distance between himself and Kit. He strategically ambled to a spot where Martin would be hard pressed to keep his eye on both of them at the same time without pivoting left and right. As soon as Mit was far enough away, klutzy Kit spilled the entire cup of coffee down the front of her sweater. Martin almost felt sorry for her in her drab, nerdilicious outfit, mousey hair that hadn't been fixed in days, bland, next-to-nothing make-up and now a huge, unsightly, dripping coffee stain to top it off.

Kit wasn't ugly. She just had a way of putting her worst foot forward. And her loose, awkward fitting clothes did nothing to enhance her image, especially when drenched in hot, brown liquid. Then there was an amazing metamorphosis that would have put the brightest butterfly to shame. Kit slowly raised her long arms up and behind her head and grabbed the gaudy, bulky sweater and began to pull it off with the slinky, sexy skill of a seasoned burlesque queen. Martin's eyes were riveted by what she revealed. Underneath the granny garb was a delicately sheer, deliciously form-fitting bra spilling over with milky white cleavage and her tight, toned abs were bordered by a waspish waist that cascaded to perfectly curved hips. Her silky smooth, taut tummy was punctuated by the cutest innie he'd ever seen. The funny thing was Mit had never seen this either and was equally captivated. He and Kit had this thing about remaining chaste. Luckily, his Vulcan logic allowed Mit to tear his eyes away for long enough to quietly reach for a heavy brass lampstand. Martin sensed something and was about to turn toward Mit and catch him in the act when Kit channeled Marilyn Monroe and said, "Oh my, would you look at that. The coffee has dripped all over my pants too."

She might as well have started singing happy birthday, Mr. President because it couldn't have been more eye catching as she reached down and began to unbutton her ghastly corduroys to reveal a glimpse of the tantalizing silk and lace panties underneath. It gave Mit just enough time to swing his willowy arm in a long arc that ended with a loud thud as the lamp crashed into Martin's temple. Kit frantically fumbled to button her trousers and grabbed her sweater as Mit pulled her toward the door. He stopped and had the presence of mind to nab the disc they'd made. Martin was only able to groan and clutch his head as they made their way out the door. They stopped at Martin's car and discovered there were no keys. Mit decided not to risk going back inside to retrieve them from Martin's pocket and headed into the woods in the general direction of the welcome center at Mt. Rushmore.

As this drama unfolded, Nick was launching into the meat of the matter with JD in his manic way … at one moment winsome and witty and spooky scary the next. Funny Nick shook his head and laughed, "It's really good to see you man. We all thought you were dead and gone. But here you are, like a bad penny."

JD tried to be funny and serious at the same time, "Don't blame me; blame God."

"Yeah, what is it with you and God? First he brings you back to life to spread his message about the end of the world then just lets you pull a Rip Van Winkle on us. Now here you are back in the spotlight with yours truly again. What gives JD?"

"I guess he's not done with me yet. He wants me to spread his message again." JD got that look on his face again and Nick picked up on the signal immediately.

"Oh no, here comes another correction right? Let me guess. You're still touchy about being called the Last Prophet. Let me see. What's your canned response? Oh yeah … you're not a prophet in the traditional or biblical sense … and certainly not the last one. You're only a prophet in the sense that you're sharing God's enduring, inspired message from the Scriptures that have been available to all mankind. Did I say that right?"

JD flashed the biggest smile, "I couldn't have said it better … thanks."

Nick was anxious to move on. "I'm dying to know what you've been up to for so long, especially since you hit us with that teaser about God saving your life a third time, but we just don't have the time. No, time's too short if we're going to get your message out today. So, speaking of the message, what's new? Is it any different than what you shared before? Do you have something new in store regarding the Anti-Christ?"

I noticed the slightest hint of panic in JD's eyes which he quickly subdued. I could imagine Cagliostro and Benedetto inching closer to their screens to hear what JD would say next. "No Nick, I'm not here to talk about the Anti-Christ, Armageddon or even the signs leading up to the end. For some reason, God wants me to focus on the last day, the final judgment."

The crowd murmured as Nick reacted soberly, "That's so very interesting JD … and scary as hell." Nick didn't dare mug at what was definitely an unintended pun. "Why do you think that God wants you to warn people about Judgment Day? Is it drawing near? Are we that close?"

You could hear a pin drop. "Nick, you should know by now that I'm not here to predict when the end will come. Scripture clearly teaches that no man will know the hour or time. It will come unexpectedly like a thief in the night." Nick nodded his consent. "That's why God tells us to remain ever vigilant and always be prepared for Christ's return."

"Yes I remember and I'm sure many in the viewing audience remember our first broadcast when you said the signs of the end have been present from the beginning to keep each generation focused on, as you put it, our Redemption which draws nigh." JD smiled and was pleased to see that at least part of his original message had sunk in. "But still there has to be a reason why God has brought you back to this topic … to doomsday."

"I've thought about this a lot, Nick. I can't say for sure but last time God wanted me to talk about things leading up to the end. By using me to help everyone look through spiritual lenses at our world in the light of the Tribulation before the end, it hopefully drew people back to the Bible and God's message of warning and hope. Now I think he wants to draw a clear line between the end times and the final judgment day. He doesn't want us to be confused about tribulation versus judgment. Our world is already in the midst of the Tribulation which you'll recall is spiritual warfare. Our world, including our churches, is steeped in false doctrine. God wants to draw distinctions between the Tribulation, including even the Little Season of Satan before the end, versus that one last day … Judgment Day. There are so many false teachings about Judgment Day. From the so called Rapture and millennialism to the JWs and Mormons, Dispensationalists and Praeterists, the churches are rife with the false hope of a second chance. This is compounded by outright denials from nihilists and atheists. God wants us to tear ourselves away from the myth of purgatory and other such lies built on the damnable doctrine of works righteousness in all its forms and see the finality of the last day. As God says in II Corinthians 6:2 'behold, now is the accepted time; behold, now is the day of salvation.'"

Nick felt the sobering reality and twinge of fear that gripped the audience. "Again JD, it not only sounds final but oh so near. God must be doing this for a reason, right now at this point in history."

JD was able to avoid the exasperation I felt. "Judgment Day could come tomorrow or perhaps a thousand years from now or more. God wants us to be prepared. Now is the day of salvation. Now is the time to accept Jesus Christ as Lord and Savior. With Christ, Judgment Day is nothing to fear but is instead a day all believers look forward to with joyful anticipation."

Nick needed to grant the audience a bit of relief from the suffocating seriousness of the moment. "Hey, are you telling me that you're looking forward to doomsday? Are you really going to try to sell me that bill of goods with a straight face?"

JD surprised Nick and everyone else. "In a temporal sense no ... I'm scared to death. Who wouldn't be? That's why people put it out of their minds or try to pretend it's just a fairy tale. But when you understand what the final judgment entails in a spiritual sense, it makes all the difference in the world. That's what I'm here to share. God's given me a fresh vision of Judgment Day. It will bring terror to some and triumph and everlasting joy to others. The good news is that, thanks to Jesus Christ, no one needs to fear Judgment Day if they have faith in the Savior."

Nick seized the moment and had JD explain how the visions came and the way JD captured them in his doomsday diary. He brought the audience's rabid interest to a climax. "Okay JD, let's get down to it. After the break, please use the time left in our last segment to outline the new vision that God has given you." Nick saw JD's frown and immediately corrected himself, "Sorry JD, I didn't mean to say <u>new</u> vision. Let's say God has shared version 2.0 of his original Revelation … kind of a fresh translation for the current generation of mankind." JD smiled and nodded as we headed into the break.

No one noticed as Al Batin's assassins made their way to the restroom to retrieve their weapons. Not a soul caught the glint of James' rifle scope from high above. Nobody paid attention as Martin returned and headed to the restroom to meet his collaborators and collect his own AK-47 from the rafters. Everyone was in the grip of Ringmaster Nick Phace as he readied them for the big finale. "Pay close attention everyone because from God's mouth to JD's lips to your ears, you're about to hear something for the first time. The Last Prophet is going to share the vision of Judgment Day that he's captured from on high in his doomsday diary." The entire viewing world was riveted because JD was authentic. Many questioned his latest miracle but no one doubted his original resurrection. It was as if Moses had come down from the mount again or was appearing transfigured alongside Elijah and the glorified Christ. At that precise point in time, JD was as close as anyone would ever come to a prophet of the Lord with the word of God on his lips. I shared the excitement of the moment but it was tempered with frustration. I thought, *if only they knew God's word of truth was right there at their fingertips ... if only they'd open their Bibles!*

Cagliostro knew he was taking a risk but a well calculated one. It was worth it to have every thorn in his flesh, gathered here in one spot, be extracted for good. He didn't worry about the horrible spectacle being played out in front of a worldwide television audience. It would be labeled another mindless terrorist attack and Al Batin would be more than happy to take the credit. Cagliostro didn't even care that JD's message would be communicated to Nick's audience before his death. He knew that once he was gone, it would fade from public consciousness in no time. He was confident the masses were fickle and would soon latch onto the next big thing in the twenty-four hour news cycle. The only loose ends would be Jude, Hugo and Adeline. They would meet a different, quieter fate. No eyebrows would be raised and they would vanish without a trace in total obscurity. Of course, Benedetto had an understanding with Brutus that James and Martin were expendable. They'd have to take a big one for the team ... no loose ends could be permitted. It was all very tidy in Cagliostro's mind. If the people wanted a sign, they'd give them one ... it doesn't pay to rock the boat, challenge the status quo. If you play with the bull, you'll get the horns.

Nick cut JD loose, "JD, please tell us about the visions."

"Nick, it's weird but they're like a modern remake of parts of Revelation, Thessalonians, Daniel or Matthew. I saw everything in today's terms. I don't think it necessarily meant the end is very near but instead was intended to help us capture the meaning of God's word regarding the final judgment in a way that's easier for us to understand. It made me think of that passage in I Corinthians 13:12, 'for now we see through a glass, darkly; but then face to face: now I know in part; but then shall I know even as also I am known.' The veil was lifted for me from some of the darker passages." Nick nodded attentively. "Some of the messages were made abundantly clear while others remained a bit shrouded. Also, just like in Revelation, some of the visions were repeated. I received some of the messages multiple times from different perspectives."

Nick wanted to let JD run but this puzzled him. "I'm not sure what you mean JD. Can you give us an example?"

"Okay, but first let me start at the beginning. Remember that there will be great tribulation before the end and it will intensify (Matthew 24:21). And as Inky pointed out in regard to America's problems, the worst aspect will be spiritual in nature … God's saving word of truth will be in jeopardy. Just when it seems that all is lost, the end will come … the final day of earth's history." JD paused to let this sink in. "It's clear from Scripture and the clarifying visions I've received that Judgment Day will literally be one, single day in history and will commence with Christ returning the way he left. The Lord will descend from heaven, from the clouds in a dramatic fashion that will not escape anyone's attention (Revelation 1:7). It will not be subtle. The day will commence with the sun and moon being darkened and stars falling from the sky and the earth's foundations being shook (Isaiah 13:10, Revelation 6:12-14). In my vision it was one of those mornings where the sun is up but the moon still appears in the sky. Suddenly, the sun turned dark but not like an eclipse. It was as if black paint were poured over the sun. And the moon was covered in blood. The whole earth was gripped in violent tremors and skyscrapers toppled like thousands of World Trade Centers and the surrounding mountains collapsed around us."

Nick interjected, "Can you tell us what city was in your vision?"

"No, I'm sorry but I can't. It was a huge metropolis much bigger than New York City but surrounded by mountains like Salt Lake City. The vision reflected our world as we know it but, in a way, every city." Nick nodded to urge JD on. "Next, the sign of the Son of Man appeared in the sky for all to see (Matthew 24:30). In my vision, it was a huge, gleaming cross that shone like the sun."

Nick had to interrupt again, "I'm sorry JD but why are you referencing Bible passages? Are these your visions or are you repeating what's already in the Scripture?"

"I'm glad you asked that question, Nick. These are the visions that God shared with me. But I went back when I was assembling the diary and cross referenced the Scriptures. I think it's important to show that this is not a new message but completely consistent with God's word of warning and promise through the prophets, apostles and inspired writers. Also, I want these references to appear in the transcript from today's show for the guidance and edification of everyone watching."

"Okay, thanks JD … it's duly noted."

"Christ is coming back with a bang (I Thessalonians 4:16, I Corinthians 15:52). No one will miss it. In my vision, I heard an ear shattering shout and a trumpet blast that sounded like a James Brown guttural grunt backed up by Chicago's horn section, only amplified like the sound of a thousand tornados. Then a massive bank of clouds steamrolled the sky putting to shame anything Hollywood has envisioned from Close Encounters to Independence Day. The clouds opened and a host of angels streamed forth so great in number I could not count them. They were nothing like the angels you might see atop a Christmas tree. Although spirits, they were manifested as males arrayed in glorious splendor in shockingly white, flowing robes adorned with swords, belts and other paraphernalia suitable for battle. They possessed no wings but levitated effortlessly in defying gravity. These magnificent creatures, full of great power and might possessed grace that inspired awe rather than fear. Then came Christ in the midst of them as if lowered on an invisible string (Matthew 24:30, Acts 1:11, Mark 13:26). The vision was so odd. It was a feeling I can't describe. With all of these amazing things that occurred … the blotting of the sun and moon, stars falling, the earth shaking, the cosmic clouds, sonic sounds and heavenly host arrayed in white … the Savior's appearance made them all seem small and insignificant in comparison. With such a miraculous scene splashed across the heavens, no eye was distracted. Christ was the center of everything. My eyes could not move from his presence."

Nick was captivated … no small feat for anyone including JD. "I'm having a really hard time grasping this JD. How could everyone alive on the earth see this at the same time?"

"I can't tell you how many times I've asked the same question. It boggles the mind but it's going to happen. To this there can be no doubt. It's even tougher to comprehend when you combine this with what happens next. The bodies of the dead, everyone who has ever lived, will be raised (John 5:28-29, Romans 8:11) and brought together, along with all the living, in one massive gathering before Christ on the judgment throne. How can this be with people and bodies scattered all over the world; a round globe where our vision is limited by the horizon? Now I'm finally going to get to your question about multiple visions I saw for the same event. Let me share two of the visions to give you an idea of what I mean. In the first one, bodies rematerialized from the grave, sea, ashes and scattered remains as if being reconstituted in a Star Trek transporter, from energy to matter. It all happened so quickly, almost instantaneously with the dead believers rising first (I Thessalonians 4:16, John 6:40, I Corinthians 15:20-23) and then the believers alive at the time were transformed in the blink of an eye and caught up in the air with the resurrected believers to meet with the Lord (I Thessalonians 4:16-18, I Corinthians 15:50-54). In this vision, there was something like a parabolic screen encircling the earth and projecting Christ's image to all. In the second, the glorified bodies possessed supernatural powers and were able to transport themselves in what might be called a telepathic manner to a place above a huge plain that stretched out below the judgment seat."

Nick was transfixed like everyone in the audience but didn't interrupt. "I think God showed me multiple visions to let me know that what's important in this instance is not the how but instead the what. Everyone will witness the judgment. Every knee will bow and every tongue will confess that Christ is Lord (Romans 14:11, Philippians 2:10). That's the truth to be taken away. The visions, I think, were figurative in a sense to let us know that we shouldn't dwell on knowing how God will accomplish this feat. He just wants us to trust him and have faith in his power and promise. It's like the question raised in I Corinthians 15, 'But some man will say, how are the dead raised up? And with what body do they come?' God answered that it's foolish to dwell on such things ... have faith and trust in his word of promise. God also wants us to know that none of this will be accomplished at man's hands. He doesn't need everyone glued to the TV to witness Christ's return. God tells us that he, Jesus Christ, is not confined to six feet of space in heaven. No, he says that Christ is everywhere at all times. Specifically, he teaches us in Colossians 1:17, 'and he is before all things, and by him all things consist.' Don't worry about how just know that God will get it done."

Nick felt the urge to voice what he thought the audience was feeling. "This is a hard thing to accept. How could billions and billions of resurrected people suddenly be gathered together in one spot to collectively witness Christ's return? It doesn't seem possible."

"Of course it's not possible. Neither is the resurrection of the body. But it happened. Christ rose from the dead. God raised me from the dead. You saw it. Just take it on faith that, as he says, with God all things are possible." Nick shrugged and conceded the point for the sake of time. "We've got to remember who God is. We have this terrible habit of making God too small; of trying to fit him into a tidy, little box. God put it this way through Isaiah in 29:16, 'surely your turning of things upside down shall be esteemed as the potter's clay: for shall the work say of him that made it, He made me not?' We're the clay and God is the potter."

Nick only conceded for the sake of time because his natural instinct was to challenge and question. "Okay JD, we've got to give God his due. But we've also got to give unto our sponsors so let's move on and wrap up your doomsday vision."

JD tried not to seem hurried. "I understand, Nick. Thanks for keeping us on track." For the first time, JD turned his attention away from Nick Phace and panned the audience and gazed directly into the camera so as to speak directly to the hearts of everyone watching and listening. "This is where the visions changed and took on a decidedly modern view of an ancient concept as old as time. My mind was transported to a great courtroom, so expansive as to contain all the multitudes of mankind from beginning to the last day, extending as far as the eye could see. The great, high walls which stretched unfathomably high were etched with the word of God, from Genesis through Revelation, word for word, with the Ten Commandments in bold font in Exodus and Deuteronomy. At the center was a colossal throne of finely polished alabaster and gold that was suspended from the heavens high above. Upon the throne sat the final judge of all, the last Word. It was not God the Father but God the Son, Jesus Christ who sat in judgment (II Corinthians 5:10, Romans 14:10, Acts 17:31, II Timothy 4:1)."

"I have never felt such dread. For the purposes of this vision, I was allowed to experience the terror coursing through the hearts of unbelievers. Hoards of people, some of whom had been very powerful in the earth, tried to scatter like frightened rabbits to hide from the terrible wrath of the stern judge they faced (Revelation 6:14-17). As they rushed toward the immense doors to seek their escape, there was no place to go. The entire world surrounding the great courtroom was engulfed in flames and the mountains and hillsides were collapsing in utter destruction. They stared in helpless resignation as the whole earth burned. There was a terrible noise of hissing and loud wrenching as if a billion demons were twisting steel girders into pretzels and raking their claws across a celestial chalk board. The earth turned to white hot, molten goo and melted down to the very elements. The enormous, towering doors were closed with a booming thud of inescapable finality and the ominous proceedings commenced with a thunderous gavel clap."

JD paused to catch his breath amidst the deafening silence. "There in front of the judge were all the billions and billions of unrepentant sinners who had rejected the free gift of salvation … all those that elected to stand on their own merit, had followed the false teachers, rejected the truth, followed false gods and man-made religions and turned their back on the true God who had sacrificed everything to provide a way of escape. It was too late. The words now echoed in their minds, 'and as it is appointed unto men once to die, but after this the judgment' (Hebrews 9:27). Yet there were many others who were full of joy and peace. All the believers were gathered together by the angels of God and taken in the air to be with the Lord around the throne. They would be judged too but by a completely different standard. I was allowed to see from their perspective too and when they looked at Jesus, the judge appeared as a defense attorney, a kindly advocate full of grace, mercy and love."

JD hit his stride as the viewers were held in rapt attention. "Then massive books were opened and each person faced the judgment alone. The books were like a list of criminal charges but interminably long. Every harsh word, every lie, every sinful deed, each transgression of lust, greed, anger, hatred, jealousy and pride were recorded. Every sinful thought was brought out in the open. Every good deed done out of self-righteousness, every act of phony piety done for self-gain or aggrandizement was revealed in the light of day. Every pharisaic pretense was exposed as an offending stench to God. Every hypocritical Christian was unmasked (Matthew 7:22-23)." JD shifted gears ever so slightly to save time. "I know what some of you are thinking. How could Jesus go through this lengthy adjudication process for billions of people in a single day? I only have one answer for you. Trust in the Lord who turned water to wine, walked on water, fed the five thousand, gave sight to the blind, hearing to the deaf, helped the lame to walk, raised the dead … and created the heavens and earth and everything in it by the command of his voice. He hears and answers the prayers of billions every day simultaneously. By him all things consist and he holds the world together by his omnipotent power. He is omniscient and knows all things down to the very number of hairs on our heads."

"So this one day judgment is literal by some miracle and you're asking us to take this on faith?

"Yes, you should accept this by faith and in accordance with the word of God. On Judgment Day, no one will question how it was accomplished. It reminds me of the loaves and fishes. They started with five barley loaves and two small fishes but Christ used his creative power to feed five thousand men and probably a like number of women and children. No one saw how it was done but afterward they collected up many baskets of leftovers. Did they demand to know how? No, they simply believed and marveled at Jesus' miraculous power. He is the Creator. It's by his power that the dead bodies of everyone who has ever lived will be reconstituted and quickened. And by his power, there will be a new heaven and earth. Certainly someone who possesses such power can judge the masses in one day."

"For all believers, there will be judgment too … but of a very different sort. The books will be opened on our lives and deeds too. But all of our sins will be completely blotted out by the blood of the Lamb, Jesus Christ. Only those truly good works that we accomplished by the sanctifying power and grace of the Holy Ghost out of gratitude and love for God will be revealed. These are the things which were not some kind of quid pro quo done in exchange for our salvation but in response to God's saving grace, out of God-given faith. These fruits of our faith will be trumpeted to God's glory, not ours. While unbelievers will be judged according to the law, believers will be judged according to the gospel. Though we do not deserve it, out of grace, mercy and love, Christ's perfect righteousness is imputed to us. Instead of seeing our sins, God will only see Christ's righteousness when it comes to believers (Philippians 3:9). Rather than judging us, Christ intercedes for us. In the courtroom I saw in the visions, the case against believers was dismissed because the penalty we owed to the court had already been paid in an amount that none of us could ever afford. For us, another book was opened: the book of life. In my vision, when the book of all the names of the elect chosen by God before all time was opened, an endless cornucopia of the bread of life spilled out and a never ending stream of living water flowed."

JD's expression changed to one of genuine wonderment. "The next scene in the vision was truly amazing. For all the believers, it was miraculous enough that all of our sins were redacted from the court records and our judge, Jesus Christ, stood in for us as our advocate. But in a twist that was just as mind boggling, we were separated and taken up from the unbelievers by God's holy angels and placed above in what can best be described as an immense jury box. We who could have been judged but were spared were allowed to participate in the judgment of the unbelievers."

Even being short on time, Nick couldn't resist, "Now hold on a minute JD; where did you come up with that one? Christian believers will judge unbelievers? I thought you said Jesus Christ was the final judge of all?"

"I hear you Nick. I was perplexed by this too. But when I went back and studied God's word, I found that it's true. God tells us in I Corinthians 6:2 that the saints shall judge the world. Now, it's important to remember that all believers are saints in God's eyes, in spite of our past sins, because of the righteousness of Christ that is imputed to us. The vision was very appropriate when you think of it. It showed believers participating in the judgment, not executing the final judgment. That role belongs to Christ alone. I guess that's why I saw us in a jury box. As jurors we were able to hear the evidence and see the iron clad case against the unrepentant sinners who rejected God's grace and mercy and declare the verdict. But it was Christ the judge who exercised full authority over everyone in the courtroom and passed sentence over the unbelievers." JD then went on to describe the grim details of how Satan, his evil angels, the Anti-Christ and all unbelievers were sentenced to hell and dispatched there by God's bailiffs, his Holy Angels. "In the vision, all I could see of hell was a huge opening to a bottomless pit. It resembled the gaping maw of a monstrous fish. The inky black darkness was pierced periodically by tongues of fire that leaped from the depths below as a sulfurous stench belched from the cavernous bowels from whence pitiful cries and wailing emanated."

Nick was fascinated and frightened at the same time. "Did everyone receive the same sentence?

Did anyone try to appeal or throw themselves on the mercy of the court?"

"Here's another example of the alternate visions I received. Earlier I mentioned how I saw the books being opened with all the charges painstakingly enumerated like an incredibly voluminous subpoena. In another view, the record was presented like one of those stoplight camera violation videos. You know, it's hard to argue when you're caught in the act on film. In the vision, it was similar except that it was much more detailed and included audio. Imagine how creepy it would be to have someone play back a recording of every bad thing you ever did and an audio tape of every sinful thought that ever crossed your mind. Every dark secret was brought into the light of day for all to see. It truly would make you want to crawl into a hole or hide under a rock."

"So as you can imagine, no one challenged the authority of the judge. His omnipotent power and unquestioned authority permeated the courtroom. A few begged for mercy and tried to appeal to the judge on the basis of their own merit. They were categorically denied. All who had decided to stand on their own merit rather than Christ's were held to God's standard of perfection that Christ met.

They crumbled under the weight of their own folly and futility in the face of perfect, divine justice. As for receiving the same sentence, no they did not. You might think that being sentenced to hell; eternal torment, darkness and separation from God would be enough but some punishments were somehow harsher than others. Those that had harmed little children and the unborn were held accountable as such. Special punishment was also meted out to the hypocrites and leaders of false religions. The harshest treatment was reserved for those that had known the truth but sinned against the Holy Ghost and devoted their lives to leading others astray. They were deemed the true servants of Satan."

Nick pressed further, "What about the believers. Did they all receive the same reward?"

"No, similarly there were differences. Of course, no one was unhappy about eternal life in heaven but some of the saints received special recognition. The funny thing was that no one was jealous and the recipients didn't deem themselves better than anyone else. People were happy to see the good works of God honored, like Paul's unparalleled missionary accomplishments. All of these great deeds were seen as personal triumphs but as evidence of God's goodness and his power in the lives of his people. Everyone, including the recipients, was happy to give God all the credit and glory."

Nick turned devilish, "JD, we're coming up on our final break but can you quickly tell us about any of the people you saw in the visions? You know, can you name names?"

"To be very honest, I recognized some people but, by and large, I wasn't afforded the opportunity to see the identity of most people. Among the unbelievers, I saw founders and leaders of false religions and some famous purveyors of false doctrines through the ages. There were many people who had committed suicide, most notably Judas. There were unrepentant sinners of every stripe: homosexuals, abortionists, adulterers, robbers, murderers, hypocrites, liars, fornicators and the like. I saw these same types of sinners among the believers too. The difference was that they acknowledged their wrong doing, repented ... had a change of heart rather than trying to justify or deny their sins ... and turned to Jesus Christ as Savior for forgiveness. They were just as filthy as the unbelieving, unrepentant sinners but were washed clean in the blood of the Lamb."

"Of course, it was easy to pick out Satan, his evil angels and the Anti-Christ among the condemned. Granted the Anti-Christ was not an individual but consisted of many people who served under the system of lies in drawing souls away from God's truth. The most regrettable thing was seeing the vast legion of unbelievers who rejected the truth and followed the false teachers and practiced the false religions of all sorts. They learned on the last day, when it was too late, that all steeples do not point upward and all roads do not lead to heaven. No one was brandishing their Coexist bumper stickers on Judgment Day. Everyone knew the truth that there is none other name under heaven given among men whereby we must be saved other than Jesus Christ."

In spite of this sobering truth, Nick's journalistic instincts didn't desert him. "C'mon JD, you can name names."

"Okay, I'll give you a few but don't read anything strange into this. Heaven and hell are determined by the simple truth of Mark 16:16. Don't go off on any tangents." JD paused as he reviewed the images in his head. "Some of the people I saw were not surprising: the apostles Paul, Peter and John for instance and Moses, Elijah and

Stephen the Martyr. Martin Luther was also among the redeemed. Sadly, Tetzel, Eck and Charles V were not counted with the sheep. The odd thing was that I knew all of them without being introduced. The saying 'I didn't know him from Adam' was rendered obsolete. He was there and I knew him instantaneously as I did with Eve and Abel."

"Many of my relatives were among the believers but with them too I knew people I had never met before, people that had died long before I was born. And still, the reunion was oh so sweet. Job was there and so was Noah but not all of Noah's family members were with him. Some counted among the elect would shock you. For example, I encountered the notorious serial killer, Charles Darwin Cane. He certainly was not saved on account of his own merit. He repented and came to faith in Christ by the grace of God. On the flip side, I was stunned to find some folks who were counted among the goats rather than sheep. One immensely popular personality famous for his prosperity gospel was doomed. A 'saint' famous for her lifelong charitable endeavors was condemned in accordance with her own merit which was found lacking apart from Christ. Gandhi, in spite of all his laudable works, was convicted in his unbelief and rejection of Jesus Christ."

JD forged on in spite of the stunned silence and palpable sense of growing anger and outrage. "Among the damned, I saw legions of hypocrites who used their false piety to foster blasphemous causes in the name of Christ. There were many who had clung to what they called social justice, collective salvation or the social gospel which, in the light of judgment, were revealed to be motivated by hatred, greed, anger and envy. The visions of the final judgment were filled with bitter irony and heartbreaking tragedy. Gandhi was not only among the goats but was singled out for special punishment for leading so many millions down the broad path to destruction. His motivations were revealed to all. His acts of kindness while well intentioned in a sense were not done purely out of love for God and gratitude for Christ's atoning sacrifice. He believed in a system of works righteousness and expected spiritual rewards for his deeds. God tells us in Isaiah 64:6 that all our righteousnesses are as filthy rags. This means that all the laudable things we do in trying to barter for our salvation apart from Christ are reprehensible insults and a stench to his nostrils."

JD carried on in spite of the unrest that stirred in the audience. "The tragic irony extended well beyond Gandhi. I saw Mary among the saints but she was not celebrated as some kind of mediator between God and man. God was glorified by the reading of her record, most pointedly by her great profession of faith in Jesus as recounted in Luke 1:46-47, 'My soul doth magnify the Lord, and my spirit hath rejoiced in God my Savior.' She knew she was a sinner in need of God's plan of salvation. Mary knew that being chosen by God to be the vessel for the virgin birth was not a reward for her own goodness but was an honor and great privilege bestowed upon her by God. Sadly and regrettably the legions of the doomed were filled with misguided souls who bought into the lie that Mary was Co-Redemptrix. They were fooled into believing in a confusing, hapless system of works righteousness. Their eyes were blinded from the truth that there is only one Mediator, one way to heaven; through the all-availing sacrifice of the God-man, Jesus Christ."

Many in the audience gasped. Nick's face was twisted by the seeming incongruence of JD's revelations. "JD I think you just lost many of us. It just doesn't make sense." He tried to throw JD a lifeline, "Are you sure these last few images were literal or figurative … or perhaps more your imagination than part of the vision God provided?"

JD was not deterred by the simmering anger and mounting rejection and wanted no part of Nick's rationalizing. "It's possible that these images were figurative in nature but I don't think so. God was careful to shroud most of the peoples' identities from me but allowed me to clearly see certain specific, recognizable figures. It may seem illogical or unreasonable in a worldly sense. How could Gandhi or anyone so devoted to charity, fighting poverty, injustice and illness or pursuing world peace wind up in hell? But we've got to see things from God's perspective. He's the final judge. God is the one who has done everything necessary to secure our salvation, at an infinitely high price, and has made it effortless on our part. God also shared his plan of salvation with us from Adam on down so that none would need to be lost. Yet, so many decided to go their own way in spite of God's patient warnings and endless calls to repentance and free redemption. He warned over and over of the coming judgment, not to frighten but to enlighten. God would not be just, honest or trustworthy and go back on his word. The unbelievers have no one to blame but themselves. God's will is that all would be saved … Jesus proclaimed, 'and this is the will of him that sent me, that everyone that sees the Son, and believeth on him, may have everlasting life: and I will raise him up at the last day."

This did not appease or please the crowd but at least silenced them for a time. Nick broke the stalemate, "We're almost out of time so we'll have to leave it there and move on. When we come back for the last segment, please tell us about the close of Judgment Day and what follows after the end."

During the break, Mit returned. He was haggard but relieved by what he perceived to be the safety in numbers. Kit was with him, disheveled in her frumpy sweater with the unsightly brown stain that looked like a Rorschach test gone awry. Mit was anxious to reveal the plot against Kit and seek help from the authorities but knew better than to cause a scene at this pivotal point in the proceedings. He laid low out of respect for JD's message which was coming to a fitting climax. When touchy security personnel approached, he was able to produce his staff credentials but, of course, Kit had none since she was thought to be at home in St. Louis. Mit tried to explain without causing a stir but the distraction caught Nick Phace's eye and he motioned for both Mit and Kit to be escorted up on stage for the final curtain call. This provided just enough diversion for Al Batin's assassins and

Martin to draw near with their weapons. They awaited instructions from James who was perched above. He was prepared to pick off any security agents who might intercede so that the three men below could focus their fire on the targets. It made their mission that much easier to have JD, Mit, Kit and me gathered together so conveniently on stage. It would be like shooting fish in a barrel.

As we prepared to wrap things up, we didn't know at the time that James hoped to wait until just after the show to close the final curtain on us, so to speak. He figured there would be a minute or two after we went off the air where the group would still be gathered together onstage as sitting ducks. Why commit such an atrocity in view of the cameras during a live broadcast if it could be avoided?

Nick was now intent upon keeping us on track and squeezing out as much pertinent information as possible. "Thanks for sticking with us. Whether you agree or disagree with his interpretations of the visions he received and whether you believe or remain a skeptic, I'm sure we can all agree on one thing. This has been an incredible show and I'm guessing that, like mine, many lives have been changed forever." The crowd acknowledged Nick with respectful applause. "Now, as promised, the Last Prophet, JD Uticus, will tell us what's to come, according to his visions, after the final judgment. Then, if we have a few minutes, I'd like to give the audience a chance to ask some questions."

JD took his cue and wasted no time, "In my vision, it was clear to me that all matter was not annihilated. Just as God reconstituted all the dead and reunited them with their immortal souls, he used elements from the previous heaven and earth to form the new heaven and earth." JD picked up on the confused frown emanating from Nick's face. "I know this may sound inconsistent with other things I've shared from the Scripture but please let me explain. First, in glorifying our bodies, the vision depicts that God used the dust from whence we originally came but it's freed from the corruption of sin that had clung to our flesh. Think of it as God restoring us to our former, perfect state. Our glorified bodies were not only endowed with amazing powers but rendered pure and sinless. All the former corruption was eradicated; not only illness and disease but all forms of immorality in thought, word and deed. When I saw heaven and earth being burned and melted down to the elements, the corruption and sinfulness that also infected all of creation was completely burned away forever leaving only the original perfection God intended. From these elements, God displayed his amazing, omnipotent creative powers in bringing a new and perfect world and universe to life. At this point, God chose to limit my view as if I was again viewing things through a glass darkly."

Nick interjected quickly, "Why would God withhold a clear view of heaven?"

"I'm guessing that it's just one of those things that we'll have to wait to behold. Maybe it's impossible to comprehend in our current state. I don't know. But God did give me a peek into our glorious future. It was not a vision but rather a feeling, call it a spiritual picture. God let me feel the perfect peace and joy that we'll experience. It was an incredible, indescribable feeling that I'll never forget. These words echoed in my mind at the time, 'and there shall be no more curse: but the throne of God and the Lamb shall be in it; and his servants shall serve him' (Revelation 22:3). Somehow, in a spiritual way, I was able to experience what it will be like to live in God's presence in perfect harmony. It was incredible beyond words. However the best is yet to come because, in that day, we'll see God and Christ with our own eyes, with us clothed in glorious new bodies built for all eternity."

In spite of the sand running out of the hour glass, Nick paused for a good twenty seconds to let everyone reflect on the amazing revelation that had just been shared by the Last Prophet. The unrest had subsided and an unearthly calm had descended over the proceedings. Then, as promised, Nick turned things over to the audience. He figured they might have enough time for one or two questions before going off the air. "It's amazing folks, just amazing. I don't know about you but I'm having a hard time catching my breath. But before we go, would anyone like to ask a quick question?"

Many hands shot up and Nick selected a man near the front row who seemed to have a look of sincere urgency on his face. "JD, I really want to believe you but I feel so conflicted by some of the things you've shared. What can you do to help? Is there another sign you can give us … please?"

JD was about to reiterate the unsatisfying, harsh truth about signs and wonders and point everyone back to God's word, the Holy Bible. But in spite of his druthers, James noticed a disturbing development from his towering vantage point. One of the security guards caught a glimpse of Martin's weapon which he had tried to conceal by his side and was moving swiftly toward him. James immediately blurted a red alert into the tiny receivers inside the ears of his co-conspirators and ordered them to attack. Martin and Al Batin's two men stepped forward and trained their rifles on our tight knit group up on the stage as James fixed his scope on the approaching security guard. He dropped him with a neck shot that whizzed from the sky like an angry hornet. Then the three assassins opened fire on us with a burst that echoed throughout the valley bringing an ear shattering, startlingly swift plague of terror and panic upon us all. There was no time to react. We were mesmerized with fear.

JD had no intention of calling upon the Almighty to satisfy Nick, the questioner from the audience or any of the other doubters or skeptics. To him it was strictly a matter of faith. But, on that day, God had other plans for the Last Prophet. Without anyone touching the control panels, the jumbotrons popped up out of the floor and the following message appeared, "Be not afraid nor dismayed by reason of this great multitude; for the battle is not yours, but God's (II Chronicles 20:15)." One of the screens was positioned just right so as to block us from James' view. Not to be deterred, he turned his sights toward the other security personnel, confident that his three collaborators would take care of us up on stage. He would have been correct judging from the hail of bullets they launched at us. That's when God intervened in a most miraculous way. They wanted a sign? Well, so be it. Energy itself cut a muster in front of us forming a semi-transparent shield that performed like a thick gel. Rather than scattering, the audience was transfixed by the unbelievable scene. The bullets were halted, caught in the gelatinous force field leaving clear traces of the paths they followed in geometric trails revealing how they would have decimated us as targets. Jaws dropped in amazement as the hand of God once again stretched out to rescue the Last Prophet, and this time his companions, from death. No one fled even though mortal danger still lurked in our midst in the form of the three heavily armed madmen.

God's word proved true again. The battle was not ours but his. He clouded James' vision with confusion and when he pulled the trigger again, it was not a security guard but Martin's head that exploded like a melon. So too were Al Batin's vicious henchmen brought to judgment, by their own hands. When they looked about to repel the security forces and make their escape, God clouded their minds so that they saw their comrade as the enemy and cut each other to ribbons in their final act of bloody disarray. The only threat that remained was James. God had a different end in store for him. He must have dispatched a holy angel, perhaps the one that had frightened the Ghost to death outside my home. In any case, the vision of terror that confronted James Mason was so incomprehensibly frightening that he rushed toward the precipice to escape and plummeted to his death in full view of everyone assembled. Every threat was removed by God's miraculous power and a feeling of awe and peace hung over the dumbstruck crowd. There had been only one casualty. However, in the pandemonium, no one noticed how this shattered individual was miraculously mended. Whole again, he stood up; transformed in a way that only JD could understand because of the way the Last Prophet had originally been resurrected after his fatal fall years before.

Epilogue

"And God shall wipe away all tears from their eyes; and there shall be no more death, neither sorrow, nor crying, neither shall there be any more pain: for the former things are passed away" (From the vision given to the Apostle John exiled on the Island of Patmos as recorded in the Book of Revelation 21:4 during the first century A. D.).

Just like he did with Elijah and the Prophets of Baal and King Jehoshaphat and the multitudes among the children of Moab, Ammon and Mt. Seir or on so many other occasions; God had demonstrated his power in a dramatic, undeniable fashion. Thus everyone believed and the world lived in perfect peace and harmony anxiously awaiting the victorious and glorious return of Jesus Christ. End of story, right? I'm sorry to burst your bubble but it didn't happen that way. In spite of another miracle involving the Last Prophet, a sign from God viewed widely by an international audience, nothing really changed, I regret to say.

Yeah, it had an impact on our lives for a while. JD enjoyed tremendous notoriety again. Maybe enjoy is the wrong word. There were many times that he longed for his old life as a recluse in the Smokey Mountains. But ever faithful to his calling, he used his fame to spread the gospel to the glory of God. As for me, it certainly helped book sales. American Phoenix: Resurrecting the Dead Republic was a big hit, for a while. The blog thrived too. Mit and Kit took the big leap and got married soon after as Mr. and Mrs. Malcolm Ives Trimble and started popping out cute little nerdkins right away. I had the privilege of serving as best man. Life was good in a temporal sense and our success allowed us to keep the creditors from our doorsteps. I almost said it allowed us to keep the wolves at bay but that might have confused you. It was true too but all of that credit belongs to God. Any remnants of Brutus' rogue operation were shut down and the wary government-types kept an eye on American Phoenix and let it run its course. This was wise because, in spite of its measure of success, like most things it didn't start a movement but faded away. Fame is fleeting in our high tech world where one day something goes viral and then shortly thereafter it's replaced by the next flash-in-the-pan phenomenon. People have short attention spans and need constant gratification from the next new thing.

The real wolves were another matter. Cagliostro dropped any plans aimed at Jude and the kids after witnessing what happened at Mt. Rushmore. He consoled himself with the knowledge that JD had kept his word about keeping mum about the Anti-Christ and speculation regarding the Papacy. Of course, he was not happy when he learned how Mit had been able to save a copy of the Marchetti file before his minions could destroy it. For the time being, all he could do was try to cover his tracks. This was bad news for Benedetto whose antennae were not as sharp as

Marchetti's had been. He was lost in a tragic *accident*. The best laid plans didn't suit Cagliostro any better than they had Riccardi. In due time, he met the same quiet fate as the real power brokers cleaned up the mess he had created. We were not out of the woods completely with Cagliostro's demise. That would never be the case but the imminent threat was gone. Life returned to normal or at least as much as it could for the Last Prophet and me, his best friend.

That year ended with unrest spreading across the Middle East in violent, anti-American tones and a changing of the political guard in Washington. Many reformers were lulled back to sleep. Everyone forgot the warning that had been issued by Washington and Lincoln on down to Reagan: the United States would never be toppled by a frontal assault ... we could only be defeated from within. It was so easy to sooth many troubled souls with materialistic things. As the Dow rose, unemployment dropped, gas prices settled back and a charade of fiscal sanity played out, people got comfy again and it was life and politics as usual. Like JD, I don't claim to be a prophet. But many of the things I envisioned on the basis of common sense proved inevitable. It happened sooner than I anticipated though. Our crushing debt caught up with us. Our dependence upon government freebies betrayed us. Our ability and will to arm ourselves militarily left us defenseless. Our abandonment of the Constitution and free market principles that had been a part of the American fabric from the beginning sounded a death knell. But more than anything else, our downfall could be attributable to losing our national soul. Just as I had warned against in American Phoenix, we were doomed by turning our backs on God.

This brings me back to where we started. America's doomsday started on a Friday. The financial house of cards collapsed and the ensuing worldwide depression was worse than the first. This led to chaos and anarchy, then a police state and finally a totalitarian regime where freedom died. How did we survive under these conditions? Believe me it was not easy emotionally, psychologically, economically, mentally or physically. But we did survive. There was one freedom that could not be taken away ... spiritual freedom and Christian liberty. In a way, it was good for us. It helped us to put our priorities back in order. We still had the things we cherished most; each other and faith in God. They could not take our hearts and souls.

I often think back to those days in 2012. The lesson God so graciously taught us through his servant, the Last Prophet, still echoes in my heart and mind. I was spot on in warning about America's demise and offering practical and spiritual solutions to our nation's woes in American Phoenix. But this was dust in the wind compared to God's biblical message of warning and hope that he so graciously shared in such a special way through his servant JD Uticus. There's a final day of judgment coming that is infinitely more important than any temporal doomsday in America or elsewhere. Let every ear hear that Jesus is most certainly returning on that appointed day. To some this will regrettably and justifiably bring terror, judgment and a casting out into everlasting darkness and torment apart from God. But to all believers who put their faith and trust solely in the merit, work and atoning sacrifice of our Savior, Jesus Christ, Judgment Day will only bring triumph, glory and everlasting joy. This is our legacy and hope. I cannot tell you when the end will come. It seems closer than ever now. Yet JD Uticus remains alive and well by God's grace, power, might and purpose. So we look forward to the end with great joy and anticipation and, in the meantime, wait patiently to see what God has in store for the Last Prophet.

FINAL WORDS OF WISDOM, HOPE AND JOY EVERLASTING ...

Wherefore, Job, I pray thee, hear my speeches, and hearken to all my words. Behold, now I have opened my mouth, my tongue hath spoken in my mouth. My words shall be of the uprightness of my heart: and my lips shall utter knowledge clearly. The spirit of God hath made me, and the breath of the Almighty hath given me life. If thou canst answer me, set thy words in order before me, stand up. Behold, I am according to thy wish in God's stead: I also am formed out of the clay. Behold, my terror shall not make thee afraid, neither shall my hand be heavy upon thee. Surely thou hast spoken in mine hearing, and I have heard the voice of thy words, saying, I am clean without transgression, I am innocent; neither is there iniquity in me. Behold, he findeth occasions against me, he counteth me for his enemy, He putteth my feet in the stocks, he marketh all my paths. Behold, in this thou art not just: I will answer thee, that God is greater than man. Why dost thou strive against him? For he giveth not account of any of his matters. For God speaketh once, yea twice, yet man perceiveth it not. ***In a dream, in a vision of the night, when deep sleep falleth upon men, in slumberings upon the bed; then he openeth the ears of men, and sealeth*** *their instruction,* that he may withdraw man from his purpose, and hide pride from man. He keepeth back his soul from the pit, and his life from perishing by the sword. He is chastened also with pain upon his bed, and the multitude of his bones with strong pain: So that his life abhorreth bread, and his soul dainty meat. His flesh is consumed away, that it cannot be seen; and his bones that were not seen stick out. Yea, his soul draweth near unto the grave, and his life to the destroyers. If there be a messenger with him, an interpreter, one among a thousand, to shew unto man his uprightness: Then he is gracious unto him, and saith, Deliver him from going down to the pit: I have found a ransom. His flesh shall be fresher than a child's: he shall return to the days of his youth: He shall pray unto God, and he will be favourable unto him: and he shall see his face with joy: for he will render unto man his righteousness. He looketh upon men, and if any say, I have sinned, and perverted that which was right, and it profited me not; He will deliver his soul from going into the pit, and his life shall see the light. Lo, all these things worketh God oftentimes with man, to bring back his soul from the pit, to be enlightened with the light of the living. Mark well, O Job, hearken unto me: hold thy peace, and I will speak. If thou hast anything to *say, answer me: speak, for I desire to justify thee. If not, hearken unto me: hold thy peace, and I shall teach thee wisdom.(Almighty God, Creator and Redeemer, Book of Job, Chapter 33)*

Other books by Steve Stranghoener ...

- Murder by Chance: Blood Moon Lunacy of Lew Carew
- Asunder: The Tale of the Renaissance Killer
- The Last Prophet: Imminent End
- Tracts in Time

These books are available at

www.amazon.com.

Made in the USA
Charleston, SC
01 October 2012